All characters appearing in this work are fictitious. Any resemblance to real persons, living or dead, is purely coincidental.

A CIP catalogue record for this title is available from the British Library.

BOUGHT AND PAID FOR

ANNA-MARIA ATHANASIOU

CONTENTS

To Nonna –
who loved to read romance novels,
but sadly never got to read any of mine.

FOREWORD

What was that age-old saying? Money can't buy you love. Of course that was true; even The Beatles wrote a song about it. How could anyone's feelings be bought? Feelings were priceless, right? Beyond monetary value, true love came from the heart and no amount of cash could bring you love... well, sort of...

It all started with a generous payout of £50,000 for an hour and a half of undivided attention. Time could be paid for but would what had been bought be worth it?

Miles and Louisa's story began ten years ago, before any money changed hands...

PROLOGUE

TEN YEARS AGO.

"IT'S THROUGH HERE, MADAME." Louisa nodded at Brian and gripped Celeste's small hand tightly. *Why had she even agreed to this?* She looked down at Celeste, who beamed up at her, excitement written all over her face. That look was worth having to sit through a two-hour concert, surrounded by teenage girls screaming at a four-piece, 20-something boy band. Okay, maybe boy band was a bit harsh. Keane Sense were in their mid-20s now, just a handful of years younger than Louisa, and she had enjoyed their music herself. She'd heard nothing else over the last six months since their new album had come out. Celeste played it all the time, knew all the lyrics and every detail about every band member. Her room was covered in everything Keane Sense, but her main focus was on the lead singer Miles Keane. His all-American-boy, wide smile, golden tan and floppy dirty blonde trademark hair, that was always smoothed back to reveal handsomely sculptured features, was all Celeste talked about. The various shirtless photos Louisa had seen of him, in low-hung jeans, showcased a perfectly toned torso and his voice was a perfect mix of smooth and gravel.

"Monsieur Dupont asked that I take you in with our team. We just need to pass through the backstage security," Brian said tightly. It was obvious he wasn't used to having to ask permission to do anything, let alone pander to some two-bit pop group's security. He worked for the billionaire Gerard Dupont, a man who rubbed shoulders with the elite, had the private numbers of governors and senators, had dined several times at the White House and had connections to the aristocracy. He'd even pulled strings to ensure this band played at the celebrated Madison Square Gardens, so his beloved daughter Celeste had VIP seats and a backstage pass to meet her idols. Brian clenched his jaw as he spoke into his sleeve to the rest of his team, as his patience began to wane.

"It won't be long, sweetheart." Louisa smiled down at her daughter, sensing her impatience.

"They're just getting ready, my lady." Brian said softly, though it was obvious he wasn't best pleased having his employee's wife and nine-year-old daughter waiting in a draughty corridor, even though he had three other members of his team with him.

Eric looked around the room and blew out a gust of air. The ten percent he earned from managing Keane Sense sometimes didn't feel enough for the amount of shit they put him through. The band had, over the last six months, risen to being one of the best-selling bands in the US and they were due to start their debut European tour in two days. Their clean-cut image appealed to parents of the young teenagers who adored them, and their good looks and songs drew in hordes of female fans. Trying to keep quiet any scandal related to the band was a logistic nightmare and this scene Eric had walked into was exactly what he'd tried his damnedest to avoid.

Louis Keane was at the far end of the dressing room, talking on his phone. This was his usual MO. As soon as he finished a gig, he rang his wife the second he entered the room, totally oblivious to his other band members. He was the only band member with his head screwed on right; the older brother of Miles and the glue that kept the three other Keane Sense band members together.

Miles Keane was slumped in one of the comfy couches, shirtless. His dark blonde hair, damp with sweat, was being gripped by a scantily clad groupie while she straddled his lap, kissing him violently, totally oblivious to the room's occupants.

At the other side of the room, Josh poured out shots of vodka from the hospitality table for four 20 something girls, while the final band member, Mick was rummaging in one of their many holdalls. He stood up abruptly when he'd found what he was searching for and shook a small plastic bag of white powder.

"Mick! Put that away." Eric's sharp tone jolted all four band members. He strode over to the docking station that was playing their latest number one track and turned down the volume. "Ladies, I'm afraid I'm going to have to ask you to leave."

There was a collective groan and the start of objections by Mick, Josh and Miles, but Eric ceased them with a raise of his hand. Louis quickly finished his call and turned his attention to his manager.

"Ladies, if you'll be kind enough to wait in the adjoining room." He signalled to a door at the far end of the dressing room. "I just need a few minutes with the band."

The four girls by the hospitality table gave Josh and Mick a questioning look. The boys gave them a reassuring nod and a wink and they reluctantly stepped towards the now open back door.

"Ma'am?" Eric focused his attention on the blonde still plastered all over Miles. She made an indecent show of writhing over him as she gave him a goodbye kiss, then haughtily strutted in the same direction as the other groupies. Eric strode over to the door and closed it with a bang, muttering to himself. As soon as the door closed, Mick, Josh and Miles started to protest.

"Fuck's sake, Eric, this is our last night in the US!" blew out Josh.

"Nothing like a buzz kill," ground out Mick.

Miles stood up from the couch and sauntered to where the drinks were laid out on the table. He swiped up the vodka bottle and put it to his lips, then took a few large gulps and slammed down the bottle in adolescent defiance. "What the fuck crawled up your ass and died?" he sneered.

"Miles." Louis said in warning, stepping up to his brother.

"What? We just completed thirty-two dates of this US tour and we can't kick back on our last night?"

Eric huffed. "You kick back practically every night, Miles, and I'm there to clean it up!"

Miles steely-blue eyes hardened. He was getting a little tired of being told what to do and when to do it. He was twenty-five years old and was expected to behave like a monk.

"I didn't come to break up your party. I'm here because we have a VIP guest who wants to meet you. It'll take fifteen minutes tops of your precious time and then you can do whatever and whoever you want, but for the next fifteen minutes, you're all going to behave like the Keane Sense members the public know you as. Is that clear?" Eric eyed each member and waited for a positive response. He wasn't a big man, average height and build, but what he lacked in size he made up in assertiveness and a sharp mind. He was the best in the business, he knew how to promote – but more importantly, he knew what to hide.

"Who's the VIP?" asked Louis.

"Celeste Blackthorn-Dupont."

"What is she, some socialite?" Miles muttered, still not on board with the turn of events.

"She's the daughter of Gerard Dupont." Eric raised an eyebrow at Miles, indicating he should know who that was.

"Who the fuck's Gerard Dupont?" he grunted.

"He's the billionaire who got us the gig here." Louis shook his head in exasperation at his younger brother.

"Oh." Miles shrugged.

"Is she hot? Maybe she'll stay for the after party. I wouldn't mind screwing a billionaire's daughter. Another thing to tick of my bucket list," sniggered Mick, trying to bring some levity to the conversation.

"She's nine years old." Eric said through gritted teeth.

"For fuck's sake, Eric! I could've been having my dick sucked off by Candy right now but instead *I* have to suck up to a nine-year-old billionaire brat!" Miles picked up the vodka bottle again but before it reached his lips, Louis pulled it out of his grasp.

"Knock off the booze. Let's just do this and then, like Eric says, you can party," Louis said, calmly holding his brother's gaze. Miles sucked on his teeth and gave a curt nod, then ran his fingers through his hair.

"Go put a shirt on." Eric focused on Miles, then turned to the rest of the band. "Clean yourselves up and use some mouth wash. Remember, it's because of *brats*," he spat out the last word, "like Celeste Dupont-Blackthorn that you guys are topping the US and European charts. Don't forget who put you at the top. They can as easily bring you back down again."

"Give us a couple of minutes, Eric. We'll be ready." Louis reassured him. Miles muttered curses under his breath, then swung around and headed to the bathroom, taking his holdall with him.

Miles looked at himself in the bathroom mirror as he braced his arms on either side of the sink. *Fucking Eric was worse than his father. "Stop drinking so much," "Stop partying so hard," lecture after lecture. He was twenty-five years old, for Christ's sake, not fifteen!* He splashed water on his face and roughly dried it, then swilled his mouth out with mouthwash. He then reached into his bag and pulled out a clean T-shirt and dragged it on. The T-shirt clung to his torso, which was still damp from the sweat after his performance. Miles then pulled out the small packet of cocaine he had wedged inside his jeans pocket and tapped out a small amount on the counter.

"All ready, my lady." Brian held out his hand, signalling Louisa to follow two of his team through the door.

"Is it really necessary for two of your security to accompany them?" Eric almost hissed at Brian.

"Absolutely. Mr Dupont insisted on it."

Eric shook his head in exasperation. He didn't know what was worse: pandering to four prima donna band members or some billionaire's wife and his entitled child. He plastered on his best professional smile and welcomed Louisa and Celeste as though they were royalty.

"I'm so very pleased to meet you, ma'am. I'm Eric Schultz, Keane Sense's manager." He held out his hand for Louisa to shake, which she did firmly. "And you must be Celeste." Celeste beamed up at him as she shook his hand, but then quickly let her eyes dart through the open door, betraying where her attention really was. "Please come in and meet the band, they're looking forward to it." Louisa smiled at Eric, knowing he was talking her daughter up and she was grateful for his tact.

The room had thankfully been put into some semblance of order. There were still pieces of clothing strewn over the chairs and the six bottles of Grey Goose vodka had been lined up on the table, but at least the smell of alcohol and cigarette smoke had been muted by the over-zealous spraying of men's cologne.

Celeste couldn't contain her glee, seeing Louis, Mick and Josh, who immediately stood up from the couch to greet her. She peppered her gushing thanks with superlatives such as "awesome", "sick" and "lit", that seemed to be favoured by the younger generation, as she described the concert. All three band members made a fuss of her handing her various signed promotional merchandise, which she accepted, but her focus shifted the minute the bathroom door opened and Miles stepped out. She let out an audible gasp as he gave her his best mega-watt all-American-boy smile that blasted across the room. If there were music to accompany his entrance, it would have been a heavenly choir of angels, as his unworldly form graced the rather drab and basic dressing room.

"Miles!" she gasped. This was who she'd been desperate to meet. She'd been crushing on him from the moment she'd seen his first video. Her room had his posters pinned on every wall; her tablet and phone had his roguishly handsome face as their screen saver. She had every album and video downloaded, which she played and watched incessantly. Miles couldn't have timed his entrance more perfectly.

Celeste lost all sense of decorum her parents had tried hard to instil in her, and all but ran to him, flinging her arms around his middle, knocking him off-guard.

"Well, I'm pleased to meet you too," he drawled and his eyes darted to his other band members, as he patted her back like a dog. Louis glowered at him and rubbed his nose, indicating his brother should do the same. Miles rubbed away the light dusting of white powder he'd carelessly left behind under his nose, just before Celeste looked up at him, but not fast enough for Louisa not to notice.

She narrowed her eyes at him and stepped forward. "Celeste, sweetheart, shall we let Mr Keane come and sit down?" she urged and her daughter reluctantly peeled herself off his middle and took a step back.

"Erm sorry, I'm just so excited to meet you," Celeste blurted out, then flicked her eyes at her mother, her fair complexion reddening against her blonde long hair.

"That's okay, Celeste. Let's go sit down like your mom said." Miles tried to train his focus on the woman who was looking at him disapprovingly but it was hard after a quarter bottle of vodka and a line of coke. His eye caught sight of Louis glaring at him and he knew he had to sober up and fast. "Um, pleased to meet you, Mrs Blackthorn-Dupont." Miles extended the hand he'd just wiped his nose with towards Louisa.

She arched a disapproving brow at him and turned her attention to her daughter, effectively ignoring him. *Who the hell did he think he was?* Louisa thought to herself. If it wasn't for Celeste's obsession with the band and her good breeding, she would have told Miles Keane exactly where he could put his hand. Miles huffed at the brush-off and staggered further into the room.

"What about a picture with the band, Mrs Blackthorn-Dupont?" Eric stepped up, clearly flustered at her blatant snub of the most volatile member of the band.

"Oh Mummy, please! Can I?" Celeste looked up at Louisa expectantly with big pleading eyes.

"If it's alright with the band, sweetheart." Louisa gently stroked back a golden strand of hair off her daughters face as she spoke, her previous annoyance forgotten.

"Of course it's alright. Why don't we get you to sit on the couch with Louis and Miles on either side of you and Mick and Josh behind. How does that sound?" Eric suggested, jerking his chin in the direction of the couch so Miles would get the hint.

"Oh, yes!" Celeste skipped to the couch as the band members arranged themselves, then sat down on the edge of the seat. She placed her hands on her lap and made sure her ankles were together. She was the perfect lady even at nine years old, dressed in ripped jeans, a Keane Sense T-shirt and pink converse.

"Right, are we all ready?" Louisa lifted up her phone and let it focus. The band members all gave varying answers that they were and then Louisa looked at Celeste over her phone and said, "Smile, baby."

"Well, seeing as you asked so nicely," Miles retorted and gave Louisa a cheeky wink.

Louisa's eyes darted to the arrogant smirk that played over Miles's lips. She ignored him, thankful that Celeste's innocence hadn't picked up on his blatant flirty remark and took a number of pictures. Lady luck was on his side again. If Celeste wasn't here, she would've slapped that smirk clean off his chiselled face. *The nerve of the man!* Louisa caught sight of her security team eyeing up Miles and she was almost tempted to let them warn him but it would only upset Celeste.

"What about a picture with your mom?" Miles fixed Louisa with his blazing eyes, daring her to object. He took in her striking features – even in the inebriated state he was in, he could see she was a stunning woman, a little uptight maybe, but her air of dignity matched her equally dignified perfectly tailored trousers with a matching top. She was understated but somehow stood out and had a confidence that only came from good breeding. Louisa's ability to not rise to Miles's blatant taunting showed a confidence that only came from someone who had been trained and well educated in the art of social etiquette.

"That's very kind of you to offer, Mr Keane, but tonight is all about Celeste." Louisa dropped her phone into her understated designer bag and nodded at the security guard. It was his signal that they would need to leave in five minutes. Louisa beckoned Celeste to get up from the couch where Miles had now slouched back and spread his legs, taking up half of the seating area. He narrowed his blue eyes at her and tried to place her accent. His brain was fuzzy but he knew she wasn't American.

"Why don't you go and say bye and thank the band for spending time with you?" Louisa said quietly in her ear.

"Okay, Mummy." Celeste turned and paced over to Louis first who stood up as she held out her hand for him to shake. "Thank you for seeing me," she said sweetly and Louis bent down and kissed the back of her hand.

"It was a pleasure to meet you, Celeste. You're a lovely young lady. One day I'd love to have a daughter just like you," he said sincerely. Celeste then moved on to Mick and Josh who were equally as courteous, telling her they hoped to see her again soon. She then turned her attention to Miles, who had been watching the sweet child's interaction with his fellow band members. He was a little in awe of how well she was behaving and his previous comments about her being a brat came unbidden to his mind. Celeste was anything but a brat; she was polite, sweet and above all, genuine. He stood up on shaky legs as she approached and tried to control his body from swaying.

"Thank you for seeing me," Celeste gushed and held out her hand for him to shake.

He took it, then pulled her into a hug and kissed her reddened cheek, then before security could react, he pulled her back at arms-length and bobbed down so their eyes were on the same level. "It was a pleasure to meet you too, sweet Celeste." He then let her go and tugged off his T-shirt and handed it to her. "Here's a souvenir of our own little after-party." He winked at her and she looked at the white, slightly damp garment, then turned to her mother for approval.

"Say thank you, sweetheart," Louisa prompted her dumbstruck daughter.

"Thank you!" she cried and grabbed the T-shirt, pulling it to her chest.

Miles tweaked Celeste's cheek and then shifted his gaze to Louisa, who stifled a smile. He was doing whatever he could to get a rise from her but there was no way she'd bite.

"Now don't sell it on e-Bay." He chuckled and Celeste's brow furrowed, clearly confused at his comment.

"What's e-Bay, Mummy?" she whispered to her mother, which caused Miles to grin wider.

Of course, how would a billionaire's daughter know about e-Bay? Miles thought to himself.

"I'll explain later, sweetheart." Louisa shook her head, then turned to thank Eric for organising the visit. She then went to every band member and shook their hand, thanking them for their time.

"Mr Keane, thank you for making tonight special for Celeste," she said tightly to Miles, shaking the hand she'd only fifteen minutes ago refused. But this time, it was on her terms.

"It was a pleasure to meet Celeste, and you too, of course." He tilted his head to the side as he spoke and made a show of taking her hand. "Please call me Miles, though. Mr Keane makes me feel old and I'm not big with titles."

"It was... interesting meeting you, Mr Keane. You're everything I expected and *miles* more. Have a good evening." Louisa pulled her hand from his grasp. She turned away from him, heading straight to the door while gripping Celeste's warm hand, and without looking back at the stunned expression that had replaced Miles Keane's trademark wide smile.

1

THE DATE – THE APERITIF

PRESENT DAY

MILES LOOKED AT HIS watch again. It was ten to one as his taxi pulled into Blacks Club. He was early, which was good for him. Normally he would be a few minutes late but since he'd started living in London this last couple months, he still couldn't get to grips with how close everything was. Miles took in the white columns and façade of the revered club at the end of the driveway. Club was a bit of an understatement. This was an estate right in the heart of London. *How was that even possible?* he thought to himself. He'd lived in England for the last three years and he still couldn't get over the grandiose buildings steeped in history that were everywhere, even in the centre of this cosmopolitan capital. California felt so new in comparison.

The taxi driver had told him it was a private club where only the elite went. Membership was by referral only and as far as he knew, they hadn't taken on any new members for a few years now. Miles marvelled at the titbits he'd picked up from the black cab drivers. They knew everything about everything and over the last two months, he'd picked up a plethora of interesting but often useless facts.

After passing through a security gate, the taxi drove down the wide driveway, which led to the main impressive house. His door was opened by the smartly dressed doorman and Miles quickly paid the driver, gathered his gift bag and stepped out onto the perfectly kept courtyard of this exclusive club.

On the whole, it didn't take much to intimidate Miles. He'd played live to audiences of thousands, met music legends, actors and been interviewed countless times on live TV. He'd even played to billions at a televised concert. But stepping through the highly polished black door of Blacks Club had him feeling a little apprehensive.

He'd never been good at following the rules. His past bad-boy image was well-documented proof of that. As life experiences and time had gone by, though, he'd matured enough, becoming less rebellious. So when he received an email instructing him to dress appropriately for today's lunch date, his initial reaction was: *screw it! He'd wear what he damn well liked.* Looking at the highly polished marble floor and the ornate mouldings of the grand entrance that showcased exquisite artworks, he was glad he'd put on one of his designer suits, even if he had made a point of omitting the tie.

The maître d' looked up from his desk and gave Miles a courteous smile. "Good afternoon, Mr Keane, welcome to the Blacks Club. Would you please follow me to your table?"

"Erm, yes, sure. I mean, thank you," Miles answered, a little surprised that the maître d' knew who he was. He was used to being recognised; it was part and parcel of being a celebrity, even if it had been four years since Keane Sense had released any new material, but he was a little taken back that the stiff middle-aged maître d' knew him.

Miles followed the maître d' through the beautiful dining room that was already half-full and took a seat at the secluded reserved table, placing his gift bag on the adjacent seat. After ordering a mineral water, he pulled his phone from his inside pocket and let his eyes gaze out of the window, which overlooked the extensive grounds. *This place was huge,* he thought to himself, then turned to his phone and quickly tapped the number. "Hey, I'm here." He spoke quietly, not wanting to draw attention to himself. That was all he needed, some fan coming over and asking for an autograph.

"What's it like?" asked Lottie.

"Well it's very... um... English. I feel like I've been transported back in time. I still don't get why a nineteen-year-old fan wanted to have our date here." Miles shifted his gaze to the diners who were far too engrossed in their own table to even notice him or what he'd just said. He blew out a breath in relief. Margot and Amanda would kill him if he screwed this up.

"She'll be some la-di-da rich daddy's girl, that's why. You know what snobs they are. 'We dine at our private club.'" She put on a fake posh accent as she spoke the last line, causing Miles to chuckle.

"Well I suppose I'll find out in a few minutes. So remember, at half past two, call me and I'll make some excuse to leave. I'm supposed to spend an hour and a half with her and then I can go. It'll make it less awkward."

"Sure. Then, are you coming over? Or shall I come over to yours?" Lottie said seductively over the phone and Miles knew that she'd be pouting.

"Erm, I'll call you, okay?" he replied. The last thing he wanted was to spend a whole afternoon and evening with her. Lottie was good to look at and happy to sleep with Miles whenever and wherever he wanted but other than that, they had very little in common. She was his go-to date if he needed a plus one and a guaranteed booty call. The arrangement suited them both. Miles didn't need to be with someone who wanted a commitment. He had enough on his plate at the moment without that complication.

After finishing his call, he quickly checked his emails and messages, then took a sip of his water that had discreetly appeared.

He put down his phone and glanced out at the cars parked outside. *Jeez, every car was better than the next.* Miles had seen plenty of expensive cars. His pop-star lifestyle had meant he could have whatever car he wanted, but these cars were understated and elegant. They weren't flashy stretch limos, Bugattis or pimped-out Mercedes that were the norm in Los Angeles.

Miles's attention was drawn to a black Bentley pulling up to the entrance. The doorman smiled widely as the car's chauffer opened the rear door and the occupant stepped out. The door obscured Miles's view of whoever had exited the car but as soon as the chauffer shut the door, he caught a glimpse of a red coat and dark glossy hair stepping in through the entrance and disappearing from view.

Miles checked his phone again. It was one o'clock. Hopefully his date would arrive soon. He already felt uncomfortable in such aristocratic and refined surroundings.

"MR THOMAS, IT'S GOOD to see you back. Did you enjoy your holiday?" Louisa stretched out her hand for the maître d' to shake.

"It's good to see you too, Lady Blackthorn. And yes, Florence was most enjoyable, thank you for asking. Your guest is already here."

"Thank you."

"Let me take your coat." Mr Thomas helped Louisa out of her red coat and passed it to a member of the cloakroom staff. Louisa thanked them both, then turned to face the middle-aged man she'd known for over ten years.

"Mr Thomas, I know we've had this conversation before and you've made it clear that it's against protocol, but could you please ask your staff to call me just 'madame' today?"

"My lady, as you are aware…" Mr Thomas began to protest.

"I know Mr Thomas, I know it goes against etiquette but my guest… well, let's just say he's unaware and knowing may cause him some discomfort. So for today, could you do me this favour?" Louisa pleaded. She knew Mr Thomas would find this request hard; he was a stickler for formalities but she really didn't want her identity to be revealed. Well, not yet anyway.

"Lady Blackthorn wouldn't like it." Mr Thomas arched his brow at her and she chuckled.

"I won't tell my mother if you don't," Louisa answered dryly.

"As you wish my la… as you wish, madame," Mr Thomas conceded.

"Thank you, Mr Thomas. I owe you one."

Mr Thomas chuckled and shook his head. "If you'd like to follow me, madame."

"That's alright. I know the way."

MILES LOOKED UP TOWARDS the entrance, wondering where his date was, and watched the maître d' talk to a woman with long dark hair. If he wasn't mistaken, it was the same woman from the Bentley. She turned and started to walk in the direction of his table. Walk wasn't the right word; she glided. For a moment he just stared at her, transfixed by her poise and air of sophistication. The fitted dress she wore skimmed over her frame showing just enough of her curves and the length hinted at lean toned legs. It was chic and elegant and had it not been for the deep red colour and five-inch leopard print killer heels, the look would've seemed a little conservative. Miles blinked, then averted his eyes, realising that at any moment she would catch him out blatantly staring. He turned his attention back to his phone and wondered where the hell his date was. He wasn't used to having to wait for anyone.

"Mr Keane?" A soft cultured voice made Miles jerk his eyes

away from his screen to rest on the woman in red standing a foot away from his table.

"Yes," he answered, clearly puzzled as to why she was addressing him.

"I'm Louisa, your lunch date." Louisa put out her hand for him to shake.

It took Miles a few seconds to register what she'd just said. "You're my date? I thought you were nineteen," he blurted out. Louisa's eyebrows rose in surprise, causing Miles to blanch, realising how his comment sounded. He shot up from his seat to shake her hand, hoping it would rectify his faux pas, but in his haste he knocked the table, which caused his water glass to topple and pour its contents over the linen tablecloth, splashing across the front of his trousers.

"Fuck! I mean sorry. Shit," Miles muttered, mortified he'd behaved like an ass, cursing in such a dignified establishment and now he'd messed up the table.

His eyes shot up to Louisa as she stepped around grabbing a linen napkin and handing it to him. "Here, use this." Her eyes darted to Mr Thomas, who was already pacing over with two waiters in tow. She placed her red leather clutch on the table, then took the napkins from the waiter and told Mr Thomas and his staff they were fine, effectively dismissing their help.

"I'm so sorry. I don't know how that happened," Miles blew out, dabbing the napkin over the front of his trousers, where a large wet patch had appeared over the crotch of his stone-coloured suit trousers.

"No point crying over spilt mineral water," Louisa said dryly, which caused Miles to pause and look at her. She gave him a smile. "Now if it had been a 2003 Chateaux Lafite Rothschild, well that would have been different," she said with a smirk as she blotted the table with her elegant hands.

Miles let out a chuckle, pleased she didn't seem offended and had diffused his embarrassment with humour. "I've no idea what that is but I'm assuming it's an expensive bottle of wine." He placed the damp napkin on the table.

"You would be right and it is absolutely exquisite," she added, taking her seat as the waiter pulled out a chair for her. He then left the menus and collected all the damp napkins from the table. "Not sure if they have any bottles here, though, but I know they have the 2016."

"Maybe we should give it a miss, unless you like to live dangerously? Thirty seconds into the date and I've already caused mayhem." Miles shook his head.

"So, I take it you were expecting someone younger?"

Miles cleared his throat and gave a nod.

"Sorry to disappoint." Louisa smoothed back her fringe and lifted her bag off the table, placing it behind her, then rested her hands on her lap.

"Erm no, believe me, you haven't disappointed me." Miles edged forward in his seat and Louisa blinked at him, waiting for whatever blunder was going to come out of his mouth next. "It's just Margot said the date was won by a nineteen-year-old fan." Miles shrugged.

"Well, Margot is half-right. I bid on the date for my daughter, who *is* nineteen. But she was unable to make it, so rather than have you waiting here and being stood up, I came in her place." Louisa gave a discreet signal to the waiter when she finished her rather thin explanation. She didn't want to bruise his ego with the truth after he'd just embarrassed himself.

"Oh. Won't she be disappointed?" Miles asked still puzzled.

"I'm not sure," Louisa muttered, then turned to the waiter. "I'll have my usual please." The waiter nodded and looked expectantly at Miles.

"What's your usual?" Miles asked.

"An old fashioned but with Scotch, not bourbon." She frowned, even at the thought.

"I'll have the same, please." The waiter nodded and left them to peruse the menus. "You don't like bourbon?"

Louisa shook her head. "No."

"Too American?" Miles accentuated his American accent, then smirked.

"Something like that." Louisa stifled a grin and opened up her menu.

Oh crap, she was here by default and probably duress, plus she wasn't a fan of America. This lunch date was going to be a disaster, thought Miles. He was going to have to make amends and fast. The last thing he wanted was an hour and a half of awkward conversation. If he'd been with a gushing fan, he wouldn't have had to do much at all. Just listen to them talk and ask him lame questions like, "How long does it take you to write a song?", "Do you really play all those instruments?" or worse: "Do you want to come back to my place?" The stunning woman in front of him was refined, obviously well bred and well educated. He couldn't impress her with his usual repertoire of sexy smiles, double entendres and name dropping. She would find that behaviour vulgar. It was time to up his game.

"I feel like we need to start from the beginning." Miles placed his menu on the table and gave her that famous smile that had made him a teen heartthrob. He then put out his hand for her to shake. "Hi, I'm Miles Keane but please just call me Miles. I'm not a fan of titles. Mr Keane is for my father." He smirked.

Louisa took in a sharp breath at his unintentional second faux pas in the last five minutes. *Didn't like titles, eh? Yes, she remembered that from their first meeting.* She put down her menu and eyed his hand and gave him a wry smile. For a moment, she was transported to ten years ago when she'd first met him in a sweaty, smoky dressing room that had been over-sprayed with men's cologne to mask the smell of alcohol. At least this time he wasn't wasted. "I know who you are and I think you'd better leave your hands at your side of the table. Just so we avoid any unnecessary spillages."

Miles let out rich laugh, grateful his lunch date had a sense of humour. He retracted his hand and fixed her with his bright blue eyes that perfectly matched his open-necked shirt.

"Good point. So tell me a little about yourself Louisa. Other than you obviously know a lot about expensive wine, you don't like bourbon and you have a nineteen-year-old daughter, which by the way you don't look old enough to have, I know nothing about you."

Louisa placed her hands on top of the menu and Miles's eyes dropped to her hands. He noticed the distinct lack of a wedding band, though her right hand had a beautiful diamond ring in an antique setting. It was big enough to be noticed but not so big to be showy. Perfectly elegant.

She ignored his compliment about her age and leaned a little closer before she spoke. "Well, you also know I paid fifty thousand pounds for an hour and a half of your undivided attention. I didn't pay that amount so I could talk about myself. I know everything about me. This date, *Miles,* is all about you, so..." She made a circling gesture with her right hand, encouraging him to talk. Miles took in a deep breath, caught completely off-guard by her unexpected direct comment, but was saved by the waiter coming with their aperitifs and to take their order.

"My la... erm, madame are you ready to order?" the waiter stuttered.

"I am, but I think Mr Keane hasn't had chance to look at the menu."

"I'll have whatever you're having. I think I can trust your judgement. You seem to know this place pretty well." Miles closed his menu and sat back in his chair. He'd had a quick glance but half of the menu was in French, which he didn't understand, plus there were no prices, which made him wary. He ate anything, so whatever Louisa chose would be fine.

"Well, if you're sure."

Miles gave her a nod and watched her closely as she ordered their meal.

"So we'll have the seared scallops to start, followed by the slow roasted beef fillet and beef cheek and for dessert, the coffee bean brûlée."

"An excellent choice as always, madame, and for the wine?"

Louisa glanced at Miles, who was still studying her. "I think we'll have the 2016 Lafite."

He suppressed a grin and handed his menu to the waiter. "Are you sure that's wise?" Miles arched a questioning brow at her.

"Let's live dangerously, shall we? And anyway, it goes so well with beef."

Miles chuckled and in his American drawl he answered, "Ma'am, I'll have to take your word for it." He shook his head, then lifted up his glass and waited for Louisa to do the same. "It's a pleasure to meet you, Louisa. I'll try not spill anything else."

Louisa picked up her glass and clinked it against Miles's. "I'm hoping you'll at least *spill* a little about yourself, though," she retorted with a tilt of her head.

"I'll make sure you get your money's worth."

"I'm banking on it."

This was going to be fun. Melissa was right: an hour and a half of making a pop idol squirm in a situation he was unfamiliar with, with a guest he wasn't expecting, plus she'd given him carte blanche to talk about himself. He was bound to say something inappropriate. Louisa almost felt sorry for him. Well, almost. He still had that cocky edge to him simmering under the surface but he seemed to have it under control, unlike that night ten years ago. He'd aged well, considering what he'd been through. His addiction to A-class drugs had been front and centre of the news four years ago. He was a classic case of super-talented singer songwriter letting fame go to his head. Maybe that was unfair. He'd suffered from tragedy too and so publicly, which must have been hard to cope with, even without media scrutiny. It was one of the reasons Louisa had made a point of keeping her identity unknown and avoiding situations that might shine the limelight on her. It also helped that she was well connected too; money could buy you ambiguity but connections were what guaranteed it.

That might change when she took over from her mother's role. Up until now, her mother had been the patron for CASPO, the Children, Adolescent and Single Parent Organisation, hosting fundraisers and bullying her connections for hefty donations that had kept the organisation afloat. Wasn't that why she'd decided to come on this date, to see if working alongside Miles Keane was something she'd be able to do? It was part of the shake-up of the charity, bringing in new blood, celebrity blood to up the donations, reaching out to a wider audience. He appealed to the young and glamorous, while she would give the charity gravity. Her family's title was the golden seal that would guarantee the wealthy aristocracy's contributions. They'd be a dream team.

Louisa had monitored the charity over the last few years and had seen donations stay at roughly the same level. She'd often discussed new strategies with her mother, exploiting the knowledge she'd garnered from the extensive charity work she'd done while living stateside. The truth was when the charity started, her mother was younger and her father had been alive. She'd had the energy and the drive to ensure the charity thrived, but since The Earl of Blackthorn's early death and then Alistair's accident, Lady Alice Blackthorn had lost her killer spirit. Now that Louisa was divorced, back in the UK and didn't have to look after Celeste, it seemed to be the perfect opportunity, plus Lady Alice Blackthorn was adamant she take on the role.

Louisa sipped her old fashioned, then placed it on the table. Miles nervously turned his glass with his thumb and middle finger. She wanted him to talk about himself. What on Earth would she find even remotely interesting about him? They were polar opposites. It suddenly became apparent to Miles that he wanted to impress her. He'd never had to impress anyone before – just walking into a room, onto a stage or a TV set was enough. His musical talent and good looks were his ticket, and everyone lined up for one – everyone except the beautiful woman sitting opposite him. She wasn't impressed with him; she was tolerating him and he'd never been so nervous or thrown off-kilter as he felt at this moment, but he'd be damned if he'd let her see that. "So, Louisa, what would you like to know about me?"

"Well I know enough about your career, your success, your net worth, where you grew up and your education. I know about all the scandal that has surrounded you," Louisa paused for a second as Miles eyes widened with every word that came out of her perfectly formed lips. "Which women you... dated. A simple search gave me all those facts and figures."

"You googled me?" Miles gasped incredulously.

"Of course; you were supposed to meet my nineteen-year-old daughter," Louisa retorted as though it was obvious.

Miles leaned forward and narrowed his eyes. "Is that why you came instead?"

Louisa's lips curved into a smile. "No. Celeste is more than capable of looking after herself, believe me. I don't stop her seeing her friends or boyfriends, even if they have a colourful past. But I do like to be informed."

"Well you seem to know everything about me."

"I want to know the things that aren't in Wikipedia."

"Like?"

"Why you stopped writing music, performing and what your plans for the future are?"

Miles was spared answering her comment by the arrival of their first course, which was accompanied by two glasses of white wine.

"Mr Thomas suggested the Pouilly-Fumé to accompany the scallops, madame," said one of the waiters.

"Thank you. Perfect choice." Louisa gave a discreet nod over to Mr Thomas who was observing their table from his post at entrance.

"How do you know so much about wine?" Miles asked, drawing her attention back to him.

She gave him an enigmatic smile and picked up her glass. Miles knew she wouldn't answer his question. She'd made it clear this date was all about him. "Try it. It's a light dry wine that pairs well with seafood." Miles did as he was bid and took a sip. He nodded, indicating he liked it. "Are you a wine drinker?" Louisa took a sip of wine and then laid her linen napkin across her lap.

"Sure, I drink wine. I know the basics. Though I have to say this wine is a lot finer than the ones I've tasted."

"So you drink...?" Louisa left the sentence hanging, waiting for him to fill in the blank, then picked up her knife and fork.

"That didn't come up on Wikipedia?" He chuckled.

"Vodka?"

Miles eyebrows shot up in surprise. "That's on Wikipedia?" he said, clearly shocked.

Louisa smirked and shook her head. "Lucky guess." She narrowed her eyes, indicating she was thinking, then added, "Grey Goose?"

"Whoa, how the hell did you know that?" Miles stared at the coolly confident woman in front of him slicing through her scallop, a little stunned. *Maybe he should start googling himself again*, he thought. He'd stopped reading anything related to him or his family almost five years ago. His phone lit up, indicating he had a message, and his eyes darted to it for a second, then he looked back at Louisa.

Louisa just shrugged and placed the morsel of food in her mouth.

2

GOODBYE – HELLO

FOUR MONTHS AGO

LOUISA WALKED AROUND HER elegant lounge, taking in the features that had become so familiar to her over the last nineteen years. When Gerard had bought the town house, just after their engagement, she'd found its eleven thousand square feet small. The six-storey house probably wouldn't fill the east wing of Holmwood House, but the location on the Upper East Side meant they were steps away from Gerard's offices on Fifth Avenue. Their home stood just off the stretch of Museum Mile that is resident to the world famous Guggenheim Museum, as well as New York City's top-tier stores and restaurants on Madison Avenue. As if that wasn't enough, Central Park was also just on their doorstep.

Their first few years in their house had been an adventure, happy times and even though the following years had turned sour, Louisa could still remember those good days when she was madly in love with her French gentleman and he doted on her every word.

It took a year to redecorate and refurbish the 1900s building and they'd just completed it in time for Celeste's arrival. Louisa found it charming that their home was classed as old. It felt almost contemporary compared to the 18th-century house she'd grown up in. Louisa filled her days with looking after her daughter and discovering New York. The four staff they employed meant her evenings were dedicated to Gerard, dining together, taking in shows and accompanying him to business functions. This had been the life she'd dreamed about; the three of them blissfully happy, living a charmed life in the vibrant city of New York.

Gerard had slipped comfortably into his family's business, broadening the French-based company and bringing it to America. The Dupont family had expanded their chemical and solvent business into disposable packaging in the early 90s, all down to their forward-thinking son. The boom in takeout coffee and food-on-the-go had bolstered an already thriving business, seeing the American Dupont empire skyrocket into a multi-billion corporation. Gerard Dupont was a shrewd businessman. He sold the company when it was at its peak, then invested in real estate when the property market slumped. Always looking into the future, Gerard invested in a new company that researched and developed biodegradable packaging, effectively competing with his old company. It wasn't a glamorous business to be in or even a business that caught media attention, like all the dot-com companies that had blown up over the last couple of decades, but it was highly lucrative and almost gave Louisa the kind of life she'd been accustomed to.

"You're sure you don't want the house, *cherie*?" Gerard's deep accented voice pulled Louisa out of her thoughts. He still called her *cherie,* even after almost living separate lives for ten years. Even though they'd signed divorce papers that very morning and her settlement had been wired to her account. Even though today she was flying to London in Gerard's private plane to start her new single life back in England. He said that she would always be his *cherie,* that that would never change and Louisa knew he meant it.

Louisa shook her head. "I'll buy an apartment for when I'm over. Celeste can use it too." She didn't want their home. For all its elegance and desirable location, the last ten years living here had been lonely. Louisa wanted a fresh start.

Gerard gave her a nod as he observed her with sad eyes. "Celeste can stay with me when she visits."

Louisa turned to look at him taking in his handsome face. His dark hair immaculately styled as always, his almost black eyes searching over her face. "I think she'd rather be on her own, Gerard. She likes her privacy and so do you." It was a subtle hint that Celeste wouldn't accept whichever one of Gerard's lady companions he was seeing. Celeste had her father on a pedestal and when she'd found out he wasn't quite the perfect man she thought he was, it had affected their relationship for a while. Now it was a case of ignorance is bliss. Celeste didn't want to meet or know about who her father was "dating" – ever.

"You know you don't need to leave straight away. We could dine out together tonight and you could leave in a day or two." Gerard took a step forward and Louisa answered him with a slight shake of her head. He was still trying to keep her here, a last ditch attempt at having a few more days. He was a gentleman in every possible way, except in the way Louisa valued most.

It had taken Louisa seven years to come to terms with Gerard's propensity for dabbling away from home. It was something he found acceptable, a distraction and pastime, normal behaviour for a man of his standing. Louisa, on the other hand, found it outrageous. It was a cultural divide that they never bridged in their marriage and though Gerard tried to conform, there was a wedge between them: he would never be loyal and she would never accept it.

Their good breeding and determination to keeping up appearances meant they came to an understanding. As long as there wasn't any scandal and Gerard didn't rub his dalliances in her face, Louisa would stay married to him until Celeste was ready to leave home. The house was big enough for Louisa to have a whole floor to herself and she had her charity work to keep her busy. It wasn't how Louisa envisaged her life when she first married Gerard but it meant Celeste had a stable home life where she saw both her parents. Gerard kept his word and to the outside world, they had a perfect life and marriage.

"It's time, Gerard. We both knew this day was coming." Louisa picked up her coat and Gerard took it from her.

"I'm going to miss you, *cherie*," he said softly as he opened it up for her to put on.

"Perhaps." She sighed. She'd miss him too. They'd been together twenty years. They were friends, above all, even if their marriage had ended up being one of convenience over the last ten years. He was so familiar to her. She knew his ways, his thoughts, how he liked his eggs and coffee, which tailor he used and where he bought his bespoke shoes. She knew everything about him and yet the comfort that that should have given her only made her sadder.

"I still love you." His voice was hoarse with emotion. He couldn't believe she was really going to leave him, even after she'd told him repeatedly over the last ten years that she was here only for Celeste. He'd hoped she'd forgiven him, come round, even, but when she'd asked him to start the divorce proceedings, a month before Celeste left on her six month voluntary work in Peru, he realised he'd always been on borrowed time. She'd sacrificed ten years so that Celeste would live with both her parents. She'd sacrificed her life so that he was in his daughter's life every day and because of that he couldn't deny her.

"I know." *Just not enough*, she said to herself, as she did every time he told her.

There was no battling over assets. No big court case to determine the settlement. No lawyers fighting for a larger payoff.

The paperwork was completed quietly, civilly and with the utmost dignity in Gerard's lawyer's office. Louisa took whatever she brought into the marriage, which was her sizeable inheritance from when her father The Earl of Blackthorn died. Their home was valued and Louisa received just under $15 million for her share. Gerard then transferred $100 million to Louisa, $5 million for every year they'd been together. Louisa didn't ask for or need the money; her inheritance had grown to five times that amount, but Gerard was fair and the ultimate gentleman. He didn't want her walking away from him without some financial remuneration.

A discreet cough from the lounge door caught their attention. "Your baggage is in the car my lady. Whenever you're ready."

Louisa thanked their driver and picked up her handbag, then turned to Gerard. This was going to be a hard goodbye. This man had once been the love of her life. He'd broken her heart, then tried every way possible to mend it. They'd spent almost twenty years together and raised a beautiful, vibrant daughter. Their life together had been on the whole good, even if it hadn't been perfect and however much Louisa wanted to move on, it was one of the hardest decisions she'd ever made. The truth was she still loved him and she'd second-thought today's decision again and again. She was setting out on her own, changing her life and starting afresh at the age of thirty-eight. All she'd ever known was her parent's home and then the home she'd made with Gerard. What she did know though was that she wanted more.

"Call me when you arrive in London." Gerard took her hands in his and gave them a squeeze. "I'm sorry, *cherie*. I'm sorry I couldn't be who you wanted."

Louisa knew he meant every word. "I'm sorry too." She could still see a glimmer of hope in his eyes.

"*Cherie,* you were everything I wanted – needed."

But not enough, she said to herself. "Goodbye, Gerard. Look after yourself." Louisa leaned in to him and gave him a soft kiss to the cheek, feeling her heart break a little more.

"Au revoir, cherie."

"THERE YOU ARE. Welcome back." Alistair's familiar large frame seemed to dwarf the plush private arrival suite Louisa had just stepped into. His wide smile and outstretched arms were enough to shake off Louisa's melancholy journey. The ten hours she'd spent on the luxurious plane had been lonely with only her disturbing thoughts and baggage for company. Seeing her beloved brother standing in his usual uniform of Barbour jacket, khaki cargo trousers and walking boots lifted her spirits. He hugged her tightly and rubbed his bristly jaw against her smooth cheek and she squirmed.

"Stop it! I'm not fifteen," she mock-chastised him, loving the fact he still liked to tease her, even after all these years. He was her big brother, regardless of what had happened to both of them over their lives, and Louisa felt unrivalled comfort in his loving embrace.

"You're still my baby sister Loulou."

"You didn't need to meet me."

"Sure I did. I wanted you to travel back in style. Needed to compete with the high-flying New York lifestyle you've gotten used to." He gave her a grin and she rolled her eyes at his teasing. Alistair was always joking with her about the glitzy lifestyle she'd had.

"Ha ha, you're so funny." She linked her arm with his. "So you're driving me home in the Land Rover, then?" she said with a huff, knowing this was Alistair preferred mode of transport around Holmwood House and anywhere outside of the grounds, regardless of the garage full of luxury cars. Though it was practical, it was anything but stylish.

"Noooo, we're taking the new Koala."

Louisa stopped mid-stride. "It's a forty-five minute drive from the airport to Holmwood and you came in the helicopter?"

"Just keeping up with Duponts," he said dryly.

"Alistair, you have nothing to keep up with," she sighed.

"I know but I just wanted to take you back home with a bit more panache." He gave her a smirk.

"How very uncharacteristic of the Blackthorns. Mama will be appalled at your flashy show."

"I think she actually likes that I'm..." He rocked his head from side to side, trying to find the right words.

"Living it up a bit?"

"Yeah."

"Well I'm glad too. You breathe, drink and eat Holmwood House. It's time to look after yourself too, be a little indulgent."

"I'm getting there," he said quietly as a number of emotions passed over his ruggedly handsome face.

"Come on, then, fly me home, *action man*," she teased, using his childhood nickname and nudging him.

"You mean robo-man now," he said dryly, knocking his chuckles on his left leg, referring to the new nickname a ten-year-old Celeste had come up with when she'd first seen her uncle complete with his prosthetic metal blade.

Alistair had been in charge of running the Holmwood estate for the last eight years since their father had been taken ill. The role of The Earl of Blackthorn had been unexpectedly thrust upon him once his father had died after a short battle with cancer, at a time when he himself was still in recovery. It was a role he knew would be his in the distant future when he retired from the military. But his critical accident ten years ago, during active combat, meant his successful military career had been cut short. The awards and accolades he'd received for gallantry did little to compensate for the loss of his left leg and two years of recovery. Spinal injuries due to shrapnel had meant he was unable to walk for six months, and the loss of his leg, making recovery even more arduous, along with the long-term psychological after-effects of post-traumatic stress disorder. As if that wasn't enough to contend with, he was told that due to his blast injuries, he would never be able to have children.

Money and position could secure many things, open hundreds of doors and give endless opportunities but they couldn't reverse the damage of bomb blasts. Alistair had undergone countless examinations and seen the top specialists from around the world, but the results were always the same; he would never be able to carry on the blood line of Blackthorn that could be traced back over five hundred years.

Alistair was The Earl of Blackthorn by birthright but he had taken the decision to pass his title and inheritance over to Louisa. She had already secured their bloodline with Celeste and to Alistair, it made perfect sense. Louisa had no desire to take on the Holmwood estate; apart from the fact she was in New York, her brother had turned their family home and lands from successful to highly lucrative. Where many stately homes and estates had suffered from mismanagement, depleting revenues and natural threats over the last handful of decades, Holmwood House, the home of The Blackthorns, had survived, due to the late Earl's forward thinking and business acumen. Alistair continued his late father's good work and expanded it even further. So Alistair and Louisa came to an agreement that Alistair would run the estate for as long as he wanted, even though Louisa was now the rightful heiress and the Countess.

In the last eight years, Louisa had seen how much running Holmwood House had given her broken brother a new lease of life. He'd always aspired to move up the ranks within the military. His love of jets and planes had steered him to a career in the RAF but even as a boy, he'd always been active and loved any kind of outdoor activities. He was lucky to have the grounds and facilities of Holmwood House to facilitate his interests. He could ride a horse by the age of five, was driving Land Rovers around the private grounds as soon as his feet could reach the pedals. He was an excellent marksman and even beat the late Earl at clay pigeon shooting in his teens. He'd fearlessly climbed rock faces and liked to live rough in the extensive woodlands on the estate with his friends, camping out with make shift tents. It was these very activities that prompted Louisa to christen her brother action-man. He was an adventurer and a risk taker and had it not been for his remarkable skill as a pilot, nine men of his squadron would've been killed in action.

Alistair had thrown himself into the role of landowner and, due to the advances in prosthetics, he was still able to enjoy the many activities that had become second nature to him. But the after-effects of his final tour had not only changed him physically but mentally, from outgoing and sociable to a withdrawn version of himself.

Lady Alice Blackthorn had never been comfortable with her son's need to push the boundaries but after seeing him change into a shadow of the vibrant man she loved and admired, she actively encouraged him to pursue whatever brought back that twinkle in his eye, even if she thought it was a little brash. Today was one of those days. She practically insisted that he took out the helicopter to pick up Louisa, using the excuse that after such a long flight, Louisa would be happy to get home as fast as possible. Alistair mumbled something about the expense and the cost to the environment, to which his mother replied that if Gerard could send her home in his private plane, the least they could do was fly her home in the same style.

After arranging for Louisa's luggage and possessions to be put through customs, they headed to where Alistair had set down the impressive AW119 Koala. He'd recently traded his original helicopter and invested in a newer model.

"She's a beauty, Alistair, much swankier than the last one." Louisa grinned at her brother, pleased to see his face light up.

Louisa was thankful that his past experience hadn't put him off flying. As soon as he was fit again, Lady Alice had insisted they invest in a helicopter as part of one of the many attractions and features of Holmwood House. Her ulterior motive for the frankly frivolous buy had been to see her son regain his love of flying but it had in fact ended up being a good investment. Alistair used it to take paying guests around the extensive grounds, it was used for weddings and other private functions plus, as a side business, he was often hired to move VIPs around. It was amazing how many of the rich and famous liked the idea of a war hero like Earl flying them around.

"This must be a hell of a babe magnet." Louisa winked at Alistair as he helped her up. "I mean, flashy cars are so passé but a swanky helicopter, well..."

"Yeah, stop fishing. I'm not seeing anyone. And just so you know, I will be interrogating you about my ex brother-in-law." He gave her a pointed look, then shut her door. Since he'd started filling his days and nights with the running of Holmwood, Alistair hadn't really had time to date, or rather he'd avoided the whole scene. He had had various girlfriends before his accident and a couple afterwards but he knew that they never had a long-term future.

Louisa sighed as she strapped herself into her seat. The last thing she wanted to do was talk about Gerard. To her family and everyone around them, it was a shock that they'd divorced, but Louisa would bet her inheritance that Alistair wasn't surprised.

"Hey." Alistair squeezed her leg, drawing her attention away from the window and to his handsome face. "I just want to make sure you're okay. I'm sure you had your reasons. I'm not here to judge anyone. You want to talk about it, then I'm your guy. I'm here for you; that's all."

"Thanks, but to be honest, I really don't want to talk about it. It is what it is. We're still friends. It's not a sudden thing..."

"Okay. But you need anything, anything at all, you come to me."

Louisa nodded and gave him a tired smile. "I will."

He gave her a nod and started his checks. "It'll be good to have you home. You can help around the estate. I'm getting pretty sick of doing all the work around there and you getting the glory and title." He smirked, hoping his joke would bring back the sparkle in her eyes.

"Shut up, you love it, riding around on horses, Land Rovers, tractors and helicopters. You're so much like papa." Louisa shook her head at him.

"Yeah, I do."

"Take me home, *Parker,*" she replied dryly, making a reference to one of their favourite childhood TV shows, and Alistair grinned, then reached over and squeezed her leg again.

"Good to have you home, *my lady*."

HOLMWOOD HOUSE SEEMED TO rise up from behind the canopy of the woodlands that marked the parameter of the estate. It was a magnificent building, which had been rebuilt in the 18th-century, set in over 500 acres of land. The French-inspired mansion, designed in the 1830s, had replaced the old, dark and dingy house and a number of new features had been added, such as the Versailles-like view of the central gardens and magnificent baroque pavilion.

The classical building was comprised of a central block between two matching bays, flanked by slightly projecting wings, all three storeys high. As Alistair flew towards the south of Holmwood House, which was actually the back, the unarguably impressive gardens came into view. Even on a cold February morning, the Italian and French-inspired grounds looked beautiful. The long canal that paved the way to the pavilion built at the end glistened as Alistair lowered the helicopter over it, causing the water to ripple. Louisa grinned at him, knowing he was showing off a little and no doubt causing their mother to tut at such a display. Lady Alice would no doubt have something to say about Alistair's showy display, even if she preened in private at his exceptional flying skills. Louisa peered out of the window, taking in the grounds that were so familiar to her and had been her home for eighteen years. There were so many good memories growing up in such a privileged environment with her family. Many might have found the grand house foreboding, even imposing, but to Louisa, her grandiose Holmwood estate felt like home.

Alistair hovered a little to the right wing of the house, where the integrated conservatory was, before setting the helicopter down gently. The household staff appeared almost instantly, happy to have their Countess back home, even if it was under sad circumstances.

Over the years, Louisa and Alistair had tried to become more relaxed with protocol and though there were certain formalities, they had managed to make their staff feel less alienated from them, as was often the case in noble households. Their parents had instigated the shift in behaviour when the late Earl had inherited Holmwood at a relatively young age.

Within a few minutes, Louisa had warmly greeted her mother and staff and was now sitting in the parlour enjoying the heat from the fire and a steaming cup of tea. Most stately homes were cold and badly insulated but after a million-pound refurbishment almost seven years ago, the 18th-century grand house had been brought into the present day. Alistair had implemented the most up-to-date ecological systems in the house and the grounds, ensuring the house could work off a high percentage of sustainable energy. Lady Alice Blackthorn lived in the west wing of the house, leaving the main body of the house and the east wing to her children. But today they were using the main house parlour.

"Have you decided where you want to live?" Lady Alice asked after they'd caught up on the latest news from Celeste. Louisa's mother was referring to where Louisa's main base would be, now she was permanently in the UK. Louisa had a house in central London that she used when she came over from New York. It was a more convenient location, seeing as Gerard and Celeste had always wanted to see the sights while they enjoyed their short visits to the UK. Holmwood was usually where they stayed in the summer months.

"I think I'll be here for now, until I settle, and then I'll probably spend most of my time in London." Louisa flitted her eyes between her mother and brother, wondering how long it would be before her mother started to probe further. Alistair paced over to the large window and stared out at the gardens, hoping the pep talk he'd given his mother before leaving that morning was enough to stop the many questions she wanted answering.

Lady Alice turned to face Louisa and put down her teacup. "You know I need you. I know you've just arrived and I promised Alistair I wouldn't push you, but CASPO needs you; I need you. I'm getting too old to run around and since... well, the last eight years have taken their toll."

Alistair sighed and turned to face the two women. He gave a pointed look to his mother, which she ignored, and then he gave Louisa a resigned smirk.

"I know, Mama. And I promise I'll come on board but I just need some time to adjust. I've just changed country and home, waved bye-bye to my daughter for six months and divorced, all in the last month, so bear with me," she said dryly.

Lady Alice gave her a small nod and picked up her teacup. To most people, Lady Alice Blackthorn was a formidable woman, tough on the outside and with a no-nonsense attitude but both

Alistair and Louisa had never been intimidated by her because they knew this was just the image she liked to portray. Being married into nobility had an inordinate amount of privilege but it also came with a huge amount of responsibility too, and that meant that Lady Alice had to grow a thicker skin and be fearless. She'd been lucky to have The Earl by her side to love, guide and support her but she still felt the need to keep up a sterner façade.

"So Celeste is back at the beginning of July? She'll miss the summer garden party for the first time," Lady Alice stated with a sharp sigh, making it obvious she wasn't happy about the fact her only grandchild wouldn't be at one of the most revered events of the summer.

"She will, but we'll have her for the whole summer before she goes off to university," Louisa said softly, hoping that would soften the blow.

"And Gerard won't want to spend time with her?"

"I'm sure between us we can arrange that. We're still friends, Mama, really." Louisa's gaze darted to Alistair who was now almost glaring at his mother.

She looked suitably chastised for a millisecond and then continued. "Hmm, good. He's a very good father and he was part of our family for years."

"I know and he loves you very much, Mama."

"And you, do you still love him?"

"Of course."

"Just not enough to stay together?"

"Mama…" Alistair barked, stepping forward, totally frustrated with his mother's inquisition. Lady Alice head snapped sharply towards her son. He towered over her slight frame but she just waved her free hand at him dismissively. "I'm her mother. I'm asking out of concern. And by the way, I saw how low you flew. Don't think I didn't."

"I know what I'm doing, okay?" he said with a scowl, then raised his eyebrows at his mother and said, "She's just walked through the door and you're starting with the twenty questions!" He threw an apologetic look in Louisa's direction and she shook her head, indicating she was fine.

"Mama, what you need to know, both of you," Louisa shifted her eyes between them, "is that Gerard and I still care deeply about each other but we grew apart. That's all, and it just seemed only right that we divorce while we still had the chance to meet someone else."

Alistair nodded his silent approval but his mother furrowed her brow. "Very modern of you."

"Just practical and realistic. I'm lucky I had such an understanding husband," Louisa said with a little force, still wanting to defend her husband in his absence.

"He was lucky to have such an understanding wife." Huffed out Lady Alice.

"Mama, he's still important to me, and he's Celeste's father, so I don't want you being difficult."

"I won't. I like Gerard, even if he is a little too suave for my liking," she said tightly. It wasn't a lie. Gerard was one of the few men who could charm Lady Alice and over the twenty years he'd been in their family, he had been a model father and had stood by them all when The Earl had died. When Alistair was injured, he had researched all possibilities to ensure he recovered as quickly as possible, even arranging doctors to fly in from all over the world to Holmwood to examine him.

"Right, I'm off back to work." Alistair rubbed his hands together. "I'll let you settle in and then I'll come and take you around – in the Land Rover this time." He gave Louisa a wink.

"Maybe you should have a nap," Lady Alice suggested, seeing her daughter give Alistair a weary nod.

"No, if I've learned one thing, it's that you need to power through the jet lag. Give me an hour."

Alistair paced up to Louisa and gave her shoulder a squeeze.

"Go freshen up and I'll honk when I'm here. I want to show you what we've done with the bathhouse."

"It's finished?"

"Yep… fully heated, complete with Jacuzzi." He gave Louisa a broad smile.

"Your brother has been busy," Lady Alice said proudly. "I'll arrange a nice lunch for us in the conservatory, if that's alright with both of you."

"Sounds perfect."

3

THE DATE – THE STARTER

"THIS PLACE," Miles picked up his knife and fork, then paused. "You're a regular here?" His bright blue eyes fixed on hers while he waited for her answer that never came. She gave an enigmatic smile, then forked up some more of her starter. Miles sighed; she was too good at this, keeping her distance, controlling what she said. It felt like she must have been schooled in the art of avoidance. It seemed to come naturally and her almost aloofness should have got his back up, annoyed him even, but in fact it was doing the exact opposite. It was frustrating but at the same time, it made Louisa that much more attractive. The mysterious veil she clouded herself with only made her even more alluring and unattainable, and if there was one thing Miles loved, it was a challenge.

"Why don't you start at the beginning?" Louisa's cultured voice interrupted his thoughts. "Tell me about how you got into music."

"Didn't that come up on Google?" he asked dryly, then he cut through his starter and ate a piece.

Louisa grinned at his obvious irritation. This was a man who was used to being in control. If he knew how much Louisa really knew about him, he'd probably get up and leave on that impulse he was renowned for. "Some parts, but I'm sure there's more. Your father is head of music at the University of Southern California. He also writes music scores for films and your mother lectures in acting, sometimes doing voice work for corporate and promotional videos. So I suppose it was inevitable that you and your brother would follow into the arts."

"The arts? You make us sound so scholarly." He laughed to cover up his shock at how well informed she obviously was. "We were in a boy band, Louisa; we didn't play in the New York Philharmonic," he huffed, arching his brow at her.

"But you could've." She tilted her head a little as his eyes widened in shock.

How could she even know that? Only a handful of people knew they'd been approached as soon as they'd qualified. Miles put down his cutlery, then reached for his wine and took a large gulp.

"Both you and Louis went to Juilliard. You both finished in the top two percent. You could have gone to any one of the top orchestras in the US – the world, in fact. I've no doubt you were approached by many of them. You came from a top musical stable and yet you chose the contemporary option; one that gave you fame, the big bucks and adoration." She paused for a moment, taking in his perfectly chiselled jaw, which was twitching. She was making him uncomfortable and suddenly she felt like a prize bitch. That wasn't how a lady behaved. She reached for her wine glass and took a sip to moisten her dried-up mouth. Her mother's words came unbidden into her head: "A lady or a gentleman always makes someone feel comfortable, whoever they are." If her mother were here now, she would be tutting under her breath. Louisa put down her wine glass and took a sharp breath.

"Man, you really did your research," he drawled with a slight shake of his head, making Louisa feel even worse.

"I'm sorry. I didn't mean to be so… blunt," she said softly.

He gave a nod and picked up his knife and fork again. "Don't sweat it. I've had far worse interrogations, believe me." He forked up some food, then lifted his slightly regretful eyes to hers. "I mean, I was in the media spotlight for ten years, drinking, partying hard, womanizing and then after…" he took a deep breath, "…and then I ended up in rehab." He popped his food in his mouth and chewed slowly. Louisa lowered her gaze to her half-empty plate, feeling awful at how hard she'd sounded. His deep voice pulled her attention back to his handsome face. "So don't worry, ask whatever you want; I've been grilled by far worse," he said with a cheeky wink. "And after all, you have to get your money's worth." He widened his eyes dramatically, which caused Louisa to laugh softly. He was using self-deprecating humour to diffuse any tension and Louisa thought that his behaviour was more befitting of a gentleman, while she'd behaved nothing like a lady. The thought was sobering. "Well, you know I went into rehab." Miles had talked extensively about his time in rehab on various talk shows and articles in an attempt to help other addicts. He also wanted everyone to know that he wasn't going back to that lifestyle again, which meant that Keane Sense were never likely to reform. Well how could they, without their fourth member who had held them all together?

Louisa gave a curt nod. "I saw the articles online."

"Yeah, you can't have a major meltdown in private when you're in the biggest boy band since The Backstreet Boys."

"Nature of the business."

"Yep, gotta take the rough with the smooth." He gave her a grin, then looked down at his plate. He'd almost finished, yet he had no recollection of how the food had tasted. At least the wine was delicious and had helped take the edge off his nervousness.

Louisa watched him closely as he seemed to drift off somewhere else for a moment. She'd been too direct and she was sure the last thing he wanted to talk about was the lead-up to what had tipped him well over the edge and down the slippery slope. He'd spent months in rehab, closed off from the world, and had emerged a fresh, fit and more mature version of himself. Before he could continue, Louisa interrupted his thoughts. "You don't need to tell me about it."

Miles's gaze shot up to hers and for the first time, he saw a softness in them. She'd hidden it well behind her efficient manner and distance. His full lips curved into a smile. "Yeah, I do." He gave a lopsided grin. "I don't mind telling you about it. My story has been sold for far more than the £50,000 you paid for today. Mainly by people who knew absolutely nothing about me." He pursed his lips together and gave a one-shoulder awkward shrug.

"Then in that case, I'd really like to know the *real* story." Louisa slid some more of her starter onto her fork and placed it in her mouth and waited for Miles to start.

"I was always a bit disruptive at school. Unruly, they called me; easily distracted. I'm sure they have an official label for it now but back in the day, I was just a naughty kid. I ended up being sent to the headmaster's office many times but he liked me, so I never got suspended or expelled. Mr Cooke was a great guy and loved his rock music. I mean the really heavy stuff."

"Really?" Louisa gave him a reassuring smile and he nodded.

Miles took a quick sip of his wine and continued. "We used to talk about that when I was sent to him. He was the one that encouraged Louis and me to start a band."

"Not your parents?"

Miles shook his head, then stifled a grin. "They both wanted us to do something less… conspicuous. My father has always done well. I think he hoped we'd follow him into that business."

"Or maybe like your mother, more drama-orientated?"

"Yeah. It meant they were still in the crazy business but without all the crazy that went with it."

Louisa let out a soft laugh. "Like you ended up, you mean?"

Miles chuckled, "Yes, exactly. Anyway, we formed this

makeshift band with two of our friends from music classes. We were just in our teens then but we enjoyed just playing our favourite songs and got to play at a few parties. Then Louis got a place in Juilliard and we stopped for a bit. Well, at least, we didn't play together as a band. Without him at home and the band, I began slacking again, so Mr Cooke suggested I compose a few songs. It sort of did the trick and kept me focused until Louis was back from college. It kept me out of mischief until a couple of years later I went to Juilliard."

"How did your parents react to you playing in a band?"

"Oh they thought it was a phase, that we'd get the notion out of our system and then we'd get serious and do a proper job, so to speak. My parents love jazz music; that's about as radical as they got." He widened his eyes in mock horror, making Louisa laugh softly.

"You don't like jazz?"

"I like all music. There's nothing I particularly dislike. Jazz was always played in our house and the first instrument I learned was the trumpet."

"Oh, not the piano?"

Miles gave slight shake of his head. "I didn't like the idea of sitting in one place. And anyway, it was fitting, seeing as I'm named after one of jazz's legendary trumpet players."

"Miles Davis," Louisa said with a knowing nod.

"Uh-uh, and Louis after Louis Armstrong." Miles picked up his wine glass and drained it. Now he'd started talking about his younger years and the lead up to his stay in rehab, he wasn't so sure it was such a good idea after all. It had been a while since he'd raked over the past. The few close people he'd spent time with knew everything about him; this was the first time in three years he'd talked about the cause of his meltdown.

"Shall I order you some more?" Louisa's eyes darted to his empty glass and he shook his head.

"I love that it's acceptable to drink at lunch time here in England." He grinned.

"Oh yes, we British are renowned for our drinking," Louisa said with a smirk.

Miles's grin widened as he watched Louisa take a ladylike sip from her wine glass.

"In the US they find it... inappropriate."

"So I believe. I can think of far more inappropriate things that are done in the US than lunchtime drinking." Louisa huffed.

"Have you ever been?" Miles shuffled forward in his seat.

Louisa gave him a soft smile, then placed her cutlery on her almost empty plate. *Nice try,* she thought to herself. "So we got to you being accepted into Juilliard."

Miles leaned back and smirked. "Yes, we did." He placed his knife and fork on his plate and shook his head. She wasn't going to be that easy to hoodwink, so rather than try to press for even one small piece of information from her, he started to tell Louisa about his time at college. How he'd loved being surrounded by such adept musicians. He'd always felt a little bit of a freak at school. There had only been a few other students that were musical in high school but at Juilliard, everyone was talented and he fitted in perfectly. By this time, he was proficient at playing the trumpet, guitar, piano, saxophone and clarinet. He'd started to take composing more seriously and was vocally coached. Louis was now in his final year but was still unsure of what he wanted to do once he graduated. He'd had many offers to join numerous prestigious orchestras around the world but even though he was classically trained, Louis had always veered towards more modern music. "He met Amanda in his final year."

"Your sister-in-law?" asked Louisa and Miles nodded with a wry smile. He was soon becoming immune to Louisa's knowledge of his life. "She's British." Again, Miles nodded.

"Love at first sight." Miles eyes clouded a little as he thought about those early days when the three of them used to hang out together. They were good times, when no one knew who they were and they could have jam sessions at the bar, enjoying what they did best. The bar Louis and Miles played in was a college hangout for students who wanted to let loose and shake off the gruelling restraints that the lectures at the prestigious college put on them. The owner allowed Juilliard students to play there for free drinks, and it was on one of the nights Louis had taken over the piano when he'd first spotted Amanda.

Amanda's father had been sent by the company he'd worked for to oversee their American branch for one year. She'd found a position as a teacher's assistant in a college teaching English to foreign students. She'd come into the bar with a group of her pupils after a late class and been totally transfixed by the good-looking piano player, skilfully performing Elton John's *Your Song*.

"Is that what Louis said?" Louisa asked.

Miles gave a nod and a sad smile. "It was the truth. I witnessed it." Miles leaned forward a little before he continued. "Louis played like he was born only to play the piano. By the age of sixteen he could literally play any song. It was his party piece, if you like. Friends would say, 'Play *Bohemian Rhapsody*' and he could, or '*I Want It That Way*' – no problem. He was truly gifted." Miles shifted in his seat. It was clear that talking about his brother was still painful. "But that night when he spotted Amanda, I saw him for the first time ever, falter over the keys. Not that anyone noticed but I did. He didn't take his eyes off her until he'd finished the song and then he gave a modest bow at the round of applause and headed straight for her. And the rest, as they say, is history." He shrugged and rested back on his chair.

"So they were together from their early 20s?"

"Yes. They were together for six years. You know, it was Amanda who asked me to do this auction?"

Louisa gave him that same enigmatic smile that meant of course she knew. He really wondered why she was even asking him to recount this information about him. She seemed to know everything anyway. "She does a lot of fundraising for CASPO," Louisa said, by way of explanation.

"Yeah, well single parents have a rough time of it, especially when it's because of a tragedy. It's a charity close to her heart."

The poignant silence was interrupted by the waiters coming to clear the table ready for their main course. Once they'd left, Louisa asked, "It never bothered Amanda that Louis had all these fans chasing you all everywhere?"

"You mean *girl* fans?" He smirked, knowing exactly what she meant but he wanted to lighten the conversation. He shook his head. "No. You would've understood if you'd ever seen Louis and Amanda together. He never had eyes for anyone else. She came with us on tours even after Grace was born. She's eight this year." His face lit up when he spoke of his niece.

"And Louis?"

"Louis will be five." Miles looked as his empty wine glass and wished he'd taken Louisa up on her offer of another. Five years had passed and it still wasn't getting any easier. A change in country, lifestyle and career and it still felt so raw. His phone alerted him of another message and his eyes shot to the screen. He picked up his phone and tapped the screen before turning it to face Louisa. "Here, that's them a few months ago."

Louisa leaned forward to look at the picture of his niece and nephew. It was uncanny how much Louis looked so much like his father. "They're adorable. You're obviously a doting uncle."

"Yeah they're a handful." He grinned widely, then placed his phone to his right.

Louisa frowned a little, then asked. "So you never wanted to get married?"

Miles let out a soft laugh, showcasing his perfect white teeth and lighting up his eyes. "No. I don't think I'm what they called the marrying kind."

Louisa chuckled. He really had that whole

charm/vulnerable/bad-boy thing down to a tee. He picked up his glass of water and took a sip. "Any children?"

She stifled a grin as he choked on a swallow. "God, I hope not… I mean… well umm." He spluttered, picking up his napkin to wipe his mouth.

"So the idea of children makes you… choke?" Louisa asked dryly.

"Shit no." Miles cringed at his choice of words but she'd caught him off-guard again. "Hell… I'm just not ready for them… I suppose." He sighed.

"I can see." Louisa smirked. "Well, just so you know – for the future, I mean – way in the future obviously… you're never ready for them."

Miles chuckled back at her. She was being less aloof and if he wasn't mistaken, she was letting her guard down a little. Her smiles were coming more readily and her eyes more expressive with every minute that past. There was a definite air of elegance that she carried so well but over the last half an hour, she seemed to have warmed up and was most definitely becoming friendlier. "I think I'd like kids, one day."

Louisa pursed her lips and nodded. "You're just hoping there's no… surprises. No knock on the door in ten years' time when an 18-year-old says, 'Hey Dad, remember that blond groupie you hooked up with?'"

Miles mouth dropped open in shock and then after a beat, he burst out laughing. He didn't care that some of the dinners had turned to look at their table. He didn't care that his behaviour may not have been altogether fitting for such an establishment. What he did care about was that again Louisa had shocked him, and in a perverse way, he loved that she could catch him off-guard with such ease.

"Sorry. I didn't mean to…" Louisa covered her mouth discreetly, trying hard to keep a straight face. God knew what the rest of the dinners were thinking. She only hoped none would come over to talk to her, though she was pretty sure Mr Thomas would intercept any intrusion.

"Judge?" Miles suggested.

"I was going to say 'make you feel uncomfortable'... I try not to judge. I'm really in no position to judge anyone. Believe me," Louisa said sincerely.

"Please tell me that isn't what this date is about. You're not going to confront me about some quickie we had in a backstage dressing room?" His expression had swiftly switched from amused to apprehensive.

It was Louisa's time to laugh, but she managed to stifle it with a cough and then arched her brow at him.

"Okay, obviously I got that all wrong." Miles leaned forward and lowered his voice. "Firstly, there's no way in hell I'd forget you and secondly, I don't think a quickie's your style." He tilted his head to the side and gave a quick raise of his brow. Louisa gave him a wry smile. *He really didn't remember her – well, why should he? He was high as a kite the last time they'd met.*

The sommelier arrived with the wine Louisa had ordered. After she'd confirmed it was indeed the correct vintage, he proceeded to open the bottle and then ceremoniously decanted it. Miles eyed the sombre man as he completed the task, then looked over at Louisa. He stifled a smirk, which caused Louisa to grin back at him. He'd somehow managed to break down all her sense of decorum.

"I promise not to spill it," he stage-whispered across the table. "I really don't want to have to tell Margot that I made my date cry."

"That wouldn't look good at all." Louisa gave a chuckle, then turned to the sommelier and thanked him.

Once he'd left, Miles looked at the garnet liquid in the simple glass decanter and said, "He didn't pour us any."

"It needs to breathe," explained Louisa.

"Oh, I see."

It was obvious Miles didn't see at all. "The wine needs to react with the oxygen in the air for the full character of the wine to come out," Louisa said softly.

"I think I read about that somewhere. Anyway, where were we?"

"The idea of children made you choke," Louisa said dryly.

Miles chuckled. "Right. What about you? I know you have one daughter; are you married?" She just gave him a wry smile, enjoying every minute of their game; he was trying to catch her out again.

The arrival of their main course stopped their conversation as the waiters placed the beautifully presented meal in front of them with a flourish. The aroma of the beef was mouth-watering and Miles couldn't remember the last time he'd had such an exquisite meal, if ever. Louisa declined to taste the wine, so the sommelier poured the wine into each of their glasses and left them to enjoy their meal.

Miles reached for his wine glass and lifted it and waited for Louisa to do the same. They said a quiet cheers, and after a subdued clink, they tasted the wine.

"I'm no expert, as you well know, but that really is the most delicious wine I've ever tasted," Miles said a little in awe.

Louisa gave a shy smile and gave a curt nod.

"So where were we? Ah yes, you were about to tell me if you were married," he said with a cheeky grin.

"Nice try," she countered.

His eyes shifted to her left hand. "No ring, but that doesn't mean anything, I suppose. You could've taken it off to keep up that air of mystery." He narrowed his eyes at her but she gave nothing away. He just stared at her for a moment, taking in every one of her exquisite features. Her dark almond-shaped eyes framed by thick long lashes, the flush on her cheeks that bloomed under his scrutiny and her full perfect lips that had a natural pout. Louisa blinked rapidly unsure of how to react to his blatant appraisal of her. She wasn't used to being the focus of someone's attention, well not in public anyway and even then it had been a long time since a man had openly admired her. She was the first to look away, suddenly feeling a little flustered. She diverted her attention to the plate in front of her and picked up her cutlery.

Miles watched her closely as she cut through her beef with a less than steady hand. She wasn't as tough as she wanted him to believe. He picked up his knife and fork and sliced through the juicy meat and then popped it in his mouth.

"This is absolutely amazing." He said pointing to his plate with his knife. "I've had some good beef all over the world but this, this has to be the best."

"The chef here is very good." Louisa said feeling more relaxed now that their attention was on the food.

Miles leaned forward a little and lowered his voice and Louisa instinctively shifted towards him. "You know what Louisa?" Louisa gave a slight shake of her head as her eyes locked on his bright blue ones. "If you are married, he must be a very trusting or a decent guy to allow you to have lunch with a strange man, with a bad reputation." Louisa's eyes widened at his comment and she took in a sharp breath as he continued. "If you were my wife, I wouldn't let you out of my sight." He held her gaze for a beat then leaned back.

Holy shit!

4

NEW BEGINNINGS

THREE MONTHS AGO

THE SOUND OF SCAMPERING footsteps on the hard wooden floor echoed along the hallway. Miles smiled and shook his head at the excitement of his niece and nephew.

"Slow down," called Amanda after them but they were already in the kitchen. "They've been so excited to come and see it all finished."

"I can tell," Miles said dryly, following them into the kitchen.

Amanda chuckled and her pretty face lit up for a few seconds. "Plus the drive down had them stir crazy. They miss you."

Miles quickly put out some snacks and drinks for the children and pulled out two bottles of beer for Amanda and himself. "I miss them too, all of you." He was being sincere. The move to London had been a hard decision. Amanda and the children were his only family in the UK and been his sole company, bar a very few friends he'd made. They clinked bottlenecks and took a drink, then settled into the bar stools.

"I thought you'd have more furniture." Her eyes scanned through to the empty dining room, then she swivelled around to look into the lounge. She was pleased to see that Miles had at least bought a couple of couches and a coffee table. But other than those, the house was devoid of soft furnishings and a number of major pieces.

"I got the essentials," Miles grunted.

"Well, you're going to need more than that if you're going to entertain, Miles," Amanda mock-chastised, arching her brow at him.

Miles's brow furrowed and his face tightened. "I'll only be entertaining you and the kids right now, so it's fine."

Amanda placed down her bottle, then squeezed his forearm. Moving away from her and the children had affected him too. He needed to be on his own so that he could get on with his new life. It hadn't been easy for any of them but it was the only way they could all move forward. Over the last year, they'd both started to make changes in their lives. Watching the children grow had made it easier. Both their focus had been on the kids, but with Louis now in kindergarten and Grace in school, Amanda was determined to use her time in a positive way. In a way that would make her late husband proud.

Their small family unit had been a crutch for Miles. An easy way to shut out the world and to focus on helping his beloved sister-in-law, but even he knew that at some time, he'd have to go it alone. So investing in his own home, almost a year ago, and letting his agent put out feelers had been the first step. He'd immersed himself in the renovation of the classic white stucco-fronted, ten-bedroom house in Kensington. He didn't need such a big house but it had been a good project to keep him occupied and an excellent investment. It also meant that he had to spend more time in the capital, near many of Eric Schultz's contacts.

One of the few rooms Miles had completed was the media room, and after settling his niece and nephew into their seats to watch a much-loved movie, Miles and Amanda moved into the only other ground floor room that had furniture, the sitting room. The coffee table had Miles's laptop open on it, along with various stacks of papers.

"What are you working on?" Amanda jerked her chin towards the table.

"I've had a few offers. Eric has been trying to get me to look at some business opportunities," he said as he cleared the papers and placed them under the table making room for their drinks.

"And you're interested?" Amanda asked hopefully. She wanted him to find something that would bring him out of the melancholy state he'd been in for such a long time. He still mourned the loss of his brother and mentor; after all, he'd been there for him his whole life and the gap his untimely death had left was cavernous. Louis had been his best friend and business partner too, so for Miles to go it alone now was both unnerving and difficult and Amanda could see the falter in every move he made.

"Maybe." He sighed and gave her a soft smile.

"What's wrong, Miles? Aren't they any good?"

Miles rocked his head from side to side. "I want to do something more than just make more money, something worthwhile." He paused for a moment, focusing on the view of his small garden through the window. He pursed his lips and continued, "That charity you've been working with, you think I could get involved? Help kids, not just with my cheque book?"

Amanda gave him an encouraging smile, leaning forward in her seat. Miles had watched her become more involved with CASPO over the last year and had given her generous donations. He'd asked with genuine interest about the work they did and was pleased to see his sister-in-law start to blossom again as her involvement increased. "I think they'd welcome anyone's input. Do you want me to speak to Margot McMillan?" she asked hopefully.

"Yeah, see what they think and maybe I can help with… I don't know, a music program or something?" he said with a shrug.

"What about these?" Amanda pointed to the stacks of papers.

"I'll look at those too but I want to do something other than feed my bank balance."

Her smile widened and then she shook her head. "You know you have enough rooms in this house to have a home office, and you're using the coffee table."

"Yeah, I know. I'll get round to it."

The way he'd answered, Amanda knew he'd never get round to it. His house looked like an empty shell: no personal items, no decorations, just the bare minimum. The house was worth £25 million, yet its furnishings were more fitting of a house a hundredth of its value. "I can help if you like. You just need a few things to make it more homely and less like students' digs." She eyed the moving boxes piled up at the far end of the lounge and the various guitars and instruments he'd left unceremoniously on the floor.

"Sure." His answer wasn't convincing but Amanda nodded anyway.

"Please tell me you at least have beds for us to sleep on."

Miles chuckled. "Yeah, you have beds, complete with bedding, I'm not that useless."

AMANDA STEPPED OUT OF the cab, which had brought her to the prestigious address of CASPO's offices in Belgravia, the shiny black door a sharp contrast to the stucco white five-storey building. The charity was housed in one of the many impressive properties owned by the Blackthorns around the capital. The first three floors were taken up by the charity and the top two floors were conference rooms that the late Earl had used for business negotiations in the capital. They afforded him privacy whenever he had business dealings in the city, plus it meant he was close to his wife.

Amanda had left Miles with Louis and Grace for a few hours,

while she had her scheduled meeting the morning after her arrival in London, having spent the night in Miles's sparsely furnished house. She'd left them, suggesting he should buy a few items to make his house more homely, though she really didn't hold up much hope.

After making small talk with Melissa, Amanda was shown into the General Secretary's office. Margot McMillan ran the charity alongside Lady Alice Blackthorn and was at their offices every day, while Lady Alice came in once or twice a week. They conducted the charity's business mainly over the phone, but at least once a week, Lady Alice made the effort to come in. She found it hard to be in the offices without her late husband and over the last eight years, she'd avoided being there, preferring to be at Holmwood House.

Amanda had decided to become more involved with the charity when she'd seen an article on the work it had done, helping wives and children of servicemen who had died, as well as families who had lost parents due to tragic circumstances. Her hefty donation had brought her to Margot's attention, who had then approached Amanda, hoping she would not only carry on supporting the charity but become involved. Today's visit was part of that. Amanda had raised money in her hometown of Worcester, collecting sponsorships from businesses in the area. Margot had asked her to come down to discuss future fundraising.

"This is a substantial amount you managed to collect." Margot looked at the total Melissa had printed out for her.

"Most of them are willing to contribute on a yearly basis, which is good."

"It is. Thank you so much for all your efforts. We really value any new input and fresh ideas to help boost the charity's income."

"It's been… well, it's a cause I can relate to, so believe me when I say, this small contribution of my time is as valuable to me as the contributions are to you." Amanda gave Margot and

Melissa a soft smile and they nodded, knowing she had first-hand knowledge of tragedy. "My brother-in-law asked me if you'd be happy for him to be involved. He's recently moved to London and I think he wants to give something back. It's been a few years since he worked as such."

"You mean Miles Keane, right?" asked Melissa, a little surprised.

"Yes, that's right."

Melissa's eyes darted to Margot, who obviously didn't realise who Miles Keane was. "He's a pop star, a very famous pop star, Margot."

"Oh, I see."

"Here, let me show you." Melissa stepped up to the computer and quickly typed in Miles Keane into the search engine and then turned the screen back to Margot.

Margot's eyes widened and she leaned in to read a few of the articles and scan the huge array of photos that filled her screen. "Oh well, he's erm..." Margot, for the first time, seemed lost for words.

"Yeah, I know," chuckled Amanda. "But contrary to all those articles, he's a great guy and I think he could bring a lot to the charity."

"He'd definitely bring interest from a different demographic to the charity," Melissa said dryly. "And a whole lot of glamour too. It's what this charity needs, a sexed-up boost." Margot stared at Melissa, a little taken back by her enthusiasm. "Sorry, pregnancy hormones," Melissa shrugged and then looked back at a smirking Amanda. She'd gotten used to the effect Miles Keane had on women after the ten years of success Keane Sense had had.

"He's single, right?" Melissa asked. Amanda nodded at Melissa. "What is he willing to do?"

"Maybe something music related, help with a music program. I'm not sure really. I suppose it would be up to you to guide him."

"You know what I'm thinking? I'm thinking we could use him in the auction." Melissa looked at Margot for approval.

"Auction?" Amanda gave a puzzled look at the two women.

"Yes, we're just fine-tuning our annual auction of prizes that money can't buy. We have around fifty prizes that will be put up on our website and anyone can bid on them. At the close of the auction, the highest bid wins the prize.," explained Margot.

"What kind of prizes?"

"Well the top five prizes are: a race track day with the Jaguar team, to be at a photo shoot at Vogue, two front-row invites to the Burberry Men's Fashion Show – those are by invitation only." Melissa's eyes widened and gave a nod, indicating it was a very special prize, as she continued to count off the prizes on her fingers. "A round of golf with Martin Levy, the British Open winner and finally, two tickets for the royal enclosure at Ascot." She finished off with self-satisfied smirk.

"They're pretty incredible prizes but what would the prize with Miles be?"

"What about a date with him? Say a dinner date. An hour and a half with heartthrob and pop superstar Miles Keane. Just think of the buzz and media hype for the charity – all those girl fans." Melissa stood up suddenly and paced, clearly excited at the prospect.

"Melissa, watch your blood pressure," warned Margot and Melissa scowled.

"Do you think he'd do that?" Melissa continued.

"Well, I think he had something totally different in mind but I could ask him."

"If you'd like, I could call him too. Thank him for offering his services, so to speak," Margot offered, seeing how excited Melissa was about the prospect. She may have been in charge but Margot valued Melissa's input. She came up with most of their fundraising events and her contacts within the celebrity world helped the charity enormously. "It would most definitely draw new interest. We like big donations but a steady flow of small constant ones is just as important. It raises awareness too and brings in revenue from new donors. It's what Lady Blackthorn has been pushing for, and now with her wanting to retire, we need as many high-profile personalities linked with the charity."

"Will someone else be taking over as the patron?"

"She's working on someone who is more than capable and will bring much to the charity but it's still to be confirmed."

For the next twenty minutes the three women came up with a number of suggestions regarding the auction and Miles's input. Amanda left the offices with a promise of getting back to them as soon as possible, once she'd had time to convince Miles.

Amanda walked into Miles's home, almost tripping over a ball of brown fur. Her children then bombarded her with a blow-by-blow account of their morning, explaining that they'd gone out with their uncle and ended up at a dog shelter and decided on which dog to bring home. Amanda looked up expectantly at Miles as an amused smirk crept over his handsome face.

"Well, you said get something that'll make my house more like a home," he said with a shrug.

"So you got a dog?" She chuckled but there was no doubt in her mind that the new addition to Miles home was a good idea. His whole demeanour had lightened up.

"I'm fostering him for now." He bent down and picked up the small fluffy puppy, who was trying to jump up. He immediately started to lick Miles's face to the glee of the children. "Meet Duke."

Amanda ruffled the adorable dogs head. "He's lovely."

"We thought so too." Miles winked down at his niece and nephew. "And he'll keep me busy."

Grace and Louis spent the next couple of hours playing with Duke and rearranging his basket and the huge array of toys they'd bought for him, while Amanda and Miles made lunch together. It was then that Amanda decided to breach the subject of the auction. She opened up the conversation saying that Margot and Melissa were very excited that he wanted to be involved with CASPO, then tactfully explained all about the auction and what a huge event it was, raising a large amount of money. It was classed as very prestigious and this was reflected in the prizes. Miles listened to her enthusiastic description of her morning with genuine interest as he seasoned the steaks, wondering where his input in the whole auction would be. Amanda then went on to tell him about the idea Melissa had, and he stopped what he was doing and turned to face an obviously uneasy Amanda.

"A date? Jesus, Amanda." He let out a sharp breath.

"I know, but it'll be one and a half hours tops. And you're used to talking to fans," she said in a rush. "A lunch date. It'll be discreet."

Miles wiped his hands on a cloth, headed to the fridge and pulled out a couple of beers. He popped open the lids and handed one to Amanda. "When's the auction?"

"Next month but you can do the date whenever you want." She hadn't discussed logistics with Margot or Melissa but she was sure they'd be happy with whatever restrictions she came back with, as long as he agreed. "Just think about how much money we could raise."

Miles took a deep drink from his beer and glared at Amanda, causing her to cringe. The last thing he wanted to do was sit down with some gushing fan and make small talk for an hour and a half. When Miles had said he'd wanted to get involved with fundraising, this was definitely not what he had envisaged. "How much do they think it would raise?"

"Your date?" Miles nodded. "They think around £20,000, maybe more."

Shit, he'd write them a cheque for that and scrap the whole idea, he thought.

"But it's not just the money. You being in the auction will be good for the charity. Raise its profile."

Miles let out an exasperated huff, realising his idea of throwing money at the problem wasn't going to make this go away. Apparently there were some things money couldn't buy after all and celebrity and status were two of them. "Shit, I can't believe a charity wants to pimp me out." Amanda stifled a smirk at his turn of phrase and he scowled at her. "I suppose not much can go down in an hour and half. They'll make sure she's no crazy, right? No reporter posing as a fan or, I don't know, a psycho?" He narrowed his eyes at her, knowing he was being backed into a corner. He'd look like a real shit heel if he said no and on top of that, he'd make Amanda look bad too.

"Of course. The winner will be anonymous until after the date and then, if they agree, we can do a press piece, but nothing before."

"What about location?"

"Well let's see who wins and work from there. Margot and Melissa are not going to want any bad press, believe me, and Lady Blackthorn will literally have their heads if anything goes wrong."

"Good to know. Lady Blackthorn sounds like a badass." Miles took another swig from his bottle.

"I've only met her once and she was lovely to me, but I can tell by the way Margo and Melissa talk about her, she won't take any shit."

Miles blew out a breath and gave a slightly shake of his head. "Okay, I'll do it. I can listen to some fan for an hour and a half, make small talk."

"Yay! You're the best." Amanda clapped her hands and rushed up to him, flinging her arms around him.

"Whatever. You owe me," he muttered.

"Yeah, I do."

5

THE DATE – MAIN COURSE

"SO HOW DID YOU get into the music business? By your own admission, your parents were against it." Louisa tilted her head a little and that tell-tale smirk of Miles's skirted over his sculptured lips. She wasn't going to acknowledge his flirty remark about if she were his. She'd definitely been affected by it though. He'd seen her eyes widen and a blush boomed over her perfect cheekbones before she focused back on her meal. He wasn't flattering her; he was just being honest. How could a husband allow such a stunning woman have lunch with a strange man? As if that wasn't bad enough, she'd also paid for his time. Maybe she wasn't married after all, or maybe the husband didn't know.

Miles gave a wry smile at her dodging techniques. It was true he'd been interviewed by the best over his career but today, she was proving to be much more skilled at extracting information than any of his previous interviewers. Perhaps it had more to do with him and his willingness to be more forthcoming. Maybe it was because she appeared genuinely interested in him and his story; she didn't seem to have a hidden agenda, other than finding out more about him. Or maybe it was because he actually wanted to tell her. After not looking forward to an hour and a half of benign conversation, Miles was actually enjoying Louisa's company and even more than that, he was relishing their underlying battle of wits. The push of her questions and the pull of her attraction.

"Well it was down to Louis, really," Miles explained. He paused a moment, causing Louisa to look up from her plate. He leaned forward, ensuring he had her full attention. He wasn't sure if the couple of drinks had taken the edge off his nervousness or whether Louisa had let down her guard a little, but there was a subtle shift in their dynamic. Miles took a sharp breath and continued. "He'd always been the sensible one, conscientious, and he was determined to convince our parents that we could make it in the business. We already had a small following, nothing huge, and just around the bars in New York."

Louisa noticed the slight change in his voice as he spoke about his late brother. It was more than clear he still found it hard to speak about him without showing emotion.

"With our parents being in LA, they panicked a bit, thinking we weren't studying and basically just playing in bars." Miles put down his cutlery and reached for his wine, taking a sip before he continued. "So my father contacted an agent he knew out in New York, Eric Schultz, and asked him to check out what we were doing." Louisa gave a little cringe and Miles chuckled. "Yeah, he really wasn't happy. Anyway Eric turned up one night at a bar we were performing in. We'd decided to do a medley of 70s rock that night."

"Seventies rock?" Louisa couldn't hide her surprise.

"Yeah you know, *All Right Now, Hotel California, Smoke on the Water*, that kind of thing." He waved his hand in the air vaguely, then stopped suddenly and leaned forward. "You've heard of those, right?"

Louisa chuckled. *What did he think? She hadn't lived in some ivory tower shut away.* "What, no *Stairway to Heaven?*" She arched her brow at him and he let out a light laugh.

"Of course that's a classic. So you know your classic rock ballads then?"

"Like you, I appreciate all music."

"Good to know." He lowered his voice a little and asked. "Even Keane Sense?" And in those few seconds, before she answered, it suddenly became very clear to him that he wanted her to like his music.

"Like I said, all music." Miles gave her a wide grin and she shook her head at his obvious delight in the small piece of personal information she'd just given away. "Carry on; what happened when the agent saw you?"

"Well he was impressed with our performance and wanted to know if we had any of our own material. I had roughly twenty pieces that I'd written over my time at school. They weren't polished off yet but they were close. Eric asked to hear a demo I'd done. It was basically just me with my guitar."

"Hadn't anyone else heard your songs before that?" she asked. The more they talked and the more Louisa heard of the beginning of Miles's career, the more genuinely interested she became. This wasn't about just finding out what kind of person Miles was anymore; she was getting a highly personalised picture of his past, an insight into what drove the Keane brothers to veer off from the path their parents had envisaged for them. Louisa had read that they'd been discovered in a New York bar but now, listening to Miles explain how Eric Schultz had ended up there, it was obvious that a large portion of their documented history had either been left out or embellished.

"Louis had, but that was it, really. Eric was impressed with the very raw version of what actually ended up being some of the material we used for our first album."

"So how did you convince your parents?"

"We didn't. Eric did. He told them he thought we had a good

shot at making a name for ourselves, with his help. We needed two more members to complete the band. Louis had graduated but I was in my second year still, and of course my parents wanted me to finish, so we made a deal. Eric would get us studio time, once we'd polished off the songs I'd written. We asked our friends from back home if they wanted to join our band since we'd started off with them. My parents gave us two years to make a success out of it. If we didn't, we'd have to look at other more stable career options, plus I needed to finish my degree."

"Two years to make it big?"

"Yeah, it was non-negotiable, along with me finishing. Louis and I spent as much time as we could getting the songs studio-ready while I was studying."

"That must've been tough," Louisa said with a slight huff.

"It was but we were so driven to prove to our parents we could do it." He gave a shrug and Louisa could imagine exactly how he must've been back then, over-confident with a huge helping of arrogance.

"And the name? Obviously Keane because of your surname, but why Sense? It's almost…" Louisa rocked her head from side to side, trying to find the word.

"Ironic?" Miles suggested and Louisa chuckled.

"Well, yes. I'm sure you all didn't have that much sense back then."

Miles let out a laugh; he was enjoying her teasing him. "It was Louis actually that came up with it. We were trying to work out who should join us. When we both realised that Mick and Josh were the ideal fit, he said, 'It just makes sense.' Hence Keane Sense." He turned his palms in a there-you-are gesture.

"That simple?"

"I find that keeping things simple usually gets the best results," he said with a slight shrug, then picked up his knife and fork and continued to eat his meal.

“Perhaps.” Louisa mirrored his actions and they eat a little more of their exquisite food, commenting on how tasty it was.

“So the material you wrote made up your first album, *And So It Begins*; that went to number one, didn’t it?”

Again Miles was taken aback at her knowledge of Keane Sense’s discology. “It did, though Louis and I co-wrote the songs in the end.” He shifted to the side and reached over to lift the gift bag he’d placed on the adjacent chair. “Actually, I brought a signed platinum disc for you. Well, for Celeste, actually,” he corrected.

“That’s very kind of you. I’m sure she’ll love it, though isn’t it valuable? Are you sure you want to part with it?” She took the large bag from his hands and then reached in to pull up the framed platinum disc.

“We’re given a few when an album or single goes gold or platinum, but this one is one of the few that has all four of our signatures on.” Miles pointed to where all four signatures were.

“Thank you,” Louisa said sincerely. It hadn’t gone unnoticed that his brilliant blue eyes had a little sadness clouding over them as he focused on Louis’s signature. He took a deep breath, then dragged his gaze from the frame to Louisa.

“Just tell her not to sell it on eBay,” he said with a chuckle and Louisa again had a flashback to ten years ago. She gave him a smirk and then carefully placed the bag with the framed disc back on the chair.

“So it was your style that set the band’s genre, seeing as you wrote the first songs?”

“Co-wrote,” he corrected. “We wanted to be edgier than a boy band and softer than a rock band, kind of a cross between The Backstreet Boys and The Police.”

“The Police?” Louisa’s eyes twinkled at the mention of the band she’d practically worshipped throughout her teenage years.

“Yeah. They were one of the best bands in the 80s; so diverse and effortlessly cool.”

Louisa nodded her agreement but didn't comment. "Well, you proved your parents wrong, didn't you?"

Miles gave her a modest shrug. Success had come quickly to Keane Sense. A lot of that was down to good management and promotion but the magnitude of their success had been purely down to their musical talent and marketable good looks.

In those early days the band hadn't really appreciated how quickly they had risen to fame. Their focus was on getting good material out and having enough success to prove to their parents they could make a career for themselves. Those first two years were almost a blur for Miles and he was thankful that he had his brother for support. Amanda was now a permanent fixture in Louis's life. She'd extended her working visa, after her parents returned to the UK, and the three of them lived in a small apartment not far from Juilliard. While Miles finished his degree, Louis worked on the material Miles had produced, as well as working with Eric on what image they wanted for their band. Keane Sense wanted the traditional set up of a four-piece band but with slick style usually found in boy bands.

Both Eric and Louis knew with Miles as the front man of the band it would cement their success. He'd already garnered considerable attention when they played in bars and at Juilliard he was fawned over by every red-blooded female. His natural charisma and cocksure personality meant he was never short of girlfriends, or rather hook-ups.

"It was pretty hard in the beginning. We were so focused on getting our material out, our image right, it was just constant work and discussions. A few fights too." He gave a wry smile as a few of them came to mind.

"I suppose it was understandable. Fights about what, the image?"

"No, we all had our own individual style, so to speak, but as a band we were on the same page. There's a lot of bullshit you need to put up with when you're in a band that appeals to young girls or women."

"You mean behaving well. No scandals; that kind of thing?"

"Yeah. Especially where everyone has a camera and basically they've become the paparazzi..." Miles reached again for his wine and took another sip. All this talking about his past was making his mouth dry up and his mind remember the good times they'd had.

Over the last few years, Miles had erased those from his memory, letting the tragedy that had turned his and his family's lives upside down dominate his thoughts. He remembered how driven Louis had been, how determined to make a success of their lives without living under the shadow of their parents. He'd wanted to break the mould of the classically trained musicians that had been, up until then, the tradition in the Keane family. It was bittersweet bringing back those early memories, but he was grateful that Louisa had made him recount them all the same. "Louis had the hardest time of it. It was the only time he argued with Eric."

"They had different ideas on the band's image?" Louisa remembered reading an article that was dated at the beginning of the Keane brother's careers. Louis Keane was the driving force behind the group. He knew it was a business they were creating, an image and a brand. His presence on stage was understated in comparison to Miles's, but behind the scenes, he took the reins. He wasn't interested in the fame; he just strived to be successful and top of their game.

"No, but he was with Amanda. They were serious and Eric didn't want her to be too visible. He thought if the fans knew Louis was spoken for, the appeal of the band would suffer. But Louis wouldn't have it. He wasn't going to hide her. He also wouldn't flaunt her either, but if he was asked about his status, he was going to be honest."

"That was very noble of him and I suppose risky."

"Louis didn't see it that way. He'd found his partner for life and there was no way he was hiding it. She'd stayed in the US for him after all."

"It sounds like Louis was a strong man," Louisa said sincerely. *It must've been hard for Louis to stand up to both his manager and his parents when they were only just at the start of a risky and volatile career*, thought Louisa.

"He was." Miles's brow furrowed a little and he gave a tight smile. "He just knew we'd make something of ourselves. I wasn't so sure but he always used to say, '*When* we make it big' and never '*If*.'" Miles looked down at his plate for a moment in reflective silence and Louisa quietly continued to eat her meal. She didn't want to push him anymore. This topic was obviously hard for him to talk about. Over the last hour, she'd seen a number of sides to his personality and most of them were unexpected. Thanks to the sommelier coming to top up their glasses, the slightly sombre mood was broken.

"You were right about this wine, Louisa." Miles gave a lopsided smirk at her as he lifted his glass and tipped it towards her.

"I'm glad you like it."

"I may insist on only drinking this with beef from now on."

Louisa chuckled at his comment. He'd changed the subject and Louisa didn't have the heart to push him anymore. Maybe she should find out more about his future plans, rather than dwell on his painful past.

"How are you enjoying living in London? I should imagine it's a change from living in Worcester."

Miles let out a rich laugh and Louisa was glad she'd managed to shake off his previous pensive mood. "Just a bit. I loved being out in the English countryside. It was good to get away from LA and spend time with my niece and nephew in rural England. Where Amanda's family lives is pretty secluded, which was great for us. Then we moved into a bigger house which meant my parents could come over and visit too."

"And how long have you lived in London?"

"I bought my house over a year ago but it took nine months to get all the renovations done. I'm getting to know the area now. It's not that far from here, actually. That's another thing I'm getting used to, everything so much closer over here."

"You don't miss LA?"

"Sometimes. It's more the familiarity of it; I still have my place out there and we go over at least twice a year. I needed to be there for work but now it doesn't matter where I am and my niece and nephew are my priority. Here I'm a little lost and I'm slowly getting used to the English way of things." His eyes swept around the grand restaurant and widened his eyes at Louisa, causing her to smile. "You probably realised I'm not really into conventional; I'm more of a rule breaker."

His last comment was rewarded with a soft laugh. "So you're an American-man-in-London rather than and English-man-in-New-York then?"

"Whoa, did you just quote Sting to me?" Miles face lit up as he grinned in total surprise, almost taking Louisa's breath away. He really was a handsome man. No wonder he had droves of adoring fans, even after such a long absence from the music business.

"I blame the Lafite," she said with a wry smile and Miles chuckled, relishing seeing Louisa relax and letting out the fun side she'd obviously been reining in.

"Well if that's all you need to let your guard down, we should order another bottle," he joked. His phone buzzed again on the crisp white linen and his eyes darted to it but he left it where it was. Louisa gave a slight frown, then took a sip from her water glass and Miles cursed to himself that his email alert had caused the smile on Louisa's lips vanish. He noticed she didn't have her phone out and he wondered whether this was some English protocol that he'd missed. His erratic thoughts were halted by Louisa's next question.

"It's been over three years since any of your music has been released. Have you decided to stop in this business?"

"If you're asking whether I've retired, I can't really say. I wanted to take some time away. Reassess my life. After..." Miles blew out a breath and leaned back in his chair before continuing. "After the shooting and my recovery, I just wanted to get away. Amanda and the children needed me and that was all that mattered."

Louisa nodded. "Understandable. Family, it's the most important thing and sometimes when tragedy hits it's only then that you realise."

"You sound as if you're speaking from experience."

"I am." She pursed her lips but didn't elaborate, and Miles knew that she wouldn't. "So no more hits songs from Miles Keane?"

"I've never stopped writing but I'm not sure if I'll ever record or release them."

"So that's how you fill your time now: writing?" Louisa pushed some more of her meal onto her fork and Miles mirrored her actions. Their meal had taken far longer than it should've done and most of what they'd eaten was cold now, but neither of them seemed to mind.

"I've made some investments in property here and am looking into working with a few companies. Nothing music-related."

"What sort of companies?"

"I've been approached by car companies, a few designers, that kind of thing." He gave a shrug and popped the last of his meal in his mouth.

"Oh, I see."

They finished up the last of their meal, directing their conversation to how tasty it had been. It was strange that after knowing each other for only an hour and a half, they were feeling less awkward with each other. Their conversation began to flow without Louisa's prompting questions.

"I'm still not sure I want to be back out in the open yet, though Amanda has pushed me to get more involved with CASPO," Miles continued, referring to Louisa's question about his music career. "Use my celebrity to raise awareness of the charity, and money of course."

"And you're not comfortable with that?"

"Believe it or not, being in the public eye is never comfortable. I've been lucky; at times I didn't feel that way, but I have been. My success in my work means I can direct the spotlight onto worthy causes and make a difference to people who really need it."

"Like the auction?"

"Yes. This garnered quite a bit of interest. They told me that apart from your generous donation, there's been a distinct increase in overall donations."

"Because of your association?"

"Apparently. There've been enquiries as to what other fundraising events I'll be doing."

Louisa gave him a wry smile and Miles rolled his eyes. "And how do you feel about that?"

"Being pimped out, you mean?"

"I wouldn't put it quite so colourfully." Louisa chuckled.

"Well that is what it is, isn't it? Today is exactly that. Fifty thousand pounds bought you my undivided attention." He shrugged and then zeroed his bright blue eyes on hers.

"It wasn't for me, remember?"

"Of course," he conceded. "But that's quite a high price for…"

"A gigolo?" Louisa interrupted, causing Miles to gasp. "CASPO is pimping you out, so that's what you are then, sort of." Louisa tilted her head, amused at his reaction to her rather forward and risqué description.

He leaned forward and lowered his voice. "Hey I haven't slept with you *yet*, so it's just lunch," he said playfully.

Louisa shifted in her seat, trying hard not to focus on the word "yet". Was that his agenda? Did he think that if he charmed her today that he'd snap his fingers and she's rollover, or roll under, so to speak? Maybe if it had been Celeste here instead of her, there was probably a possibility. She was most definitely the type of woman he'd been associated with in the past. Louisa frowned at the thought of her daughter and Miles together. What she wasn't sure about was whether it was because she disapproved of him or whether she didn't like the idea of him sleeping with anyone else and especially Celeste. She marshalled her disturbing thoughts and replied. "Didn't you know, Miles, you don't pay for a gigolo or a call girl to sleep with you; you pay them so that they go away afterwards."

Miles's eyes widened and he gave a sexy smirk. "I wouldn't know. I never had to pay for it."

"Yes, I read the articles. I'm not sure what's worse though, paying for it or knowing that whoever is with you, is there solely because of who you are? At least the first option is honest, don't you think?" Louisa countered and Miles's smirk widened into a megawatt grin.

"How the hell did we get from charity work to paying for sex?"

"I don't know?" giggled Louisa.

"Blame the Lafite?" He jerked his head to the almost-empty decanter.

"Yes, definitely." Louisa shook her head slightly. It had been a while for her to have so much fun. Usually her lunch dates were stuffy, or just boring. The only people she had fun with were her family. "So CASPO? Are you going to get more involved, even if they are just going to *pimp* you out?"

"They've asked me to be one of their ambassadors."

"Oh wow," Louisa feigned surprise. "So they really are getting their claws in. And? Are you going to accept?"

"The way I see it, if you're going to be pimped out, you may as well help someone in the process." He tilted his head and grinned. "And besides, I've seen the work they do. They've helped so many single parent families, got them on their feet and out of poverty. Those kids and their parents have really had life-changing help. I reckon that's a good reason to be used and abused by CASPO. Like I said, I've been lucky and this is my way of giving back. I never need to work again, so at least I can dedicate my time to something that's making a difference."

"Here's to you and your new pimp, then." Louisa raised her glass and Miles's rich laugh caused Louisa's heart to skip a beat.

"Now there's a sentence I never thought I'd hear, especially from someone like you, Louisa," he drawled, lifting his glass and clinking it against hers. "I can't make you out. I have a feeling that's the whole point, though." He narrowed his eyes at her and she blushed under his blatant scrutiny.

"Perhaps." Louisa took a sip of her wine, keeping her eyes on his.

"There's no perhaps about it. But I have picked up on a few things."

"Like?"

Miles drained his glass and placed it carefully on the table. "You've suffered tragedy." His eyes swept up to Louisa's but she gave nothing away. "You have a lot to lose. I don't mean in the material sense, I mean you value you anonymity. Being in the limelight doesn't appeal to you but somehow you're noticed wherever you go."

"Why do you say that?"

"You've made a point of making sure I know nothing about you. You're obviously well known here, yet no one has come over to speak to you, even though they've discreetly been watching us. At first I thought it was because of me." He shook his head and pursed his lips. "I don't think anyone in here has even heard of me or Keane Sense. It's you they know."

"That's because we're British and tend to keep ourselves to ourselves. And don't worry, I'm sure they know exactly who you are," Louisa stage whispered and Miles chuckled.

"Nice try. Don't worry, my ego isn't that fragile. No, they know you don't like to be bothered."

It was unsettling how close Miles was to the truth. What he didn't realise was that it went against protocol for anyone to come over and address her. Louisa wasn't particularly a stickler for these formalities but everyone else seemed to be and, to be honest, that was fine by her. "What else have I given away?" Louisa goaded.

Miles gave her a cheeky grin. "You know your music and I think you may have been a fan of The Police. Maybe you still are." Louisa grinned at him but kept tight-lipped. "You're elegant and well-bred but have a daring side that I've had flashes of, and of course you know about exquisite wine." He punctuated his observation with an arch of his brow. "How did I do?"

"I'm obviously not as good at hiding things about myself as I thought I was," Louisa said drolly.

"Ha! Now I know you're just teasing me, but that's okay. I'm enjoying this game of ours..." The vibrating of his phone against the table halted their playful banter and Miles muttered a curse to himself when he saw the name Lottie flash across his phone and her pouting face filling the screen. His eyes darted to Louisa and they were met by a considerably cooled expression. "I'm sorry, I need to take this," he said and in that moment, he wished he'd put his phone away and never asked Lottie to call. If he didn't answer, she'd just keep calling.

Louisa rose from her chair and placed her napkin on the table. "I'll give you some privacy."

Miles scrambled to his feet, leaving the phone to vibrate and his napkin fall to the floor. "No, really you don't need to. It'll take a second, that's all," he said in a rush, mortified that he'd obviously upset her.

"It's fine, Miles. It must be urgent; whoever it is, is quite persistent." There was a hint of sarcasm in her tone, making Miles feel even more wretched.

Before he could insist, Louisa had already picked up her bag and was heading towards the exit. *Fuck!* He thought to himself. He'd pissed her off and they seemed to be getting on so well. He grabbed his phone and swiped the screen.

"Jesus Miles, how long?" griped Lottie.

"Um sorry, it was on silent," he muttered as he watched Louisa elegantly walk out of the door, after speaking to the maître d'.

"Well, you asked me to call." Miles could tell she was irritated.

"Yeah, it's okay. I'm done already."

"Oh how was it? Was she a proper spoiled daddy's girl?"

"No, um look I can't talk now. I'll call you later, okay? Thanks for calling though," he said dismissively, just wanting her off the phone before Louisa reappeared at the door.

"Oh okay…"

"Bye, Lottie." He cut her off before she could say anymore. He looked down at his screen. There were around twenty notifications and messages but he wasn't interested in opening any of them. He was momentarily distracted by the sommelier, who was now filling their glasses. He'd picked up Miles's napkin from the floor, then handed him a new one. Miles thanked him and turned his phone nervously in his hand. *What if she'd left?* he thought to himself. She wasn't pleased about the call; in fact, she seemed annoyed every time his phone alerted him. Miles slipped his phone in his jacket pocket and hoped he hadn't blown the date.

It seemed like an age before Louisa stepped back into the restaurant and the relief Miles felt took him by surprise. He was going to have to make it up to her somehow. As Louisa approached, he stood up, formulating an apology in his head but before he could say anything, she spoke.

"Everything alright?" It had annoyed her that he'd answered his phone. It was a pet peeve of hers but Miles wasn't to know. Louisa disliked phones being present unnecessarily, especially on a date. When Gerard used to take her out, she'd insisted his phone was out of sight. He was either with her for that time or not. If anything was that urgent, life or death, they had their driver or security around who could be contacted. Anything else could wait for a couple of hours.

"Um, yes. It wasn't anything urgent. Sorry," he muttered.

"Are you sure? The caller seemed quite insistent." Louisa lowered herself gracefully into her chair and placed her bag at the back of her chair, before raising her cooled expression to Miles.

"Really, it was nothing." He sat back down again and eyed his refilled glass and wished it were a shot of vodka he could knock back in one gulp, rather than a revered red wine that needed to be sipped and appreciated. He needed to get them back to their playful banter, not because he had to but because he wanted to. Maybe the honest approach would work with her. After all, she'd stressed that she'd wanted to know about him. He waited patiently for their plates to be cleared by the efficient waiters and then spoke.

"You know what Louisa, this date has been unexpectedly enjoyable." Louisa's gaze softened at his candid comment and Miles slanted his head a little to the side. "I haven't laughed like this for such a long time and even though I know next to nothing about you, you've been without a doubt the best blind date I've ever been on."

His comment brought a slight flush to her cheeks. "Really? Have you been on many blind dates?"

"Oh, I don't kiss and tell. That wouldn't be very gentlemanly now, would it?"

"I suppose not. It's more that they all kissed and told. Well, if you believe all the tabloids, that is." She smirked at him and he mock-cringed, which caused her to chuckle.

"My past is never going to go away."

"Nope."

Miles shifted forward in his seat. "You know, I wasn't really looking forward to this date."

"Hence the fake phone-call?" Her eyes darted to where his phone had been and was pleasantly surprised to see it wasn't there anymore. Miles twisted his mouth in embarrassment at being caught out.

"Busted. Seriously though, I mean it, I'm really having fun. What's not to like? I'm out in a swanky restaurant with this elegant, confident, beautiful woman who also knows about wine." He waved his hand in the air as he spoke and Louisa narrowed her eyes at him.

"I see what all those articles about you mean now."

"What articles?"

"The ones that say it's not just your chiselled all-American good looks and unworldly talent that have women throwing themselves at you. It's the way you charm the panties off every woman you bestow your undivided attention to." Her direct remark was rewarded with another rich laugh and Miles shook his head, again knocked off-kilter by the intriguing woman sitting opposite him.

"Very few people know the real me, Louisa. That was… those articles were about my past. Were there any recent articles you read on me?"

"Nothing much since you moved here."

"What, you didn't read the one that said I'd moved in with Amanda and the kids because I was banging her?" he said with a roll of his eyes.

"Believe it or not, I don't believe everything that's been written about you in the media. It's easy to make assumptions as to what is going on behind closed doors. It's even better to fabricate a story if it means more hits on a website."

"You sound as though you're talking from experience."

"I am. Things are usually not what they seem. As easy as you can make up a sensational story, you can just as easily make up a fairy tale, happily ever after story." Louisa gave an awkward one-shoulder shrug.

What? Miles blinked at her, slightly surprised at her gloomy observation. "I'm not even going to ask what you mean by that because I know you won't say, but what I will say is this, I'm really having a good time. No offence to Celeste, but I'm glad you came on this date after all." Miles picked up his glass and tipped it towards her.

"I'm glad I came too." Louisa picked up her glass and clinked it against his.

"So you are having fun then?" he asked with a cheeky grin and she couldn't help but reciprocate it.

"I'm having fun," she conceded and he gifted her with that knock-your-socks-off smile he was renowned for.

6

HIDDEN AGENDAS

TWO MONTHS AGO

LOUISA WAS SITTING IN Melissa's office while she waited for her mother to finish off her calls. Since she'd moved to her London residence almost three months ago, they'd made a point of having lunch whenever Lady Alice came to the offices. Today Lady Alice had asked Louisa to pick her up from the office, hoping to pique her interest in the many projects the team were working on. Louisa had been there an hour already and there had been a steady influx of staff popping in to talk to her, informing her of different fundraising and success stories. Lady Alice, as in all her endeavours, was relentless in her efforts to ensure Louisa would finally officially become the patron of the charity.

Louisa eyed her childhood friend, who was positively blooming, as Melissa put her hand over her mouth and shuddered.

"Are you okay?" Louisa shifted forward, concerned for her dear friend.

"Morning sickness," Melissa mumbled, then reached for a glass of water she had on her desk. Melissa and her husband Robert had been trying for a baby since the day they were married, just over five years ago. They had almost given up after a number of failed IVF treatments. Then purely by accident, or by nature, Melissa had become pregnant. She was in her third month and everyone at CASPO had been instructed not to pressure her or give her undue stress since she refused to stop working. Pregnancy suited Melissa. Her chestnut bob shone under the office lights and her fair complexion had a rosy tint to it.

"Ginger biscuits," suggested Louisa.

"I ate them all." Melissa shrugged and Louisa rolled her eyes, then reached into her bag for her phone.

"Hugh, I'm so sorry to ask you this, but do you think you could buy some ginger biscuits for Melissa's morning sickness? Thank you."

Melissa gaped at her friend as she placed her phone back into her bag. Louisa rarely asked her staff to do tasks for her, even if they were all more than willing to. "I can't believe you did that."

"Hugh's a friend, as well as my driver and security. And I'd never ask for me; this is all for you and my future godchild and he knows that, so don't worry, he won't take offence. Enough about that. Now tell me what you're working on." Louisa's chin jerked at Melissa's computer screen.

Melissa swivelled the screen so Louisa could see and started to explain about the auction. The page they were looking at had the live list of the fifty auction prizes and next to each one was the running total; the one with the highest bid at the top.

Louisa scanned the list and watched as the totals kept changing. Her eyes honed in on the top prize and her brow furrowed. "Is that Miles Keane the pop star?"

"Yes! Didn't your mother tell you? He offered to auction off a lunch date. The bids are coming in so fast for that one." Melissa sniggered.

"How long has the auction been up?"

"Three days and it'll close at midnight tomorrow."

Louisa watched the total go up in increments of ten pounds. "When's the date scheduled for?"

"Anytime. He left it open."

Louisa furrowed her brow, thinking back to that brief encounter they'd had in the smoky dressing room. He'd crossed her mind occasionally over the ten years, especially after the shooting, but it seemed he'd pulled away from the lime light of late. "It's already up to £12,000. That's more than double the next highest prize."

"I know! It's all his fans. The phones are red hot with press and enquiries." Melissa couldn't contain her excitement. Even she hadn't expected such a great response.

"Wow, that's so good for CASPO. You know if Celeste were here, she'd be bidding. She'd probably squander her whole inheritance for that date," Louisa scoffed.

"Good job she's in Peru, then, isn't it? Though she'd kill you if she knew and you didn't tell her. Maybe I could ask him to come into the offices and meet her when's she's back?"

Louisa narrowed her eyes at Melissa and wondered about her suggestion. Maybe a date with Miles Keane would be a nice birthday surprise for her daughter. Louisa was trying to convince Celeste to fly back for a few days over her birthday. It would be the first birthday she'd be apart from her. A date with her crush might just be the bait to get her to come.

"We thought we'd get around £20,000 as a final total but it seems that he still has some very loyal fans out there by the way the amount is moving up. There are bids from fans in America and Japan."

"How did they get to hear about the auction?"

"The beauty of technology. The website has all our events on and once Miles Keane's date was put on, we had a serious surge of hits and we also have an app," Melissa said proudly.

"Really?"

"Oh yes, we're very modern now. Robert and his team have

brought us up to the 21st century. You can make your bid, as well as follow on it." One of Melissa's husband's companies developed websites and apps and he'd donated his team to CASPO, giving the charity a much-needed technological shake up.

"How on Earth did you pull the date off?" Louisa asked, now genuinely intrigued as to how the bad boy of pop had somehow been cajoled into auctioning off his time.

"It was his sister-in-law, actually. She's been raising funds for us over the last year and he asked her if he could get involved."

"His sister-in-law, she lives in the UK?" Louisa remembered seeing an article on Louis Keane's widow moving back to her hometown but she couldn't quite remember if it was permanent.

"They both do, from what I gather."

"What's she like?"

"Amanda Keane? Lovely, down to Earth, but you can tell she's sad. This work has brought her out of herself, though."

"I can't even imagine what it must've been like for her," Louisa said quietly.

The whole world had been stunned at the live footage of the horrifying gunning down of nine people almost five years ago. The band had been asked to perform a small set at the graduating ceremony at Julliard, seeing as two of the band members had graduated from the prestigious college. As was expected, there was a media frenzy and their fans flocked from miles away to the school, just to get a glimpse of them. Louis Keane had been asked to give the address and then afterwards the band was to perform a fifteen-minute medley of their chart topping songs as well as debut their new single. Security had been a logistical nightmare but once the students and their guests were all in the Alice Tully Hall, there would be no disturbances from fans or press. Louisa remembered Celeste being glued to the TV screen to watch the live streaming of the ceremony and of course her favourite band. She'd begged her parents to take her to the school so she could wait and see if she could catch a glimpse of them but of course there was no way either Gerard or Louisa would agree. By way of compensation, they promised tickets for their next concert in New York. Tragically, the concert never happened.

"I met Louis Keane."

"What!"

"Actually I met the whole band." Louisa huffed.

"When?"

"Oh God, it was... it must be ten years ago now. Celeste was desperate to see them. You remember how crazy she was for them? Well, their tour of the US started – I think it was one of their first ones – and the places they played in weren't very big but had sold out. So Gerard, being Gerard, contacted their agent and managed to add another date to their tour and got them to play Madison Square Gardens for their last night in the US." It was amazing what money and connections could get you when you knew where to ask.

"Anything for Celeste. Gerard always made sure his daughter was happy."

Louisa gave a nod. If only Melissa knew that the very day of the concert, Louisa had found out that on his important business trip to France he'd been accompanied by another woman, a woman who didn't work for him but most definitely got paid handsomely.

"Exactly," Louisa said with a sigh. "We were all supposed to go but he ended up going away on business, so just Celeste and I went in a private VIP box. Afterwards, we went backstage and met them for a few minutes."

"How was he?"

"He was an absolute gentleman. In fact, he said that he hoped one day he'd have a daughter like Celeste." Louisa scrunched up her nose remembering his kind words.

"Wow, that's... well a bit surreal, seeing as he did have a daughter – and look." Melissa pointed to a picture of an eight-year-old blonde girl holding the hand of Amanda Keane. It was one of many shots that the paparazzi had taken of the family while they'd spent some time in London. "She looks a little like Celeste did at that age." Melissa peered at the screen and gave a nod. "What about Miles, what was he like?"

"The complete opposite." Louisa widened her eyes and shook her head. "He was high as a kite, if I remember correctly and behaved inappropriately."

"What do you mean?" Melissa's face dropped. This man was going to be meeting a fan for lunch. A lunch CASPO had organised and she would be responsible for.

"He was just flirty and obviously had no clue as to who we were, probably because he was drunk. I remember thinking *this is who my daughter idolises,* and I was appalled. He was sweet to Celeste, though."

"Well, by all accounts, he's a changed man now. I suppose a tragedy puts a lot into perspective."

"Not sure *that* leopard could change *that* many of his spots," Louisa said wryly and immediately felt bad for Melissa, seeing her look worried.

"Maybe we need to have the fan chaperoned, just to be on the safe side." Melissa jotted something down on her notepad.

"I'm sure he's not like that now, Melissa."

"Probably not."

"But make sure there's no chance he takes her in the toilets though," Louisa said with a chuckle.

"Louisa! Though I tell you what, morning sickness aside, I wouldn't mind being dragged into the toilets with him. He's ridiculously good looking." She sniggered.

This time it was Louisa who was a little shocked. "Jeez, Melissa."

"Pregnancy hormones." Melissa shrugged.

Their inappropriate conversation was cut short by Hugh coming in with five packets of assorted ginger biscuits. Once Hugh had left and Melissa had munched through her first biscuit and was starting on her second, the two women continued to chat about their families and generally catch up.

"How's the house? Finished yet?" Melissa asked, brushing her hands together to remove the crumbs.

"It should be finished by the end of next week. I'm living on the top floor until the last of my things have been put in. The redecoration has really changed it. I didn't realise how much difference it would make. It kept me busy too."

"Talking of keeping you busy, are you going to help me with the garden party?"

"You really need my help?" Louisa arched her brow at her more-than-capable friend.

"I *want* your help. Plus I'll be bigger then and I have to watch my blood pressure and not overdo it," she added with a smirk.

"Resorting to emotional blackmail now, are we?"

Melissa grinned at her perceptive friend who'd seen right through her hidden agenda, but didn't deny what her motive was.

"Of course I'll help, though knowing you, it's probably all organised. What other fundraising events have you got in the pipeline?"

"The annual ball mid-July. God, I'll be huge by then." Melissa made a face, then picked up another ginger biscuit.

"Any big names coming?"

"We're working on a few."

Louisa leaned over and pinched one of the biscuits and took a bite. "What do you think about asking Konran?"

"Isn't he in the middle of a world tour right now?"

"Yeah, but I can ask. And Celeste will be here then too, so... The cause is close to his heart too."

"Well to have a megastar rapper will be quite a coup for CASPO, and it'll also bring some serious attention to our charity."

"Maybe we shouldn't say anything yet. Let me talk to him

first. I think he's in Japan right now, so until I manage to actually chat to him, let's keep this between us."

"ANY CALLS, HUGH?" Louisa slipped into the back of her car and fastened her seat belt.

"Mr Dupont called, and Earl Alistair."

Louisa let out a breath, reached into her bag and looked at her silenced phone. She'd just endured a full on interrogation worthy of a murder suspect from her mother; the last thing she wanted was to talk to Gerard. She knew he was due to arrive in London for business and he wanted to see her. Why Alistair was calling, she had no idea. "Hey, you called?"

"Yeah. How was lunch?" Louisa could hear the cringe in Alistair's voice.

"Well I got the full Lady B treatment. She basically told me to get my shit together and take over from her. She said it was time to take on my responsibilities, as I was after all the Countess, and to channel all the experience and expertise I'd learned to good use. I'd done enough mooning and my recluse behaviour wasn't worthy of the Blackthorn name. She then pulled out the classic... if your father was alive he'd be reminding you who the Blackthorns are." Louisa caught Hugh's eyes in the rear view mirror as he chuckled. She grinned back at him. He'd often witnessed Lady Alice's outbursts throughout his time working for the Blackstone's and felt the utmost sympathy for Louisa.

"Oh wow, so she went for the kill then? And have you got your shit together?" her brother said with a chuckle.

"Apparently, I don't have a choice. She wants to announce her retirement after the garden party, so I will be the patron when we have the annual ball in July."

"And the board?"

"She's already told them. Everything is ready – apart from me, that is."

"Louisa, you're ready. You just got comfortable being out of the spotlight. You have totally got this." Alistair's encouraging words did little to calm the tightening of her stomach. He was right; she'd enjoyed twenty years of anonymity, only being seen by the world press when her father had died. It was time for her to be who she was born to be.

"Thanks, the same goes for you too. You need to get out more."

"Well that's why I was calling you. I'm coming down to London to meet the gang and need somewhere to crash tomorrow. I don't fancy staying in a hotel, though."

"Of course you can stay; it's our home, not just mine. I'll make sure your room is ready. Who's down then?"

"The usual suspects: Robert, Eddie, Giles and Tim. All except Gordon, because he's in Brazil." The six men had been friends from boarding school and were the only people, other than family, Alistair spent time with. Whenever there was an occasion that enough of them were in the same country, they always organised a night out. Throughout their childhood, Alistair's friends had periodically stayed at Holmwood House, throwing parties in the old dairy, spending weeks enjoying all the facilities as well as helping the late Earl around the grounds. Louisa had been around eight years old, but she remembered spying on her brother and his friends as they stole beer from the kitchen that the Earl had purposely left there for them. She wasn't allowed to join their parties, or bunk with them in their rooms above the dairy, but thankfully, they let her join in with their various games during the day.

"That's nice that you all get together."

"Yeah, well Giles is over for business and Tim is coming in especially."

"Great, so I'll see you for breakfast then, the morning after."

"Sure."

Louisa tapped on Gerard's number and waited for it to connect. Now that she'd heard that Giles was in London, it made sense that Gerard had timed his visit to coincide. Giles Dupont was Gerard's cousin and had a percentage of the Dupont Corporation in France. No doubt they were meeting in the capital to finalise some deal or another. Louisa was glad her divorce hadn't affected Alistair's friendship with Giles. It was through Giles that Louisa had met Gerard.

The trouble with the aristocracy was that everyone moved in the same circles, so the children tended to know one another and grow up around each other. This meant that they felt like family. In Louisa's case, her brother's friends had held no appeal to her as she got older, until one day, Giles had brought his cousin to Holmwood. Gerard was over on business and was at a loose end one weekend. Louisa had been only seventeen at the time but the dashing French man caught her eye that spring bank holiday. He was everything her brother's friends – and any other boy she'd ever met – weren't. Apart from his classic good looks he was mature, serious and had a presence that only came from inner confidence. He made every other man she'd met look juvenile.

Rather than spend the morning goofing around with his cousin Giles and the rest of his friends, Gerard had spent it talking with the late Earl. Louisa had watched them walk around the grounds in deep conversation while she and Melissa helped one of the hands look after the horses. After lunch, Gerard had joined the rest of the party, along with members of the household, and played cricket, but his attention had often floated in the direction of Louisa. The Earl umpired the match while Louisa, Lady Alice and Melissa watched. As soon as Gerard was caught out, he sauntered to where Louisa was sitting, helping himself to the refreshments that had been laid out. There were a few other team members standing around the table but rather than talk to them, Gerard crouched down beside Louisa. Louisa turned, surprised that he'd even noticed her. The handsome French man gave her a nod and a self-assured smile that had Louisa, for the first time, a little flustered.

"Cricket not your forte?" she asked, trying hard not to blush under his intense scrutiny.

His smile widened at her tone. "No, I prefer boules. It's a French thing." His rich accented voice had Louisa's stomach flipping.

"Yes I know, we play it here too," she said dryly.

"You know how to play?" He tilted his head to the side and waited for her answer.

"Yes."

"Would you like to play with me?"

Louisa took in a sharp breath, wondering if the confident smirk on his face was because of his choice of words or because he could see she was affected by them.

"Yes."

"Good." Gerard gracefully rose up and swiped his hand in front of him. "Lead the way, my lady."

It was over the hour long game of boules that Gerard had realised Louisa was more than just an entitled heiress. The women he had previously dated were snobs, spoilt and demanding. Louisa was a breath of fresh air. She had every right to behave as though she was superior and yet she did not. Her youth gave her an air of innocence but she wasn't as naive as she looked; her teasing of his boules skills and sharp wit kept him on his toes. He charmed her with his confident manner, he made her laugh with his dry humour and he captivated her with his full and undivided attention. Louisa had for the first time found a man amongst the many boys. By the end of their game, Gerard was also more than a little taken with Lady Louisa Blackthorn. By the end of that summer, they were engaged.

"Cherie." His slightly accented deep voice still made Louisa's heart clench.

"Hello Gerard, how are you?"

"I'm fine, and you?"

"I'm good."

"I still miss you."

"I know." She heard his resigned sigh. He would never give up on her; it wasn't in his makeup to. He'd always try to win her back and she would always try her hardest to resist him. "Are you in London?"

"Yes, and I wanted to take you to dinner tonight."

"Is seven o'clock at Blacks okay?"

"I'll pick you up."

"No need, I'll have Hugh bring me."

"As you wish." Louisa could hear the disappointment in his voice. "I'll see you at seven, *cherie*."

Louisa looked down at her phone and turned it in her hand. A myriad of emotions swept over her. In the last few months, Louisa had gotten comfortable in her loneliness, because that was what she was, incredibly lonely. She really missed Celeste, and she missed her organised life, but most of all she missed Gerard. Twenty years of love and friendship was hard to get over. He had of course been a gentleman in every aspect, calling her twice a week to see how she was, making small talk and keeping her abreast of life in New York. But his intention was crystal clear to Louisa. For twenty years she'd seen and experienced Gerard's seductive manner. He tried to coax her back in subtle ways: an exhibition she would love, a new theatre show that had opened, any way he could, but Louisa always graciously declined. Louisa was sure this trip to London was another one of his ploys to chip away at her resolve. She admired his determination and took some comfort in the fact he was still trying. But there was too much history, too much hurt that she just wasn't able to forget.

Maybe being the patron of CASPO was what she needed after all. Louisa hated to admit that her mother was probably right. It was time to get her shit together, throw herself into a new venture and set an example for her daughter. Louisa scrolled down to Konran's number and sent him a quick message.

Hey, hope the tour's going well. Give me a call when you're free x

Louisa then checked the CASPO app she'd downloaded and saw that the date with Miles Keane was now at £13,000. Tonight, she'd ask Gerard to arrange for his plane to fly Celeste back from Peru for her birthday and she would outbid anyone for the date. At least she'd have her daughter back, even if it was just for a couple of days.

7

THE DATE – THE DESSERT

THE RESTAURANT AT THE Blacks Club was beginning to quieten. The recently vacated tables were discreetly being set up for afternoon tea. From early in the morning, until late in the evening, the restaurant at the Blacks Club had a steady stream of clientele. Set in the heart of the city, it was the perfect location for business to be conducted, and the present diners certainly reflected that.

Miles watched the waiters efficiently move soundlessly to the music of Chopin as it drifted through the room. Their own table was being prepared for dessert with equal efficiency. The waiter asked whether they were ready for their next course.

Louisa shifted her gaze to Miles. "Would you like dessert now or take a little break?" she asked.

"Whatever suits you."

"You don't have anything pressing?" Her eyes twinkled as he stifled a smirk.

"No. I've nothing to rush back to."

"Then in that case, we'll wait a while."

The waiter gave a curt nod and left them to enjoy the last of their wine.

"No more questions then?"

"I think that maybe I've been a little too tough on you."

Miles twisted his mouth, indicating that she was probably right, but spared her a verbal confirmation and Louisa grinned at him. She hadn't been that hard on him, he'd just expected something different from his date. He hadn't been prepared to have his past brought up again.

"Do you think you know someone because you ask them questions about themselves?" She tilted her head to the side and Miles narrowed his eyes at her, unsure of where her question was leading. "Well, you don't. You only know someone when they volunteer information about themselves, about their feelings, dreams, their inner thoughts."

"I'm not sure I follow."

"When you ask someone, what's bothering you? How do you feel about that? They'll answer the question but it doesn't come willingly, truthfully even. It's been forced out of them. When someone decides to open up to you without prompting, you see their real candid self. That's who they are. There's a lot to be said for just being patient and listening."

"A bit like a shrink does?"

"Yes, I suppose so. I've found that if you let people talk about themselves, they reveal far more than if you'd asked straight questions."

"Are you expecting me to just talk about myself, then? No more probing questions?"

"If you'd like."

"What I'd *like* is to know more about you but I take it that that's not going to happen." Louisa gave him that enigmatic smile again and he shook his head and chuckled. "So I'm supposed to ramble on, then?"

"Well, I'm hoping it'll be more interesting than just ramblings."

"Would you like me to continue telling you about how Keane Sense started?"

"It's totally up to you. The ball is firmly in your court."

"Ha, I think the ball has never been in my court, Louisa. Okay, where were we?"

"Eric had convinced your parents."

"Right." Miles took a sip from his refilled glass and leisurely licked the remnants of the wine from his lips; a seemingly innocent gesture that had Louisa totally mesmerised for a moment, before he shuffled forward in his seat to continue his story. "Well, I ended up finishing my degree while we perfected our demo for the first album. Eric then managed to get us a recording contract, which was amazing, considering we weren't even known. It also meant we needed to get to work on polishing off fourteen of the songs Louis and I had written. It was crazy. One minute, we were just bashing out songs on a keyboard and guitar, then the next, we were in this studio with producers, sound engineers and the use of an orchestra if we wanted."

"A dream come true?"

"Exactly." His lips curved into a lopsided smile. "Within a few months, we were promoting our debut single, then the album and before we even realised it, we were number one. We weren't ready for it. Well let's say Josh, Mike and I weren't. Louis had always been level-headed. He was interested in the facts and figures, we weren't so much."

Louisa nodded at his self-scathing comment and shuffled forward in her seat. "Then came the fans?"

"Yeah. Nothing can prepare you for that. Girls screaming at you when you arrived at a studio, being followed by fans or photographers everywhere you went. We ended up being prisoners in swanky hotels and we weren't even that successful then."

"I don't think the fans were only interested in your musical talent. Your manager and his PR team knew exactly what they were doing," Louisa said with a wry smile.

"Pimping us out?"

"Pretty much. Bottom line, Miles, you were four good-looking guys who also sang and performed well. The fact you were also songwriters was just an added bonus. How did your parents react to your new-found fame?"

"I think they thought it was a little vulgar. Don't get me wrong; they were proud of us, really proud, but the adoration, the fame and everything else that came with that, it didn't really sit well with them."

"Do they still feel that way?"

Miles took a deep breath and gave a curt nod. "Especially after… My folks are low-key, quiet and our fame bounced a little their way, which meant their somewhat subdued life was disrupted."

"That must have been a bit of a shock for them." Louisa could appreciate Miles's parents' discomfort. She'd spent most of her life trying to avoid attention that came with her title. Moving to America had somewhat helped and being under the shadow of her successful businessman husband meant she could almost make herself invisible. That and not using her title helped too. Now she was back in England, though, and ready to embark on her new role as CASPO's patron, her anonymity had a very short shelf life.

"Yeah. When your trash is sifted through and you're hounded at your place of work and home it isn't easy." Miles huffed out. "We had to organise security for a while for them, which again was an adjustment. Then, after the shooting, it just got worse, and at a time when all they needed was space and time to come to terms with their loss."

They sat in comfortable silence for a while. Miles thoughts drifted back to the time when his family had been in the constant spotlight at the worst possible moment of their lives, while

Louisa reflected on how thankful she was that the hardest time in her marriage had never been exposed.

"I suppose they've got their privacy back now." Louisa's comment brought Miles back from his distracting thoughts.

"Yeah, but it's funny." He gave a humourless laugh. "In hindsight, my parents would rather Louis was here and they were hounded every second by paparazzi."

"I'm sure," Louisa said softly.

Miles shook his head in an attempt to shake off his sombre mood. "I suppose you should be careful what you wish for." He blew out a sharp breath and gave Louisa a tight smile. "Shit, I mean, sorry. I didn't mean to put a damper on our date. You see this is why my dates go so much better when I don't just focus on me." He mock-chastised her, causing Louisa to chuckle. "I'm so much better at dates when they do all the talking."

"You're a lot better than you think, Miles." Louisa gave him soft smile and Miles grinned widely at her.

"Yeah?"

"Yeah. Showing that vulnerable side to yourself is endearing. Don't you know women love that kind of thing?" she said dryly. Louisa couldn't even imagine how many women he must've been with. If she believed the tabloids, the number was in the hundreds.

Miles leaned forward and lowered his voice a touch. "So I'm endearing to you?"

Louisa kept tight lipped and glanced over to one of the waiters, who was discreetly standing a few feet away, and gave him a nod. "I think it's time for dessert, don't you?"

"Ooh, nice dodge, Louisa. Obviously we haven't had enough wine for you to admit it yet." He widened his eyes at her and she narrowed hers back at him, enjoying the way he teased her.

"Well, Miles, just so you know, for future reference that is, I have never needed wine or any other stimulant for that matter, to say what I think or feel to anyone."

"No?"

Louisa gave him a deliberate shake of her head. "Sometimes it's what's not said that holds the most meaning. And sometimes I'd rather just not say… if you get my meaning."

Miles let out a husky laugh. She was playing him at his own game and he loved every second of it. Louisa may have lightened up and warmed to him but she was still giving nothing away. Louisa picked up her wine glass and disguised her smirk by taking a sip.

"You know what I took away from that statement?" Louisa furrowed her brow at his comment. Miles leaned forward, resting his elbows on the table and clasping his hands in front of him. "*For future reference*. That means you plan to see me again." He gave her a self-satisfied smirk and kept his eyes fixed on hers.

Louisa's gaze faltered for a second, realising she'd slipped up. "Not necessarily. There's every possibility we could bump into each other."

"Really? Like where?"

"Charity functions, fundraisers. You're here in London now, soon to be pimped out by CASPO. It's highly likely at some point we'll be at the same event."

"Perhaps, though I think the version in my head, of how our future meeting would be is so much more interesting." He raised his eyebrows as he watched Louisa's cheeks heat. "And before you ask what that is, let's say I'm taking a leaf out of your book and keeping it to myself." He tapped his temple with his index finger.

Louisa suddenly felt her whole body warm up. That familiar sensation that had lain dormant for what seemed an age started in her toes and worked its way up until her whole body was tingling. Just the idea that this ridiculously handsome man sitting in front of her was thinking of how they might meet in the future, had her stomach clenching.

Her uneasy feelings were interrupted by the arrival of their third course. The waiters placed the dessert that looked like a piece of art in front of Louisa and Miles simultaneously, along with two small wine glasses half-filled with a rich gold wine.

"Mr Thomas took the liberty of pairing the brûlée with a Sauterne, madame," the waiter informed them before he retreated.

"It's a good job I don't have anything on this afternoon," Miles huffed. "What with all this fancy food and even fancier wine, I don't think I could do anything. You know, I don't think I've ever had dessert wine before."

"Well you don't have to have any if you don't want. Believe it or not, I don't eat like this every day, but it is a special occasion after all."

"A special occasion, eh?" Miles eyes lit up and Louisa clenched her jaw, realising she'd once again slipped up and revealed too much.

Rather than ignore his comment – or worse, back-peddle – Louisa decided to bite the bullet and own it. He was hell-bent on getting her to break a little, it was only fair to throw him a bone. "Well, it's not every day I get to have lunch with such a huge pop star, even if I did pay rather handsomely for the privilege."

Miles let out a chuckle. "Is that so? Well, Louisa, just so you know, *for future reference* that is, you won't need to part with a penny for our next date." He gave her a cheeky wink, then picked up his dessert wine glass.

"You're so sure we'll have a second date?"

"I'm banking on it." He threw back the words she'd said to him earlier.

Louisa tried hard to stifle her smile at his downright cockiness. Normally she would've been put off by such a blatant show of confidence, but somehow Miles's attitude did the exact opposite to her. She reached over and lifted her dessert wine glass.

"Here's to our next date." Miles arched his brow, then clinked her glass with his. There was no question in his statement. One way or another, he was going to ensure he had another date with the intriguing woman sitting opposite him, and on his terms.

"Perhaps," she countered.

"I can live with that." He blasted her with that smile again. It wasn't a no. The odds were beginning to swing a little bit in his favour. He was hoping he wasn't going to screw up the rest of their date. After Lottie's call, he'd been worried that he'd blown it, but thankfully Louisa seemed to have forgiven the intrusion of the call. He couldn't blame her – she had paid for his time after all, but more importantly, Miles wanted Louisa to have a good time. She was here because her daughter couldn't make it and purely because she was well-mannered enough not to cancel.

Miles sipped the sweet wine and furrowed his brow.

"You don't like it?"

"It's not that, it's just that… well I wasn't sure what to expect. But it's actually quite pleasant."

"When you taste the brûlée, it'll compliment it."

Miles picked up his spoon and cracked through the caramelised sugar, taking some of the creamy dessert with it. Louisa watched him as he tasted the dessert, trying hard not to focus on how his tongue swiped over his lush lips.

"That's amazing."

Louisa gave him a nod and then picked up her spoon.

"I didn't think I'd be learning the art of fine dining on this date," he drawled.

"What did you envisage the date to be like then?"

"Honestly?"

Louisa gave him a nod.

"No offence to Celeste, because I don't know her, but from experience, I expected some breathy fan who doted on my every word, asked boring questions, showed far too much skin in an attempt to lure me and giggled a lot."

"Sorry to disappoint."

Louisa's dry response was rewarded with another husky laugh that had Miles's eyes light up. "Louisa, believe me, you most definitely didn't disappoint."

Louisa's eyes darted to his and he held her gaze for a few seconds, causing her pulse to quicken. She was enjoying him flirting with her but she couldn't be sure if it was just part and parcel of the date or if he was being genuine. She decided to defuse the heated moment with humour. "Well you have to say that, don't you? After all, I paid you." She arched her brow at him and he grinned widely.

"That's exactly why we need another date."

Louisa gave a sage nod. "You mean it'll be on the house, so to speak?" She stifled a smirk and he chuckled.

"Ah Louisa, now you're just toying with me, but that's okay. Like you said, you paid for the privilege. On our next date, though, the tables are gonna turn. I'm going to be toying with you."

"That's if we have another date."

"Why, are you worried that you can't handle not being in charge? You said you were having a good time – or were you just being polite?"

Louisa cracked into the brûlée and spooned up the dessert. "Are you doubting your dating techniques?" She popped the spoon into her mouth and slowly pulled it out, then licked her lips.

Miles tilted his head to the side. "Are you doubting your level of control?" Before she could answer, he added with a cheeky twinkle in his eye, "You know that this is the hardest I've ever had to work at convincing a woman to go on a date with me. You're seriously damaging my self-esteem here."

Louisa chuckled at his attempt to ease the sudden highly charged atmosphere. He'd seen she was uncomfortable with the direction their conversation was going. He'd hit on a nerve; she was doubting her self-control. What was worse, though, was she couldn't be sure his undivided attention was purely because he had an obligation or whether he was enjoying her company as much as she was enjoying his. He said he hadn't envisaged the date turning out like this – well, neither had she. The last thing she'd expected was that she'd have a good time. Even more disturbing was the fact that the idea of a second date was becoming more appealing with every minute that passed.

"Well, if we do have another date, it'll be purely to help with your self-confidence issues," she said, stifling a grin.

"Why thank you, ma'am," he drawled in an accentuated American accent, for which she rewarded him with a soft laugh.

As the restaurant hit its first lull in clientele before the afternoon tea trade, Louisa veered the conversation to places of interest for Miles to visit in London. She'd decided that probing him further about his past understandably made him sad and uncomfortable, and unless he volunteered the information, she wasn't going to push anymore.

The couple of hours they'd spent together had somewhat made up for that fifteen-minute meeting over ten years ago. That cocky, twenty-something pop star had been tamed by circumstances and tragedy that no one should have to endure. The man sitting opposite, who was trying hard in every way possible to charm her, was a new improved version of himself. His boyish good looks had matured into chiselled jawlines and sharp cheekbones. The few lines that appeared when he smiled only made him more rugged. His bright blue eyes still had that mischievous twinkle Louisa remembered so vividly but they now had an intensity, which hinted at a much deeper soul of someone who had been through pain and survived it.

The devastatingly handsome man in front of her was a polished, mellowed, mature version of the bad boy she'd met in the smoky dressing room, and boy, did it look good on him. His flirtatious nature was now subtle, disarming in its continuous attack. He'd managed to chip away at Louisa's resolve by unwittingly revealing his sensitive side. She'd come into the date wholeheartedly expecting to dislike Miles, believing his success, super-stardom and popularity would've changed him into a worse version of the over-confident and arrogant young man she'd met, when in fact he was proving to be the complete opposite.

How much of his personality change was down to the tragic circumstances of his brother's death, Louisa couldn't be sure. If she believed what was written in the media, then it would seem it was purely because of Louis's death. But Louisa knew not to take the articles she'd read on him at face value. Her own experience and story were living proof that what got reported was a distorted version of the truth.

They'd managed to finish off their dessert and sip their way through the wine, oblivious to the sudden increase of clientele. A few furtive looks passed their way but both Louisa and Miles didn't even notice. Their conversation had moved on to the renovation of his house.

"Thank goodness for Amanda," he huffed. "When I first bought my house, I didn't have a clue. My house in California was already decorated. The only change was I added a recording studio. Thankfully, the contractor Amanda introduced me to was patient with me and to be honest, it was therapeutic."

"Remodelling, you mean?"

"Yes. I'm creative by nature but this was a different area of creativity for me."

Louisa nodded. "And you're happy with the result?"

"Yeah. I'm still furnishing it, slowly, very slowly." He chuckled. "I've got the basics, which is fine by me but I suppose it needs some personal stuff."

"You mean mementoes, photos and the like?"

"Uhuh, plus other things."

"Like framed platinum records?" Louisa gestured towards the bag.

"No, they're all in in my California home. This place is more… I don't know, classy? The house is Victorian, for goodness sake! It would be a little tasteless to decorate it with flashy awards."

"So antiques, then?" Louisa suggested.

"Possibly."

"You know, you shouldn't overthink it. When I decorated my homes, I just put things in I really liked. They didn't necessarily go together. I had a lot of family heirlooms that I loved and ended up scattering them through the different houses. Then I added pieces that I found over time. Houses are decorated, homes are a work in progress."

"Yeah, you're right. Though Amanda has insisted I get a dining room table and chairs." He rolled his eyes and shook his head.

"You don't think you need one?"

"*If* I eat at home, it's in the kitchen, so it just seemed unnecessary."

"When you invite someone home, you eat in the kitchen?" Louisa asked, careful trying not to sound surprised.

"I've never invited someone over for dinner, Louisa," he said quietly, raising his eyes to hers.

"Oh." Louisa wasn't sure what that statement implied. Did he never have anyone over or when he did, the last place on his mind was the dining room. Louisa averted her eyes and toyed with her spoon.

"I haven't invited anyone over, other than Amanda and the kids – and they're family, so the kitchen's fine. Plus with those two kids, it's important to contain the mess to one room." He chuckled and Louisa let out a sharp breath she hadn't realised she was holding. For some reason, that fact he'd just revealed made her feel relieved. Surely that was to do with him having just moved in rather than a choice, though.

"But you might one day. So I think Amanda might have a point."

"Maybe I'll invite you over." He raised his brows at her as he saw her blush and he grinned, pleased to have surprised her.

"Me?"

"Uhuh. Would you come, if I invited you?" He shuffled forward in his seat, closing the distance between them.

"For dinner, you mean?"

"Yeah. I can cook. Not fancy food like this but I can grill up some prime steaks. They'd go really well with the Lafite." He gave her that wide smile and she chuckled.

"So you're a Lafite convert then?"

"Are you avoiding my question, Louisa?"

Of course she was avoiding the question. "I'll tell you what. Buy yourself a dining room table and chairs and then, when you've got them, ask me again?" she answered with a smile, hoping she'd managed to halt any more discussion on them meeting again.

"Now there's an incentive to buy furniture if ever I heard one. If only Amanda knew how easy it was, she'd ask you to put down more incentives for me to buy more of what she thinks are essentials." He shook his head, then leaned forward, capturing her gaze with his bright blue eyes. "You realise that I'm going shopping tomorrow, don't you? So effectively, we could be having our date a lot soon than you think."

"I said you could *ask* me to come to dinner, not that I'd say yes." She stifled a grin at the shocked expression on his face. He thought he'd cornered her into a date, and a quick one at that.

"What! You'd make me spend money on a table and chairs and then shoot me down? Oh no, I need a guarantee. I can live without a table and chairs; the kitchen is fine by me." He punctuated his remark by leaning back in his chair.

"You're saying that you'll only buy the table if I promise to come around?" Louisa tilted her head to the side, bewildered at his determination. "That's a lot of money wasted on something you feel you don't need, just to get me to come around Miles. I'd be happy to eat in the kitchen," she said with a slight shake of her head. She didn't give two hoots about eating in the kitchen and she most definitely didn't want him feeling as though she needed or expected a lavish table either.

"Maybe." His expression softened and he shifted forward again. "But I wouldn't be happy having you come around for dinner without having a table and chairs for you to sit at. So it'd be worth every penny." His face had lost that humorous twinkle and in its place was total sincerity.

Louisa took in a sharp breath, caught in the intensity of his gaze as the weight of his words settled over her like a warm blanket on a chilly day. "Miles…"

"It's just dinner, Louisa, to christen my new table. It's the least I could do; a thank you for donating to CASPO, nothing more," he coaxed gently.

"I'm flattered that you're going to all these lengths just to have dinner with me."

"Louisa, it's not flattery. I really do want to see you again and not under these circumstances." He waved his hand in the air vaguely. "You're the first person I've met in a very long time that doesn't give a damn that I'm Miles Keane from Keane Sense. It's surprisingly refreshing. You have no idea what's it's like never knowing if someone is with you because of who you are, or whether they just like hanging out with you because they see past all the fame and celebrity. I'm tired of having to second-guess someone's motives. My real friends are people from my past, before Keane Sense. It's curiously challenging for me to have to work so hard to convince someone to just have a friendly dinner with me. That's all it'll be, Louisa, me cooking a few steaks in my new home."

He had no idea that his heartfelt plea was so close to the bone. Wasn't that exactly why Louisa had insisted she kept her identity a mystery today? Miles hadn't realised in his candid request that Louisa knew exactly how it felt to wonder if someone wanted her company because she was Louisa or Lady Blackthorn. Maybe this once cocky boy-band heartthrob wasn't who she'd perceived him to be after all. Maybe they had far more in common than Louisa originally thought. Maybe he even deserved a chance to redeem her first impression of him. Ten years was a long time ago, another lifetime. The last couple of hours, he'd certainly managed to change her opinion of him.

"Buy the table and ask me again," she answered softly.

Miles blew out breath, a little shocked that he'd persuaded her. "I'll take that as a yes, because you're too much of a lady to make me spend a ton of money on a table and chairs, then not come and be the first to eat off it." He stifled a grin.

Louisa's heart stopped for a split second, hearing him call her a lady, but she quickly dismissed it as a figure of speech. "That sounded like a mild form of blackmail." She arched her brow at him and took a sip of her wine.

"There was nothing mild about it," he said dryly, then grinned as he watched Louisa's cheeks blush.

Had she just agreed to a second date? Well, he had to buy a table and chairs first... Louisa nodded to the waiter. Maybe it was the large amount of alcohol they'd consumed that had broken down her resistance. *It was time for coffee.* Or maybe it was just because this handsome man opposite her had done an excellent job of convincing her.

8

HATCHING PLANS

TWO MONTHS AGO

"HEY, LADY B, HOW are you?"

"I'm good, sweetheart. How's the tour going?" Louisa grinned widely at Konran on her computer monitor. When he smiled, she could still see the skinny, sweet, fourteen-year-old boy she'd met just over ten years ago.

Konran Konjwa, or TuKon as he was now known, had been sponsored by one of the many philanthropic organisations Gerard contributed to. Louisa spent her time being involved with a large majority of them, especially ones that helped children. Konran was one of the musically gifted children who had been singled out by one of the charities. He then lived with his mother in a one-bedroomed apartment in one of the poorest parts of the city. His father had been gunned down in crossfire while walking home from his security guard job a year ago, forcing Konran and his mother to move into a smaller home. Their plight had been brought to Louisa's attention and after meeting them, Louisa set the wheels in motion to find a better home for them and fund Konran's passion for music. Konran's mother was given a job within one of the many companies Gerard owned and Konran's talent for writing music flourished, once he was placed in the right school and environment. Celeste and he became friends, an unlikely combination of rich, titled, well-bred girl and black teenage boy from the Bronx. But they bonded in the youth centre that Celeste and Louisa volunteered in, over music and being misfits. Celeste still felt like a foreigner because of her European background and Konran felt out of place in the middle-class area he was now living. The six-year age gap didn't seem to matter and over the years, their bond had become stronger.

"Man, its crazy! The Japanese are unbelievable."

"And you're doing Australia next, right?"

"Yeah, I can't wait to see a kangaroo! I heard from Celeste too this week. She's doing great work out in Peru. The education program she told me about is awesome. I'm so proud of her."

"Yes, she's a true crusader. I'm proud of her and proud of you too – your first world tour," Louisa said, genuinely in awe of how far he'd come in such a short time.

"Yeah I know, surreal. Who'd 'ave thought it eh? It's all thanks to you and Gerard."

"We just put you in the right environment, sweetheart; you always had the talent." Konran shook his head because he knew he'd never be where he was today without the Duponts. They were in his prayers every night and his heart every time he wrote a song.

"So the reason I need to talk to you is I'm organising the annual ball for CASPO and I wanted to know if there was any way you could be there for it. I know you're touring but you'll be in Europe by then."

Louisa watched Konran's forehead furrow. "When is it?"

"July third."

He glanced at something to the left. "I'll be in Germany."

"I know."

"Checking up on me?" He chuckled.

"Always." She gave him a knowing look.

"Well, it looks as though there shouldn't be a problem. I have two days off between Munich and Frankfurt."

"So you'll make it?"

"Of course; I can never say no to you, Lady B." He gave her a wide grin.

"You're the best. Celeste will be here, so it'll be a bit of a reunion too."

"Awesome. Will Gerard be there?" Konran asked softly. Konran and Gerard were close too and their divorce had been a shock to him.

"I don't know. I don't think so."

"He calls me at least once a week, you know."

"Yes, I know – he told me."

"You guys okay?" His genuine concern was etched all over his face.

"We're fine, Konran, you don't need to worry." Konran gave a nod and Louisa forced out a smile to appease him. "So, tell me more about Japan."

Konran's face lit up instantly. "Man, you'd love it, the cherry blossoms are just starting and the sushi... that stuff we eat in New York ain't nothing like this."

"*Isn't anything* like this." Louisa corrected.

"Hey, you can take the boy outta the Bronx but you can't..."

"... take the Bronx outta the boy. Yes, yes I know." Louisa finished off the well-known phrase he always quoted when Louisa or anyone else tried to correct him. For the next ten minutes, Louisa listened to everything Konran said, relishing in his success and unbridled enthusiasm. It did her heart good and made her a little proud and grateful that she had had a hand in it.

An hour later, Louisa was still sitting in her home office, waiting patiently. Her eyes were glued to the spot where the last bid of £32,000 had popped up over fifteen minutes ago. The bids had slowed down over the last two hours and Louisa was sure that no one else was likely to put in a new bid. Louisa kept an eye on the counter as the seconds clicked by, then, when it was one minute to midnight, Louisa typed in her bid of £50,000 and waited. As soon as there was fifteen seconds left on the clock, she pressed the Enter key. Her bid popped up into the box, then five seconds later, the auction site closed. *She'd got the date with Miles Keane for Celeste!*

Her momentary glee was interrupted by a noise coming from the entrance hall. Louisa quickly rose up from her chair and went to see what it was. She came face to face with a slightly dishevelled Alistair along with an obviously drunk Tim and Eddie.

"Louisa! You're still up." The two men tried to keep steady but they kept swaying as they tried to focus on Louisa to greet her.

"Good night?" she asked with an arch of her brow.

"Err, yes. I'll put them on the second floor," Alistair said as he ushered his friends into the lift.

"Glad to see you at least have your wits about you. Need any help?"

"No I'm well practiced and someone had to be the responsible one." Alistair rolled his eyes but Louisa knew that after his accident, Alistair only drank occasionally.

"I'll see you in the morning, then. Good night."

Louisa received garbled versions of good night from Tim and Eddie as the lift doors closed, then went back to her office to close up her computer.

The next morning found Louisa and Alistair sitting around the dining room table drinking tea. Both Tim and Eddie were still sleeping off their excesses. She got to hear about their antics and was pleased that Alistair had the good grace to let Tim's wife know he was staying with him. Giles had gone back to his hotel room and Robert had left early, as he wasn't happy leaving Melissa home alone for too long.

"Those two are still like lovestruck teenagers," Alistair huffed. "And now she's pregnant they're even worse."

"I think it's sweet. I didn't see that one coming at all," Louisa said, genuinely happy for her best friend and Robert's union. It had been a surprise to Louisa when she heard that they had started seeing each other once Robert returned from living in the Far East.

"Well, their paths hardly crossed while Robert was in Hong Kong. A lot changes in ten years," he said wistfully.

"It does. How's Eddie after his divorce?"

"Good, actually. Well, I think last night might have helped a bit too. I should go and wake them up."

"Yes, but before you do, I wanted to run something by you."

"Shoot."

"It's to do with CASPO."

"You're going to take over, aren't you?"

"Yes, of course." She waved her hand in the air dismissively.

"You don't want to?"

"I do, it's just I need… I don't really know what I need, to be honest. Maybe a kick up the arse," she said with a roll of her eyes.

"Well, I could do that if you like," he said with a smirk. "Is it because of what happened between you and Gerard? I know there's more to it than you said."

Louisa gave him a warning look. "We were talking about me and CASPO."

"Okay, what is it?" he sighed, not wanting to push her.

"I wanted to invite twenty kids to stay for an activity weekend at Holmwood. No press, just the kids having fun on a short break. It'll give their parents a bit of time off too. Maybe we could even sort out some adult activities for them. I thought in the summer. These families never get holidays and to stay at Holmwood on those grounds…" Louisa left the sentence hanging and tilted her head, seeing Alistair's raised brows.

"It sounds like a great idea. What are you asking me for?"

"Because you run the estate. You'll have to be involved, and your staff, and I don't want to mess up your schedule," Louisa said deliberately.

"Louisa, *you're* the Countess."

Louisa blew out a breath. "Shut up," she said in good humour.

"Okay so what activities were you thinking of?"

"Well a number of fun ideas; horse riding, because when have any of these poor kids had chance to ride a horse? We have the lake, maybe some boating. We can make an assault course. There's the pool too and for the less active maybe painting, cooking, bowling on the green and croquet, even a cricket match."

"I could take them up in the helicopter." Alistair added with a grin.

"Yes!"

"Teach the older ones to drive with Hugh maybe?"

"There are so many things we could do for them." Louisa couldn't hide the excitement in her voice. This is what all the fundraising and highbrow events couldn't achieve: giving these unfortunate cases unique experiences. Yes, the money helped them enormously, changed their lives for the better but having a small holiday, having such facilities at their disposal, money couldn't buy that.

"Barbequing would be fun.," continued Alistair.

"And a big party on the last night."

"I think it's a brilliant idea. Let me get some ideas together and rope in the gang too. It's about time they helped a bit. I might even get some of my old squadron involved." He twisted his mouth thoughtfully.

"It's a lot of work and Holmwood would need to be closed off from the public for a few days," Louisa said cautiously.

"It'll be worth it. You'd better tell Mama," Alistair said with a smirk, just as Tim and Eddie slipped into through the door. "Look what the cat dragged in. How are your heads?"

"Bloody awful," mumbled Tim, and Eddie grunted his assent.

"I'll get aspirin and some tea. Can you stomach any breakfast?" asked Louisa.

"Louisa, you're a gem," Tim said as he pulled out a chair and gave her a tired smile.

"I'll get Clair to rustle up something high carb to soak up the alcohol."

Eddie nodded and slumped into a chair and held his head. "Jesus, we were legless last night."

"Err no, that'd be me." Alistair knocked against his metal leg, which caused Tim and Eddie to bark out a laugh, then cringe in pain. Louisa had lost count of the various leg jokes Alistair and his friends had come up with over the last years. She chuckled and was suddenly transported back to when they were all in their teens and staying at Holmwood, telling inappropriate jokes to each other.

"Thanks again for letting us stay. Sorry we were in such a state. We owe you." Eddie directed his attention to Louisa.

"About that; I think Alistair may have a way you can repay me." She gave Alistair a grin, then headed to the kitchen to ask her cook to prepare breakfast.

"SO IT WAS YOU that won the date?" Melissa gaped at her friend, then slumped down in her chair dropping her bag on the floor.

"Shh, I don't want anyone to know. It's a surprise for Celeste's birthday," Louisa hissed. She quickly closed Melissa's office door. Louisa had come into CASPO's offices early, before Melissa had chance to go through all the auction bid winners, meeting her as she arrived. She didn't want anyone to know it was her that had won the top bid. Firstly because she didn't want anyone to think it was fixed and secondly, she didn't want to expose her daughter to any of the media circus around it either.

"I spoke to Gerard and he'll fly Celeste out the day before and then she can go back the day after. It also means I get to see her on her birthday too." Louisa couldn't contain her excitement.

"Will she do that?"

"I'm going to call her tonight."

"That's quite a surprise."

"I know. I miss her. She's been away three months and it's been awful." Louisa huffed as she picked up Melissa's bag off the floor and hung it up for her. "How's your stomach?" Louisa asked, seeing Melissa shudder.

"Crap. I need black tea and ginger biscuits."

"I'll get them."

"No, sit down. I'll ask Lucy. You stay put and tell me about dinner with Gerard." Melissa picked up the desk phone and quickly asked Lucy for their drinks and biscuits. "So, how was he?"

"Gerard was Gerard." Louisa sighed, thinking back to their pleasant evening. It was disarming how the familiarity of someone was so comforting, especially when you felt lonely. Gerard had been as attentive as always. He knew what aperitif to order for her, what wine she liked, how she preferred her salad dressed, what accompaniments she had with her meal; he knew everything about her and how to please her. Their conversation wasn't stilted or forced. Private jokes peppered their time together, Gerard was well versed in the art of relaxed conversation and he knew exactly what Louisa would talk freely about and what topics he should avoid. He was astute, yet smooth in his design, determined to win back the only woman he'd ever loved and the well-orchestrated dinner was his first step.

Louisa had been subjected to the "Gerard experience" for twenty years and just as he knew everything about her, she knew every move, every thought process and his end game. He was still hard to resist and familiarity was a dangerous path to retake; just because it was easier didn't mean it was right. It was why Louisa had decided to come back to the UK. She needed the physical distance to help her achieve the emotional one.

"Still trying to get you back?"

Louisa looked down at her empty finger, where her beautiful wedding band and engagement ring had sat for twenty years and sighed. "He was, as always, the perfect gentleman. We had a very pleasant evening catching up and he tried to persuade me to come to New York next week, but I told him that I was getting ready to take over here and had some plans I needed to get in motion." Melissa gave her an encouraging smile. "Well, it wasn't a total lie." Louisa gave a half-hearted shrug. "When's the garden party again?"

"June third."

"I'll be helping out with that."

"Yes, my girl is back!" Louisa shook her head at Melissa's child-like enthusiasm. "And the ball?" Louisa nodded. Melissa clapped her hands and made a happy face.

"Plus I have another idea," Louisa said with a smirk.

THJROUGH THE GRAINY PICTURE, Louisa could make out the pretty face of Celeste. The Skype connection wasn't the best but Louisa could see that Celeste's blond hair seemed lighter and she looked a little slimmer in the face.

"You've got a tan, sweetheart."

"Yes, I'm outside a lot."

"Well just be careful not to burn."

"I know Mum," Celeste said in a mildly exasperated tone. "I spoke to Papa yesterday. He said you had dinner."

"We did and we discussed your birthday."

"What about it?"

"Well Papa said he'd arrange to fly you out here the day before and then back the day after, so we can spend it together," Louisa said cautiously.

"I can't just leave for three days because it's my birthday, Mum." Celeste rolled her eyes at the suggestion.

"Well the other thing is I bought you something, and you can only have it if you're here."

"Mum, are you blackmailing me?" Celeste arched her brow at her mother. She knew she wasn't above doing anything underhand if it meant they'd spend time together.

"No, I mean... sort of. It's a sweetener." Louisa cringed. There was no getting around her perceptive daughter.

"You're terrible, you know that? So come on, tell me what is *so* special I can only have it in England."

"I won a bid on a charity auction for a lunch date with Miles Keane." Louisa waited to see her reaction.

Celeste scrunched up her face in confusion. "You mean *the* Miles Keane?"

"Yes."

"This isn't a joke?"

"No! Why would I joke?"

"I don't know. I didn't think my mum would bid on an auction for a date, *with Miles Keane!* Are you serious?"

"As a heart attack."

"Oh. My. God!" Celeste clapped her hand over her mouth, then let out a squeal. "And it's going to be on my birthday?"

"Yes, I arranged it." Louisa let out a laugh, pleased her daughter was so happy.

"Wow, I mean this is pretty awesome. A bit weird, but awesome."

"So you'll come?"

"Well I need to clear it with them here, and we're in the middle of getting the kids ready for their exams but... anyway, let me see, okay? I'm sure it'll be okay." She made an excited face and Louisa laughed again.

"Okay, sweetheart, you do what you need to do."

"Miles Keane, eh? Thanks, Mum, you're the best."

After saying their goodbyes, Louisa shut down her computer and grinned to herself. *It was the best £50,000 she'd ever spent.*

TWO DAYS AGO

"MUM, CAN YOU HEAR ME?"

"The connection is awful. Is everything okay? Are you getting ready?" Louisa grinned at the distorted picture of Celeste.

"That's why I called. I'm not coming."

"What! Why ever not?"

"We've had a break out of some bacterial disease…"

"Oh my God, are you okay?" Louisa interrupted, panicked that her daughter was ill with some South American disease and over ten thousand miles away.

"Yes, I'm fine – really, don't worry. I had all the vaccines, remember?" Louisa sighed in relief and Celeste continued once Louisa seemed to have calmed down. "But a few of our team are down with it – some of the local teachers who haven't been vaccinated. It's not serious but they've been taken away so that they don't pass it on to the kids." Celeste took a pause. She knew she was going to upset her parents but her sense of duty to the program outweighed their disappointment. "We're right in the middle of exam prep. These kids have been working so hard, doing so well. Mum, I can't up and leave them. I mean, I came here to help, make a difference; they're depending on me. What kind of a person would that make me if swanned off for three days, just for my birthday?"

Louisa took in a deep breath, trying to keep her face as neutral as possible. "Sure, of course, sweetheart, there's no question." Louisa tried to mask her disappointment but Celeste could hear it in her voice. "I'm so proud of you. You do what you need to do. I'll reschedule it for when you're back." In the back of her mind, though, Louisa wasn't entirely sure if it was possible but she would deal with that later.

"No Mum, really. Just give it to the next bidder. I mean, I really like Miles Keane, his music and that, but I'm not sure Nicolas would be all that happy if I went. And to be honest, I'm kind of over my crush on him." Through the pixelated picture, Louisa could see Celeste's scrunch up her nose.

Nicolas was Celeste's boyfriend who she'd met while training before they were sent out as a team from the US to Peru. Louisa had met him a few times and he looked to be a decent guy, a little serious maybe, but it was obvious he was more than a little taken with Celeste. Louisa couldn't see him being that happy about Celeste on a date with a pop star she'd been crushing over for almost ten years.

"If you're sure?"

"I'm sure. Anyway, I'll get to meet him at some point, now he's signed up to be one of the ambassadors of CASPO. You'll be working with him won't you?"

"Of sorts, though in reality, our paths won't really cross that much. But at events, though. That *will* be interesting," Louisa said dryly.

"Ha, you still think he's a cocky pop star?" Louisa had made it obvious what her opinion of Miles Keane was, based on her own experience, though everyone who had met him at CASPO had only good things to say about him.

"Melissa and Margot say he's not like that at all, apparently."

"You *still* haven't met, then?"

"No. He's just going to be at events and press junkets. I won't really have that much to do with him. You know how these things work; he'll be the pretty face and we'll do all the work," Louisa huffed.

"Maybe you should go in my place then, and get to know him. He might surprise you."

"I don't think so," Louisa huffed.

"Maybe not. He's *so* not your type." Celeste laughed at the very thought of her mother and Miles Keane on a date.

"Exactly."

"Okay, I've got to go. We'll chat on my birthday and I'm sorry I won't be there." Celeste made a sad face and Louisa blew her a kiss.

"That's okay, sweetheart. You did the right thing."

"Love you Mum."

"Love you more."

Louisa stared at the screen of her computer for a moment, feeling disappointed that it would be two more months before she'd have her daughter back but equally proud that she'd put duty before herself. She hoped Nicolas was a strong enough man to handle and accept the choices Celeste would make in the future. Celeste would be Lady Blackthorn one day and with that came responsibility. She needed a man who was strong enough to stand in her shadow and be happy for her to be in the limelight.

Louisa sighed, then picked up her phone and tapped on Melissa's number. She needed to see what could be done about the date.

9

THE COFFEE

"THIS PLACE IS HUGE." Miles swivelled around to take in the view of the extensive grounds, perfectly showcased by the French windows. The butter-soft leather couches and wingback chairs gave the light and airy room an old world feel, but the splash of jewelled toned furnishings added a contemporary edge.

They'd moved into the lounge area at the suggestion of Mr Thomas. It was predominately used for guests to enjoy a cigar and drinks in the evening but seeing as it was the afternoon, there was hardly anyone in there and the insightful maître d' thought it would afford them some privacy. The main restaurant had started to fill up with various high-class members for afternoon tea, the kind of clientele who might not be as discreet as the previous lunchtime occupants.

"Scratch that, this place is grand; a piece of quiet English heritage right smack in the middle of this vibrant capital. How is that even possible?" Miles shook his head in disbelief and nodded his thanks to the waiter who had just placed coffee and petit fours on the low table in front of them. He eyed the two large brandy glasses, filled with a deep chestnut coloured liquid. "No wonder there's a waiting list to be a member here."

Louisa arched her brow at his comment, surprised he was so well informed about her club.

"The cab driver told me," Miles added as explanation, seeing Louisa's reaction. "So what are we drinking?" He gestured to the brandy glasses.

"Armagnac."

Miles furrowed his brow. "Not cognac?"

"Same region, different grape," Louisa said with a grin.

"Hmm, so fancy brandy then?" Miles smirked.

"Yes." Louisa chuckled, pleased her companion was neither embarrassed to ask nor uncomfortable about his lack of knowledge.

He leaned forward and picked up both brandy glasses and handed one to Louisa. "I haven't drunk so much during the day in such a long time." He huffed. Louisa took the glass from him and raised it.

"Am I a bad influence?" she asked coyly.

He gave her a wide smile, then clinked his glass against hers. "Oh yeah, you most certainly are," he said in a low voice and Louisa blushed under the intensity of his gaze. "You know, it's usually me that's the bad influence."

"So this is unchartered territory for you, then?"

"On so many levels," he muttered before taking a sip.

"Are you sure you don't have anywhere you need to be?"

Miles shook his head and gave her a lopsided smirk. Even if he had somewhere to be, there was no way in hell he was going to leave. Prior arrangements be damned. They practically had the lounge to themselves and the couch they were sitting on meant they were now just a foot apart. Louisa had positioned herself at the edge, her elegant poise betraying good breeding, while Miles had shifted, angling himself towards her.

"What about you? You weren't supposed to be here. Haven't you got somewhere to be?"

"No."

"No? I find that hard to believe."

"Why?"

"A woman like you should be in demand."

"A woman like me?"

"Yeah. Beautiful, intelligent, successful." Louisa went to say something but Miles halted her by lifting up his index finger. "And before you say it, no, I'm not saying that because you paid me to."

Louisa chuckled at his insightful interruption. "Thank you." She lowered her eyes and looked into her brandy glass, suddenly feeling shy at the directness of his compliments. It had been a long time for someone to pay so much attention to her, and while she welcomed the excited bubble that bloomed inside her, it was still unnerving.

"You know, you could tell me a little about yourself," Miles coaxed.

Louisa gave him a soft smile and placed her glass down on the table. "Coffee?" she asked and Miles grinned.

"Another dodge, Louisa?" He let out a soft chuckle. "Yeah sure. Black, please." He watched her gracefully pour their coffee, taking in her profile, wondering why she felt it so important to keep her identity or anything about her private. She was clearly well known at the club so she wasn't totally under the radar. It was obvious that Louisa just didn't want *him* to know who she was. Louisa placed Miles's coffee cup in front of him and picked up hers and took a sip.

"Now you're living in London, will you be attending more events?"

"Events?"

"Openings, fashion shows, that kind of thing."

"I get invited to loads. There are a few companies I'm going to become more involved with, business wise, but since..." Miles faltered.

"Since?"

Miles smiled tightly at Louisa's questioning gaze. How could he mention that since he'd been associated with Lottie, he was constantly invited to very fashion show she modelled in and anything remotely connected to the fashion industry? He'd been trying to get Louisa to agree to a date for the last hour – how could he acknowledge any kind of relationship with his "go to" girl? That would make him look like a prize dick. *Who was he kidding? He was a prize dick. Why would such an elegant woman like Louisa even think about going on a second date with him?*

"Nothing. Erm, yes I'll be attending a few, Men's Fashion Week for one, plus some others."

"Well you move in *those* circles, so it was only a matter of time before they found you, so to speak."

Miles clenched his jaw a little and then sipped his coffee, effectively delaying his response. *Shit, she knew about him and Lottie – or rather, she knew what she'd seen in the media.* Rather than be evasive, Miles decided to just address the subject. "That Google has a lot to answer for," he joked, hoping to diffuse the sudden tense atmosphere. Louisa let out a soft laugh and Miles immediately felt better. "Lottie and I have an understanding."

"That sounds intriguing." Louisa arched her brow at him and waited for an explanation.

"Hell, I didn't think I'd be talking about Lottie on this date. In fact there are a lot of things we've spoken about that I would never have spoken about on *any* date." He blew out.

Louisa gave him a smug smile pleased she'd chipped through his cockiness. He looked decidedly uncomfortable as he shifted in his seat. Louisa suddenly felt bad for him. She wasn't behaving like a lady again, and though she would've liked to blame the alcohol on her behaviour, it was more than that. She wanted to know what Lottie Price, the rising star in the modelling world, meant to Miles. The few photos of him, over his last months in London, had the perfect figured and glossy blond by his side. Granted, there was no PDA, no kissing, hand holding, anything that betrayed intimacy, but they were always together.

"You don't need to explain anything to me, really," she said sincerely.

"There's really not that much to explain," he said in a rush because there wasn't. She was his fuck buddy and he attended functions with her. Well, at least on his part, that was all she was. "We just go to events together. I met her at a Christmas party held by the contractors that did the renovation on my house. She needed a date for a function that I'd also been invited to so we arranged to go together." The truth was decidedly more colourful but Miles wasn't about to divulge the frantic hooking-up in the toilets at said party that led to him then spending the night at Lottie's apartment, and subsequently more hook-ups.

"Like car-pooling then?" Louisa said dryly.

"Yeah, kind of." Miles stifled a grin, thankful that Louisa hadn't pushed the subject.

"How very… eco-friendly of you," Louisa deadpanned.

Miles let out a husky laugh at Louisa's droll remark. "I really do not have an answer for that remark, Louisa. You are without a doubt an unexpected pleasure." He shook his head in awe of how this stunning woman sitting next him had managed to probe into his private life, making him feel uncomfortable, then within a second, made him laugh out loud with some witty remark, totally knocking him off-kilter.

Louisa tried to keep her face impassive but she was surprised by his words and affected by the way his whole face lit up as he freely laughed. "So, apart from your efforts to help with global warming, the various events you're dragged to, and being pimped out by CASPO, what else do you do with your time?"

Miles couldn't stop the laugh that came freely. "You paint a sorry picture of me, Louisa." He put down his coffee and shifted a little more to face her. "What I'm about to tell you isn't public knowledge yet, so I'll need to know you can keep a secret." He leaned forward and spoke conspiratorially, then winked. Louisa arched her brow as if to question his doubt in her trust. He chuckled, "I think you could've worked for MI6, Louisa. No one's going to get any information out of you." His remark was rewarded with a chuckle. "There's a designer who wants to work with me on a clothes line and a fragrance company that wants me to be the face of their new men's range and a watch company. I'm also in negotiations with a TV channel that want me to be part of a new show."

"A show?"

"Yeah. They want to do a show on pop stars from the past who have stopped performing and recording. Sort of a 'Where are they now?' show. I'd be the interviewer."

"Oh that's sound like a one eighty turn for you."

"I'd say. But it all depends if they can get the right kind of pop stars to agree. Most of them don't want to be put back in the limelight."

"Though I'm sure there are a few that might welcome rekindling their fame."

"There is that too. There's a lot going on at the moment but CASPO is the first collaboration I've signed up for officially; the rest are still in the air. Four years away from official work gave me the time to decide which direction I should take. I literally went from school into the crazy world of music without much thought, so I want to make sure whatever I get involved with from now on is something that I'll be doing for a while and have control over."

"Well your secret is safe with me, Miles."

"Louisa?"

Louisa turned towards where a familiar voice called her name, only to see Gordon McKenzie striding in their direction. Her smile widened at her brother's childhood friend, equally surprised to see him in London. Gordon had spent the majority of his life abroad working in the diplomatic corps, and the last time Louisa had seen him was in New York last summer, a year or so after he and Emily had married. They'd been on a stopover from Brazil and Louisa and Gerard had dined with them before they headed back to London.

Louisa shot up from her seat and stepped up to him. After her initial surprise, she was now faced with the dilemma of explaining who Miles was and ensuring Gordon didn't divulge her identity. "Well, this is a surprise. What are the chances, eh? I thought you were in Brazil." Louisa accepted his kiss to her cheek.

Gordon slipped his hand around her waist and gave her a squeeze, then pulled back a little. "I've been back for a month now." He gazed down at the woman he'd been in love with for almost thirty years; since the day she'd run around the grounds at Holmwood House at the age of eight on his first visit to his best friend, Alistair's house. He'd spent many school holidays at Holmwood House while his parents were stationed at various embassies around the world. The Earl of Blackthorn and Gordon's father had been friends, and their friendship had carried down to Gordon and Alistair.

"A month?"

"Didn't Alistair tell you?" Gordon's light brown eyes searched Louisa's and he could see she knew nothing of his latest news. "Your brother is useless," he chuckled. "I've moved back home. Emily was never happy, so I'm now working in the city."

"Yes, she didn't seem to like the life of a diplomat's wife when I saw you last." Gordon's eyes darted to Miles, who had stayed in his seat, quietly observing the exchange.

In the couple of minutes he'd had to take in their interaction, Miles realised that there was a familiarity between the two of them, one that comes from many years of friendship. They were close but hadn't been intimate, though from Gordon's adoring expression, it was obvious that his feelings for Louisa were far more than just friendliness. He had a distinguished air about him that came from old money and breeding. His grey suit was immaculately cut but understated – Saville Row for sure. His light brown hair conservatively cut and his square jaw clean-shaven. This man was well bred and refined, and looking up at Louisa and Gordon, Miles could see how well matched they were. *Maybe he was an old flame after all.* Miles had listened intently to see if he could glean any information about his mysterious date, but other than picking up that Gordon was married and that Louisa had a brother called Alistair, there was nothing.

Louisa tensed for a second, realising Gordon had focused on Miles. A hundred thoughts thundered through her head. How was she going to explain Miles? How was she going to ensure nothing was given away by Gordon?

Miles's gaze fixed on Louisa's and he fleetingly saw the panic in her eyes and though this would've been the perfect opportunity for him to find out more about her, Miles could see that this was not how Louisa wanted him to. He rose up from his seat and put out his hand.

"Oh sorry, Gordon, this is Miles."

"A business associate of Louisa's," Miles offered as an explanation, seeing Gordon's questioning expression. He took his hand and shook it firmly. Miles noticed that he still had his arm around Louisa's waist. Louisa smiled warmly at Miles, grateful he'd provided a cover for their rendezvous.

"Pleased to meet you, Miles. You're over from America?" Gordon asked, picking up on Miles's accent.

"That's right." Miles gave him a tight smile, deciding not to correct him, and let his eyes rest back on Louisa, effectively letting her take the lead in the conversation.

"I'll just be a moment, Miles," Louisa said softly.

"Of course, take your time. Nice to meet you Gordon."

"Likewise." Gordon then turned his attention to Louisa. "Shall we?" He guided her towards the entrance of the lounge.

Miles retook his seat and focused on Gordon's hand that rested on Louisa's lower back as the couple walked and talked before stopping by the threshold, where they faced each other. Miles picked up his Armagnac swirled it around and took a large gulp, still keeping his eyes on the couple. The more he watched, the more Miles noted how many times Gordon discreetly touched her. This man felt far more for Louisa than just friendliness.

"It's so good to see you," Gordon said sincerely.

"Same here."

"So you're here visiting?"

Louisa narrowed her eyes and scrunched up her nose for a second, realising Gordon didn't know the reason for her being back in London. "No, I moved back to England in January," she said softly.

Gordon furrowed his brow. "I don't understand."

"I take it my brother didn't tell *you*," she said with a mild exasperated huff.

"Tell me what?"

"Gerard and I divorced and I moved back here."

Gordon's eyes widened at the unexpected news and instinctively reached out his hand and placed it on her arm. *When had this happened? Why had this happened?* He stood for a second absorbing the news in stunned silence. His manners kicked in and he began to speak.

"I'm... I..." he stuttered, trying to say the right words. He should've said he was sorry, showed some empathy, but the fact of the matter was he was anything but.

Seeing Gordon struggle, Louisa decided to explain what had happened in the last few months. Her eyes darted to where Miles was sitting and caught him staring at them, so she shifted a little so he couldn't see her so clearly. "It's fine, Gordon. I'm fine.

Celeste went to Peru for six months as a volunteer and she's coming back at the beginning of July. We're settling in here. She starts university in September and life goes on," she said in a reassuring tone, mistaking Gordon's shock of the news as deep concern for her wellbeing, when in fact, he was devastated that the one woman he'd ever loved was now free and he was not.

"I had no idea. Why?... I mean..." Gordon fumbled for his words. His stomach felt like a stone had dropped in there with this unexpected news. *After all these years together, why had they finally divorced?* There had been the odd rumour that Gerard had not been faithful and Gordon had often wondered if it was true or whether Louisa had known of it. On a number of occasions, he'd wanted to tell her, but he'd never wanted to be the man who she would forever remember as the cause of her unhappiness. Whenever he'd ever seen them together, over the years, they'd always looked happy, despite the rumours, so Gordon resigned himself to the fact that Louisa was the one that had got away and the rumours were unfounded.

"We just grew apart. We're friends; we have Celeste to think about."

"Sorry, it's just a bit of a shock. You were together nineteen years..." The words died on his lips as he realised he'd divulged how closely he'd followed her life. He gently rubbed his hand up and down her arm and stared at her beautiful face. He'd given up on them ever getting together after waiting for over fifteen years, and now it was him who was married.

Louisa, sensing that Gordon was finding her news too much of a shock, decided to change the subject. "Anyway, enough about me, how's Emily and married life?" she asked brightly.

"Erm, easier now we're back here," he said without emotion. He really didn't want to talk about his lukewarm marriage.

"And you're living in London?"

"I have my apartment here but we've moved into a house about twenty miles away from my parents."

"Oh, so not too far from Holmwood then? Good, it'll be nice to catch up properly and get to know Emily better. Apart from Melissa, I really don't have that many friends here anymore." Gordon could think of nothing worse than his wife and Louisa become friends; come to think of it, nor would Emily.

"That'd be nice," he replied without an ounce of sincerity.

Louisa turned to focus back on her date and caught Miles still watching them and gave him a tight smile. "Well, I better get back to..."

"Yes of course. It was so unbelievably good to see you again." He held her by both arms and pulled her towards him and kissed her cheek, lingering over their embrace.

"You too, Gordon. Give my love to your parents and Emily," Louisa said with a wide smile as she pulled back.

"I will. It'll be good spending time together again, like old times." He blinked down at her, holding her gaze for as long as he could.

"Yes it will, but with less running around."

Gordon laughed at her joke referring to their childhood, then she turned back towards where Miles was still sitting and gracefully paced towards him, totally oblivious that Gordon continued to stare after her.

"Sorry about that," Louisa said as she retook her seat next to Miles.

"Not at all. London is obviously a small city after all," he said dryly. His eyes flitted back to the entrance and he was pleased to see that Gordon had finally left.

"Thank you for not..."

"Making things difficult for you?" Miles suggested.

Louisa chuckled. "Yes, exactly that."

"Gordon, he's an old friend?" He hoped he didn't sound too affronted but he was curious as to who he was, and especially who he was to Louisa.

"A family friend." Her gaze moved to the empty entrance of the lounge and then back to Miles.

Miles gave a nod and decided not to comment on their unexpected visitor. The date had been going so well, he didn't want to say something that could jeopardise it. He decided to diffuse Louisa's sudden thoughtful mood with humour. "You realise I only behaved like a gentleman because you're paying me."

Louisa gave him a wide smile. "Is that so? Somehow I don't think so."

"Well, I think because I was so chivalrous, I am now entitled to my second date. I could've really put you through the ringer there."

"How exactly?" She leaned back a little to regard him.

Miles made a show of pretending to think about his answer and then lowered his voice and leaned forward. "Well, I could've said that I was your escort."

Louisa let out a giggle. He was of course just toying with her, referring back to their earlier conversation. "Or, I could've asked all sorts of questions about you." He narrowed his eyes at her as he spoke.

"Is that so? Well, Gordon would never have believed you and he's very discreet," Louisa said nonchalantly.

"Yeah, I got that."

But something in the way Miles said those last four words made Louisa furrow her brow. *What did he mean by that? He'd hardly said two words to him.*

The noise level from the restaurant had steadily gotten louder and Louisa knew that there was a good chance she might bump into someone else who knew her. She'd been lucky that it had been Gordon and not someone who was considerably nosier. "I think that maybe it's time for us to leave. This lounge will start filling up soon."

"And you don't want to bump into anyone else? Someone less discreet?"

Louisa gave him that enigmatic smile that Miles was beginning to find both frustrating and sexy. He shook his head and scanned the lounge for a waiter.

"What are you looking for?" Louisa asked as they both rose from their seat.

"I need to settle up."

"It's taken care of."

"What? No, that's not right." Miles's eyes widened in horror. She couldn't pay for the meal; that was wrong on so many levels.

"It was already arranged," Louisa said as explanation.

"Louisa..." His tone became mildly chastising. She waved her hand in the air dismissively, effectively halting any further discussion and began to pace towards the door.

Mr Thomas was there to greet them both, holding Louisa's coat and the bag with framed disc. After thanking him, they both walked leisurely to the main entrance of the club in contemplative silence, the chatter and music from the restaurant a backdrop to their final few moments together.

Louisa suddenly felt uneasy. She'd had such an entertaining afternoon, she couldn't remember the last time she'd enjoyed someone's company so much. All ill thoughts of this man had practically been erased. He'd redeemed himself of that bad behaviour ten years ago. There were still hints of the arrogance he'd possessed all those years ago, but somehow they'd morphed into self-assuredness and only made him more attractive. The notorious cocky playboy had matured into an unexpected gentleman and the thought that these were their last moments together, before he found out whom she really was, depressed her. Once he knew she was Lady Blackthorn, the Countess of Holmwood, he'd change towards her. It would never be just Miles and Louisa again. His guard would be up and that flirtatious way he'd been looking at her over the last few hours would change to reverence.

Miles felt Louisa start to slip away from him. Her stance was changing with every footstep. Back was the slightly distant Louisa he'd first clapped eyes on as he fumbled with his wet trousers. Over the last four hours, she'd let her guard down enough for him to see a glimpse of the personality she was hiding behind that detached façade she wore as amour. He still didn't know why she'd been so secretive about who she was but he instinctively knew it was for her own protection. These would be their last few minutes together and the thought made Miles desperate to prolong it or at least secure the second date they'd joked about.

They walked out into the cooler courtyard where Louisa's car was idling. A smart driver immediately stepped out of the car and opened up the rear door for her. "How are you getting home?" Louisa asked.

Miles turned to look back at the club entrance. "I'll get the efficient Mr Thomas to sort me out a cab. I don't live far from here, about a couple of miles." He gave a shrug, trying to sound breezy, but his jaw twitched; he wasn't ready to say goodbye yet. The thought of not seeing Louisa again made his insides churn. It was a feeling he'd never experienced before. What was even more disturbing was that for the first time ever, he was not in control, and the experience was both thrilling and frustrating.

Louisa gazed into Miles's brilliant blue eyes and saw a myriad of emotions swimming in their depths. Was he really interested in her or was he just playing his part, taking one for the CASPO team, so to speak? A considerable part of her wanted him to have been genuine but the other was just plain scared. Before she could analyse her feelings anymore, she turned and said, "I could drop you?"

Miles eyes widened in surprise and for a nanosecond, he was as stunned as Louisa was at her offer of a lift. All Miles could think about was that he had a few more minutes with Louisa and they'd be practically alone. He had to make those few minutes count. "Sure," he said with a wide smile.

Louisa let out the breath she was holding and gave him a shy smile, then stepped into her waiting car.

Miles told the driver his address and then slid into the luxurious interior of the car next to Louisa. Now that they were effectively alone, Louisa suddenly felt a little nervous. While they'd been in the club, there had been outside influences that they could talk about. Here in the car it was just them, no food or wine to comment on. Louisa looked out of the window and took in the familiar grounds of her club, noting that the blossom made the many mature trees look fuzzy.

"It really is a lovely place." Miles's voice broke through Louisa's thoughts.

"Yes, it is." Louisa turned to look at him and he gave her that cheeky smile she'd seen so often over their time together and wondered if he bestowed it on every unsuspecting female he encountered.

"You realise that this is again a turnabout for me?" Louisa gave him a questioning look, unsure of what he meant. "Being dropped off by my date."

"Ah, I see. You usually do the dropping off? And then what… you'd hope to get invited up for coffee?"

"I used to, yes, when I dated."

"Dated?" Louisa arched her brow at him and he laughed at her deliberate dig at his colourful past.

"Damn that Google," he chuckled and Louisa laughed softly, glad he was using humour again to cut through her nervousness. Who would've thought the arrogant pop star would turn out to be such a gentleman? "Shame we had coffee already. It means I haven't an excuse to ask you in," Miles said, looking out to where the familiar surroundings passed by as the car neared his home. He turned back to Louisa as the driver pulled up outside the large white house set back from the pavement. "But then again, I think you're too much of a lady to come in on a first date."

The driver stepped out of the car and waited discreetly on the pavement, leaving Miles and Louisa alone for the first time. Miles reached into his inside pocket and took out a pen and a small cream card, then scribbled down a number on the back. Louisa watched him, still a little surprised at his last statement. If he'd asked her in for coffee she wasn't sure she'd have turned him down after all.

"Thank you for the most unexpected blind date I've ever had. Here," he said with a grin.

"What's this?" Louisa looked at the cream-coloured business card Miles held out for her. He tilted his head to the side and fixed her with his bright blue eyes. "My number."

Louisa's eye shot up to his. They'd flirted for the last four hours and joked about a second date but she hadn't expected him to follow through. Surely he was just playing the game. "Why are you giving me your number?"

"You're too much of a lady to give me yours or ask for mine," he said with a smirk.

"Why would I want to give you my number or ask you for yours?" she said quietly, knowing full well he was one hundred percent right.

Miles reached over and gently took her hand. His fingers warm against her soft palm as he turned it over and pressed his card into it. Louisa focused on the hand he was holding, realising this was the first time he'd touched her. The thought made her stomach clench unexpectedly.

"You just paid £50,000 for an hour and a half of my time. You also paid for that amazing lunch. It's only fair that I take you on a date, to repay you. I'm buying a table tomorrow," he gave her a playful smile, "so when you're ready, call me." Louisa went to interrupt him but he stopped her with a slight squeeze of her hand. "I'm new to this city. I hardly know anyone at all. You could show me around." He gave her a cheeky grin and reluctantly let go of her hand.

"Lottie hasn't shown you the sights?" She narrowed her eyes at him and Miles's face dropped and she instantly regretted her words. Her mother's chastising of unladylike behaviour came rushing into her head.

"No, she's not big on culture," he said with a smirk. Miles reached for the door handle but the driver managed to open it before he could. He slipped out and then bobbed down a little so he could say goodbye.

"You know, you got your going rate wrong," Louisa said with a grin.

"Excuse me?"

"I paid £50,000 and got four hours."

"So you did. I'd call that a real bargain." Louisa let out a soft laugh and he shook his head, enjoying the last glimpses of her teasing humour. "Please call me. You can at least let me treat you to dinner, Miles Keane style. Then maybe you might tell me a little bit about you, Louisa."

"Have a good shopping day tomorrow. It was very interesting meeting you *again,* Miles."

"It was very intriguing meeting you, Louisa." And with those departing words, he closed the door to the car and paced quickly up to his home.

Louisa watched him climb up the few steps and unlock his door. She waited to see if he would look back at her, even if he couldn't see her through the blacked-out rear windows. If he did, she'd go on a date, if he didn't, it meant he was just playing his part. Louisa held her breath as the shiny black door opened and Miles took a tentative step inside, willing him to turn and look back. Then from nowhere, it seemed, a small fluffy dog jumped up into his arms. Miles rubbed his face into the dog's neck as the adorable dog squirmed in an attempt to lick his face. Louisa laughed to herself at this unexpected scene she was witnessing, safe in the knowledge Miles couldn't hear or see her. Miles looked over his shoulder, straight into the back of the car for a couple of seconds and for that moment, Louisa wondered whether he'd heard her. The cute dog saw his opportunity and gave Miles a good lick, which had Miles grinning as moved further in and shut the door.

"Home, my lady?" her driver asked.

"Yes, and thank you, Hugh. Did I get any calls?"

"A number, my lady."

"Anything urgent?"

"Lady Blackthorn called wanting to know if you'd finalised the garden party details today."

Louisa cringed. She'd totally forgotten she was supposed to talk with the manager at Blacks this afternoon. Miles had totally distracted her. Louisa looked back at the large house as the car pulled away and wondered what kind of dining room table Miles was going to buy.

Miles stood a little back from his lounge window and watched the sedate Bentley pull away from the curb and furrowed his brow mulling over Louisa's parting words, "It was interesting meeting you *again*, Miles." A memory grazed somewhere in the back of his mind but he just couldn't grasp it. He looked down at Duke and ruffled his head wondering if it was too late to go furniture shopping.

10

WELL SPENT

MILES STEPPED UP TO Margot's door and gave it a light tap. Her head shot up from some papers she was poring over at her desk and she gave him a huge smile through the glass wall. He couldn't believe he was here. He'd deliberated whether it was against CASPO's policy for him to try and contact a donator personally, let alone ask for personal details, but he was at a loss as to how he could find out who Louisa was. She'd given nothing away over the four and a half hours they'd spent together. He just hoped he didn't sound or look desperate.

"Hey, Margot, how are you?" Miles extended his hand to the pintsized general secretary. She'd been at CASPO since day one and was a close friend of the founder and patron.

"I'm well, thank you. What's more important, though, is how are you and how did the date go yesterday?" Her light blue eyes twinkled behind her rimless glasses. Miles chuckled at her directness. He'd just about gotten used to Margot's manner. She was a cross between a sergeant major and Mary Poppins, with a little bit of grandma's homeliness thrown in. It all depended on what role she was taking on. "It went well, I hope." Margot waved her hand, indicating Miles should take the seat in front of her desk. He shook his head; he wasn't planning on staying long.

"Yeah, there was a bit of a change, actually. The nineteen-year-old fan couldn't come but her mother came instead."

Margot leaned back in her chair. "Really? That must've been interesting," she chuckled.

"Yeah, you could say that. Anyway, I wondered if you had a contact number or email, so I could thank her. She paid for the meal."

Margot furrowed her brow. "Well, it was Melissa who organised the auction. It was all very confidential. She'd have the details."

"Oh, okay, thanks." Miles said his goodbyes and headed to Melissa's office. She was in charge of fundraising events and was also Lady Blackthorn's goddaughter. Miles walked the few feet further down corridor, then tapped on the open glass door. Melissa's head peered up from her mobile, then she dropped it on to her lap. She was just about to call Louisa to see how the date had gone, when the unexpected handsome face of Miles peeked at her through the doorway.

After Celeste's decision not to come back for her birthday, Louisa had called Melissa immediately and told her the sad news, joking with her dear friend that Celeste had suggested that she went in her place. Melissa had thought it was an excellent idea, especially as they had never met, and this would be an ice-breaker. After all, Miles would be one of the ambassadors of CASPO and even though their paths would only cross at official events, Louisa would need to know more about him once she took over as patron. This would be a perfect opportunity; no one would be around to observe them, Louisa could get to know who Miles Keane really was and it would be in a social setting. Louisa agreed but with the proviso that Miles Keane did not know who she was and the whole date was confidential.

"Good morning, Miles. This is a surprise." Melissa gathered

herself before asking, "how did your date go?" She took hold of his outstretched hand and shook it firmly. Over the last two months, since he'd been more involved with CASPO, he'd become fond of Melissa and her slightly gauche ways that seemed out of place in such an aristocratic organisation. She was the most approachable out of all the staff at the organisation and the first person he'd been introduced to.

"Good. That's why I'm here."

"Oh. Well, sit down," she urged.

Miles took the seat she'd indicated to. "Umm, Margot said you'd have a contact number or email of the winner?"

"The winner?" Melissa furrowed her brow, clearly confused.

"Actually, the woman who paid for the date. Margot said you were the one who organised it." Miles swallowed and hoped he didn't look too transparent. Melissa wasn't a fool; there really wasn't any reason for him to need Louisa's contact numbers. In all honesty, if Louisa had wanted Miles to have them she would have given them to him herself. He just hoped Melissa's good breeding and fine social skills meant she wouldn't probe the issue.

"Well, the donator wanted to remain anonymous," she said with finality and rested her hands on her five-month pregnant belly.

"Oh." Miles pursed his lips, wondering how he could get round that fact. "Well, can *you* get in touch with her then? I wanted to send her something to say thank you. She paid for the meal and then dropped me off home," he said sheepishly.

"She dropped you off?" Melissa snorted.

"Yeah, in this fancy Bentley. She was very..."

"Very what?" interrupted Melissa. Amusement skirted over her pink lips.

Intimidating, confident, alluring and sexy as hell, thought Miles but he went with, "Secretive."

Melissa gave him a shrug and turned her palms over in a

there-you-go gesture. "How was it?" She leaned forward and rested her elbows on her desk.

"It was unlike any date I've ever been on." He huffed and shook his head.

"Well, of course. She paid for you!" She let out another snort.

Miles rolled his eyes. "No, I mean any date I've been on before has been… I don't know. I suppose I knew what I was getting into. This date …" he twisted his mouth and rocked his head from side to side, trying to find the right words to describe the experience.

"She had the upper hand," Melissa said, punctuating her statement with a jab of her finger.

"Yeah, she definitely had the upper hand."

"Unchartered territory?"

Miles chuckled. Melissa had unwittingly hit the nail on the head, using the exact same words as Louisa.

"Well, I could contact her for you, or if you wanted to send her something, I could forward it on."

Miles took in a deep breath. He wasn't sure how comfortable he felt having a go-between, though if he were ever to have to have one, Melissa would probably be the best choice. She was discreet, matter-of-fact and extremely kind. "Okay, I'll have to get her something classy."

"Didn't you give her a signed platinum disc?"

Miles let out a humourless laugh. "Not exactly classy, is it?" It had been meant for a nineteen-year-old fan, not a sophisticated thirty something woman.

"No, I suppose not."

"Let me think about it and I'll let you know. She didn't give much away, so it'll be hard to get her something."

"She didn't talk about herself much?"

Miles shook his head. "That's what I'm talking about. Usually my dates never shut up about themselves." He rolled his eyes and Melissa let out a laugh. "Anyway, I'd better get off." Miles lifted himself out of the chair and reached over to shake Melissa's hand.

"I'll walk out with you. If I sit too long, my blasted ankles swell." Melissa pulled her tall frame out of her soft office chair and rounded her desk. "Have you settled in?"

"Just about. Amanda is on her way in from Worcester today. We're supposed to go and buy some furniture. She said my home looks like a student's." He chuckled. "I still have no idea where the right places to shop are. I've just about got to grips with the local stores in my neighbourhood!"

"You're lucky to have such a great sister-in-law."

"Yeah, I am." They'd reached the reception area and Miles headed for the door, then he suddenly had an idea. "Do you know of a good wine merchant?"

"Of course." Melissa huffed. "I'll forward the number to you."

"Great. Thanks, Melissa, take it easy." Miles jerked his chin in the direction of her baby bump.

Melissa grinned widely before she turned to head back to her office. She needed to call Louisa, and did so right away. "So how was it?"

"I wondered how long it would take you," chuckled Louisa.

"Well I was about to call you when I had an unexpected visitor. Miles came in this morning, asking about you. He only just left!" Melissa huffed down the phone.

"He was asking about me?" Louisa tried not to sound too eager.

"Yeah. So I take it you didn't reveal who you were or put him through the ringer either, then?"

"I fully intended to make him squirm but he was… I don't know, different to what I remember."

"Well, it is ten years ago. Are you the same person you were ten years ago?"

"No, thank goodness," Louisa muttered.

"And he's had a rough time of it too."

"True. So what did he want?"

"He wanted to contact you, to send a thank you gift, but I told him you wanted to stay anonymous. Not unless you want me to give him your details?" goaded Melissa.

"No! God no."

"Right. Well I told him I would forward anything he wanted. He was a bit apprehensive but he didn't press."

"Well, I think that maybe that's the last you'll hear of that," muttered Louisa.

"I'm not so sure," retorted Melissa. She was pretty certain Miles would be knocking on her glass door again and soon.

Wanting to change the subject of a handsome ex-pop star and renowned playboy, Louisa veered the conversation to the charity. "Anyway how's everything else?"

"Well Lady Blackthorn is in today."

"Has my mother been bending your ear?"

"Ha! What do you think? She wants you exposed and out there." Melissa snorted. "We're trying to see when it would be best to announce it. I suggested at the start of summer Garden Party next month when we introduce Miles as one of the ambassadors."

"Won't that steal his thunder?" Louisa asked dryly.

"Do you care? But now that I think about it, it would be better to wait until the ball. That way we get two opportunities to shout about the charity. We need to get as much exposure, so the money starts to come in." Louisa could almost see Melissa rubbing her hands together in glee. She'd been badgering Louisa to get fully involved with CASPO for years and now she was back in the UK, Melissa had become as subtle as a sledgehammer. "We need to increase donations. It's all well and good that the Blackthorn family fund most of the work at CASPO, but we need to get money in from other sources too."

Melissa was right, of course: the higher the profile of the supporters, the higher the donations. Charity was like any other business; targeted PR and marketing got you increased revenue and if you had high-profile supporters, then the earnings were guaranteed. Miles Keane was their golden goose and she was the new blood that would pump life into the rather staid charity.

"I'll talk to Mama and Margot and they can put it to the board," Louisa said with a resigned sigh.

"You think anyone would dare to cross your mother?" snorted Melissa.

Louisa chuckled, then added dryly, "Probably not, but there is a protocol and you know how my mother is a stickler for protocol."

"SO, HOW DID THE date go? You were very sketchy on the phone." Amanda eyed Miles over her coffee cup. At Miles's request, Amanda had come down for the day. She'd been a little surprised at his sudden urgency, seeing as she'd been asking him for over two months to buy some more furniture to fill out his large house.

"Good, well... unexpected."

His uncharacteristic nonchalant manner caused Amanda to narrow her eyes at him. "What are you hiding, Miles?"

His eyes darted to his perceptive sister-in-law and let out sigh. "Okay, the nineteen-year-old couldn't make it, so her mother came instead."

"What? You got stood up?" She found the idea amusing.

"I suppose so. Anyway, it was fine," he said dismissively.

"Fine? You said good and unexpected." Amanda placed her cup on her saucer and arched her brow at an uncomfortable-looking Miles.

"Fuck. Alright, she was actually really nice. Very... sophisticated."

"Well she's a mum... what did you expect?"

"She wasn't old, if that's what you mean."

"How old was she?"

"I don't know; it's not the kind of thing you ask, is it?" Miles furrowed his brow, he'd thought of many things he'd wanted to know about Louisa, but he'd never once thought about her age. "I'm not sure. She looked my age but she must've been older, I suppose." He got up from his stool, collected the empty cups and placed them in the sink.

"Where was the date?"

Miles paused for a moment, then turned and leaned against the sink. "At The Blacks Club. Very classy and very English, I was so out of my depth."

Amanda nodded. "Makes sense. The Blackthorns owns it." She watched as Miles looked down at his feet, lost in his own thoughts. "What aren't you telling me, Miles?"

Miles raised his head and pursed his lips together. "I… I really liked her. She was like no one I've ever met before. I mean, apart from being smoking hot, she was confident and elegant, surprisingly easy to talk to and she was… I don't know… fun."

"Are you going to see her again?"

Miles blew out a breath. "That's the problem; she gave nothing away. I don't even know if she was married. I went into CASPO to get her phone number and Melissa said she wanted to be anonymous. Though she said she'd contact her for me. I gave her my number but, I don't know, she's not the kind of woman who'd call, so…" He shrugged, leaving the sentence hanging.

"Is this why you want to buy furniture?"

Miles huffed. Amanda knew him too well. He explained about the joke they'd had about a second date and buying a table and Amanda chuckled. *Maybe this woman was what Miles needed,* thought Amanda. Someone who had him chasing, rather than the other way around. Hopefully, this woman might steer him away from the usual women he spent time with, ones who only saw Miles Keane the sexy pop star. He was so much more than that.

Over the last four years, he'd proved that to himself and everyone who really knew him, and had it not been for his selfless support, Amanda knew she'd have never survived and come out the other side. Amanda gave him a reassuring smile. He really was affected by whoever this mystery woman was.

"Okay then, let's go find you a table and a few other bits and pieces."

Miles and Amanda spent the next few hours scouring some of the high-end furniture shops, searching for suitable pieces befitting of his classically decorated house. There was a huge array to choose from which at first seemed daunting. Then Miles remembered Louisa saying something about just buying what you liked and the task suddenly became easier. The only frustrating part was that it would be two weeks before delivery, as the chairs needed to be upholstered.

Miles dropped Amanda at the station, after they'd had a late lunch as a thank you, and then headed back home; his pocket almost £15,000 lighter and his mood decidedly more optimistic.

The next thing Miles needed to do was organise his gift. He slouched into his sofa and called the number of the wine merchant Melissa had given him. After introducing himself, Miles asked about the 2003 Lafite Louisa had mentioned.

"We have two bottles in stock. For a larger order, we need four to six weeks." The slightly stern man said over the phone.

What? Miles scowled. He wanted to send her a case. "Okay, fine, I'll take them. I have my credit card."

"Splendid. That will be £2036 in total."

"Sorry?" Miles spluttered.

"That's £2036," repeated the wine merchant.

"That's over a thousand a bottle." *Surely there must be a mistake.*

"It is a vintage year, sir."

Miles swallowed. He was so in over his head. *Who paid that kind of money on wine?* "How much is the 2016?"

"Also a very good vintage, sir. That's £632." *Holy shit!* Miles quickly did a rough calculation in his head. The meal must've cost over £1000! "Do you have a case of that?" he asked, thinking he needed to put something in his presently empty wine cellar, plus there was the possibility that he'd have a dinner guest over soon.

"As a matter of fact, we do."

"Great, add that to my order. I hope you at least gift wrap?" Miles said dryly.

"All are wines are packed in specialised wooden boxes, sir."

"Of course they are," Miles muttered. "Okay. Erm... I'm kind of new to this, as you might have guessed, and I have this empty wine cellar. Do you have a... like a beginner's pack, Mr...?"

"Chapman. Is this for an investment or for drinking?"

"Drinking. I need a bit of everything."

"Of course, Mr Keane. How about I bring over a selection for you when we bring your order? We can discuss them and you can decide which you'd like."

Discuss them? Fuck: so in over my head. "Okay, sure."

Miles sat back and surveyed his empty house and scratched under Duke's ears, realising that this was the most preparation he'd ever done and the most money he'd ever spent to get a second date. He just hoped it would all pay off.

11

A DEAL'S A DEAL

LOUISA LOOKED DOWN AT the wooden box and read the card again.

Just something to say thank you for lunch.
I think you called it "exquisite" – like our date.
By the way, I've been shopping!
Miles

He'd sent her two bottles of the 2003 Lafite! Louisa shook her head in disbelief. The parcel had been brought in by Hugh, after Melissa had called to inform her that a gift was waiting for her at CASPO offices. Louisa didn't know what to make of it and she most definitely didn't know what to make of his note. He'd gone shopping. Did that mean he'd actually gone out and bought the table after all? Louisa turned the card in her hand. She had two choices: send a thank you via Melissa or contact him directly to say thank you herself. Louisa looked at the back of the card again. She knew she wasn't going to ask Melissa but she wasn't ready to call him either; it felt too soon, but she could at least send him an email. An email was safe.

Louisa stepped into her office and logged into her private email account that was reserved only for family and close friends. Her fingers hovered over the keys in apprehension, then she began to type.

To: Miles Keane
From: Louisa
Subject: Exquisite taste

Dear Miles,

Thank you for the Lafite. It was an unexpected surprise.
I hope your shopping trip wasn't too tedious.

Best wishes
Louisa

Louisa re-read the email, pleased that it sounded friendly without being too familiar. She clicked on the send icon and let out a breath, unsure why she felt nervous. *It was a simple thank you note, for goodness sake. He probably wouldn't even answer.*

"Madame?" Hugh's voice pulled Louisa's attention from her screen.

"Yes, Hugh?"

"Clair needs to go over the menus for next week before we leave for Holmwood."

"Of course. Whenever she's ready, Hugh."

The computer indicated a new email and Louisa's eyes darted to the screen. Louisa smiled at the subject title.

To: Louisa
From: Miles Keane
Subject: Exquisite date!

Dear Louisa,

I'm glad I can surprise you, for a change. I also bought myself a few bottles of the 2016, plus a selection of other wines with the help of a Mr Chapman because, as you know, I have limited knowledge of wine. So at least my wine cellar is at least being filled. As for filling the rest of my house, shopping wasn't as tedious as expected.

I shall keep you posted.

Miles

Louisa let out a soft chuckle. Well, he hadn't said that he'd bought a table but his sign-off indicated he would. A soft knock drew Louisa's eyes to her cook Clair, who stood at the threshold.

"Come in, Clair, sit down."

Over the following week, Louisa had a steady stream of amusing emails from Miles. Their joke had now become a private game, where Miles sent various pictures of comical dining room tables and chairs asking for her opinion. The first one he'd sent was of a brightly coloured children's set with the simple question: "What do you think?" Louisa had laughed softly to herself, seeing it and answered: "I feel that the colours may clash; maybe something subtler."

After a couple of days, Miles sent another picture of a white plastic garden set with the simple message: "Is that subtle enough?" Louisa immediately sent her reply: "Though white is a neutral colour, I feel the material may not be fitting for indoor dining."

Miles chuckled at her eloquent replies and could practically see her stifling a grin as she gracefully answered each email he sent. She was playing him at his own game. Every inappropriate dining room picture set he sent her was met by a well-thought-out objection without ridiculing his choices: perfectly ladylike in its delivery. The latest reply he'd received, after sending her a picture of a rough wooden table with benches for chairs, made him laugh loudly:

To: Miles Keane
From: Louisa
Subject: Hard to bear

Dear Miles,

Though your latest choice of material is by far the best so far, I do feel that the seating may prove a little harsh on your guests' behinds. May I suggest something with padded seating?

I applaud your perseverance and look forward to your next proposition.

Louisa

Miles quickly typed a reply.

To: Louisa
From: Miles Keane
Subject: Sore behinds

Dear Louisa,

Thank you for your concern about my future guest's (note singular) behind. The last thing I'd want is for her behind to suffer in anyway. Her comfort is of the utmost importance.

You do realise that you're the guest I'm talking about, don't you?

Patiently waiting…
Miles

Louisa read the new email and swallowed. Up until now, their emails had only been about the ridiculous furniture pictures, but reading his last one made Louisa suddenly feel uneasy. He still wanted a date and on his terms. She read through it again, trying to analyse what it meant. He wanted her to be comfortable; had he picked up on her apprehension? And what was he waiting patiently for? For her to say she'd come on a date? Louisa stared at the screen and for the first time, she was unsure of what to say. She'd been happy to play along with their game, and looked forward to whatever inappropriate picture Miles sent, but this last email had shifted their light banter to something more, something more like the conversation they'd had at Blacks. That was when he was Miles and she was Louisa on a blind date. Where he'd joked with her and flirted, showing her his vulnerable side, and over the four and a half hours, he'd managed to change her lowly opinion of him. When he'd meet her again, he'd know who she was and Louisa knew that everything would change; the thought depressed her. Maybe she was just reading far too much into the email, overthinking its meaning. He was playing their game, answering her comments with humorous banter and she was over-analysing it. Maybe one more date with him wouldn't be such a bad idea after all.

Miles waited for a reply that never came and he cursed to himself. *Had he pushed Louisa too far this time?* Over the past week, he'd managed to coax responses to each one of his emails but his last one had more than hinted that he was expecting to see her again. He waited a few more minutes, then stepped out of his office. He'd send her something more fun later on and try and get back to how they were before. He just hoped he hadn't blown it.

In the week after his shopping trip, he'd managed to set up one of the rooms on the first floor as an office. The dining table had been delivered, along with the sideboard and a piece of furniture that could be used as a bar; a discreet cabinet that opened up, rather than the brash open bar units Miles was used to seeing. The dining chairs were due in a few days, so in the meantime, he'd set up his instruments in what was the drawing room, including his piano that Amanda insisted she send down, now he had space for it. His house was by no means finished but at least the storage boxes weren't on display in the sitting room anymore and the echo around the three reception rooms had definitely been reduced. The only homely element to Miles's home was the dog basket near the marble fireplace in the sitting room, and the scamper of Duke's feet against the polished wooden floors. Miles scratched behind Duke's ears, then headed out of the front door to his business meeting.

THE VIEW OF HOLMWOOD House never got old for Louisa. Hugh drove up the wide road that led the way to the grand house, through the canopy of trees and the lush grass that seemed to go on for miles. In the distance, she could see Alistair galloping down the length of the lake towards the house and she shook her head at his recklessness, but smiled to herself all the same. It was good to see him being the Alistair she knew and loved: a risk-taker and daredevil.

Louisa had decided to spend a couple of days at Holmwood so that she could get the wheels in motion for the activity long weekend. Alistair had come up with a few ideas and managed to get his friends and old colleagues involved too. Melissa and Margot were also on board with the idea and were now processing through their lists of candidates.

Lady Alice was happy to have her home host the holiday,

especially as it meant both her children would be involved. When the late Earl had been alive, he'd regularly hosted weekends for his employees and their families as a thank you, but since he'd died, and after Alistair's accident, Lady Alice hadn't had the heart or energy to start up the tradition again. This activities weekend was certainly the first step towards that, though, with the next generation of Blackthorns at the helm.

"This is nice. A family dinner; just Celeste missing," Lady Alice said, placing her napkin on her lap. "Melissa tells me all's well with the garden party."

"Yes, there'll be around a hundred attending, which is more than last year." Louisa smirked.

The Blackthorn's garden party was always held the first week in June at The Blacks Club. It was a very prestigious event the Blackthorn family hosted to thank the most generous supporters of CASPO. They also invited a number of the people who had benefitted from the charity so that the donators could see first-hand how their donations had changed lives.

"I think it's because a certain celebrity will be there," Louisa said wryly.

Lady Alice arched her brow at Louisa. "Yes, Mr Keane has certainly helped the charity's coffers. He's definitely garnered more interest this year. I don't know why we never thought of bringing in someone so..."

Alistair and Louisa threw each other a look, then directed their attention to their mother who seemed to be struggling to find the correct adjective.

"So what?" prompted Alistair.

"Famous," Lady Alice said with a nod.

"Hmm – or infamous," Alistair muttered under his breath. "He does have rather a large following." He smirked at Louisa.

"He's actually a very nice man too. When he came into the CASPO offices, he brought flowers and for Margot and Melissa, plus some cakes for the rest of the staff. What's more important, though: our donations have gone up since the auction."

"Well that is the whole point."

Lady Alice ignored Alistair's comment and continued, "And after the official announcement at the garden party, I'm sure we'll see another significant spike."

They were served their meal by the discreet staff and said a subdued cheers once the wine was poured. Louisa forgot how much her mother enjoyed dining in the dining room. When it was just Lady Alice and Alistair, they ate in her wing of the house, but once Louisa came to stay, Lady Alice liked to use the main dining room. It was an impressive room with gilded cornices and lofty ceiling, which had three magnificent chandeliers down the centre. The large table could easily seat twenty four and on occasion had been extended to seat thirty two.

Louisa's thoughts drifted to another dining room table, one that had been preying on her mind the whole day, and the talk of the garden party in a few weeks only made Louisa more uneasy. Maybe she should just bite the bullet and say yes to Miles. No one would know and it could be the right time to come clean about who she was.

Lady Alice continued as she always did, oblivious to Louisa's introspective mood and Alistair's indifference. "It'll be a perfect opportunity for you to meet the board members and donators too, Louisa. It's been a few years for you to be at one of our garden parties."

"I know who's on the board, Mama."

"Yes, but you'll be meeting them as the future patron this time. At least you'll be on your own turf, so to speak."

"And our expense," coughed Alistair.

Louisa stifled a grin. Alistair wasn't a huge fan of the social side his title burdened him with. He had little time for sucking up to rich and entitled people so that they'd part with money they'd never even valued or earned. He knew it was ironic for him to feel this way, being as he was the Earl of Holmwood. The difference, though, was he'd also worked away from his estate, amongst ordinary hardworking people. He'd lived, worked and suffered alongside them and that had grounded him. His father had always worked hard, expanding the Holmwood estate and their various businesses, setting him an example, and after Alistair's military career was cut short, he vowed to keep up his late father's good work.

"I hope you didn't bully anyone into accepting me," Louisa said sharply.

"The Blackthorns *are* the patrons of CASPO, Louisa. Without us, the charity wouldn't exist. The board knows that; there was no bullying at all. I think they're actually relieved, to be honest."

"Relieved?"

"Well, I'm getting too long in the tooth and Alistair's never been too good at being a diplomat." Lady Alice pursed her lips as her son rolled his eyes.

"I leave all that schmoozing to you two," he said. "I just turn up, smile at everyone, shake a few hands, slap a few backs, then bugger off."

"And you do that so well," Louisa said sarcastically.

"Why thank you, *my lady*."

"You two are incorrigible," Lady Alice said.

The dinner proceeded leisurely as they talked about a number of ideas for the weekend. Lady Alice enjoyed seeing both her children become actively involved with such a worthwhile event. Their good humour and constant ribbing of each other had Lady Alice laughing softly. She'd missed having her family around her, missed seeing Alistair so relaxed and genuinely happy. Louisa was the only one who seemed to bring that side of him out again.

It was close to ten by the time Louisa headed up to her suite. She looked around at the familiar room and saw her laptop set up on the antique desk. She paced over to it and switched it on, then waited for her email account to load. Within a minute, her emails filtered through and her heart jumped when she saw one from Miles. He had attached a photo of a low wooden table with cushions all around, similar to ones found in the Middle East.

To: Louisa
From: Miles Keane
Subject: Comfort first

Dear Louisa,

In the interest of comfort, I thought this might be appropriate.
I would, as always, appreciate your valuable input.

Miles

Louisa smiled to herself. Even via email, Miles was being a gentleman. He didn't even mention that she hadn't acknowledged his last email and he'd carried on their game. She quickly typed a reply.

To: Miles Keane
From: Louisa
Subject: Comfort v practical

Dear Miles

Though I don't doubt the seating will be comfortable, I feel it maybe a little difficult for your guests to get up, especially after a meal and a few glasses of wine.

Traditional seating might be the way to go.
Keep trying.

Louisa.

Miles looked down in relief when he saw his phone alert him to an email. She'd finally answered him. "Keep trying," she said. Well, he wasn't about to give up now, especially since he was expecting delivery of his chairs in two days. He picked up his beer and took a drink.

"Good news?" Lottie asked, seeing Miles's wide smile.

"Yeah, just some email I was waiting for."

"Want to celebrate?" She wiggled her eyebrows at him and Miles instantly wanted to leave the fashion event he'd accompanied her to and go back home, alone.

TWO DAYS LATER

Miles's fingers hovered over the keys. He'd never felt so nervous about sending an email.

To: Louisa
From: Miles Keane
Subject: Personal approval

Dear Louisa

After your valuable input, I've finally invested in a suitable table and chairs. Of course I would welcome your opinion.

I kept my side of the deal. I really hope you keep yours.

Miles

P.S. No picture included. They need to be viewed personally to be fully appreciated.

Louisa read it holding her breath. He'd backed her into a corner without even realising it. If she avoided him, his opinion of her would plummet when they finally officially met at the garden party. He'd probably think she was a snob. If she declined the invite, he was sure to think it was ungracious of her, especially after their teasing emails over the last ten days. Either way, she would come off looking bad and the last thing Louisa wanted was for Miles to think badly of her. That thought alone had Louisa both confused and uneasy.

Louisa let out a breath, knowing her nervousness was because she really did want to see Miles again and not in an official sense. It had been hard to admit to herself that those four and a half hours with Miles had had such an impact on her. On top of that, he'd been consistent in his pursuit, which had only fuelled the effect, even if he'd disguised it in light-hearted banter.

To: Miles Keane
From: Louisa
Subject: Personal inspection

Dear Miles,

If you knew me, you'd know I never back down on a deal.
I look forward to seeing your new furniture.

Louisa

Miles blew out a relieved breath as he read the email. *That's the whole point,* he thought to himself. He didn't know her but was determined at least this time, to rectify that.

To: Louisa
From: Miles Keane
Subject: A deal's a deal

Dear Louisa,

I knew you were too much of a lady to go back on our deal.
And that's the whole point... I don't know you at all.

How does 7pm Friday sound?
Dinner Miles style, dress code casual. You can do casual, right?

Miles

Louisa snorted at his question. *He did think she was a snob.*

To: Miles Keane
From: Louisa
Subject: Casual dining

Dear Miles,

Yes, I can do casual.

See you 7pm Friday.
Louisa

She said yes! Now he had three days to get everything in order. Miles sent back a simple "Looking forward to it", then scooped up Duke, giving him squeeze.

Louisa sat back in her chair, then furrowed her brow. She needed to organise the perfect house-warming gift.

12

UP CLOSE AND PERSONAL

HUGH SMOOTHLY PARKED THE car and waited. The only sound in the car was the rhythmic swish of the wipers as they cleared the light rain that continued to fall. Louisa looked up at the classic white house and her stomach flipped. For three days, she'd tried to convince herself it was just a casual dinner. It was a case of her simple good manners, accepting the invitation of a future ambassador of her charity; a chance to get to know him and for him to learn a little about her. She looked down at her cream fitted dress and black suede stilettoes and blew out a breath. It wasn't exactly casual. Louisa had contemplated going back home to change, after her meeting at Blacks had overrun, but that meant the early evening London traffic would've made her late.

"Ready, my lady?" Louisa caught Hugh's eye in the rear view mirror and nodded. He stepped out of the car and opened up a large black umbrella, then opened up her door. Louisa stepped out under its shelter, taking the impressive bouquet of flowers and sliding a large gift-wrapped box towards her. Hugh immediately took the box from the back seat so she could adjust her bag and thin coat.

"I'm not sure how long I'll be."

"That's fine; I have a TV series downloaded on my iPad that I want to catch up on."

Louisa gave him a thankful smile, then reached out to take the box. "I'll text you when I'm ready to leave."

"Of course; let me help you." Hugh shut the door but held onto the box and umbrella and Louisa's eyes darted to the black shiny door nervously.

Being part of the aristocracy didn't afford you any privacy. There was always someone either tending to your needs or watching over you. Louisa had been accustomed to that way of life for many years, though she had managed to keep some of her life in the US totally private. Here, though, her every move was monitored and though Hugh was as discreet as he could be, given the circumstances, Louisa would've still preferred that he didn't accompany her up the four steps to Miles's front door.

"I'm not sure that's such a good idea."

"Believe me, it is." Hugh gave her a wry smile, then stepped to the side. "After you, my lady."

Miles checked the warmer where he'd placed the various sides dishes he'd prepared, then set the bottle of wine on the kitchen island along with the decanter he'd recently bought. Over the last three days, he'd expanded his crockery and glassware collection, along with any other items he thought he would need for home entertaining. *Thank goodness for Internet shopping and next-day delivery,* thought Miles as he readjusted the napkin in his newly acquired bread basket.

He'd specified it was a casual dinner but the lengths he'd gone to over the last two weeks suggested the opposite. His home was starting to take shape. He'd added a large mirror over the fireplace in the sitting room, bought a few more pieces of furniture and hung up a few pictures in the music room. Miles looked outside at the rain and huffed. He hoped it wasn't a bad omen. He was just happy his barbeque was undercover. The light ring of his doorbell alerted his eyes to the kitchen clock. Seven o'clock. *Bang on time*. He took in a deep calming breath and blew it out while he quickly paced to the door.

"Hel-lo Louisa," Miles stuttered; his eyes flitted between a tightly smiling Louisa and an impassive Hugh who were standing in the shelter of the umbrella.

"Hello, Miles. Hugh was just helping me."

Hugh noticed the look of relief on Miles's face and arched his brow.

"Oh, err, come in," Miles said in a rush, forgetting his manners and stood back, allowing Louisa to step into the hallway and out of the rain. "Here, let me take that." Miles reached over and took the large gift-wrapped box from Hugh.

"Thank you, Hugh," Louisa said softly and with a curt nod, Hugh stepped back, gave a stern look to Miles, then headed back to the car.

Miles quickly shut the door and turned to Louisa. "Let me take your coat." He placed the box on the central round table and helped Louisa out of her coat, hanging it unceremoniously on the banister.

"If this is your idea of casual, I'm intrigued to see what you call dressing up," he said with a smirk as his eyes raked over her, causing her cheeks to redden. She looked perfectly put together, the cream dress fitting over every curve, and her stilettoes matched her small black bag.

"I came straight from a meeting."

"Oh, I see." Miles held her gaze and Louisa's heart rate rocketed. *What was she doing here?* They were alone in his house with no distractions. She hadn't done this in a very long time. Who was she kidding? She hadn't done this before *ever.* Her years at Holmwood House had taught her how to behave in difficult situations, be calm and collected at all times and never let down her guard – all part and parcel of being a Countess, but the way Miles was looking at her right now, her whole body felt like it was glowing and this was just at the start. Louisa held out the bouquet for him to take, just so he would break eye contact with her.

"These are beautiful."

"They're for the table. Well, you can't have a dining room table without a vase of flowers on it," Louisa said lightly, hoping talk of the dining room table would diffuse the highly charged atmosphere.

"Thank you." He threw her a lopsided smile. "What's this?" Miles pointed to the large box.

"A house warming gift, but please open it after I leave."

"Okay… it isn't a vase, is it?"

"No."

He twisted his mouth and shrugged. "Shame; I could do with one right now. I don't have one for these."

Louisa covered her mouth with her hand to stifle a grin. "Oh, I didn't think."

Miles let out a soft laugh and shook his head, then put out his hand, an invitation for her to step towards the kitchen. "Don't worry; I'll find something. Come on through." Miles opened the door leading into the kitchen and they were met by a very excited Duke. The adorable puppy jumped up at Louisa and she immediately crouched down to pet him. "Meet Duke."

"He's gorgeous."

"And big trouble." Duke rolled on to his back and accepted the belly rub from Louisa. "He's a rescue that I'm fostering, though I think he's a keeper. Grace and Louis would never forgive me if I gave him back." Miles opened one of the kitchen cupboards and pulled out a stainless steel wine bucket. "Ah, this might work."

Louisa straightened and rounded the island. "Here let me."

"Oh, thanks."

Louisa set to work on filling the bucket with water, happy to have something to occupy herself with, then opened up the bouquet and started to arrange the flowers. Miles leaned his hip against the island, taking in her profile. It was a surprisingly domestic scene but the way Louisa looked and was elegantly arranging the flowers, she was anything but domestic. She gave him a sideward look and smiled shyly.

"You want the grand tour or a drink first?"

"A drink?"

"Sure, what can I get you?"

"Whisky, straight."

Miles gave a nod. "I think I can manage that." He paced towards the sitting room, then looked back over his shoulder at Louisa. She'd paused for a beat and momentarily closed her eyes, letting out a breath. Miles furrowed his brow and headed towards the drinks cabinet. By the time he returned to the kitchen, the arrangement was finished.

"Wow, they look amazing. Thank you. Here." He handed Louisa her drink, then pulled out a beer from the fridge. Once he'd popped open the lid, he raised it and clinked it against her glass. "Welcome to my home. Let's go through to the sitting room."

Louisa let him lead the way into the sparsely furnished room. The large windows showcased the private garden at the rear of the house and lit up the pleasant room even on such a drizzly day.

"Would you like to sit down?" Miles hovered by the fireplace and watched Louisa gaze out into the garden, framed perfectly by the window.

"You have a garden too. That's unusual for this area." She ignored his invitation to sit and turned towards him as he joined her.

"Well, it's more like a large patio. I'm used to a bigger back yard... garden," he corrected himself and Louisa grinned. "But it's manageable and I can grill outside too. Thank you for coming."

"Well you kept me very intrigued. With all the furniture

choices – and I'm a woman of my word." Louisa took a sip of her drink and Miles nodded sagely, then gave her a wide smile.

"I'm worried that this whole table-reveal thing will be an anti-climax."

Louisa let out a chuckle. "I'll let you into a secret, Miles. Though I'm happy you bought a table, I couldn't care less where we ate, so this date's success doesn't hinge on your table choice."

"Well, damn, the table was kind of my guarantee to impress you. Now that just made me more nervous."

"You're nervous? Of me?" Louisa couldn't hide the surprise in her voice. This was Miles Keane, cocky, sexy pop star, who clicked his fingers and women clawed over each other to get his attention and get into his bed.

"Unchartered territory." He fixed her with his eyes and Louisa felt that unnerving pull again.

"Are you *that* worried I won't like your table?" she joked and Miles let out a husky laugh, glad to see she'd relaxed enough to start teasing him.

"Yeah, that's exactly why I'm nervous," he drawled and took a drink from his beer.

"Well, if it makes you feel better, I'm a little nervous too. I haven't had a man cook for me who I didn't pay."

Miles nearly spluttered his beer at her comment. "I really don't know what to make of that revelation, but I assure you my cooking isn't that bad and remember, this date is on the house."

"Show me your table."

"I thought you'd never ask." He gave her a cheeky wink and Louisa let out a soft laugh, then followed him through to the kitchen. He set down his beer and scooped up the wine bucket full of flowers. "This way." Louisa placed her glass on the island and walked behind him towards a dark wooden double door.

"Ready?" Louisa nodded and then Miles opened up one of the doors. "Ta-dah!"

The room was as bright and airy as the sitting room and

decorated in muted neutral tones, with a large window letting in the natural light from the garden. From the ceiling a rectangular chandelier hung directly above the dining room table, which gave the room a dramatic flair. The table itself was simple solid walnut, from what Louisa could tell, and the fourteen padded chairs around it were upholstered in light silver-grey velvet, adding a touch of luxury.

"You set it already?" Louisa eyed the two place settings that glinted under the lights at one end of the table as Miles placed the flowers in the centre.

"Well, I did invite you to dinner."

"It's a really lovely table." Louisa stroked her fingers over the smooth tabletop.

"I know; I was very well advised, plus the flowers set it off, don't you think?" He tilted his head to the side as he regarded her and she gave him a smile. "Now you've seen the *pièce de résistance,* I think the rest of the house may disappoint you."

"Shall I be the judge of that? It's a lovely room, Miles. I think you've got the decorating thing down to a tee."

"Ha, thank you for the vote of confidence." He signalled Louisa to follow him into the hallway and they began to descend one floor. "Well, you've seen the sitting room and kitchen, this is apparently a drawing room, whatever that is," He shrugged and stepped into the room. "But I made it...

"Your music room," finished Louisa as she took in the array of musical instruments on display, a black grand piano taking the centre stage.

Miles paced around the room, readjusting a framed picture of himself with Louis in an unguarded moment. Louis was sitting at a piano, not dissimilar to the one in the room, and Miles was standing in that cocksure way he had been known for, holding his trumpet and laughing at some inside joke.

"It still needs an armchair, maybe a rug and some more things on the wall. Do you play any instruments?"

"A long time ago. Piano, but it's been a while. It's been a while to do a lot of things," Louisa said with a huff.

"Like?"

"Dating. I'm recently divorced."

Miles gave a slow nod, then said, "I should say that I'm sorry but I'd be lying."

Louisa's eyes widened at his candid comment. "I didn't want you to think I was the kind of woman who cheated on her husband," she said quietly.

Miles stepped up to her and rested his hand lightly on her arm. Gone was the confident woman who had strode into Blacks two weeks ago and in her place was an uneasy, nervous one. Miles had been so focused on his own apprehension, he hadn't foreseen that Louisa would also be anxious. All he wanted was for her to relax and have a good time, to enjoy his company – not because she'd been backed into a corner, like their first date, but because she genuinely liked him. Miles hadn't realised how important that fact was to him.

"Louisa, you really don't need to tell me anything about yourself if you don't want to." He bobbed down to catch her gaze and she lifted her head.

"Thanks."

"Come on, let me put on the steaks and we can just keep it casual, eh?" he said brightly. "I can show you the rest of the house later."

"That's sounds perfect, as long as you let me help."

Miles gave her that wide smile that had all ages of women swooning at his feet, but it faltered when he spotted something out of the window. "Is your driver still outside?" They made their way up the stairs to the hallway.

"Yes."

"Why?"

"He'll stay there until I'm ready to leave. So the kitchen's through here?"

Miles nodded, unsure of what to make of that information. She had a car on standby. *Was it for a quick getaway or was he security too?* His eyes drifted over Louisa, taking in every detail and for the hundredth time in two weeks, he asked himself: *Who was she?*

"Right, so I got some filet mignons and there's a pepper sauce if you'd like. The sweet potatoes are in the oven. Green salad that just needs dressing and steamed asparagus, plus I grilled up some vegetables; they're in the warmer."

"Sound delicious."

Miles opened up the fridge and took out a large bowl of salad and a plastic box with the steaks in and placed them on the island. "How do you like your steak?"

"Medium rare, more rare though."

"Okay, then, so I'll fire up the grill."

Louisa followed Miles out into the back garden, where a huge stainless steel barbeque was housed under a wooden canopy.

"That's some barbeque."

"Yeah, I had it especially brought over." He quickly lit up the burners, then stepped back into the kitchen. "Maybe I should open the wine?" He gestured to the bottle of Lafite and Louisa grinned at him. He worked off the foil and uncorked the wine and then poured it into the waiting decanter. "Don't be too impressed. The good Mr Chapman told me how to do this."

Louisa let out a chuckle, then stepped up to where the salad was. "Shall I dress the salad?"

"Yeah, what do you need?"

"How about I look in your cupboards?"

"Knock yourself out." He picked up the box with the steaks in and watched her look through his relatively empty cupboards. "These will take all of ten minutes."

Louisa told him that was fine and grabbed the olive oil and balsamic vinegar. Louisa quickly rustled up a dressing and tossed the salad, glad she was given a few moments alone. She glanced through the kitchen window at where Miles was now standing. The light blue polo shirt fit snugly over his toned chest and his slightly worn jeans hugged his behind perfectly. He'd looked good in a suit, but it was obvious that this more casual look was who Miles was – and boy, did he wear it well.

"You look very at home there." Louisa had stepped back into the garden.

"Well, it's one of the things we Americans know how to do. My family were big on outdoor eating. The weather helped, out in California."

"Not so much here, though." Louisa looked out where the drizzle was still falling.

"That's why I added this extension. What about your family?"

"Do they like to barbeque?" Louisa gave him a confused look.

"Well that's a start, I suppose."

"We have done. My brother Alistair is big on outdoors – more of a campfire kind of thing, though."

"You just have one brother?" Louisa gave him a nod. "Is he married?"

She shook her head. "He's six years older than me and was in the military, RAF, actually." Miles flipped over the steaks and the sizzle distracted Louisa for a second.

"Oh wow. Was?"

"Yes, he had an accident on his last tour, which meant he had to cut his career short. He now works in the family business."

"And what's that?"

"Erm, property management," Louisa said cagily.

"Hmm." Miles furrowed his brow, knowing her answer was probably not altogether the truth but rather than push, he directed her attention to the steaks, keeping to the safe topic of food. After a few minutes, Miles lifted the meat off the grill and placed them onto a warmed dish. They both gathered up the various dishes from the kitchen, taking a few trips until everything was set out on the new table.

Miles pulled out the chair at the head of the table for Louisa to sit at and then took the seat to her right. "*Bon appetite.*" Miles lifted his glass and Louisa clinked hers against it.

"Everything looks delicious. I didn't realise how hungry I was. So how are your business propositions coming along?" Louisa asked as she began to cut through her succulent steak.

"I signed up for a watch company this week and it looks like the show might be going ahead. It seems you were right; there are old celebrities who want the limelight shone on them again."

"That's a new role for you then, being a presenter. Are you nervous?"

"Apprehensive. It's been a while since I was out there. I feel better that's it's in front of a camera, rather than… well, let's just say I'm not so good at being front of a large audience anymore."

"Well, I think anyone would feel daunted at being in front of thousands of people, even without what you went through," Louisa said softly. Miles gave a one-shoulder shrug and averted his eyes from Louisa's sympathetic gaze. "I can't even… I'm sorry. Maybe we should change the subject."

Miles shook his head, indicating he was fine, when he was anything but, then reached for his wine. He hadn't spoken about that horrific day in over three years, not since his time in rehab. She'd opened up the sensitive subject, when most of the people he'd met knew about it and avoided bringing it up at all. He caught their condoling looks though. People treated him differently now. Before, he'd been welcomed with huge smiles and hard hugs and Miles had revelled in it; now, the smiles were softer and the hugs had been replaced with respectful handshakes. It took Miles a while to get used to the change but every time it happened, it reminded him of why. His gaze lifted to Louisa's concerned expression and for the first time in a very long time he felt empathy. There wasn't pity in her eyes, there was understanding and Miles rarely saw that. "You know, the day it happened – the shooting – it's five years next week."

"Oh I didn't realise, I'm so sorry."

"It's okay, you weren't to know." He took a deep breath and gave her a tight smile. "That day we were so excited to be back at Juilliard. Seeing our old professors. It was a huge honour for us to be asked."

"I'm sure."

"Louis had practiced his damn speech over and over so many times that Amanda and I knew it by heart. He was always so meticulous; it used to drive me crazy." He huffed and shook his head. "We were so stoked that our parents would see it streamed live too. They couldn't make it out because they had their own students' graduation over the next few days. In hindsight, I now wish it hadn't been. Can you imagine seeing your son gunned down in front of your eyes?" Louisa closed her eyes for a second and swallowed, trying hard to keep her emotions in check. It was every parent's nightmare, to lose a child but to witness the brutality of it; how could they ever erase that image?

"I remember hearing the first shot and it just didn't register, what had happened, until I heard the second and the screams started. It was mayhem. Everyone running for cover and still the shots kept coming. We were sitting ducks on the stage. Thank god Mick and Josh got down. Everything became slow motion. I remember Mick and Josh screaming at me to get down but I just ran to Louis and tried my hardest to stop the bleeding, but there was just so much blood. I didn't even feel the shot that went through my shoulder, it was only when I realised I couldn't press down with my left arm that I saw the blood – my blood."

Louisa remembered seeing the live footage. The heartbreaking image of Louis's limp, blood-soaked body being held to Miles's chest as he rocked his brother, sobbing uncontrollably. That image had gone viral until the worldwide press realised it was tasteless and appalling to exploit such a tragic moment and took down the footage. Louisa's eyes welled up and she tried hard to blink them back as Miles continued.

"The shooter was shot by one of *our* security guys, who was guarding one of the doors from the outside. Thankfully, he managed to get in before the shooter reloaded. No one thought for a moment that someone who'd been invited would be armed, or a risk to us or anyone else."

Louisa took a sip from her wine in order to moisten her dried up mouth and steady her voice. "I read he was an ex-student, an older brother of one of the graduating class."

"Yeah, he'd been in my year and failed in his second semester. He had all sorts of mental issues. No one knows if he was out for revenge on the college, the students or us." Miles blew out a breath and gave a slight shake of his head, surprised at himself. He hadn't expected to talk about that awful day tonight. Maybe it was because he wanted Louisa to know him better, see past his celebrity persona, or maybe it was because the anniversary was coming up and he needed to talk about it. Whatever the reason, Miles felt both uneasy that Louisa had unwittingly drawn out the story from him and unexpectedly glad that she knew the truth.

"Two professors, six graduating students and Louis died that day."

"It was a horrific incident."

"Everyone focused on Louis and me but the facts were far worse. Those other eight innocent people also died."

"You did a good thing, though. You raised so much money for the families." Louisa's voice wavered a little, clearly moved by Miles's description of that fateful day's events.

Keane Sense had donated the proceeds of their final single, aptly titled *Lost Love,* to the families of the victims. The single had topped the charts for twenty weeks.

"Wow. I didn't mean to get so morbid. I haven't talked about that day in a very long time." Miles roughly ran his hand over his face and shook his head. He gave Louisa an awkward smile, then picked up his wine glass. "I can't even blame the Lafite this time, seeing as I've only had a couple of sips."

Louisa smiled softly at him. He was disguising his discomfort with humour again and Louisa wasn't about to make him feel any worse. "Well, there you are then. You need to drink a bit more."

Miles's smile widened and he took a deliberate drink from his glass, which made Louisa chuckle. "Shit, I really didn't mean to upset you. I was hoping this date would be even better than the last one, but I seemed to have messed up there."

"You haven't messed up, Miles. Thank you for sharing something so difficult," she said sincerely.

"Okay, enough of all the sad stuff. What about this table, eh? Pretty special." He rubbed his palm over the surface, widened his eyes and gave a knowing nod. Louisa laughed at his exaggerated performance.

"Pretty special, and I have to say the food is excellent too."

"Aww, Louisa, that's because it free."

"Oh, I think there's more to it than that."

"Yeah?"

"Yes."

13

WORTH THE RISK

"SOMEHOW, I DIDN'T EXPECT you to know how to load a dishwasher."

They'd finished their pleasant meal and, on Louisa's insistence, they cleared the table. The conversation over their leisurely meal had been more light-hearted. They'd stuck to safe, neutral topics. Miles told her about his shopping trip and ideas he had for his home. He'd made her laugh, explaining how the delivery of wine had come with a rather stiff Mr Chapman. At the end of his crash course in wine appreciation, Miles was now on first name terms with the wine merchant. Louisa asked him about his collaboration with the watch makers and generally let Miles dominate the conversation. It still felt as though Louisa was almost interviewing him, but he realised it was her tactic to avoid giving too much away.

Miles had garnered some information from her, though. She lived not far from Westminster and her daughter was due back at the end of June from Peru, which went to explain why she was unable to come on the date.

"Are you suggesting I'm incapable of doing domestic chores?" Louisa asked dryly.

"Let's just say, I have a feeling this isn't something you do on a regular basis." Miles grinned at her and she gave him a nod. It was true she hardly ever did any domestic chores, though she was more than capable. Her whole life, she'd been tended to by various staff but that didn't mean she expected it – it was more that her staff expected to.

On Miles's suggestion, they had moved to the lounge where it would be less formal. The drizzle had changed to rain now and Miles lit the fire, which instantly transformed the airy room to cosy. Louisa sat at one end of the settee while Miles went back into the kitchen.

"Dessert," he explained and placed a box along with plates and cutlery on the coffee table. "So, I didn't make dessert, but I did get these absolutely delicious éclairs from this shop I discovered on my shopping trip." Miles flipped open the lid to reveal six éclairs that looked like works of art.

"They look too good to eat."

"I know. This one's my favourite: Tahitian vanilla and pecan éclair. But they're all pretty special. We can cut them up so you can try them all. Coffee?"

"No thank you, it's a bit late for me."

"Herbal tea, then? Or a brandy."

"A brandy would be lovely."

Miles stepped over to his drinks cabinet and said a silent thank you to Charles Chapman for suggesting he had a few good bottles of cognac, Armagnac and port in his cabinet. Miles poured two generous measures into two brandy glasses and then set them on the table. "Why the secrecy, Louisa? I've been trying to work out why you won't tell me who you are and my mind has come up with some pretty farfetched scenarios." Miles cut the pastries into pieces, then gestured to Louisa to help herself, then sat down next to her.

"That sounds interesting. Like what?" She peered into the box and selected a piece of the éclair Miles had said was his favourite, plus another two, which looked equally delicious.

"You're a spy for MI6," Miles deadpanned and Louisa let out a soft laugh. "No? Okay, your family is in exile?" he said with a shrug, trying hard to keep a straight face.

"Nope." Louisa cut through a piece of éclair and forked it into her mouth. It was exactly as he said: delicious. She pointed to her mouth as she chewed and nodded her approval.

"I know, they're really good." He helped himself to a couple of pieces, then leaned back into the settee. "So, not a spy or in exile." He made a show of thinking. Louisa giggled at his imaginative theories. The truth was of course, far duller, but she was enjoying this new game of theirs. It had been a long time for Louisa to enjoy someone's company so much. Miles was fun. He made her laugh and had a knack of making her feel comfortable yet special at the same time. He was laid back, yet still paid attention and in his own unique way, he'd coaxed out a side of Louisa that she'd reserved for very few people. Miles had again surprised her. He was nothing like the young arrogant man she'd met ten years ago and everything like the kind of man who appealed to her. The thought both unnerved and excited her. She knew the dynamic of their relationship would change as soon as she told him who she was. It was inevitable.

Louisa took in Miles's handsome face as he chewed on his dessert. His bright blue eyes sparkled at her mischievously as he concocted a new scenario, and Louisa knew she wasn't ready to lose this. The way he looked at her had her heart racing and her skin tingling and she wanted to hold on to Miles and Louisa for just a little longer.

"I know," Miles said with a wide smile. "You witnessed a murder and you're in the witness protection program?"

Louisa laughed again at his effort. "Maybe I'm the murderer and I'm on the run, hiding from the authorities?" She gave him a knowing look.

Miles narrowed his eyes at her and then shook his head. "Nah, but you're hiding from someone or something, that's for sure... but I'm not sure what."

"Or maybe I'm an eccentric recluse who has one hundred cats named after the ancient gods," Louisa said playfully. This time, it was Miles who laughed, making his whole face light up and taking Louisa's breath away.

"Somehow I doubt that very much, though I do have you down as an animal lover. You know it's not fair, don't you? You know so much about me and I know hardly anything about you." Miles shuffled forward on the settee, closing the distance between them.

"You've got to know Louisa, and that's who I am. And yes, you're right: it isn't fair at all, but I want it to stay like this for just a little longer, if that's okay?"

Miles narrowed his eyes at her. *What was she hiding? Why was it so important for her to keep her identity from him? Maybe she was married after all.* Louisa held his gaze and Miles saw a myriad of emotions pass through them. She was worried and this was a plea for him to give her time.

"I'm enjoying just being Miles and Louisa. It's been a long time for me to be just Louisa."

Miles reached over and took her hand, rubbing his thumb over her knuckles, and gave her a reassuring smile. This secrecy was important to her and he was sure she had her reasons, even if it was frustrating for him. He wasn't ready to lose what they had either. Miles wasn't even sure what exactly it was that they had; all he knew was that since the day he'd met Louisa, she'd been in his mind constantly and that had never happened before.

"Well how can I deny you that, *just* Louisa? I still think you're a spy, though. I like the idea that you could kick my ass if I overstepped the mark," he said with a cheeky smile.

Louisa let out a breath and grinned at him. "I *could* kick your ass and I most definitely would if you overstepped the mark," she deadpanned and Miles dropped her hand and put both of them up as a show of surrender. Louisa laughed at his over-dramatic reaction.

"I'll bear that in mind."

And just like that, they were back to having fun. Louisa picked up her plate and forked up some more éclair. "You were right, these are delicious."

"I know. So, *just* Louisa, when can I see you again? Next week?" Miles tilted his head to the side as he gazed at her.

"I'm out of the country for a few days."

"A secret mission?" he said dryly.

"Not quite. I have an obligation that I can't get out of." Louisa scrunched up her nose and Miles nodded.

"So the week after next?" He tried hard not to sound too hopeful but he wanted to know when he would see her again. Louisa gave him a small nod, and he smiled widely. "What about your number? I could call you and we could talk about safe topics like food and drink, or interior design." Miles saw apprehension in her eyes and cursed himself for pushing her. Before she could say anything he continued, "No? Okay we can stick with emails. It's kind of romantic anyway and I'm less likely to screw it up."

"Miles Keane likes romance, eh? Somehow, I didn't have you down as a romantic." Louisa chuckled.

"I'm an artist. We are the embodiment of romance – didn't you know that? So, I can email you then?"

Louisa put down her plate. She was being selfish and unreasonable and he was being anything but. She felt like a prize bitch again and she was worried that it might be her that screwed it up, not him. There was only so much a man could put up with and she was asking far too much of him. Louisa stood up from the settee. It was time for her to go before he asked her to, or before she said or did something they both might regret. She wanted Miles to remember her like this: having fun and joking about.

Miles shot up from his seat. *Shit, had he blown it by asking her for her number?*

"Where are you going?"

"It's late and I've an early call... I'm sorry I'm being so..."

"Mysterious?"

Louisa nodded and Miles stepped a little closer to her.

"I just need to know one thing, Louisa. Am I wasting my time?"

"I wouldn't be here if you were wasting your time." Miles let out a relieved breath. "It's just my life... things are a little complicated and I need to be careful. Meeting you, getting to know you has been unexpected and strangely enough, exactly what I needed, but I really need to go."

"Well, you are no doubt the most interesting woman I have ever met, Louisa."

Louisa gathered up her bag and headed to the hallway. She should text Hugh but she didn't want to linger any more than she needed to. Miles reached for her coat and held it out for her to put on. He wanted her to stay a little longer and the thought that it might be a couple of weeks before he saw her again frustrated and saddened him. He'd never felt so out of control. They paced slowly up to the door and Miles opened it. The rain was still coming down and Miles frowned, then scanned the pavement to see if Hugh had noticed them.

"Thank you for dinner."

"No need to thank me; the pleasure was all mine," he said sincerely, not wanting her to leave.

"I was very impressed with your culinary skills."

"Just my culinary skills?" he arched his brow at her.

"No, the table was pretty impressive too."

Miles chuckled, pleased she was teasing him again. He still wasn't sure why she felt the need to leave but he wasn't about to blow it again by trying to make her stay. She obviously had her reasons and she'd agreed to see him again. If she wanted to go slow, he could do slow. It would probably kill him, but looking down at Louisa's beautiful face, he knew it would be worth it.

"Thank you for being patient," she said softly and he gave her a nod.

"Hang on, I'll just go get my coat to shield you and take you up to the car. You'll get soaked.

"Don't bother; it's just a bit of rain. I'll run." Her eyes darted to the waiting car and Hugh caught her eye. He immediately got out of the car with the umbrella, but she put up her finger, signalling him to wait. She turned to Miles who had furrowed his brow, unsure as to why she'd asked her driver to hang back. "You want to kiss me?"

The unexpected question threw Miles but he only hesitated for a second. "Yeah, I want kiss you." Because it was all he'd been thinking about all evening.

"I thought so." She gave a wide smile, then hoisted her coat over her head and dashed down the stairs.

"What?" Miles stared after her, totally confused, as he watched Hugh quickly pace up to her with the open umbrella.

"Goodnight, Miles," she called over her shoulder.

"What, that's it?" he said incredulously.

"You missed your window," Louisa called, back turning around.

"What? There's a kiss window?" he said, clearly confused.

"Uhuh. You've got to go after what you want, and you missed it," Louisa said with a wide smile as she took a couple of steps backward, heading towards her car. Hugh stifled a grin at her savvy comment.

"*Fuck*." Miles ran his fingers through his hair in frustration. He'd missed out on kissing her. Louisa turned around and paced to the car.

"Madame, you didn't call…" Hugh started to apologise for not being at the door when he reached for the car handle. Before

Hugh even realised, he saw Louisa being span around and pressed up against the car.

Miles grasped the side of Louisa's stunned face and crushed his lips to hers. After a beat, she slipped her arms around his waist and began to kiss him back. This wasn't a gentle kiss; it was one born from frustration, desperation and pure desire. Miles held her tightly as though he was worried she'd push him away, but once Louisa relaxed against him, he held on to her because he just didn't want to let go. Hugh discreetly turned around, giving them as much privacy as the bizarre situation would allow, still holding the umbrella over the two of them. They reluctantly pulled away from each other, both breathing deeply. Miles rested his forehead against hers, still holding her face.

"You like to live dangerously. Hugh is armed, you know," Louisa said, gazing into his blazing eyes.

Miles pulled back and stared down at her as she stifled a smile. "That kiss was worth the risk." He bent down again and gave her a tender kiss, coaxing her lips against his. Her stomach clenched as a low rumble in the back of his throat vibrated over her, as the kiss deepened. But it was over far too soon. Miles dragged his lips from hers and stepped away. Hugh coughed and turned back around, trying hard to keep his face impassive, but was failing miserably. He'd worked for Lady Alice Blackthorn for ten uneventful years; he had a distinct feeling that the new countess was going to keep him on his toes.

Miles reached out his hand and Hugh took it, giving it a firm shake. "Thank you for not shooting me."

"You're welcome, sir." He gave Miles a smirk, then opened up the back door of the car.

"I'm sorry," Miles said softly to Louisa as he helped her into the car.

"You're sorry you kissed me or because it was inappropriate?"

Miles leaned down and fixed her with his brilliant blue eyes. "Oh, I'm not apologising for kissing you." He straightened, then stepped back. "Goodnight, *just* Louisa, until next time." He shut the door and turned to head back to his house. Louisa let down the window as Hugh began to follow him with the open umbrella.

"Sir, let me…"

"I'm fine, Hugh, it's just a little rain."

"Next time?" called out Louisa.

Miles turned around, the rain falling hard on him, and he blasted her with his mega-watt smile. "Oh yeah, that kiss means that there will *definitely* be a next time." He gave her a cheeky wink and Louisa grinned back at him. He then put his hands in his jeans pockets and slowly walked backwards to his front door, whistling *Singing in the Rain*. Louisa laughed at his nonchalant performance, indifferent to the rain pouring over him and his blatant disregard for decorum. Louisa closed up her window, leaned back into the plush leather seat and let her fingertips drift over her lips.

Until next time; when everything would inevitably change.

14

MILES TOO MUCH

MILES PULLED OFF HIS soaked shirt and toed off his wet shoes, before peeling himself out of his drenched jeans. *That kiss was most definitely worth the risk,* he thought to himself with a smirk. Leaving his shoes by the door, he gathered up his wet clothes and headed to the laundry room. His eye caught sight of the housewarming gift Louisa had brought him, sitting on the table. He scooped it up and, after dropping off his wet clothes, he headed into the lounge.

It was beautifully wrapped in silver paper and a white bow. Miles pulled at the ribbon and let it drop to the floor, then made quick work of the silky paper, only to reveal a cardboard box. He prised open the top and peered inside. The first thing that struck him was the worn state of the black leather case the box housed. He carefully pulled out the case and rested it on the coffee table, staring at it for a second. The small brass plaque with The Martin Committee logo made his pulse spike as realisation hit. His impatience got the better of him and he flipped open the brass clasps, opened up the case and took in a sharp breath. There, nestled in slightly worn blue velvet, was a beautiful brass trumpet with distinct mother-of-pearl keys. Miles took in the engraved detail of the magnificent instrument and let his fingers flutter over the letters. It was every trumpeter's dream to own a Martin, but this was so much more. Miles lifted out the cream envelope with the Sotheby's logo on it and carefully opened it up. His hands trembled a little as he pulled out the weighty certificate of authenticity and read it. The beautiful trumpet had been one of Miles Davis's, custom-made by The Martin Committee, complete with serial number, along with the legendary musician's name engraved beneath their logo.

Louisa had bought him one of Miles Davis's trumpets! How had she even... where did she...? Miles slumped back into the settee, totally stunned. It was rare to find a Miles Davis trumpet for sale; they had often been gifted by the musician to friends, so to find one was in itself exceptional. Added to that, the instrument was worth a small fortune but to Miles, it was priceless.

LOUISA STARED OUT OF the window as the rain poured down with a soft smile on her face. *He'd kissed her!* Louisa couldn't remember the last time a man had kissed her so forcefully, without a care in the world as to who was watching or who she was. Her stomach flipped just thinking about it. Louisa's eyes flitted to the rear view mirror where she could see Hugh's focused attention on the road ahead. *What must he be thinking?* It was hardly ladylike behaviour, being kissed passionately in the middle of the street in the pouring rain. But wasn't that the whole point? Miles didn't *know* who she was and didn't give a damn that she was a countess.

Her attention was drawn to her phone, indicating an email, and she glanced at the screen to see who it was from. Miles Keane's name flashed on her screen and she immediately opened it up.

To: Louisa

From: Miles Keane
Subject: Miles too much!

Dear Just Louisa,

I am very rarely lost for words but somehow you have rendered me speechless. Thank you. Your housewarming gift is far too generous and will have pride of place in my music room.

I hope I can do the prestigious instrument justice when I play it to an audience of one: you.

Thank you for tonight. Thank you for the priceless gift but most of all, thank you for the kiss in the rain.

Until next time...
Miles

Louisa smiled down at her phone. *Miles too much?* Yes, that was exactly what he was; he was definitely far, far too much.

15

MILES AWAY

"SO, WHAT THE HELL do you do at a garden party?" Lottie adjusted strap of her bra under the silk slip dress she was wearing. She'd been tempted to go braless but since she'd be meeting the Countess of Holmwood today, she thought a display of nipples might be inappropriate.

"I've no idea. You're the English person here; you're better equipped for this than me. Drink tea I suppose and eat cucumber sandwiches." He shot her an irritated sideward glance and instantly regretted inviting her to the event.

He'd hardly seen Lottie apart from accompanying her to a boutique opening a few days ago. Today's invite, he now realised, was clearly a mistake. Her presence was already annoying him.

Miles pulled his shirt cuff straight and brushed down his trouser legs nervously. He'd just picked up Lottie from her flat and was on the way to the Blacks Club for the garden party hosted by Lady Blackthorn. The prestigious event was held in early June to mark the beginning of summer, but today, CASPO was also officially introducing Miles as the new ambassador of the charity.

He felt nervous and it was probably because he knew he'd be a little out of his depth again at the illustrious venue. The last time he'd been there was on his blind date. It probably also had to do with the fact he'd have to give a small acceptance speech. This would be the first public event he'd be speaking at since the shooting. He'd spent the last five years avoiding events where there were crowds. Lottie was oblivious to his nervousness. He'd only invited her at the last minute because Amanda couldn't make it, as Grace was unwell. Miles had hoped he would've been able to ask Louisa, seeing as she knew the venue and the charity, but from the tone of her emails over the last week it was obvious she had a heavy schedule. There was also the fear of rejection too. Their emails had been light-hearted, as Miles had kept to safe topics, discussing his recent visit to Worchester and Duke's antics.

Miles had spent the few days after Louisa's visit with Amanda and the children. They had fallen into a routine of either Miles travelling up to Worchester for a few days or Amanda and the children coming down to London every couple of weeks. Miles was still very much part of their lives. He was the father figure they needed and a constant reminder of where they came from. For Miles, it was his way of clinging on to the brother he missed every day. He'd confided in Amanda about Louisa, omitting too many details, mainly because he didn't actually have any. He scowled as Lottie adjusted her far-too-low-cut dress, and again second-thought his decision to invite her.

"Believe it or not, not all English people live like the Blackthorns." Lottie rolled her eyes at him. "And why are we in a cab?"

"I didn't feel like driving. The traffic is awful on a Saturday and to be honest, I only drive when I'm going out of London." The last thing he wanted to do while he was nervous was to drive around in London and then avoid alcohol all afternoon.

"What's Lady Alice like, then?"

"She a very nice lady. Today isn't only to introduce me. She holds this event as a thank you to the donators."

"Oh, I see. Well, I'm looking forward to seeing inside the exclusive Blacks Club."

LOUISA SMOOTHED DOWN HER pretty, feminine dress as she stepped out of her car. Hugh gave her an appreciative nod. She'd decided to wear a lace dress that was fitted around the bodice and flared out from the waist. She'd replaced her usual stilettoes for a high, thicker-heeled sandal, seeing as she would be walking over the grounds today.

"I'll be close by, my lady, if you need to leave." Louisa gave him a relieved smile. Today was going to be the first public event Louisa was attending since coming back to the UK. The people she would be meeting were known to her, but this would be her first outing as the returning, divorced Countess of Holmwood.

Louisa hadn't realised how much having Gerard by her side had become a habit; someone to hide behind or lean on. Her recent trip back to New York for the yearly dinner of one of the charities she and Gerard championed – an obligation her good breeding and sense of duty couldn't avoid – had compounded that. It was frighteningly easy slipping back into her role as Gerard's partner, and Louisa had a distinct feeling that that was the whole point of Gerard's invitation – another of his subliminal messages that he wanted her back.

Hugh gave her an encouraging smile and she took comfort in the fact her loyal driver, bodyguard and friend had her back. She was ever grateful that Alistair had recommended his ex-military friend to her family.

Louisa stepped into Blacks and her stomach clenched. Today would also be the day Miles Keane found out who she really was. Their last few emails they'd sent to each other had been fun and flirty. He'd asked about her trip and she'd brushed it off, avoiding any details, but it hadn't deterred him. The last email he'd sent mentioned the garden party and Louisa was tempted to tell him that she'd also be there but she decided against it at the very last minute.

Mr Thomas gave her a wide smile and quickly went over a few details with her before she was escorted into the garden. The gardens looked beautiful. Lush grass stretched out, topped with the various trees in full bloom. Blacks Club was a piece of English countryside right in the heart of London. Over the years, many investors had tried to buy the prestigious property, from other rich families to Arab sheiks and more recently Russian billionaires, but the Earl of Holmwood would never part with what used to be his ancestors' London home. He'd converted it into the exclusive club in the early 80s, when all the socialites were spending obscene amounts of money. It was an instant hit, providing exclusivity and of course privacy. Now the club was more like a private country club that also welcomed families to use some of the facilities.

Louisa scanned the grounds where various marquees had been set up and the croquet lawn was being arranged. There would also be the reinstating of the annual polo match where the Blackthorn team played against the donator's team. This was the one area Alistair enjoyed and probably the only reason he was attending today. Louisa spotted Alistair checking his horses at the far end of the field and waved to him. He smiled widely and jogged up to her.

"Hey, how are you feeling?" He bent down to kiss her cheek, then gave her cheek a quick rub with his beard.

"Stop it! I'll be all red. And I'm feeling nervous enough already. Where's Mama?"

"In the lounge, knocking back Pimms with Margot. Melissa is flapping around and Robert keeps trying to calm her down. It's like an Oscar Wilde farce, so stay out here with me and let's go check out the Champagne tent," he said with childlike enthusiasm.

"Sounds like a brilliant idea. Who's playing on your team today?" Louisa eyed her brother. It would be the first public match Alistair would be playing in since his accident.

"Eddie, Tim and Gordon. Robert's going to be umpire." Alistair picked up two Champagne flutes and passed one to Louisa.

"Gordon's here?"

"Not yet, but he will be – that's if he and Emily haven't had another fight." He rolled his eyes and Louisa's brow shot up. "Don't ask." He made a face and shuddered. "So are you ready for this?"

"I will be. We've been lucky with the weather." Louisa shielded her eyes as she looked up at the clear sky.

"We sure have. Flying in this was a dream." Alistair grinned at his sister.

"Do not tell me you flew Mama in?"

"Yes, I did."

"How was that?"

"Surprisingly good. Oh watch out, her she comes." He nodded to where their mother was coming out of the French windows of the lounge and onto the stone-paved terrace. Alistair and Louisa set off towards where the tables had been placed and where Lady Alice had decided to sit.

"Hello darling, you look absolutely lovely."

Louisa kissed and greeted her mother affectionately and took in her flushed cheeks. "How many Pimms have you had Mama?"

"Don't be ridiculous. Only a couple." Lady Alice waved her hand dismissively. Louisa guided her mother into a chair and grabbed a few glasses of water from a passing waiter. "Have you checked everything's in order?"

"Mama, Melissa is an excellent organiser and Mr Thomas has the most efficient staff. You sit here and enjoy yourself with

Margot and let them take care of everything," Louisa said, giving her a reassuring pat on her shoulder. This was the first garden party her mother had taken a back seat to. Margot made a huge fuss of her friend and Melissa made a point of explaining what order the various events would take place in, just so she felt part of the day.

As soon as the clock stuck three, the first of the guests began to arrive. Louisa knocked back her Champagne and gave Alistair a grim look, then headed towards the guests. Alistair called out behind her, "Work it baby," and Louisa threw him a thunderous look over her shoulder, which only made him laugh loudly.

Miles paid the taxi and helped Lottie out of the car. She tried hard not to look too dumbstruck as she took in the impressive club and the vast grounds, which were beautifully decorated. They were guided towards the terrace and welcomed by Mr Thomas, who pointed out to Miles where Margot and Lady Alice were. As soon as Miles walked out of the main building and on to the terrace, there was a distinct shift of everyone's attention. It was a subtle change in some and blatant in others, but regardless, Miles Keane had made a definite impact on the guests of the party. The women straightened their posture and fluffed their hair and the men regarded him warily, seeing how they measured up to him. Most didn't.

"This place is so classy," Lottie whispered to Miles, her eyes as wide as saucers as she watched the army of waiters gracefully walking around the many guests with silver trays laden with Champagne, Pimms and a colourful array of canapés. "No tea or cucumber sandwiches in sight, and they've got horses too – look." She pointed to where the polo field was and Miles blew out a sharp breath. *He was so out of his depth.*

"Come on. We need to go and say hello to Lady Alice." He guided her to the terrace. "Now remember, you call her Lady Blackthorn, my lady or madame." Miles reminded her, not wanting to offend anyone.

"Okay. Shit, I'm nervous. This is way more posh than I expected. Do I look alright?" Miles gave her a reassuring smile. The woman earned thousands walking down catwalks and was photographed half-naked, yet a garden party hosted by the aristocracy had her second-guessing her appearance. Miles shook his head at the very idea.

"Oh, Mr Keane, it's so nice to see you again." Lady Alice offered her hand and Miles took it, giving it a gentle shake.

"Thank you, Lady Blackthorn. It's pleasure to see you again." He greeted Margot who was to his right and then introduced Lottie to them both. She nervously shook their hands and then accepted a glass of Champagne from a waiter.

"You must meet my son." Lady Alice's eyes lit up as Alistair approached them. "Darling, this is Miss Price and Miles Keane, our new ambassador."

Alistair gave the couple a polite smile and shook both their hands. "Welcome to Blacks."

"Thank you, sir. It's a pleasure to be here; the gardens are beautifully transformed."

"Well my mother knows how to throw a great garden party," Alistair said wryly.

"Oh, this is nothing. When James, my late husband was alive, we used to throw some very grand parties at Holmwood. All sorts of people used to come, remember? Hopefully, now my daughter's back, she'll start up the tradition again."

"Your daughter?"

"Yes, she's the actual Countess of Holmwood now and she's recently back from America." Lady Alice's attention was diverted for a moment as a waiter collected the empty glasses off the table. "You'll meet her soon. I think she was talking to one of our big donors."

"Yes, my sister knows how to work an event and get more pledges. The Blackthorn women are born charmers; unfortunately, the Blackthorn men are less so," Alistair said with a wide grin and a hushed tone. Miles took an instant liking to the Earl Blackthorn. He was approachable and was less intent on ceremony, plus he seemed to have a wicked sense of humour. "Well, that's what we're all here for isn't? Boost the charity – and thanks to Mr Keane here, we've seen a distinctive jump in revenue." Margot gave Alistair a stern look and he winked at her.

"I was trying to place you and then I remembered that my grand-daughter was a huge fan of yours. She had a poster of you pinned up in her room at Holmwood. Do you remember, Alistair?" Lady Alice looked to Alistair for confirmation.

"I do."

"I feel like I should apologise," Miles chuckled.

"I think my niece might be over it now, though. That was over five years ago."

"Is she here?"

"Celeste? Sadly, no. She's away doing a grand job volunteering in…" Lady Alice paused for a moment as she tried to remember where Celeste actually was. Maybe Louisa was right: she should probably lay off the Pimms. "Erm, in South America somewhere at a school, but she'll be back for the ball though."

Miles furrowed his brow at Lady Alice's comment. *Did she just say her grand-daughter's name was Celeste?*

Miles's confused thoughts were disrupted by the sound of Melissa's distinct voice. "Gordon's just arrived, thank goodness." She rolled her eyes at Alistair, then turned to greet Miles and Lottie. Miles narrowed his eyes at her, blindly shook her hand, then introduced Lottie but his mind was trying to process what he'd just heard. He suddenly had a very bad feeling. His eyes darted from Melissa to Alistair and then to Lady Alice.

Before he could process his erratic thoughts, Lady Alice spoke. "Oh, there you are, darling. Come and meet Mr Keane." Miles's eyes shot up to where Lady Alice was looking just over to his left. There, through a sea of guests, a familiar beautiful woman stepped towards where Lady Alice was now standing.

Miles's eyes widened and he was sure all the blood had drained from his face. *It was Louisa, his Louisa.* She looked stunningly elegant in her ivory dress as the sun shone behind her, picking out the auburn flecks in her hair. He stared, dumbfounded, as his brain started to piece everything together. When he'd heard the name Celeste, that was the first warning sign; it wasn't a common name, and paired with Alistair… *what were the chances?* Miles blinked rapidly behind his sunglasses, glad Louisa or anyone else couldn't see the shock reflected in them.

"Mr Keane, may I present my daughter the Countess of Holmwood."

Louisa was about to say that they'd met, but Miles's hand shot out for her to shake. "Pleased to meet you, Lo… my lady."

"And you, Mr Keane." Louisa stared at the handsome face of Miles and her heart plummeted. He hadn't even acknowledged that he knew her. He'd almost gaped at her and then his stance had changed immediately. It wasn't a subtle change. He'd stiffened the second realisation hit. Gone was the charming Miles who'd flirted with Louisa, and in his place was a man in awe of the Countess of Holmwood.

"And this is Lottie Price."

Louisa forced herself to look at the young woman her mother was introducing her to, who was standing by Miles's side. She'd seen Lottie many times in all the photos at various events she and Miles had been photographed at. Unlike herself, Lottie Price was a face everyone knew. "I'm pleased to meet you, Miss Price." Louisa shook her hand, wishing she was somewhere else entirely.

"Likewise, my lady."

"I was just telling Mr Keane here about Celeste."

"Is that right?" Louisa shifted her attention to her mother and plastered on a fake smile, the one she'd used on every donator for the last hour.

"Celeste is your daughter?" Miles asked, wanting to make sure this wasn't a dream – or rather a nightmare – he was in.

"Yes, that's right, but she's away at the moment," Louisa said stiffly.

"Lady Blackthorn said she was volunteering in Peru."

Alistair narrowed his eyes for a moment and darted them between Louisa and Miles. His mother hadn't said Peru. He furrowed his brow and tried to work out what he was missing.

"That's it, Peru!" Lady Alice said, oblivious to the awkward atmosphere. "Louisa will be taking over from me as patron of CASPO, though we won't officially be announcing it until the ball."

"I see." Miles swallowed hard. *Was this why she'd kept her identity a secret? Had she wanted to see who Miles Keane was before CASPO confirmed he was the new ambassador? Was their whole interaction purely a fact-finding mission?* Every question that exploded into his head made him second-think what had happened between them. *Had he really read all the signs so wrong?* He scrambled to remember conversations they'd had but his mind was both in shock and confused.

He focused back on to what Lady Alice was saying. "So you'll no doubt be bumping into her at various functions and events."

"I'm sure we will." Miles shifted his gaze onto Louisa again and was met with a stiff smile.

"Well, it was *interesting* to meet you, Mr Keane, Miss Price, but I'm afraid I'm needed elsewhere." Louisa gave them both an insincere smile, then turned away and headed towards the Champagne tent. Something in Louisa's manner grazed Miles's mind but he just couldn't grasp it.

His jumbled thoughts were interrupted by Alistair. "I need to go and change out of this for the match. It was a pleasure to meet you both," Alistair said in a rush, then jogged up behind Louisa.

Louisa slipped on her sunglasses and tried hard not to succumb to the wave of disappointment that washed over her. She was on duty and she couldn't let Miles's blatant brush-off affect her. This was an important day for CASPO and her personal feelings needed to be shelved, for now. But however much she tried to internally manage her emotions, the bottom line was he'd behaved exactly how she'd expected. He'd forgotten who he knew and saw someone entirely different; added to that, he hadn't even acknowledged that they'd met before. As if that wasn't enough to make her feel wretched, he'd brought along a date, and not just any date, his go-to girl. Louisa all but marched to the tent and grabbed a fresh glass of Champagne and took a deep breath. She was a fool. *What did she expect?* The man was a serial man whore. *Why on Earth would he be even interested in her?*

"Want to tell me what that was about?" Alistair had caught up to her and was giving her a quizzical look.

"Just drop it, Alistair." Louisa took a drink from her glass and blinked back the tears behind her sunglasses.

"Oh, now I'm really intrigued. Do you know him?"

"I thought I did."

"You've lost me."

"Never mind; I'll tell you later." Louisa nodded to three men who were heading their way. "Duty calls."

Alistair grabbed hold of her arm. "Are you okay?"

"Yes, just a little disappointed. Let's just get through this blasted thing and I'll tell you all about it." She gave her brother a soft smile.

"Do I need to kick his ass?"

"God no, he has been the perfect gentleman – well, until now," she said with a sigh.

"Okay, I'm off to change. I expect you to cheer for me."

"Always."

The garden party was a great success. For the next hour, Louisa played her role and moved around the grounds, taking time to talk to the large donators and privileged guests who had been invited. She divided her time between the special guests who had benefitted from the work CASPO did and the ones who had generously donated. Lady Alice watched on as her daughter slipped easily into the role, a true professional, playing her part of stroking egos and flattering, all in aid of CASPO. The men stood taller when she spoke to them, laughed at her jokes and preened at her compliments. The women spoke kindly to her, hoping they'd be accepted into her tight inner circle, and Louisa listened intently to their opinions and observations, all part and parcel of making them feel important. It had been Lady Alice's role for over thirty years but she was more than happy to pass the reins over to her daughter. Louisa would bring a new energy to the charity and with the introduction of Miles and his showbiz appeal the charity would go from strength to strength.

Miles moved around the guests with the effervescent Melissa by his side. She made the necessary introductions to the many donators and Miles played his part as the new ambassador, but his attention was never far from Louisa. He watched on as she spoke to the various well-to-do gentlemen, all clearly entranced by Lady Louisa Blackthorn. They were polite and respectful in their stance and manner as they leisurely chatted but their eyes reflected their appreciation of the stunning woman in front of them.

Their paths hadn't crossed since their awkward introduction. Louisa had glided from guest to guest, giving everyone her attention, except him of course, and once again Miles felt out of his depth. He didn't know what the protocol was for demanding a countess talk to him, to ask her the hundreds of questions he couldn't stop asking himself. He looked down at the Champagne glass in his hand and sighed. *Had he blown it with her?* His gaze drifted around the party, taking in the well-bred aristocratic guests that Louisa seemed so comfortable with. He was nothing like them. This was who Louisa was. These were the people she'd grown up around and obviously where she belonged.

His attention was drawn to Lottie's girlish giggle. She'd been asked by one of the CASPO staff to join them in a game of croquet and she was enjoying the attention, away from Miles.

Lottie was used to being the centre of attention whenever they were at an event and if she wasn't, she made sure she became it. Miles was sure her over-enthusiastic display was part of that. Lottie had garnered some of the spotlight but it paled in comparison to the attention Louisa seemed to inadvertently command.

Miles made his way back to where Lady Alice and Margot were sitting, guided by the now rather tired Melissa. They were to go over the order of events regarding the official announcement of Miles's ambassadorship.

"So, Mr Keane, are you ready to be thrown to the wolves?" Lady Alice's eyes twinkled as she spoke and Miles chuckled.

"Well, if I wasn't nervous before, I certainly am now, my lady." His palms were sweating at the thought of standing up in front of the hundred or so guests. It wasn't a large crowd by any means. It didn't compare to the tens of thousands Keane Sense had performed in front of but nevertheless, it was still daunting.

"All a bit much?" Lady Alice waved her hand in the direction of the guests.

"You could say that. I'll be honest; I'm a little out of my depth." He hoped Lady Alice couldn't detect the real apprehension in his voice.

Lady Alice's eyes softened at his candid comment and she immediately felt for the handsome man. "You know I married into all this?" Miles furrowed his brow, unsure of what she meant. "The aristocracy."

Miles said a silent "Oh," realising she'd mistaken his unease with the environment, rather than the situation he was in. She wasn't completely wrong but there was more to his discomfort than being surrounded by the aristocracy.

"My family were lawyers. My father worked for the company that dealt with my late husband's businesses. He wasn't even a partner. Margot's father was one of the partners though." Margot nodded in confirmation.

"So how did you meet the Earl?"

"Remember those parties I mentioned at Holmwood?" Miles nodded. "Well it was at one of those. James suggested to the then Earl, his father, to throw a garden party for his employees and their families. Margot's father and mine were invited and so were we."

"Oh, I see."

"I'd never met an Earl before; I hadn't even known who James was. I remember Margot was engaged to Charles by then." Lady Alice looked to Margot for confirmation.

"Yes, that's right. He was the other partner's son. Alice was a bit out of sorts because she knew no one except me and I was with Charles." Margot chuckled at the memory.

"I was. This huge stately home with acres of land and all the gentry around, it was so daunting – and a little boring. Anyway, I went for a walk along the lake and generally had a snoop around and ended up at the stables. Well, James came into the stables all dressed up ready for the polo match, and I was immediately taken with him. He introduced himself as just James and we chatted for a while. He was so charming and easy and of course so handsome."

"He was very handsome," agreed Margot and patted her dear friend's hand.

"I had no idea he was the Earl's son, heir to Holmwood. He spent far too long talking to me, considering he had guests and a game to play. Imagine my surprise when I later found out who he was."

"I can imagine," Miles said dryly and his eyes flitted to where Louisa was now crouched down, talking to a man in a wheelchair.

"I probably wouldn't have spoken to him if I had known. Anyway, to cut a long story short, we ended up getting engaged within six months. So don't think that this has always been my way of life. You just get used to it."

"I'm not sure I could ever get used to it, my lady."

"Ever is a long time, Mr Keane. Come on, I think it's about time you were made official."

Lady Alice made her way to the small raised portion on the terrace, where a podium and microphone had been set up. The guests immediately gathered around to listen to the revered countess. After a few words of thanks to everyone for their support, she then made a short speech, proudly introducing Miles as CASPO's new ambassador. She presented him with an official plaque, which he accepted graciously to a very enthusiastic round of applause.

Miles stepped up to deliver his acceptance speech and held on tightly to the sides of the podium, to stop his hands from shaking. He took a deep breath and tried to focus on the few guests he'd spoken to, hoping their familiar faces would anchor him and make the whole ordeal less terrifying. He delivered his well-practiced speech without a hitch. It was eloquent and humorous, showing that well-documented charm he was known for, and every guest was mesmerized by his smooth delivery. This was a man who was used to attention, a man who had thousands of fans enthralled with every performance. Tragic circumstances and five years away from the limelight hadn't quashed that unique gift. Louisa watched him speak with sincerity about the work CASPO did and how he felt honoured to be part of such a worthy cause, a cause close to his heart. Louisa caught a glimpse of the Miles she'd spent time with while he'd cooked dinner and served her éclairs. Her stomach clenched at the memory of who they'd been for those few hours and she sighed, knowing they'd never be like that again.

Miles began to relax as he spoke, his unease dissipating with every second that passed. Today was a personal milestone for him. It may not have been a huge event or audience but it was a definitely a start. He allowed his eyes to scan the crowd of people in an attempt to spot Louisa. He finally found her off to the side, standing with Alistair. Her expression gave nothing away and when he ended his speech, she applauded along with the rest of the guests.

Miles stepped down and had the sole intention of going over to speak with her but he was immediately drawn into the crowd of guests, who were intent on officially congratulating him.

As Louisa made her way to the polo field with Alistair, glad to have a small respite from socialising, they were joined by Gordon and Emily. After the usual pleasantries and brief catch-up, Gordon lifted his chin in the direction of the terrace. "You were with Miles last time I saw you here."

"Yes, that's right. We were discussing him being an ambassador. It was very hush hush, then," Louisa said as an explanation, then immediately turned to Emily who looked bored and asked her about moving back to the UK. She wasn't all that fond of Emily, who always seemed to be either unhappy or indifferent and any conversation with her seemed to be forced.

"Sorry to hear about your divorce," Emily said and her sincerity took Louisa by surprise. Gordon's attention shifted from Alistair, hearing his wife's comment, and he momentarily looked uncomfortable.

"Thank you. It is what it is," Louisa said with a slight shrug, feeling that it was a little odd that Emily would mention it, then turned her attention to Gordon. "So, are ready for the match?"

"Yep. It'll be good to play with this rabble again." He gestured to Alistair, Eddie and Tim, who had now joined them, all kitted out in their black and white uniform.

"Well, we'll be cheering you on and I hope you win. It'll be me presenting the trophy and prizes."

"Well that's an incentive to win if ever I heard one," Gordon said with a wide smile and Emily's face dropped.

The polo match was watched with great enthusiasm. The guests marvelled at the skill of the players as they galloped and controlled their horses with incredible proficiency. It was both thrilling and entertaining. It was good to see Alistair display the adventurer side of himself again, with that Blackthorn flair he'd always had. Louisa gave her mother's hand a squeeze as she gasped at a rather reckless manoeuvre her son had executed.

"He's determined to give me a heart attack today," Lady Alice muttered. "What with the helicopter ride and now showing off on the polo field."

Louisa chuckled. "He's just being Alistair again, Mama. I think it's time, don't you?"

Lady Alice gave her daughter a warm smile. "Yes, it's been long overdue and I think it has a lot to do with you being back."

The crowd cheered at a masterful stroke that secured the Blackthorn team's victory, and Louisa and Lady Alice jumped to their feet and joined in the jubilation.

Miles watched Louisa hand Alistair the impressive gold cup, hugging him tightly and whispering something to him. He thanked her and smiled widely down at his sister. It was obvious that they were close and when they turned to have their picture taken, Miles noticed that they still held on to each other in silent solidarity. He also noted that when Louisa congratulating each of the winning team members, Gordon let his hand linger around her waist, confirming his previous suspicions: Gordon saw her as more than just a friend.

The team members were the centre of attention and Louisa stepped back, allowing them to enjoy centre stage. It did her heart good seeing Alistair genuinely happy. He avoided public events and Louisa knew he'd only agreed to today because she was there and he was surrounded by his friends and family. She took the opportunity to slip away and headed towards the club in the search of a stiff drink.

"Louisa!" Louisa stiffened at the sound of Miles's voice calling out to her. She marched on without breaking a stride, ignoring him. "Lady Blackthorn." She flinched at the use of her title. It was no use; he was just a couple of feet away from her now and she didn't want to draw unnecessary attention.

She came to a halt and pivoted around to face him. "Not now, Mr Keane," she said with more force than was required.

"Stop with the 'Mr Keane'. I'm Miles, remember?" he said with frustration and he ran his fingers through his hair.

"I remembered just fine. I think it was you that forgot," Louisa bit back and Miles clenched his jaw and had the good grace not refute her comment.

He momentarily closed his eyes, then blew out a breath. "Sweet Jesus, all this time... man, I didn't see that coming." He stared at her stony expression still trying to come to terms with this curveball he'd been served. "You're the Countess of Holmwood," he said deliberately. "Why the fu... why didn't you tell me?"

"That right there is why I didn't tell you." Louisa narrowed her eyes at him.

"I don't understand."

"The way you're looking at me now, I'm not *just* Louisa."

"I was shocked. Shi..." He paused for a second, gathering himself. His natural instinct was to curse and he was having a hard time reining that impulse in. He didn't know much about the aristocracy but he was pretty sure cursing in front of them was against protocol. "I thought it was because you were still married and hadn't finalised your divorce. I thought... God knows what I thought, but it sure wasn't this." Louisa let out an appalled huff. "What is it? Why are you so... I don't know... angry?"

"I'm not angry at you."

"Really? Well you sure as hell *ain't* happy," he said accentuating his American drawl. "Did I offend you? Me not acknowledging that I knew you – offended you?" he pushed, stepping closer to her, but she stood her ground.

"I'm not offended. I don't get offended. I'm disappointed. I misjudged… forget it. How do you Americans say it… *My bad.*" Her tone was mildly sarcastic.

"Louisa, I can still call you Louisa, right?" Louisa clasped her hands together, blew out a breath and nodded. This is exactly why she had said nothing. Everything had changed. He didn't even feel comfortable calling her by her name. "I was caught off-guard. You weren't exactly forthcoming about who you were. What did you expect? You knew I was coming today, that I'd meet you." Her flippant remark, at their first date, about bumping into each other at events made perfect sense now. "Why didn't you tell me who you were?"

Louisa swallowed, suddenly feeling bad that she hadn't been up front with him, but she had her reasons. "Because I knew you'd look at me differently, like you're looking at me right now?"

"How am I looking at you?" Miles stepped a little closer, they were only a couple of feet apart now and Louisa felt her heart start to beat faster. There was no point in hiding why she'd withheld her identity. He knew who she was and everything was different; he may as well know how she felt.

"Like I'm untouchable. Like I'm some delicate creature that you need to approach with caution, with consideration and reverence. Like I'm some object to look up to, and not like I'm *just* Louisa who loaded your dishwasher and ate your steaks." *Who you kissed in the pouring rain.* "I wanted that to last for as long as possible because I knew that after today, you'd never look at me that way again."

"Louisa, I…"

Before he made some excuse that was purely to placate her, she interrupted him. "Look Miles, its fine, really. I understand. You go back to whatever and whoever and I'll get on with my role. We had a couple of dates; it was fun. But right now, I need to be the Countess of Holmwood. I don't have time for this." He went to say something but she stopped him again with a nudge of her chin, towards where Lottie was obviously searching for him. "You've abandoned your *date,* Mr Keane."

Miles shifted his gaze and saw Lottie trying to walk as elegantly as possible in her stiletto heels that kept sinking into the grass. He turned back to where Louisa was standing. "Louisa, can we just…"

"It was interesting while it lasted, Mr Keane. I'll see you around." And with those parting words, Louisa turned around and walked into Blacks, leaving a frustrated and crushed Miles. *He'd blown it.*

16

LOST FOR WORDS

NOT EVEN DUKE COULD pull Miles out of his cheerless mood. The puppy jumped about in welcome as Miles stepped back into his otherwise empty home. He threw his keys on the table, then bent down to ruffle Duke's soft brown coat. After he had spoken to Louisa, she spent the remaining hour flitting from one guest to another. She was never alone, not even once. Whether it was intentional or coincidence Miles wasn't sure, but either way, he knew they couldn't have a private conversation with so many people around observing them. He resigned himself to the fact that whatever they needed to say had to be said another time, without an audience. One way or another, he was going to get to talk to her and if it meant badgering her with emails until she conceded, he wasn't above doing that – protocol be damned.

The remainder of the garden party had gone smoothly and once the clock had struck six, the guests began to leave. Miles dropped off a cranky Lottie. She'd hinted that she wanted to see his house, but the last thing he wanted was Lottie's company or her anywhere near his home. Miles sauntered into his lounge and headed straight for the drinks cabinet. He needed a stiff drink. He still couldn't believe Louisa was *the* Countess of Holmwood. After pouring himself a large vodka, he made his way into his office and fired up his laptop. Well now he knew who she was, he may as well find out everything about her. It only seemed fair, seeing as she'd done her own meticulous research on him.

The first thing that struck Miles was how few photos were out there of her. There were a number of pictures of the family, when Louisa and Alistair were young. These were mainly official photos, taken over the years when the Earl had been featured in magazines and newspapers. There were also articles documenting Alistair's illustrious military career. The heir to the Blackthorn estate definitely looked the part of dashing pilot, all geared up in his RAF uniform with a crew cut and clean shaven, in complete contrast to the bearded, longer-haired man he'd met this afternoon. Miles scanned the few articles that praised Alistair as he'd moved up the military ranks, until he came across one reporting that Alistair had gone missing in action, not far from the Pakistani border. Miles clicked on the following links, which detailed the plight of the future Earl and his squadron. The story reported that due to Alistair's skill and bravery, he'd managed to land the damaged helicopter and save his nine-man squadron but had sustained serious injuries. No details were given but as Miles scrolled down, he came across a number of blurry photos obviously taken from far away. He looked the shadow of the cheery man Miles had seen in the previous photos. Gone was his wide smile and fearlessness and its place was a badly bruised, bandaged-up, broken man in a wheelchair. Miles read the attached article and gaped. He then zoomed in on the grainy photo. *Alistair had lost his left leg!* Miles sat back in his chair and replayed the afternoon in his head. At no time had he even noticed that Alistair was missing a leg. *He'd played polo, for goodness sake!*

Miles scanned for more articles but only came up with one in *The Telegraph* that mentioned Alistair had been decorated for bravery. Miles took a drink from his glass, relishing the burn it gave him, and mulled over what he'd read. Louisa's hint of having experienced tragedy now made sense. A few of the articles had mentioned her coming back from the States to support her family, though there were no photos of her until her father had died a couple of years later. *She'd lived in America?* Miles furrowed his brow at this new piece of information and huffed to himself. He was pretty sure he'd asked her if she'd ever visited the US and she'd declined to reply.

Miles zeroed in on another grainy photo taken of her. Again, it must've been from an unofficial photographer but even blurry, he could recognise her distinctive posture and beautiful face sitting next to Alistair and Lady Alice, in what looked like a private cemetery. To the left of her was a very distinguished looking man who looked at least ten years older than her. Miles enlarged the photo so he could get a better look, but the photo was just not clear enough. The links underneath the article had Gerard Dupont highlighted and Miles immediately knew that this man was Louisa's husband. He wasted no time in clicking onto the link and was hit with over three million results. *Whoa! Who was this guy?*

The ring of his telephone in the quiet of his office made him jump. He looked at the screen and saw that it was Amanda. "Hey, how's Grace?" he asked.

"A bit better. Her temperature has dropped, thank goodness." Miles could hear the relief in Amanda's voice. "So tell me about the party; how did it go?"

"It went well. Lady Alice was very gracious and she sure knows how to do English garden party with style. They had a polo match and a croquet game set up. Who the hell still plays croquet? I felt like I was in Downtown Abbey, for Christ's sake!"

Amanda chuckled down the phone, imagining how out of his comfort zone he must've been. Barbequing in jeans and a T-shirt, knocking back a few beers was more Miles's style and she felt a tinge of guilt having abandoned him to cope on his own. "I'm sure you charmed everyone."

"I did feel like the freak show but I did tone down the American in me, just a bit," he said with a smirk.

"And your speech?"

"Went great, though I was a bit nervous," he said dismissively, catching Amanda's concerned tone. He didn't want to get into his hang-ups on public speaking right now. His eyes flitted to the screen, where hundreds of photos came up of Gerard Dupont and he pursed his lips. "You remember that date I had? The mom?"

"Uhuh, the auction date? You didn't really elaborate on your second date, though," Amanda teased. She'd asked him how it had gone and he'd brushed it off, so she'd not pushed for more details.

"Yeah well, funny thing is, I found out why she was so evasive about who she was."

"Oh, and?"

"Are you sitting down, 'cause you're never going to believe it?"

"I'm sitting down, just tell me!"

"She's Lady Louisa Blackthorn."

Miles was met with silence and he looked at his phone screen thinking he'd lost signal. "Amanda?"

"Sorry? As in Lady Alice's daughter?" Amanda asked deliberately, unable to mask her disbelief.

"The very same."

"I... but..."

Miles huffed. He could visualise Amanda's shocked face as she stumbled over her words. "Yeah, my reaction was pretty much the same when we were introduced. Didn't see that one coming."

For the next few minutes, Miles went over what had happened that afternoon. Amanda listened intently, still stunned that Miles had had two dates with the Countess, one in his home no less, and he had been none the wiser.

"So now she's pissed at me for, I don't know, not saying that I knew her or being shocked – or fuck knows. All I know is she was wasn't happy."

"Miles, you're going to have to make up."

"Make up! Did you not hear what I just said? She's angry at me and I can't very well go and knock on her door and demand to see her can I? She's... she's... fuck." His eyes homed in on a picture of Louisa and Gerard at some event with the Prince Albert of Monaco.

"What? She's what?" Amanda insistent tone pulled his attention away from the computer screen.

"She rubs shoulders with royalty, for Christ sake. Have you met her?"

"I did very briefly. I was at the offices when she came to take her mother out for lunch one time. She was really nice and made a point of coming to speak to me."

"Was this before or after my date?"

"Err, before... I think so, anyway."

"Shit, Amanda, I don't know what to do. I've been trolling the Internet trying to get as much information about her as possible."

"And, did you learn anything?"

"A bit. That's what I was doing when you called." He ran his fingers through his hair in exasperation. The more he thought about their time together, the more he felt wretched. He was pretty sure he must have offended her on so many levels during their dates and she'd had the good grace, or the audacity, depending on how you looked at it, not to say anything. He cringed, thinking about the blatant flirting, then he squeezed his eyes shut, remembering he'd mentioned something about hating titles. *Fuck!*

"Hang on. Let me get my laptop and we can do it together," Amanda suggested.

She was met with a grunt. While Miles waited for Amanda to return, he clicked on the various links and articles that detailed Louisa's succession to the Blackthorn estate and title. There was no reason given, only that Alistair Blackthorn, the present Earl of Blackthorn, had handed his title and inheritance to his younger sister. Miles found the information unusual but then wondered whether it had something to do with his accident.

"Her husband is really good looking," Amanda said, pulling Miles out of his thoughts.

"*Ex*. And that's not helping," he said mulishly.

"He's French and a billionaire businessman," continued Amanda.

"Yeah I see. Still not helping," he growled and Amanda smirked to herself. This was the first time she'd ever witnessed Miles unsure of himself. The man was the biggest player she'd ever met – women literally threw themselves at him. It was refreshing and amusing.

"She doesn't like the limelight. Most events they're at have him in the forefront and they don't refer to her as Lady Blackthorn, just Mrs Blackthorn-Dupont."

"Hmm, maybe she didn't want to laud it over everyone." Miles twisted his mouth, thinking over Louisa's behaviour. It had been obvious, even to him in his total ignorance, that she was well bred, but she didn't seem to stand on ceremony. Not in the restaurant and most certainly not in his home.

"Maybe, or maybe her husband didn't want her title to overshadow him?"

"Considering her title and his position, I would've thought they'd be more photos." Miles scrolled down, finding very few photos, not even a wedding picture.

"I think that they're not the kind who like their life looked at too closely. There isn't even anything about their divorce. No scandal. Nothing."

"How very civilised," Miles said dryly.

"So what are you going to do?"

"I'm not sure. But one way or another, I need to talk to her. How, I'm not sure. At least now I know more about her. Things make more sense."

"Like?"

"Her driver or bodyguard, why she was well known at the Blacks Club, why she's so… I don't know, knowledgeable. Christ, she loaded my dishwasher and dressed the salad. She must have an army of staff that do all that for her." He blew out a breath, trying hard to remember what other faux pas he must've have done.

"You like her, eh?"

"Yeah, I do."

"And knowing who she is, does it change that?"

"No, I just feel like its… I don't know… weird."

"Weird?"

"She's a countess, Amanda. Have you seen Holmwood? They have their own lake, a pavilion, even a pet cemetery… and so much more shit I don't even know what they are. What the hell are an orangery and a bathhouse? Man, I'm just getting to terms with the fact I've got a drawing room – which, by the way, I still don't know what it is – and from the spec I'm looking at on Holmwood House, they've a shit ton more: they have a library, a drawing room, formal sitting room, the Countess's sitting room, an anteroom, which I've no idea what that is either. And loads more rooms, that's without the gazillion bedrooms, plus an east wing and west wing! And staff? They have a whole army…" Miles ranted as every image relating to Louisa's life came at him. She was so out of his league. She was used to finery and an aristocratic lifestyle surrounded by class and steeped in a rich history. *The country he was born in was younger than her family heritage!* The Blackthorn name and estate, where Holmwood House was built, could be traced back to the 1300s.

"Miles, I get it, it's a big house. I can see it."

"Big house? Now that's an understatement."

"You're shocked."

"Shocked! No, I'm way past shocked. This is a whole new level we're talking about. Shocked was when I found out she was Lady Louisa Blackthorn. Now I know what that means, I'm astounded."

"Miles..." Amanda could hear the frustration and despair in his voice and it broke her heart, knowing that he was beating himself up about how he'd behaved. He'd changed over the last few weeks and Amanda knew it was all down to meeting Louisa.

"Amanda, I had this woman in my house. A woman who has hundreds of staff to do everything for her, and she arranged flowers in a wine bucket for me! I ran after her in the pouring rain and kissed her. *In the middle of the street, while her chauffeur held an umbrella for us!*"

"You did that? Wow, Miles, you really are a romantic," Amanda said in awe.

"Apparently, I could've been shot."

"What?"

"Never mind."

"What are you going to do?"

"I don't know."

"She is still just a woman you met and know. She must've liked you to go on a second date, go against protocol. Maybe you should just be how you were with her, like nothing's changed."

"But it has changed."

LOUISA RE-READ THE EMAIL that she knew would inevitably pop up. It had surprised her that it had taken Miles almost a day to send it, considering his tenaciousness in the past. Maybe he was too busy. Maybe he had plans after the garden party that ran into the next day. Louisa sighed – *who was she kidding? Of course he was busy; there was no maybe about it.* He was obviously busy with the skinny blonde model who seemed to be permanently attached to his side. *What a cliché!* Pop star and model, a match made in heaven.

Alistair peered at her over his teacup. "What's got you scowling first thing this morning?"

Louisa's eyes shot up from her phone to meet his arched brow, then she darted them towards her mother, who tilted her head towards her, waiting for her daughter to answer. Louisa had gone to Holmwood House after the garden party, deciding she needed to be away from London for the weekend. It also meant she could spend time with Alistair, putting together the plans for the activities weekend.

"I'm surprised you have that with you at the breakfast table. Don't you hate phones when you're dining?"

"Yes, just an oversight," Louisa mumbled. Her mother was right. It was a pet peeve of hers but after yesterday's fiasco, she'd secretly hoped to receive some sort of communication from Miles. She'd held on to her phone, like one of those thousands of people she abhorred, as though their whole life depended on it. "I'm off for a ride. I think I need some fresh air."

"I'll join you." Alistair rose from his seat before Louisa could object. "I'll get Martin to get Roxy saddled up for you until you change."

"Thank you, I won't be long."

Louisa all but dashed out of the door and headed to her suite. Once she was inside, she opened up the email again and read it for the third time.

To: Louisa Blackthorn

From: Miles Keane

Subject: Where and when?

Dear Louisa,

I've spent last night trying to find the right words to say and in the cold light of day, I'm still at a loss, and that's a first for me. Words usually come easy to me... except when directed at you.

What I do know, though, is that I want to see you, desperately so. You told me you were a woman of your word and, if I recall, you said you would see me again.

Tell me where and when.

Miles

Where and when? He made it sound so simple and why was he so desperate to see her? Louisa's head span with a hundred unanswered questions. The problem was she wasn't sure if she wanted all the answers. *A woman of her word* – he was blackmailing her into another meeting. Her first impulse was to send a curt refusal and be done with it but she knew that was her pride steering her. *She had him tongue tied? At a loss for words?* Louisa thought back over their first date when he'd fumbled at the start, then at the garden party when his surprise had made him falter. She should've felt some satisfaction in his unease but the truth was she didn't. Initially, she'd wanted to make Miles Keane, the cocky pop star, squirm as payback for ten years ago. Now though, having gotten to know him a little better, her thoughts had changed.

Louisa wasn't entirely sure what had made her so angry, because she had been. She'd denied it of course; ladies didn't get angry, didn't show extreme emotion, and were calm and controlled. But seeing him at the party, witnessing his shock, him not acknowledging that he knew her and, to add insult to injury, bringing a date, it was enough to forget her ingrained control and ladylike behaviour. A ride around the grounds and fresh air would hopefully bring her some much-needed perspective. Louisa set down her phone and changed into her riding clothes and quickly made her way to the stables.

"So, that Miles Keane was quite a success yesterday." Alistair gave Louisa a sideways glance. They were riding side by side at a leisurely pace around the estate's perimeter.

"Subtle, Alistair, really subtle." Louisa shook her head, knowing there was no way she'd get away from her brother's questioning. She was frankly surprised he'd taken so long.

"Subtle isn't my style. So, what's the deal between you two, then?"

"There's no deal. We've met before. Twice, actually." *Three times.*

"I don't understand; he made out he didn't know you."

"He didn't."

"Okay. Now I'm really confused. You've met him twice but he doesn't know you?" Alistair pulled up his horse until he stopped, causing Louisa to do the same. He cocked his eyebrow at her, waiting for an explanation. "Spill."

Louisa sighed and gave her brother a condensed version of Miles and her two dates. She omitted a few personal details, like the exorbitant housewarming gift she'd bought him and the reckless kiss in the rain but other than that, she'd given him all the facts.

He listened in silence and when Louisa finished, he blew out a sharp breath. "Wow. That's a bit underhand." He tilted his head at his sister.

"What?"

"Come on, you go on two dates with the guy. The first one he's expecting someone entirely different and no doubt he was shocked. He asks you out for a second one, after sending you a classy and expensive thank you present. So, the guy obviously liked you and then, knowing that at some point he's going to find out who you are, you don't give him a heads up? He must've been gobsmacked. Poor bugger."

"He turned up with a date." Louisa glared at him.

"And you kept your identity a secret," he countered. "I don't think there was much between them anyway – well, nothing serious. He probably had it arranged from before." Louisa snorted and Alistair chuckled at her reaction. "What's bothering you the most, that he didn't acknowledge you or he brought a date?"

Louisa's eyes shot up to his amused expression and she sighed. Her perceptive brother had hit the nail on the head. Yes, it had bothered her that Miles hadn't acknowledged her but seeing the stunning blonde model next to him had cemented all her deep-seated insecurities. She'd had over ten years of self-doubt in a marriage of convenience. Her self-confidence had been gradually worn down. Miles had given her the impression that he liked her, but seeing him with Lottie Price made her think that maybe he was just playing her after all. *Why bring a date?*

"The whole thing is bothering me." She gazed out over the lake to Holmwood House and sighed. "But probably the fact that things won't be the same."

"Well, of course it won't be. The guy is probably drowning right now. It's quite a big revelation, you know. Not only are you the Countess of Holmwood, you're the patron of the charity he's just committed himself to." Alistair watched Louisa look out over the green lawns and out to the woodlands that marked the end of their estate. It was obvious to him that Miles Keane had had an impact on his normally composed sister. "And he's been in touch since yesterday?"

Louisa nodded. "Yes. He wants to meet up. But I don't think it's a good idea."

"Because?"

"Because he's Miles Keane who no doubt has a little black book full of 20-something models, actresses and pop stars who he can call. He's not going to be interested in a divorced countess, in her very late 30s, with a daughter."

"He knew you were divorced and had a daughter before and he was still interested."

"He'll look at me differently."

"Probably."

"You're not helping!"

"Louisa, you're the countess. Whoever you meet is going to look at you in a different way. At least with Miles, he got to see who you were first."

"I'm not sure if I'm ready to get involved with anyone."

"You wouldn't have gone on a second date if you weren't ready." Alistair gave her a knowing look. "Give him at least the chance to explain himself."

Louisa blew out a sharp breath and then pursed her lips. She'd have to see him at some point. They'd have a number of events to attend and it wouldn't do to have an atmosphere. The problem was she was scared. If they met up, he might just politely apologise and back off and she couldn't very well ask him out.

Alistair nudged her, bringing her back from her erratic thoughts. "Come on, I'll race you back." His eyes widened in mischief and she was transported back to when they were children. He always goaded her into racing him, letting her almost win, then pipping her to the post right at the end.

"You'll win, Alistair, you always win."

"Come on, I'll give you a ten-second headstart," he teased and before he finished his sentence, Louisa tapped her leg against her horse and galloped off.

ALISTAIR OF COURSE WON, but it was still fun to gallop a little recklessly over the grass to the house. It had been a while for Louisa to spend time on the estate. She visited often but spent most of her time seeing to the business side. Alistair would meticulously walk her through every aspect and discuss future plans. Now that summer had arrived, the house would see a huge influx of visitors, meaning part of the house would be open to the public. Security was doubled and Louisa would now be confined to the top floor of the house, using the back stairs and a private entrance.

Holmwood House attracted a huge amount of tourism, plus it was hired out for events throughout the year, from weddings and parties to hosting various festivals. The estate also supported local businesses that sold produce and crafts in shops that were housed in what used to be the old dairy. There was a tearoom too, and Alistair had plans to convert some part of the house into an exclusive restaurant, all subject to Louisa's approval.

Louisa gazed out of her sitting room window and watched Alistair as he spoke to the various staff before the gates were opened at ten. For the next nine hours, the house would be on show. Gardens would be walked through, the rooms and antiquities would be admired and the facilities would all be well used. Alistair had employed many ex-service men and women, as well as locals to run the estate and had a stellar team that were both loyal and professional. From late March to the end of October, Holmwood House opened its gates to the public and every year, there had been a steady increase in visitors, all down to Alistair's forward thinking and hard work, and Louisa couldn't be more grateful.

She paced over to her phone and picked it up and opened up her email account. She needed to answer Miles. Alistair was right; he did deserve to explain himself. Her anger had cooled from yesterday, but she was still apprehensive. As for seeing him again, she wasn't sure if she was ready. Apart from her hesitance, Louisa had a full couple of weeks, organising her official takeover of CASPO as well as spending time at Holmwood. She would also be tied up in meetings with sponsors, press releases and organisation for the annual ball, which was in a few weeks' time, and Celeste was due home too. Duty came first. She was the Countess of Holmwood; where and when with Miles Keane would have to wait. Louisa looked down at her phone again and her stomach clenched. Everything had changed.

17

SURPRISE

HOW LONG DID YOU have to wait before sending another email? Was there a rule somewhere that specified the exact waiting period? Miles sipped his coffee and stared at the clouds floating across the sky, mulling over what his next move should be. His whole weekend had been consumed with Louisa. Had it been any other woman, he wouldn't have put so much thought into it. She would have been forgotten by now and he would have moved on. But Louisa wasn't any ordinary woman, she was extraordinary; added to that, she was the Countess of Holmwood.

Miles had woken up late and rather than go for his usual run, he'd used his personal gym and pool to release his frustration. The hour-and-a-half workout did little to rid his continuing thoughts of her. After showering, he threw on some grey lounge pants and headed to his music room; he always found the room comforting and calming. Music was where he found peace; whether he played or listened, he could lose himself amongst the melodies, empty his mind and find much-needed clarity.

Miles thought about talking to Melissa but then changed his mind. The less people knew about what had happened between

Louisa and himself, the better – and he had a distinct feeling Louisa wouldn't appreciate her private life being discussed. It had been two days since he'd sent the email and he'd heard nothing, not even a scathing reply which, right now, he'd have taken. Anything was better than this silence. His eyes drifted over to the beautiful trumpet Louisa had sent him. Maybe he should send it back; that might make her contact him. He placed his cup down on the wide windowsill and picked up the instrument. It was truly a magnificent trumpet. He'd tried to find one over the years but they were so very rarely put on the market. The cost would have been insignificant to Miles – he would've paid anything for one – but it was clear that Louisa must have pulled some serious strings to get this. Money couldn't always buy you want you wanted; it was connections – and from the look of it, Louisa most definitely had them.

Miles had spent the best part of his weekend doing as much research on Louisa and the Blackthorn family as he was able. He was never going to be so unprepared again. But as Amanda had said, there wasn't a huge amount about Louisa specifically. It seemed that her connections had kept her private life exactly that: private.

He scrolled over the few pictures that had been taken at the garden party by the one official photographer. They'd been posted up on the official CASPO site. The pictures were mainly of him and Lady Alice, seeing as it was the day they officially announced his ambassadorship but there were a couple of Louisa as she handed Alistair the polo trophy. She really was a stunning woman, elegant in an understated way, and yet she inadvertently drew everyone's attention.

Protocol be damned! He wasn't going to just let her slip away. He was sure he hadn't misjudged the connection they'd had. Miles stormed up the stairs to his office and brought his computer to life with a sharp shake of the mouse. He'd blackmail her, coerce her, guilt her and badger her into a response. He wasn't above any of it. She was the one with class… him, not so much! *What was the worse she could do? Ghost him? Maybe have Hugh shoot him? He'd been shot at before and survived – had the scar to prove it.* Louis's words came unbidden into his head, his brother's mantra when they were first starting out; "You have to believe it to achieve it." He'd said those words over and over to Miles, and proved their worth when his vision of their band became everything Louis had hoped for and much, much more. Well it was time to put those wise words into practice.

Louisa. Miles shook his head. It was beyond bizarre that her name was the female version of his brother's. *Was it an omen, some other worldly sign?* Did she come into his life to bring him out of the vast void he'd felt over these last five years? She certainly brought him hope, and for the first time, a woman had played him at his own game. Two dates they'd had and she was constantly in his thoughts. *He was so screwed.* Well, he hoped she was ready for the challenge, he wasn't above playing dirty to get what he wanted.

To: Louisa Blackthorn
From: Miles Keane
Subject: Precious gift

Dear *Just* Louisa,

I'm faced with a dilemma. Where do I send the beautiful housewarming gift you gave me? I don't think it's right that I keep it under the circumstances. I could give it to Melissa to pass on to you or just leave it at CASPO's offices. Maybe you could forward your address and I'll have it delivered.

Miles

If she didn't respond, he'd turn up at CASPO with it and give it to Melissa. If she was going to ignore him, there would be consequences. She wasn't going to call the shots anymore.

Louisa looked at her phone and her heart lurched. *He wanted to give back his gift? Was he trying to insult her? And what did he mean "under the circumstances"?* Louisa clenched her jaw. This was because she hadn't replied to his email. He was throwing a tantrum. She'd had every intention of replying but she wanted to be less emotional when she did. She needed to be objective and have time before she replied. This email, though, had her emotions all fired up again. *Just Louisa? What was that for? A reminder of what they'd been?* Louisa looked out of the car window as Hugh negotiated the London Monday morning traffic and sighed to herself. She didn't want the trumpet back. She'd pulled in favours and called in on her prominent contacts to coax the seller to part with it. The cost was trivial to her; it was the sentimental value it held for Miles that had mattered and she'd wanted him to have it. Now it seemed he felt it was what... inappropriate? She was going to have to respond before he did something stupid.

To: Miles Keane
From: Louisa Blackthorn
Subject: Precious Gift

Dear Miles

The gift was meant for you. I thought you would appreciate it. If you return it, I will feel obliged to send back the two bottles of Lafite. If that is what you want, then I shall send Hugh to drop them off.

Please don't do this.

Louisa

His response was immediate.

To: Louisa Blackthorn
From: Miles Keane.
Subject: Backed into a corner.

Dear Louisa

I don't want to do anything but you've cut me off. I don't know what to do.

I need to talk to you, see you. I don't care about who you are and I haven't a clue what it means either. I got to see Louisa for those two dates and that's who I want to spend time with. Don't just throw it away.

I want our "until next time... "

Miles

The honesty of his response made her stomach tighten. There wasn't anything she wanted more than their next time. All Louisa had done since the party was go over their conversations and she'd constantly wondered whether Miles would want to see her again, once he knew. She'd been harsh with him at the garden party, a reaction to his behaviour. Alistair had been right, Miles deserved a chance to explain. The email he'd sent had gone a little way to quash some of her doubt, but his last response meant he wasn't letting her have total control. Miles wasn't going to let her ignore him, and that thought alone made her have a slight hope that what had passed between them wasn't just in her head.

Louisa had never been an impulsive woman. Her life hadn't allowed her that privilege. Days were structured, planned and then organized. There was a procedure that needed to be followed. Appointments and meetings were arranged weeks in advance and free time was slotted in accordingly. The next few weeks had her busy from the morning until early evening and today was the start of her taking on the role of CASPO's patron. Her first meeting was in an hour with the board, but she had decided to go in a little earlier, meaning she had a little time to spare. *Damn protocol.*

"Hugh?"

"Yes, my lady."

"Can you take me to Miles Keane's house?"

Hugh's eyes snapped up to the rear view mirror, catching her gaze. "If that's where you'd like to go." He tried to mask his surprise but he was sure Louisa could see it.

"I just need to..." Louisa looked out of her window as the words of her explanation died on her lips. *What was she thinking?* She couldn't just turn up at his home unannounced and uninvited.

"I'll have you there in five minutes. If we leave from there in twenty minutes, we can still make your meeting with the board."

Louisa's gaze shifted back to the rear view mirror. She couldn't see Hugh's face but from his eyes she could tell he was smiling. "Thank you, Hugh."

"Madame, is he expecting you?"

"No."

"I see. Forgive me for saying, but hasn't he had enough surprises?"

Louisa smiled at her driver. He was right of course. It was only right that she give him fair warning. "Perhaps. I'll let him know." *Thirty seconds should be enough.*

MILES LEANED BACK IN his office chair and stared at the screen. She wasn't going to respond. The unexpected ring of his doorbell set Duke off barking and Miles rose from his chair, wondering who it could be at this hour on a Monday morning. His picked up his phone and headed to the hallway, when his phone signalled a new email. He opened it up as he paced to the front door. It was from Louisa and simply said, "Where and when? Yours and now."

What?

Miles opened up his front door and was faced with the stunningly elegant vision of Louisa, dressed for business in a form-fitting cobalt blue dress.

"Good morning. Is this a bad time?" Louisa raked her eyes over his tanned bare chest and took in every contour before Miles was able to respond.

"You're here," he blurted out, his eyes wide in shock.

"It would seem so." She arched her brow at him and waited.

It took him a few seconds before he realized he was supposed to invite her in. "Fuck, I mean hi. Shit, come in." Miles stepped back so she could step in, clearly knocked off-kilter by this unexpected visit. His eyes flitted to the street and spotted Hugh leaning against the Bentley, watching him. Miles gave him a nod as a way of greeting, then shut the door.

"Hello Duke, at least you're pleased to see me." Louisa crouched down to ruffle Duke's head.

"I… shit, I wasn't expecting…" Miles ran his hands through his hair, still stunned she was here.

Louisa straightened and gave him a soft smile. "Miles, I have 15 minutes. You said you needed to talk to me. So here I am."

"Jeez, you really like throwing those curveballs, don'tcha? Are you trying to keep me on my toes?" He let out a sharp breath and shook his head. She looked even more beautiful, if that was even possible, and her formal manner just made her feel unattainable, just out of reach, which only made her even more alluring.

"Is that coffee I smell?" She smirked at him, pleased she'd caught him off-guard.

"I'll take that as a yes and yes that's coffee. Would you like one?" he said dryly.

"I would."

Miles held out his hand signalling for her to go on ahead of him towards the kitchen. *He couldn't believe she'd come to see him.* In his surprise, he'd forgotten he was only wearing a pair of lounge pants.

"Maybe I should go put something on. I'm not sure this is how I should be dressed in front of a countess."

Louisa turned around and grinned at him. "Hmmm, well not in public, anyway. In private, though, there aren't any hard-and-fast rules, so don't change on my account." Her eyes danced mischievously and Miles chuckled at her response. *How could she be so precise and yet sexy at the same time?*

"Okay then, coffee," Miles said with a smirk. He pulled out a cup and saucer, then poured Louisa a cup as she settled herself into one of the bar stools around the island, placing her bag behind her.

"Shouldn't we go into the lounge?"

"I'm fine here." Louisa took the cup from his hand and thanked him. He seemed to have recovered from the shock of seeing her but his eyes still looked confused.

"So you were in the area?" Miles lowered himself into the stool next to her.

Louisa scrunched up her nose and rocked her head. "Sort of."

Miles chuckled, then moved around so he was facing her. "So, you're a countess." Louisa nodded, then took a sip from her cup, glad she had it as a distraction. It wasn't a question but rather a statement, and suddenly the mood of their conversation changed from playful to honest. "I did a lot of research on you, since I found out."

"I'm sure you did. It's only fair, seeing as I did a fair amount on you. And?"

"It's a lot to take in." Louisa sighed and pursed her lips, then averted her gaze from him before answering.

"That's subjective." She took another sip of her coffee. He obviously found the whole situation daunting. Well, there was no point in beating about the bush; she needed to know if her position was too much for him. "The question is, is it *too* much to take in? Alistair told me I should at least hear you out. He seems to think I may have been a little irrational – hasty even." She turned towards him, trying to gauge his reaction, but her eyes kept involuntarily drifting over his exposed torso.

Miles spotted the moment she noticed the one-inch scar on his shoulder; it was only for a second and then she dropped her gaze to her twitching fingers. Louisa clasped her hands together and placed them on her lap, hoping it would stop the urge she had to touch him.

"Alistair is quite a guy."

Louisa looked up again and smiled. "He is."

"A lot of what we talked about makes sense now. That must've been a hard time for you all: the accident and his recovery. He's a true hero."

"He doesn't think so but I'd have to agree with you. He has his ups and downs, but I'm pleased to say there are more ups now."

"I'm still finding it hard to get my head around you being Lady Blackthorn."

Louisa nodded. This was the part where he was going to tell her that the title and all it encumbered was too much for him to deal with. There weren't many men who could accept what her title and position meant. Gerard had been used to being surrounded by aristocracy when he'd met her. She was also a good deal younger than him, so he felt less threatened by the power she could, if she wanted, wield over him. Added to that, she wasn't the heiress to the estate then, so he'd never felt undermined by her. This situation was entirely different though.

"You remember at Blacks how you said that Google had a lot to answer for?"

Miles nodded, unsure of where the conversation was going.

"Well who that is, who you've read about, it's just what I represent, my job, but it's not all of who I am. I'm still the woman you met at Blacks." She blinked up at him, taking in his handsome face. This would probably be the last time they'd be alone together. The idea had her heart sinking and Louisa began to doubt her past actions. Maybe she should've been honest right from the start. If she had been though, their relationship would've been completely different. Their date at Blacks would've been polite, shorter, without any flirting whatsoever, and ended with a shake of hands and parting of ways. They would've then met up at the odd function for CASPO and been courteous to each other and under no circumstances would there have been a second date. At least she had that to hold on to. Now all she could think about was – what could've been.

Miles nodded. "I get that, believe me, I really get that. But you have to understand I was shocked, Louisa. It was the last thing I expected." Miles ran his hand over his face in frustration. "You know I was going to ask you to come with me? To the garden party." He let out a humourless laugh. "That's why I was asking you about your plans in the emails. And you didn't say anything to me, not even then." Louisa dropped her eyes from his questioning gaze.

"I was hoping that when you saw me, you'd be surprised and then we'd laugh about it. But you froze and everything changed." She looked back up at him. "And then you were with…" Miles gave a slight wince at the mention of Lottie and once again, he mentally kicked himself for taking her. "It seems like I read that whole situation all wrong."

Miles reached over and took Louisa's hands and she swallowed. His hands felt so warm and strong in hers. She couldn't remember the last time a man had held her hands so lovingly. "I only asked Lottie because I wanted someone familiar with me. Amanda was supposed to be with me but then at the last minute couldn't come, and I couldn't ask you. I wish I hadn't brought her along. Really she's just..."

Louisa wasn't sure she wanted to know any more details of his and Lottie's relationship. And to be fair she really didn't have any right to be annoyed. They weren't a couple, they were barely friends, and what little they had was based on a few hours in each other's company and a dozen emails. It was hardly a relationship. "I don't need to know." She tried to pull her hands away, but he held onto them tighter. "Miles, I don't do this kind of thing. I've never done this."

"You mean date?" His eyes widened.

"Sort of. Date, see someone who isn't preapproved. Turn up on someone's doorstep unannounced, when they're practically naked." She huffed and Miles let out a soft laugh. She was adorable when she was flustered.

"Distracting you, am I?" He tilted his head to the side, then gave her that bright smile that stunned every female in a ten-mile radius.

"I don't think you need your ego boosted anymore," she said dryly. He brought her left hand up to his lips and kissed the knuckles.

"Is this distracting too?"

"Miles..."

He pulled her right hand up to his lips and brushed them against her skin. "Yes, my lady." His gaze rose to catch hers, then he shuffled forward in his seat and trapped her knees between his.

She grinned at the use of her title, feeling her cheeks redden. He didn't need to try very hard to distract her, she'd already forgotten why she was even cross at him. "I'm just Louisa."

"Yes, you are." His gaze was steadfast on hers. Gone was the Miles who'd been surprised at her impromptu visit and in his place was a confident, sexy man. Louisa pulled in a shaky breath, totally entranced by the way Miles was looking at her. He wasn't pulling any punches. "I need an answer to the same question you asked me."

"Ask away."

"Am *I* wasting my time?"

Miles sculptured lips curved into a smile. "Absolutely not. I've had a shitty weekend. I didn't know what to do, how to get hold of you after you didn't respond to my email."

She could see the sincerity in his expression and a wave of relief washed over her. "Is that why you wanted to give back your gift?" she asked softly.

"I wanted to get your attention."

"It worked."

"So it seems, though I didn't expect this."

"Surprised?"

"All you seem to do is surprise me, Louisa, in every way. I'm hoping you've no more up your sleeve, even if I did like this one." Miles slipped off the stool and looked down at her.

"Yeah?"

"Oh yeah." Miles urged her off the stool with a slight pull on her hands and she stood, with just a few inches separating them. "I'm glad Hugh is in the car for this one. Please tell me he won't be around every time I want to kiss you."

"That depends where you want to kiss me."

"Are we talking location or on your body?" Miles lowered his head to her ear. "Because you know I want to kiss you all over, right?" He traced his fingers up her arms slowly and she shuddered. "Will that get me shot?"

"That depends on whether I want you to." Her voice was barely audible.

"Do you want me to?" he rasped as his nose grazed over her ear and across her cheek. He gently clasped her face and let his lips hover over hers. Their eyes locked onto each other's, Louisa's wide with anticipation and Miles's heavy with yearning. Slowly, he lowered his lips to hers and brushed the gentlest of kisses against them. Louisa's hands slowly smoothed around his waist and he groaned at the feel of her warm palms sliding against his skin. Miles tighten his grasped on her and deepened the kiss.

In the background, he could hear a phone ringing and he willed it to stop but Louisa tensed, then pulled away. "I have to go."

"*Fuck!* What? Why?"

"I need to be at CASPO by ten."

Miles made a frustrated noise and his eyes searched hers. He didn't want to let her go. "Are you ever going to give me your number? How am I supposed to get in touch with you?"

"I'll get in touch with you."

"Is this part of being a countess or you wanting to be in control?"

Louisa gave him that enigmatic smile and reluctantly stepped away from him. She lifted up her bag from the stool, pulled out her phone and tapped the screen. She quickly told Hugh she'd be out in two minutes, then dropped her phone back into her bag. "I'll call you."

"Louisa..."

"My private phone is monitored." She looked embarrassed and gave a shrug. "Security. I need to just clear it and then you can call me."

"Oh wow."

"All part of being Lady Blackthorn."

"Shit, I'm so out of my depth here." Miles stared at the stunning woman in front of him and wondered if he could handle everything that came with Lady Blackthorn.

She stepped forward and placed her hand on his chest. "I'm just Louisa."

"Until next time?"

"Yes. Until next time."

LOUISA TRIED HER HARDEST to concentrate on her meeting with the board. She nodded in the right places and she was sure her well-practiced expression gave nothing away, but the truth was all she could think about was the 15 minutes she'd had with Miles. She was beginning to understand what was so appealing about impulsive behaviour. If she hadn't acted so spontaneously she wouldn't have caught Miles in his semi-naked state; that alone was worth any security risk.

Her following meetings with sponsors didn't go much better either. It seemed that no one was any the wiser and she was thankful that Melissa was on hand to refresh her memory later of the important facts. Louisa wasn't particularly interested in how the charity raised funds; she knew that this was crucial and without it CASPO wouldn't exist, but what concerned her more was how the money was spent. Her main interest in her charity work was the good that came out of the hard work the staff at CASPO put in.

Louisa's twenty years in America working alongside various charities had been the perfect training ground for her. She'd seen first-hand which systems worked and which failed. It was easy to throw money at a situation but more often than not it was time, patience and expertise that ensured any monetary hand out made a life-changing difference.

By the time Louisa made it home after a dinner with another generous donator, it was late. She prised off her shoes and flexed her toes into the thick carpet of her office. A slight tap at the door had her attention shifting to Hugh standing by the threshold.

"Will there be anything else, my lady?"

Louisa's eyes darted to the recent email she'd received from Miles. It was time to broach the subject of her phone. "Come in, Hugh. Please sit down." Hugh gave a curt nod and lowered himself into the chair in front of her desk. "Would you like a drink?"

"Not on duty, madame."

"You're off duty now. I'm not leaving and I'm sure Thompson is on duty now; it's after ten." Louisa stood up from her chair and turned to the mahogany cabinet behind her desk, where she kept a small selection of drinks. "Whisky?" she asked.

"Thank you, madame." Louisa poured their two drinks and turned, only to find Hugh standing again. She handed him his drink and after he'd thanked her, she told him to sit down.

"I want Miles to be able to contact me, so I will be giving him my private number." Hugh gave a soft smile and nodded. "I'm presuming you've already done security checks on him because of CASPO."

"Yes, madame." They raised their glasses in a silent cheers and took a sip.

"My phone is monitored?"

Hugh gave her a nod. "All incoming calls are monitored."

"Not outgoing?"

"They're not recorded, madame, just logged."

Louisa narrowed her eyes. "I see."

"Your phone is also tracked, so we know your whereabouts at all times, madame."

She furrowed her brow at this new information. "But you're with me, or one of your security staff is with me all the time."

"It's just a precaution, madame."

"I didn't realise."

From the look of confusion on her face it was clear to Hugh that Louisa didn't know the lengths her late father had gone to, to protect his daughter. When Hugh had first started working for the Blackthorns, it was post-9/11. The Earl had concerns about the safety of his daughter and only grandchild living stateside. He'd insisted in the latest technology to keep tabs on them. When the Earl died, Alistair had continued his father's vigilance. "When the Earl was alive, he insisted."

"You mean my phone was tracked while I was in America?"

"Yes, madame."

"Did Gerard know?"

"Yes, madame."

Louisa shot up from her chair and Hugh immediately stood up. "That's outrageous! Sit down." She waved at him. "It's just you and me now. Why was I never told?" She began to pace, clearly irritated at being kept in the dark.

"Your late father was worried about your safety. It was when America was targeted by terrorists and then there were the shootings. He spoke to Mr. Dupont about security and he assured him that you had an excellent team but he understood your father's concerns and agreed to the tracker. When Alistair – sorry, Earl Alistair..." Louisa waved her hand again, dismissing his mistake of not using Alistair's title. She had never been a stickler for protocol. "When he took over, the tracker stayed on, up until you returned to England. The new phone you were given was automatically tracked and monitored."

"I'm not sure what to make of it all." Louisa sat down in her chair again and took a drink from her glass. Gerard knew this and kept it from her. He probably had her phone tracked too, maybe even recorded her calls.

Hugh watched Louisa as she processed the information. He hadn't realised she'd been kept in the dark. "Madame, it was purely for your safety. You should also know that Lady Celeste has a tracker too."

Louisa let out a humourless laugh. "She won't be pleased about that." The thought did give Louisa peace of mind, though. She knew Gerard had a team in Peru watching over the camp she was at, which had appalled Celeste, but a tracker too would really rile her. "Anyway, about Miles."

"You'd rather his calls weren't recorded."

"Yes. No offence, but it's bad enough you're privy to what goes on in my private life. I'd really like some of it private."

"I understand. I'll see to it."

"Thank you, Hugh."

"If that'll be all, madame." Hugh rose from his seat and placed his glass on the desk.

"Yes, goodnight Hugh."

"Goodnight, my lady."

Louisa's eyes focused on the glass he'd left behind. He hadn't touched it after his initial sip. It seemed Hugh was always on duty.

18

BITTER STING

"YOU KNOW THIS IS torture, right?" Miles stretched himself out on the king-sized bed and let his gaze drift over the stunning view of Lake Geneva. It was breathtaking during the day but at nightfall, the sparkling lights that shimmered on the lake's surface made the view spectacular. He'd arrived the previous day to shoot the new campaign for the luxurious watch company. Since Louisa had given him her number, they'd chatted every evening. It was fast becoming an addictive habit for Miles.

"I wouldn't call being put up in the Royal Suite of Four Seasons in Geneva torture," Louisa said dryly.

"It is when you're on your own and wish a certain *lady* was with you to appreciate it."

Louisa couldn't think of anything more she'd rather do than spend a few days and nights away with Miles. Hearing him say he felt the same way only made her wish for it more.

It was curious how their conversations had taken on a more familiar tone. Gone was the polite distance and in its place was an alluring warmth, an intimacy that usually came from a couple who'd shared more than a few weeks together. Their nightly conversations had a lot to do with that. Being on the end of a phone rather than face to face meant they could be candid. Louisa relished every minute of their conversations. Miles's teasing and flirting were both refreshing and infectious, and Louisa found herself being pulled in deeper every day.

"I remember the view of the lake and the *Jet d'Eau* as being quite beautiful from the Royal Suite." Louisa flexed her toes, trying to ease the stiffness as she lay on her bed. She'd been from breakfast meetings, to more meetings, to lunch meetings, to conference calls, then to a working dinner. The beautiful heels she'd worn for fourteen hours had taken their toll on her poor feet. It had been that way for the last five days and even over the weekend, she was going to be rallying around to get donators and sponsors, as well as thrash out details for the activity weekend with Alistair.

"You've been here?"

"Yes, though it was a while ago."

Miles heard the sound of ice against glass down the phone and he pictured Louisa's perfect lips on expensive crystal, as she sipped her drink. "Of course you have. I sometimes wonder if there's anything you haven't done or any place you haven't experienced." Miles muttered as he shifted to pick up his beer bottle from the nightstand and took a swig from it.

"I've never been on a blind date before, or loaded someone else's dishwasher, or been kissed in the rain, for that matter."

"Really?"

Louisa smiled, pleased she caused his mulish tone to change. She couldn't alter her past experiences or who she was, but at least there were things she'd only done with Miles and she wanted him to know that. "Yes, really."

"You realise I'm grinning now."

"I'm pleased I was able to ease your torture and that I can make you smile," she said dryly, though she was secretly happy she'd eased his surprising insecurities.

"I love it when you talk all precise and ladylike; it's sexy as hell." He heard Louisa huff down the phone. "But Louisa, you talking to me over the phone like that is seriously torturous too. It's been over a week since I saw you and these daily phone calls are amazing, but they're no substitute for seeing you in the flesh."

"Well, you're in Switzerland for another few days, right?"

"Yeah. We're filming on the lake tomorrow and then some more at night. It's a very adventurous advert. Slick and stylish. They've got me doing all sorts."

"Like what?"

"Water skiing, for one thing."

"Really? Do you know how to?"

"Yeah."

"Wow. A man of many talents." He tried hard not to preen over the fact that Louisa was obviously impressed at this. He liked it when he could surprise her. "Good job, though what's that got to do with a watch?"

"They're showing that it's waterproof. Sort of a 'you can wear it anywhere, anyhow' kind of campaign. All in the lap of luxury though."

"Well of course," Louisa chuckled. "What else?"

"Driving through a windy mountain road, then skiing. And before you ask, yes, I can ski too."

"Sounds very 007. Do you get the girl at the end too?"

Miles let out a laugh. "Of course. I mean, seriously, I went through all that. And I'm Miles Keane, didn't you know? I always get the girl!" Louisa let out a chuckle enjoying his playful tone.

"Is that so? I'll need to remember that."

"You just do that," he said a little softer. "You know they asked me to compose and play the theme music too?"

"Oh Miles that's... well, that's truly incredible. A creative input you're perfectly qualified for. They knew what they were doing when they approached you."

"Thanks." Miles smiled, even though he knew Louisa couldn't

see him. Her comment affected him far more than it should. Miles had never sought approval but hearing Louisa affirm his talent had his heart soaring.

"Have you started working on that yet?"

"I've a few ideas. Now I know the concept. It will be a completely different direction to any music I've been known for before."

"More classical?"

"Uhuh."

"I'm looking forward to hearing it. This will be the first piece you'll have released in a while. There will be quite a buzz about it."

"Well that depends if it's any good." Miles chuckled nervously. This was a big step for him and the idea of having his work out there again, without his brother by his side, had him uneasy just at the thought.

"Miles, this campaign is really no different to a music video. From what I remember, you were pretty good in those."

"Why, Lady Blackthorn, are you admitting to watching my videos?" He smirked to himself and took another drink from his beer.

"Stop changing the subject. Yes I did, mainly because Celeste played them incessantly. You were good in them." Louisa relished the burn of her drink as she took a sip. *Thank goodness he couldn't see her blushing,* she thought. She wasn't about to admit she'd watched a few of them more recently too.

"As good as Sting was in his?"

"Don't tell me you're jealous of my crush on Sting!" She let out a soft laugh.

"I'll let you into a secret, Louisa, I'm jealous of anyone who captures your attention."

The sincerity in his reply caught Louisa off-guard. *How could he be jealous of anyone?* "Miles…"

"I mean it, Louisa. When can I see you?"

"I'm flying out to the States the day before you come back."

Miles's stomach dropped. "Oh. Business?" He hated how needy he sounded but he had to know if she was seeing Gerard.

"No. Celeste is coming back from Peru and she arrives in New York then. We're going to spend a few days there. So she can spend time with Gerard before she comes back home with me."

Miles drained his beer and eyed the bar, thinking he could do with something much stronger. Of course she'd be seeing her ex. They had a daughter together, after all. It still didn't take the sting out of the revelation though. "I see. You must be very excited to have her back." He tried to sound neutral but even he could hear the tightness in his tone.

"It has been the longest six months of my life! And then she'll be off again at the end of September."

"You never wanted more children?"

"Yes. Just not with Gerard."

"I don't know what to make of that revelation. I thought… well, I presumed you had a happy marriage – well, at least until recently."

"Don't believe everything you read in the media, Miles." Louisa let out a breath and Miles recalled her saying something similar on their first date. *So her marriage was far from idyllic, yet they would be spending time together?* Miles furrowed his brow, unsure of what to make of the whole scenario. The only positive note he took away from her comment was that she hadn't wanted more children with Gerard. What that meant he wasn't entirely sure.

"But your divorce is amicable, right?" he asked, trying to piece together the parts of her puzzling relationship.

"Yes, didn't you know when you're well bred, you do everything with the minimum of fuss and attention? Having your dirty laundry aired in front of the whole world is just not done. We protect our privacy and trust very few with it. Rumours are quashed before anyone digs too deep. It's a very tight circle, the aristocracy, and if you haven't been surrounded in it, it's hard to understand the loyalty that comes with that. You have so many privileges but they come at a price. Everything always comes down to a price you need to pay, and more often than not, the cost has nothing to do with money."

Whoa! What did that even mean? The more Miles got to know about Louisa's way of life, the more he became astonished and in a strange way even more intrigued. The life of a pop star had always garnered a huge amount of attention. Very little was kept secret. His whole career had been under a spotlight and when things turned sour for him, that spotlight changed to floodlights. He understood about paying a price more than anyone. "Jeez, Louisa. I can't even begin to get my head around what you just said."

"I'm sorry. Ignore me. I'm not usually this candid but it would seem you bring that out in me," she said softly.

"Oh god, Louisa, I hate that these conversations we have are when we're miles apart." He made a frustrated noise and Louisa grinned to herself. "When are you back?"

"Next Saturday."

"*Fuck*. That's in ten days. And then you no doubt have the run up to the ball, so you'll be busy."

"My calendar is… it's just hectic, but we'll see each other at the meeting two days before the ball."

"Oh wow, that sounds wonderful. You and me, surrounded by CASPO employees. How romantic." He couldn't squeeze more sarcasm in his tone if he tried. "I want it to be just you and me, Louisa."

"I want that too. Look, I'll see if I can move things around when we get back from New York. What's your schedule like?"

"God, this shouldn't be so hard." Miles dragged his hand through his hair in frustration. "I'm at a number of events once I get back from here. It's Men's Fashion Week and I'll be at some of the shows and dinners."

"Oh, well Celeste will be home, so..."

"Louisa, just tell me when and where, and I'll try my damnedest to be there."

"It'll have to be somewhere discreet."

"I'm sure we can manage that."

THE SUITE AT THE bold and lavish Mark Hotel of course lived up to its description. The elegant yet high-tech suite overlooked the town-house garden views and dark ebony and sycamore furnishings ran throughout the four-roomed suite. Being situated on the Upper East Side meant that Louisa was in walking distance of her previous home – not that Gerard would've allowed her to walk. She would have a driver on call 24 hours of the day, all seen to by her ever-attentive ex-husband.

Gerard stood by the window, patiently waiting for the hotel staff to finish unpacking Louisa's luggage. He was still a handsome man, impeccably dressed in a black three-piece suit, a conservative look he managed to make look chic with stylish accessories. The flecks of grey in his dark hair only added to his appeal. The few creases he sported made his Gallic good looks less smooth and a little bit rugged. His stance had always been confident, years of good breeding had instilled a distinguished air about him, and where many of his fellow countrymen were renowned for a quick temper, Gerard had mastered the control of his emotions. He reserved his passion only for the bedroom.

Gerard took a sip from his coffee, then turned his attention out to the view. It was obvious to Louisa he wasn't pleased that she had again insisted on staying in a hotel. After 20 years together, she knew the subtle signs, the tightness in his jaw the constant rubbing of his thumb and forefinger ever present when he felt out of control. Louisa moved around the luxurious and unnecessarily large suite, setting up her laptop and thanking the staff. Gerard had insisted on organizing the booking for her. Louisa would have been happy with smaller accommodation but her ex-husband wouldn't hear of it. The second bedroom was superfluous, seeing as Celeste would be staying at his home.

"I still don't understand why you're in a hotel." Gerard turned from the window as soon as the last of the efficient staff had left. "Your rooms are the same as when you left them."

"I told you last time I was here that I wouldn't be staying at the house again. And anyway, I don't want to encroach on your time with Celeste when she arrives tomorrow. You'll be able to spend time with her."

"I thought it would be nice to be altogether." He placed his coffee cup down on the antique table with a little more force than necessary.

"Gerard..."

His dark eyes darted up to Louisa's and he cursed himself for letting his feelings show. He wanted to make the next few days perfect for the three of them and he'd already ruined it within the first hour of her arrival. "I know. It's not the same anymore."

"No, it's not," Louisa said quietly. Maybe her coming out here had been a bad idea. She should've waited for Celeste in England. The last thing she wanted was to give Gerard mixed messages. She was here for Celeste, no other reason other than to make sure their daughter had both her parents with her at important stages in her life.

"Will you at least dine with me tonight?"

"Here at the hotel?"

"If that's where you'd prefer." Louisa gave a nod. At least here she could excuse herself. She had a distinct feeling Gerard was going to pull out all the stops on this trip.

"You're looking good, *cherie.*"

"Work is keeping me busy. I like the challenge and now that I'm back, Mama is passing more over to me."

Before Gerard could answer, Hugh knocked against the open lounge door. After apologizing for the disturbance, he handed an envelope to Louisa.

"Any important calls?"

"There all written down, my lady."

Louisa's eyes scanned the list and zeroed in on the couple of calls from Miles. She thanked him and Hugh retreated as quickly as he'd appeared.

Gerard's gaze drifted to the direction of the door and frowned. "Does he go everywhere with you?"

"Him or a member of his team, yes." Louisa folded away the list and placed it on the desk. "He told me about the phone tracker. Why didn't you?"

Gerard paused for a moment before answering, uncomfortable with the way their conversation was heading. "Your father was insistent that you and Celeste had trackers on your phones. I wasn't going to go against his wishes. It made sense."

"I don't dispute the reason behind it. I know the dangers and risks. I've been surrounded by it my whole life. What I'm asking is why the hell you never told me?" Louisa crossed her arms and waited for a response but Gerard's jaw tightened even more. He hadn't been prepared for a cross-examination on this trip. Louisa stepped forward, unwilling to back down, but her voice softened. "He spoke to you, because you were my husband. You should have informed me. Did you record my conversations too?"

Gerard swallowed and softly said, "Not all of them."

Louisa blew out a sharp breath but kept her cool, even though inside she was fuming. He'd monitored her calls and though Louisa rarely confided in anyone, especially over the phone, it still hurt that he'd been privy to private conversations. "It makes sense now. How you were always a step ahead of me. How you hid things from me." Gerard watched her carefully, knowing he'd hurt her once again. She'd learned over the years to keep her expressions neutral, but he caught the slight tremor in her voice and it made his chest ache. He'd wanted these few days together to go smoothly, a snap shot into their possible future together. The last few months without her had been miserable for him and he was determined to try and win her back. "But I still found out about... I may not have seen or heard anything but I just knew."

"*Cherie,* please don't do this. I was an idiot." He moved closer to her. The few feet between them seemed too far for such an emotional conversation.

"I'm never coming back to you," she said with finality and this time it was Gerard who took a sharp breath.

"Twenty years is a long time, *cherie.*"

"It was five years for me. The rest... it was never *just* us."

Gerard's chest tightened at her subtle reference to the mistresses he'd had over their marriage and had the good grace to look contrite. "I made mistakes."

His declaration was laced with regret but it gave Louisa little comfort to see the strong man she'd once adored look so sorrowful. "I'm glad you've realised. Don't let them tarnish your relationship with Celeste."

LOUISA HELD TIGHTLY ONTO Celeste, breathing in her familiar scent as she buried her nose into her silky hair. There was seriously nothing better than hugging your child. It didn't matter how old they were, the feeling never changed. She hadn't realized how much of a relief she would feel, having her daughter back safely. Louisa had never stopped Celeste doing anything. When she'd wanted to skateboard at the age of six, Louisa took every precaution she could to ensure Celeste could learn as safely as possible. Her next passion was dirt biking. By the age of eleven she was racing through rough terrain while Louisa and Gerard had their hearts in their mouths. Louisa swore she was more like her uncle Alistair than either her or Gerard. Celeste started kickboxing at age thirteen and had broken her nose by fifteen. Thankfully, it healed back perfectly. There were no ballet lessons for Celeste; for all her poise and ladylike traits, Celeste had never wanted to pursue any activity that was more conventionally suited to a future Lady Blackthorn. Louisa would have even welcomed hip-hop but Celeste was never interested. Her only consolation was that her daughter learned to play the piano. That was the only ladylike or sedate hobby she had.

Celeste loved her time at Holmwood as a child because her grandfather and uncle encouraged her to be adventurous and they gave her every opportunity. Assault courses were built, rock-climbing walls were erected, zip lines were hooked up, and rifle ranges created, all for Celeste to fulfil her adventurism.

When she was seven years old, Celeste had wanted to be involved with her mother and father's charity work. It was on one of her mother's visits to an after-school music club, funded by one of their charities, that Celeste met Konran Konjwa. They became firm friends, even though they were from different backgrounds and had six years between them. They spent time together at the club and out, bonding over their love of rap music. Her six months in Peru was a perfect pairing of Celeste's sense of adventure and her charitable nature. When she had suggested her plans, both Louisa and Gerard knew there would be no stopping her. Now that she was safely back, Louisa would make the most of their time together before she embarked onto the next chapter of her life.

Louisa took a back seat during the daytime, allowing Gerard to spoil his only daughter with his undivided attention. He had three days to spend with her and, as was his usual style, he'd planned every minute. In the evenings, they met up for dinner, which meant Louisa could hear all about their day.

They dined out at the most celebrated restaurants in New

York; no expense was spared, but every night, Louisa was driven to her hotel. Gerard would see her into the lobby, even though Hugh or one of the security team was with her at all times. Part of it was because he was always the consummate gentleman, while part of it was that he wanted as much time as he could with her, without their daughter as a buffer.

Their first night dining alone had been polite. Louisa kept their conversation light. After their heavier conversation earlier that day, she didn't want to revisit parts of their life together. It was over for her and there was no point rehashing or reliving the reasons why. They had a beautiful, vibrant daughter together and their relationship needed to be at least pleasant so as not to make future events difficult. Louisa was a master of masking her emotions and no one had managed to break her – well, at least not in public.

Gerard again arranged his private jet to take them back to London; an over-the-top luxury that Louisa both appreciated and accepted for the sake of her daughter. As Gerard embraced his daughter tightly before they boarded, Louisa felt more than a twinge of guilt for taking her away from him. His eyes glistened with the bitter sting of tears he was determined not to shed and he promised to come out for a short visit in the summer.

"Au revoir, cherie," Gerard said softly as he kissed Louisa's cheek, letting his hands linger a little longer in hers.

"Take care, Gerard." Louisa turned and headed up the stairs, reining in her emotions before Celeste could see. It should have gotten easier every time she said goodbye but it never did. Gerard was right – 20 years was a long time.

"HOW'S THE JET LAG?" Alistair grinned at his sister as she scowled and tried to stifle a yawn at the same time.

"I'm just going to power through it. If I sleep now, it'll just take longer."

"Just overdose on coffee." He shifted in his chair, then pointed to the computer screen. They were going over the plans for the activity weekend. Alistair had plotted the various activities on a virtual model of Holmwood House and the grounds. They were able to accommodate just over 30 children and their parents. Apart from the Holmwood House staff, Alistair had recruited his friends and some of his military buddies to help out. Louisa watched her brother as he explained every area. It was obvious that this whole project was more than just a duty for Alistair. His enthusiasm for every one of his carefully thought-out plans radiated from every pore. This project mattered to him, not only because he was the Earl of Holmwood, but because it meant he was physically able to help. He'd always been so active and though running Holmwood House was a full-time job, Alistair missed using his physical strength rather than just his business acumen.

"That's amazing. Really. And you're sure 32 children aren't too many?"

"No, we've enough room. We'll use the old dairy to accommodate the older children and the 17 parents with younger children will use the old staff quarters and the other rooms in my wing."

"Are you sure? I mean they'll be putting you out."

"Don't worry about me. Remember, I'm used to roughing it. Besides, I'll be bunking in your part of the house." He flashed her a grin.

"Not roughing it at all then?" she chuckled.

"You forget, I'm a cripple. My roughing days are over." He knocked his knuckle on his prosthetic leg, then winked. Louisa rolled her eyes at him but she knew behind his joking there was a little sadness.

"You know there's a good chance Konran will be here too."

"Really? I thought he was on a world tour."

"He is. He's coming over for the ball as a surprise, in between dates. He was supposed to have some recording time when the weekend is on but he's trying to reschedule that so he can be here. Well, at least for some of the time, anyway."

"That'll be some surprise for the kids. Maybe we can get him to do a music activity. Can you imagine the famous TuKon jamming with them?"

"Jamming? Are you brushing up on the music lingo?" Louisa joked.

"Talking of music lingo, how's Mr. Keane?"

"Subtle as always. He's fine." She brushed off his question and redirected the conversation. "You're coming to the ball, right? I mean, I need a date?"

"Not my thing, Louisa. You're so much better at all that than me; all that glitz and glamour. Schmoozing and sucking up to people, I leave all that up to you and Mama. I did however get all my gang to buy a table. This," He swirled his finger in front of the computer screen. "This is what I like to do. And besides, isn't Mr. Keane going to accompany you?" he asked, flashing her a cheeky smile. Louisa furrowed her brow.

"I'm not sure. Melissa is in charge of all that."

"Hmm, I see." He stifled a grin and gave her a knowing look.

"Shut up."

"So come on, how are things in that area? From your slight blush I'm presuming better?"

Louisa let out a resigned breath. "We speak on the phone but he's been busy, I've been busy." She gave a half-hearted shrug. "I've never done this before so I'm kind of… shit, I don't know Alistair. I've too much going on, professionally, personally." She scrunched up her nose and he slipped his arm around her shoulders and gave her a squeeze. He knew she wasn't comfortable talking about her private life, but if there was one thing his accident had taught him, it was you needed to talk things out.

"Well there's nothing wrong with taking it slow." Louisa nodded and he gave her quick kiss on her head, then pulled back. "How was New York?"

"Oh you know. Fancy?"

"No, I don't." Alistair snorted, then added, "And Gerard?"

"He's good. He's going to miss Celeste. It's cost him, her leaving."

"I'm sure, but I think its cost him more losing you."

"Perhaps." Louisa looked out of her office window at the grounds, it was late afternoon and she was really beginning to feel the effects of her lack of sleep. "Marriage, eh? It's not easy for me either," she said quietly, then turned to her brother and gave a wistful smile.

"Louisa, I don't know what..." Alistair's phone vibrated against the desk and he glanced at who it was ringing. "What the hell does Gordon want?" He swiped his screen to answer the call. Alistair grimaced at whatever his friend was saying and from what Louisa could tell, Gordon wasn't altogether happy.

"He's had another row with Emily. He's on his way here.," said Alistair once he'd finished his call.

"Another row?"

"Yeah, things aren't good between them. Like you said: marriage."

ALISTAIR WATCHED GORDON AS he waved off Louisa. She was on her way back to London. Her eagerness to leave had her brother curious as to whether she had arranged to meet up with Miles or that the presence of Gordon and his marital problems was just too close to home for her. Gordon had arrived in the late afternoon and ended up spending the night. Alistair had noticed that his friend had unmistakably perked up once he'd known Louisa was at Holmwood. He'd always wondered if his good friend had ever gotten over his crush on his sister. A few minutes with Gordon and Louisa in the same room was enough to confirm to Alistair that his friend was in fact still totally enamoured with her. It wasn't any wonder that Emily disliked Louisa so much and Alistair didn't hold back pointing this out to Gordon once they were alone.

Louisa had left them for the most of the evening. She'd used the excuse of jet lag finally making it hard for her keep awake, but Alistair realized she was being tactful, allowing Gordon to talk through what problems he was having at home.

Celeste had decided to stay at Holmwood House, rather than go to London with her mother. She knew that Louisa would be working long hours with the last-minute organization of the ball and Celeste wanted to take advantage of the fact that her grandmother would fuss over her for a while, especially after being away for the last six months. Lady Alice of course was thrilled to have her granddaughter's full an undivided attention for four days.

Louisa was still feeling the lingering aftereffects of jet lag as she worked in her office. Her eyes flitted to the empty coffee cup on her desk and she contemplated a refill to get her through the next few hours. She was hoping she'd have a chance to speak to Miles tonight. He was in the middle of London Fashion Week, which meant he would be at a number of events all day as well as the evening.

Louisa had been following his appearances, which had been well documented across every media platform, especially since he'd been announced as CASPO's ambassador and was now the new face of the luxury watch brand. Rumours were also out that he would be presenting a new TV show, so Miles Keane was one of the hottest celebrities in the audience of the many shows. He looked comfortable in the spotlight, dressed impeccably in varying outfits, from casual jeans and shirt to perfectly tailored three-piece suits. In many of the photos, Miles was accompanied by an older man. The caption under one of the photos revealed it was Eric Schultz, his long-time friend and agent.

It was nice to be back in her London residence after almost a week away. The house had always been in her family but over the last few months, it was finally feeling more like her home.

A message rang through on her phone and Louisa's eyes darted to the clock on her computer screen. It was almost ten. Her heart skipped a beat, knowing it was Miles. She opened up her phone and read the simple message.

I'm home. Can you talk?

"You're in the music room?" Louisa squinted at the screen of her laptop. They'd started to video call since she'd been in New York. It had begun with Miles wanting to show Louisa how he'd managed to train Duke to sit. Louisa had reciprocated by showing him the view from her hotel and they had continued from then on.

"Yeah, I thought you might like to hear the music I composed for the advert."

Louisa could hear the apprehension in his voice. This was a big deal for him and Louisa couldn't believe he was trusting her with something so important. "I'd love to."

"I'm not sure the acoustics are that good but you'll get the feel of it. Just give me a moment to set up the backing." He'd propped up his laptop on the piano, from what Louisa could tell, then moved out of the camera range. After a few seconds, Miles's handsome face popped back into view and he swivelled the screen so Louisa could see he was standing, holding a trumpet. Not just any trumpet, but the one she'd gifted him. "I thought I'd give it a spin," he said with a cheeky grin and Louisa chuckled. "So, you have to imagine that I'm water skiing on this gorgeous lake, looking all athletic."

Louisa's eyes widened and she shook her head. "I don't need to imagine too hard. Remember, I've seen you topless."

Miles let out a laugh. "Maybe I should take off my shirt now so you can get the feel of the advert."

"Umm, it's not one of *those* kind of video calls, Miles," she mock-chastised.

"Maybe next time." He gave her his mega-watt smile and Louisa squirmed in her seat.

"Carry on."

"Right, so as I'm climbing back up on deck, they zoom in on the watch, then zoom out, and I'm now driving along windy mountain road, then to the slopes. It goes on like that. Does that make sense?"

"Perfect."

"Okay."

Miles lifted up a remote and pressed it, then from the screen, Louisa could hear a beautiful melody beginning, played on the piano. Her eyes were transfixed on the screen as Miles lifted the trumpet to his lips. It was mesmerizing to watch how his whole demeanour changed, like he was alone and unguarded, totally in the moment. The somewhat mellow beginning had smoothly moved to a faster pace with the introduction of the trumpet, bringing a slight sense of urgency. Louisa could envisage the scenarios Miles had described, racing through the mountains and skiing down snowy slopes. The music tempo gradually changed to a slower pace until it gently ended, leaving Louisa in awe of how the short piece had managed to incite so many emotions. Louisa had only ever seen Miles as a pop star, hugely successful in that particular genre, but hearing the piece of music he'd composed and performed so expressively, it was obvious his talent far surpassed that title.

"That was incredible, Miles. I'm literally speechless."

"Yeah?" He smiled shyly at her, his initial nerves subsiding at her heartfelt comment.

"Yes. What does the watch company think?"

"They haven't heard it yet. You're the first person I've played it to."

Louisa's eyes widened as the weight of what Miles had just said sank in. "Oh, I'm... I don't know what to say. I'm honoured."

"Thanks." Miles gave her a slightly embarrassed smile and ran his fingers through his hair. Her genuine reaction was all he'd needed to ease the knot in his stomach. He hadn't realised how much of an impact her words would have on him until he'd heard them.

"They'll love it," Louisa said, mistaking his nervousness for doubt.

"It's just been a long time... since... well, this will be the first piece I've put out." He took a deep breath and shrugged.

"I see. Well for what it's worth, I think it's a brilliant piece and from what I remember of Louis, I think he'd think the same too."

"Thanks."

"And, you know... it's probably the best way for you to get back into the music business. Less visual, if you get I mean?"

Miles eyes widened at her perceptiveness. "Yeah, that's what Eric said. He really pushed me to do this."

"I think your agent knows exactly what he's doing."

"I'll tell him that. He'll get a kick out of it." Miles chuckled, then gave her a crooked smile. "That trumpet though, eh? Pretty awesome."

Louisa let out a soft laugh. "I think its awesomeness has a lot to do with who's playing it."

"So I'm awesome?"

"Miles, are you fishing for compliments?" Miles chuckled knowing she was on to his game. "Yes you're awesome."

He grinned at her and added, "But not as awesome as Sting."

Louisa laughed and shook her head. "No, but you're getting closer."

19

ANOTHER DATE?

VULNERABLE WAS AN EMOTION Louisa had experienced for the last 15 years of her married life. When you've allowed someone into your life, loved them completely and let them see every part of you, it's devastating when they use that against you; used the fact that you trusted and loved them unconditionally. Louisa had hardened up over those years until a certain pop star had accidently come into her life. Over the last few weeks, Louisa had let down her guard little by little. It was hard not to. Miles was everything she wasn't; bold, unguarded and approachable. He wore his heart on his sleeve, saying whatever was on his mind, and for Louisa it was refreshing. That's why when Louisa saw the many pictures at the closing dinner of Men's Fashion Week of Miles and Lottie Price, in a barely-there dress, those very familiar feelings hit her like a wrecking ball. It didn't help that every caption under the photos speculated if they were *still* an item. Louisa hadn't realised that they'd *been* an item or that the media had known about Miles and Lottie's arrangement. Maybe it was pure conjecture, a juicy piece of sensationalism to get more hits on a website. It was even possible that Lottie's team were feeding the media tit bits to aid her career. Miles was certainly the hot ticket of the moment and Louisa was sure Lottie's association with him would up her status even more.

Louisa really didn't have any right to even be upset. There wasn't even anything officially between them. They'd seen each other three times in total and spoken almost every night on the phone for the last two weeks. It was hardly a relationship. The fact was, Louisa hadn't really thought about what they were to each other. While their liaisons had been private, without prying eyes, she'd never put a label on it. Friends, maybe – or associates? Well, she'd never kissed one of her friends like she'd kissed Miles, or one of her associates, for that matter. There was definitely more to their relationship, but they'd both done a good job of side-stepping it, rather than laying it on the line – or maybe that was just her doing. All Louisa knew was that seeing Miles and Lottie together, looking like the perfect celebrity couple, made her stomach tighten and her blood begin to simmer. That alone confirmed to her that he already meant more to her than maybe he should. However, she rationalised her feelings and their situation, the bottom line was she was hurt. Miles was obviously still cosy with his go-to girl. Louisa had spoken to him late after the very event they were photographed at and he hadn't mentioned Lottie. If there was nothing going on between them, surely he'd have said something. The fact he hadn't only compounded her uneasy thoughts.

Louisa rubbed her forehead in frustration. It was Miles Keane: playboy, pop star, serial man whore. *What made her think he had changed?* He was coming out of the other side of his hiatus from fame and obviously slipping back into his previous habits. She was just lucky she hadn't let things go further between them. Well, she would be the perfect lady and behave professionally and politely around him and let him carry on with whomever he pleased.

Louisa blew out a breath and picked up her phone. There was

a message from Miles saying he couldn't wait to see her tomorrow, which she'd ignored. She'd thought about skipping going into the office tomorrow, just so she wouldn't have to see him, but that would be unfair to Melissa. They had a full few days and her good friend needed her, not to mention it wouldn't look good that the patron was slacking off. Louisa sometimes wondered whether being accessible was such a good thing after all. She shook her head determined to rid her mind of all thoughts related to Miles; she had a job to do and she'd wasted far too much time already. She checked her watch, then tapped through the call and waited.

"Hey, Lady B." Konran's familiar deep voice made Louisa smile in spite of her bad mood.

"Morning, Konran, I hope it's not too early for you."

"Nah, I've been up a while. My body clock is all over the place with this tour."

"I've seen the reviews. You're *smashing it,* apparently," Louisa said dryly and Konran laughed at her choice of words.

"Yeah, it's going good." Konran described a few of the places he'd been to and Louisa lapped up every moment, revelling in his meteoric success. He'd moved a long way from the one-bedroomed damp flat in the Bronx he'd shared with his mother.

"So your manager has all the details for Saturday. He said they'd be a total of four of you coming out."

"Yeah, that's okay, right?"

"Of course. Are you still fine with staying with me, because I can arrange a hotel?"

"No, the guys are stoked that they'll be staying at your London house and Celeste will be there too. Unless you'd rather we stayed in a hotel."

"Not at all. It'll be almost like old times." Louisa chuckled. Konran had stayed over many times when he'd been younger and had even come out to Holmwood House and London over the time they known each other. They chatted easily talking about old times. For all his superstar status, to Louisa he was lanky Konran, who took time out to talk to Celeste the first time she'd visited the music workshop.

Their conversation shifted to CASPO and her new role there. "So you'll be the official patron after the ball?"

"That's right."

"And Celeste told me about Miles being the new ambassador." He let out a laugh. "Who'd have thought it, eh? Celeste's crush being part of CASPO. Joking aside, he's cool and a great pull, though he hasn't performed or released anything since the shooting."

"I think it's still hard for him," Louisa said softly.

"Yeah, I totally get that." If there was anyone who could understand Miles, it was Konran. He'd been ten years old when his father had been gunned down in broad daylight, caught in the crossfire of rival gangs. He'd turned his grief to composing rap songs about his pain and anger. Now his songs had messages of hope and optimism and finding the good in whatever life threw at you.

"If anyone understands, it's you, Konran."

"Will he be at the activity event?"

"Erm… we haven't really had time to go over it with him yet. But I'm sure he will."

"That sounds awesome. I know I'll only be there for just over a day but I'll make it unforgettable; maybe we could do something together."

"That's sounds like a good idea. Maybe you could suggest it to him."

"Yeah maybe I will. Wow, Miles Keane and me."

"Miles Keane and *I*!" Louisa corrected.

"Yeah, yeah, whatever. Look, there's something else I wanted to run by you."

"Sure, what do you need?"

"Well, this album has gone through the roof. Sort of set me

and my mom up for life." Louisa congratulated him again on how well he was doing, then asked him about his mother. He'd set her up in a nice house, as well as his aunt and their family, so that they'd be close by. "And I still love writing and recording, so that ain't ever going to stop."

"That *isn't* going to stop." Louisa corrected and Konran chuckled, thinking she was never going to give up on correcting his grammar.

"So I want to do more than just give big donations."

"Well, your time is just as valuable, Konran. Coming to the activity weekend will be huge for the kids."

"I know that too but I was kinda thinking that... from now on, any money I make from future albums should go straight to charity, to CASPO and the one you were part of that helped me in New York."

"Konran, that's very generous." Louisa gasped. He was talking about a few hundred million and though Louisa would've welcomed the donation, she wanted to make sure he was being advised properly. "Have you talked it over with your manager?"

"Yeah. He was a little shocked but bottom line, it's my decision and I want to give back. I never need to work a day in my life again, even if I have ten kids. I'll make money on the concerts plus a few endorsements I'm looking at. Louisa, they need it more."

"Konran that's... I'm so honoured to have met you, got to see you grow up into this incredible *awesome* man. I don't know what to say," Louisa choked out, clearly moved by this grand gesture.

"The honour was mine, Lady B, it's always been mine."

MILES STEPPED OUT OF his cab and looked up at the CASPO building, wondering why Louisa wasn't answering his calls or messages. He knew she was busy with the ball preparations but

Miles had a niggling feeling it was something else. Maybe spending time in New York with Gerard had caused this change of heart. Miles scowled at the thought. He needed to clarify exactly what was going on between them. He knew he wanted more than late night phone calls and secret kisses and though he hadn't a clue on what was the correct protocol when trying to date a countess, he wasn't going to let that stop him. Regardless of his determination, Miles still felt uneasy as he walked through the reception area of CASPO's offices. The girl on the desk greeted him with a huge smile and asked how he was, while her cheeks blushed uncontrollably. Miles was used to women being flustered around him and made an effort to be gracious, even if it became tedious after a while. The receptionist guided him to Melissa's office, which was in complete disarray. There were hundreds of gold bags on every surface and three of CASPO's staff were placing varying items into each one. The staff stopped what they were doing and stared unashamedly at Miles.

"Morning, Miles, welcome to the chaos that is my office," Melissa snorted. She'd resorted to wearing unflattering smock dresses and ballet shoes, now she was bigger.

"Morning." Miles greeted the staff and gave Melissa a kiss on the cheek. "What are these for?"

"The guests at the ball. Gift bags for each one of them." Miles peered inside seeing a hard-backed copy of the latest bestselling autobiography, his and hers designer fragrances, a box of exclusively handmade Champagne truffles, a bottle of 30-year-old single malt and a sleek power bank.

"A power bank?" Miles asked.

"Oh yes, very useful. It powers up all phones, tablets and laptops. They're the most powerful one on the market," Melissa said with pride, then turned her attention to the CASPO staff who were still drooling over Miles. "Chop, chop, we haven't got all day."

"Cool."

"You want one? We've a whole box over there." Melissa pointed over to the far side of her office. "One of Robert's companies imports them."

"Oh, thanks."

"Come on, we'd better get to the meeting. If you stay in my office any more, they'll never finish," she said dryly and hefted her heavily pregnant self out of her chair.

"So it's been pretty busy then?" Miles asked as they made their way to the boardroom.

"Oh yes, we've been rushed off our feet. Robert keeps dragging me out of here at seven but I hate leaving Louisa to do it all."

"I think Robert's right. How long have you got to go?"

"Eight blasted weeks. I feel like a whale as it is." Miles chuckled and said something on the lines of that she was blooming and Melissa scoffed, knowing he was just being kind.

They entered the boardroom, where Margot and a few of the senior CASPO staff were already seated. After greeting everyone, they began the meeting, going over the order of events, timing of arrivals, which media channels and publications would be there and the current total of revenue the ball had brought in so far. Margot added that there was a step up in security measures, not only because of the celebrities attending but also members of the aristocracy and leaders in industry.

Miles wasn't entirely sure why he'd been included in the meeting but he was glad that CASPO had asked him all the same. It gave him an insight as to how this kind of event generated donations. Apart from the price of each ticket, there were sponsors of the event too, which was great exposure for both the companies and CASPO. Miles was surprised Louisa wasn't at the meeting and decided to see if she was in her office but before he could leave, Margot caught up with him.

"Will you be bringing a guest? Because we can squeeze another place on your table. Though it'll make it an odd number."

Margot twisted her mouth as she thought about it, tapping her pen against her clipboard.

"No, why would you ask?" Miles thought the question was odd, seeing as they'd clarified he wasn't bringing anyone the previous week.

"Louisa was under the impression Miss Price would be accompanying you."

Suddenly Louisa's lack of communication became crystal clear and Miles silently cursed the press and Lottie's publicist. She'd seen the photos at the closing dinner and jumped to conclusions. The wrong conclusions. "No, I'll be alone," he said tightly.

"Oh, well that won't do."

"I'm sorry?"

"It's bad enough Louisa is refusing to have someone to accompany her, something about it being the 21st century." Margot gave a huff, waving her hand in the air. "And now you too." She tutted, clearly unhappy.

"Maybe they could be each other's date." Melissa chimed in hearing their conversation.

"Excellent idea, our new ambassador and the new patron. Melissa will send you the times and I'll let Louisa know," Margot said to Miles without discussion and marched out of the boardroom.

Miles turned to a smug-looking Melissa and narrowed his eyes at her. Either Melissa knew more than she was letting on or she was just playing matchmaker. "I wanted to speak to Loui… Lady Louisa. Is she here?"

"I think she's in her office with Hugh. Come with me, I'll take you in." They paced down to where Louisa's door was slightly ajar where Miles could hear Hugh's hushed voice. Melissa rapped her knuckles on the door, then opened it. Louisa was behind her desk, looking as stunning as always in a yellow shift dress, her thick hair styled in an up-do, showcasing her slender neck and for a second, Miles faltered. He greeted them both, noting Louisa widening her eyes in surprise at seeing him.

"Miles wanted a word," Melissa said with a bright smile, then turned to Hugh. "Hugh, can I borrow you for a moment?" Within a few seconds, Melissa had ushered the efficient head of security out of Louisa's office and shut the door behind her. Miles couldn't have liked her any more at that moment.

"I have the distinct feeling you're trying to avoid me." Miles stepped towards her desk and Louisa stood up, not wanting him to look down on her.

"Miles, I have a lot to get through today..."

He cut her off before she could brush him off with any excuses. "If you're pissed at me you should at least tell me what I did."

"What or who?" she said in that precise ladylike tone Miles was beginning to know too well.

"I see." He pursed his lips together and shook his head. "You think that all because I'm at the same event as Lottie, that I automatically slept with her?"

"You know what, Miles, it really doesn't matter. I have absolutely no right to presume, judge or speculate. After all we're just..."

"Just what?" He arched a brow at her and paused for a beat. "What exactly are we, Louisa? Friends? Well friends wouldn't be so quick to jump to conclusions. Colleagues? You wouldn't be so upset if we were just colleagues, now, would you?"

"I'm not upset," she shot back, though it was obvious she most certainly was.

"Really? Well you're nothing like the Louisa who loaded my dishwasher or who listened to me play my music to her a few nights ago."

There was a hard knock at the door and Miles cursed under his breath. *Why was it so damned hard to have a few minutes alone?* Louisa beckoned whoever it was to come in.

"Oh sorry, I didn't realise you were still here; am I interrupting?" Melissa said with zero concern.

"No, Miles was just leaving." Louisa glared at Miles.

"Actually it's good you are here. Seeing as you're both going solo to the ball, Margot thought it'd be fitting for you to be each other's date…"

"*Date?* I'm not…" Louisa shifted her glare to Melissa.

Melissa ignored her friend's objection. "It also means we can have you both use the same car, so it makes my life easier," she said dramatically and Miles stifled a grin. "That isn't a problem, is it? I just talked it over with Hugh and he says that works fine. Also helps to cut down on our emissions and all that. Got to think of the environment," Melissa said in a rush, leaving Louisa no room for discussion. Louisa gave a curt nod, knowing her dear friend had backed her into a corner. She'd look petty if she objected, but she would definitely be giving Melissa a piece of her mind at her meddling ways. Miles said he was fine with whatever arrangements.

"Excellent! I'll send you both the time of pick up. Shall I walk you out?" Melissa beamed at Miles.

"Of course, after you, Melissa."

They set off towards the entrance, dropping by her office to pick up the power bank she'd promised him. Melissa gave him a sideward glance and they walked to the reception as she chatted away in her usual friendly manner, but she could see his mind was elsewhere.

"Thanks for this," he said as he reached the door.

"You're very welcome – and not just for that." She nodded at the box in his hand.

Miles furrowed his brow, unsure of what she was referring to.

"Let me give you a little bit of advice, Miles. Louisa isn't your usual kind of woman." Miles face dropped and Melissa waved her hand dismissively in the air, indicating she didn't mean anything bad by her statement. "I've know her all my life. She trusts four people in her life. Melissa put up four fingers and ticked off each one. "Lady Alice, Alistair, Hugh and me. She's trusted in the past and been stung, in the worst way, so you're going to have to be patient with her. That frosty exterior she puts up is purely for protection. You've managed to melt through it, though." She gave him a wry smile and he let out a sharp breath. "Give her a bit of space; she's a lot on her plate right now, and... well just so you know, I'm totally on your side. You're exactly what she needs."

"So you orchestrated all that, then?" Miles jerked his head towards the offices beyond the reception area. Melissa tapped her nose and said, "Like I said, you're welcome."

Miles leaned down and gave her a peck on the cheek. "Thanks, I think I need all the help I can get."

"Oh, you're not doing too badly."

Miles took hold of the door handle and opened the door.

"You know, I can't drink at the moment, so a bottle of Lafite is out of the question. But I do like éclairs though." She grinned at Miles and his jaw dropped for a second as he realised Melissa obviously knew far more than she was letting on. He chuckled and made a mental note to order a dozen éclairs to be delivered as soon as possible.

20

THE BALL

MILES ADJUSTED HIS BOW tie for what seemed like the hundredth time as Hugh drove through the early evening London traffic. He eyed the back of the driver's head and wondered whether he should ask him about Louisa. She'd ignored his calls and message since their brief talk at CASPO's offices and Miles was convinced that she was going to make new arrangements for tonight's ball but at six o'clock, on the dot, Hugh arrived in her Bentley. Miles was both relieved and nervous, hence his constant fidgeting. He'd played to thousands of fans in concerts and been live streamed to billions, yet an evening with Lady Louisa Blackthorn had him jumpy. Miles couldn't believe he was reduced to this. The feeling of uncertainty was alien to him. He'd never had to try and win a woman over and if he'd felt a bit of resistance, he'd tended to move on without a second thought. There had always been plenty to pick up the slack. Louisa had changed that. From their first meeting, he was constantly doing the chasing, trying to impress her, learn more about her but she always seemed just out of reach. Miles wondered whether that was what was drawing her to him, the allure of her unattainability. His ego refusing to let go. Miles looked out of the window and sighed; it was more than that and he knew it. Since meeting her, she had become a constant and captivating thought and there was rarely a moment she was far from his mind.

Tonight was going to be hard enough without a frosty Louisa by his side. This was the first official event he was attending for CASPO. He'd have to circulate and rub shoulders with the kind of people Louisa was used to spending time with. He'd never been one to conform, he'd always been a take-me-as-I-am kind of guy, but maturity and experience had rubbed away that rougher edge to him. He was here for a good cause, and important one, one that would change the lives of children and if it meant he'd have to suck it up, he'd do it. The upside to this stuffy and aristocratic event was at least he'd be in the same room as Louisa, and at some point, he would make sure she heard him out.

After Miles had realised it was because of the photos of him and Lottie that had upset Louisa, he'd tried to call her to explain that it was purely by coincidence. It was inevitable that he would bump into Lottie at Men's London Fashion Week, and the handful of pictures taken were literally during a couple of minutes within the five-day event. The price of fame was that pictures and quotes were taken out of context and normally, Miles wouldn't care how he was perceived – until it affected his possible relationship with Louisa.

Louisa had ignored his calls, so he'd reverted to sending a message, but again she hadn't responded. So Miles decided that rather than badger her anymore, he'd do as Melissa suggested, and give her some space, but at some point during the evening he'd make sure she knew that Lottie meant nothing to him. How he would do that he wasn't sure. One way or another, he wanted Louisa to know that there was no one in his life, but he hoped there would be.

Hugh slowed down and parked up the car outside what could

only be described as a palatial stately home in the heart of London. Miles held back from whistling out loud. He'd seen Holmwood House when he'd searched for information on Louisa but he hadn't seen Louisa's London home. He stared up at the four-storey 20th-century mansion and again felt out of his depth. Miles had never really seen Louisa in her own environment, only at Blacks Club, and then he hadn't known who she was. Seeing her home for the first time made Miles realise that Louisa's life was as far removed from his at it could be. He had a big life, full of anything he could ever imagine, and could buy whatever he wanted, but Louisa's life wasn't only big, it was grand and gilt-edged in privilege.

Hugh turned and explained he'd be a moment, then stepped out of the car. Miles kept his eyes on the double dark wooden door and wondered whether he should get out and accompany Louisa. But before he could suggest it, Louisa's statuesque form appeared. Miles stared unashamedly at the stunning vision of Lady Louisa Blackthorn gliding towards the car, flanked by two suited men. Her sapphire ball gown with off-the-shoulder structured drape was both dramatic and elegant. The dress's asymmetric pleats and demure side slit made it chic and modern, displaying Louisa's flair for style. Hugh opened the door for her and softly complimented her appearance. She thanked him, then smoothly slid into the plush interior. Hugh spoke briefly to the two men, who then left and got into a black car in front of them.

"Louisa, you look breathtaking," Miles said as his gaze swept over her serene expression.

"Thank you." The slight tilt of her head caused the low early evening sunlight to catch her diamond and sapphire earrings, sending a sparkle around the car. Miles's eyes flitted to the back of Hugh's head and he once again wondered if he'd always be around at the most private moments of their time together. Before Miles could say any more, Hugh spoke. "My lady?"

"Yes, Hugh."

"Lady Alice and Lady Celeste will be arriving at Blacks at 6:35, five minutes before our ETA."

"Celeste will be at the ball?" Miles asked, shifting a little so he could look at her better.

"Yes." She gave a tight smile, then added, "She's been staying at Holmwood since we returned from New York."

"I'm looking forward to meeting the woman who stood me up." Miles gave her a wide smile, hoping his joking would melt through her frosty exterior. Louisa's lips twitched at his comment and she allowed her gaze to skim over him. Her fleeting glimpse noted his break-from-tradition midnight blue tuxedo, which hugged his body perfectly. She wouldn't have expected anything less from Miles, the ever rebel and non-conformist. It surprised her how much it pleased her that he didn't feel the need to follow the rules.

"My lady?" Hugh's voice brought Louisa's attention to the front of the car and Miles clenched his jaw. He'd hoped that during the ten-minute drive they'd clear the atmosphere, but the interruptions were making it harder. "Mr Konjwa's flight is on time."

"Excellent." Louisa reached into her blue clutch bag and pulled out her phone, then proceeded to rapidly type on it. Miles narrowed his eyes and focused on her elegant hands. This was the first time he'd seen her use her phone. He remembered asking her about it on one of their many late night conversations. Louisa had stated that she wasn't a huge fan of phones but she understood that they were now essential. The idea that moments were constantly interrupted by calls or messages irritated her – hence she thought having your phone out in company was bad manners. Her comment had explained why on their first date Louisa had seemed displeased at the sight of Miles's phone.

"I thought you didn't look at your mobile when you were on a date." Miles tried to keep his tone neutral, but even he could hear the edge in his voice. He felt that she was purposely snubbing him.

Louisa paused for a beat and tilted her head towards him and locked her gaze on his piercing blue eyes. "Is this a date? I thought we were just carpooling," she said in that precise tone that both annoyed and aroused Miles in equal measures. He gave her that cocky smirk she knew meant she'd upset him, and for a split second, Louisa regretted her unladylike behaviour, not because he was rattled but because her remark confirmed to him that he'd hurt her.

Miles's stomach dropped at the not-so-subtle reference to their conversation about his and Lottie's relationship. "Louisa –"

Before Miles could continue, Louisa cut him off. "This is work, Miles." She was already on edge about this evening. It would be the first major public event she was going to since her divorce, plus she would be under the spotlight, something she wasn't altogether happy about but she had her eye on the bigger picture. Added to that, she was still harbouring feelings of disappointment towards Miles. Her tone was calm but Miles could feel her underlying unease. "For the next five hours, we're on duty. Being Lady Blackthorn doesn't give me the privilege to throw a tantrum and storm off when something or someone pisses me off. We get on with it; struggle through. I'm not a diva who can go and cancel an appearance on a whim or just behave badly. It's just not done." She paused for a second to collect herself. Louisa hadn't wanted to show how vulnerable she was feeling, but sitting at such close quarters to Miles had her emotions coming up to the surface. She just couldn't have this conversation with him now; there were too many other things going on for her personally and professionally. "This is who I am. I will smile, be polite. Do what's expected of me, my duty, because my title comes with this cost. Believe me, the last thing I want to do now is be on show – and not only because of whatever is going on between you and I."

Miles saw the struggle in her beautiful face and gave her soft smile. The last thing he wanted to do was make tonight harder for her.

"This is not about me, or you or us. This is about going out there and doing our duty so children have a decent education, they're taken from abusive parents, their lives are changed for the better and for good. You think you can do that?"

"Of course. Louisa –" Her name was a soft plea.

Hugh interrupted them again. It took every ounce of self-control for Miles not to tell him to shut the fuck up. Hugh informed Louisa about the arrival of some other VIP guest. Miles presumed his team were sending updates which Hugh needed to convey to Louisa but it didn't lessen his annoyance. He clenched his jaw and stared blindly out of the car window, deciding whatever he had to say to Louisa, he'd do without an audience, someone overhearing it or interrupting.

The car started to make its way up the familiar driveway to the Black Club and in the distance, Miles could see that the whole entranceway had been transformed with black velvet ropes leading the way. On either side of the newly laid black carpet, that paved the way into the club, were huge elegant flower arrangements on golden pedestals. There seemed to be a mass of security men guiding prestigious cars in the right direction, which confirmed the type of guests who would be at this illustrious affair.

Louisa caught sight of Miles's shocked expression and realised that he was probably feeling nervous. They were here to do a job and it wouldn't do for him to be uneasy. She needed to put her personal feelings to one side and make this evening as comfortable as possible for him. Miles turned as Louisa's voice cut through the unnatural quiet of the car.

"I know Melissa sent you the itinerary for tonight but once we're in there, you'll probably forget it all. It can be quite hectic." She gave him a reassuring smile and he nodded. "There will be a number of Black's staff who will be on hand to keep you informed. We tend to get waylaid talking too long. We've 30 minutes tops before we go in for pre-dinner drinks."

"I've done red carpets before, Louisa," Miles said with smirk, though he had to admit this was nothing like those.

"Of course. This one's *black,* though." She arched her brow at him and he chuckled.

"Louisa –"

"Not now, Miles. Remember, this is what I do. This, right now, is what's important." He gave her a nod. She was right of course and he marvelled at how she was able to detach herself. Gone was *just* Louisa and in her place was the elegant Countess of Holmwood.

"Game face on, then," Miles said as he playfully widened his eyes. Louisa stifled her smile, grateful that her rather terse words hadn't fazed him. He was diffusing the tense atmosphere in his unique way.

As Hugh brought the car up to the edge of the black carpet, Louisa leant forward and handed him her phone. "Alistair's been informed of Konran's ETA. I've seen to all the logistics. If there is anything pressing, you know where to find me." Louisa's fingers drifted over the beautiful bracelet she'd worn, a subtle reference to the tracker Hugh had hidden behind one of the sapphires.

Hugh then got out of the car and opened the door for Miles to step out. "Mr Keane, enjoy your evening," Hugh said with a smirk.

"Thank you, Hugh," Miles said, then bent down and extended his hand to help Louisa out of the car. They were in full glare of the guests, who were already walking in, and the privileged photographers and journalists who had been given the exclusive rights to the event. But for all the sudden frenzy of activity behind them, Miles's focus was on the beautiful woman who had clasped her hand in his and risen out of the car. It felt like a bolt of electricity had shot through them and their eyes locked conveying so much in a few seconds. They may have had personal issues but right now, in this very moment, they were united in duty and a joint team.

I've got your back.

Don't worry.

I'm glad you're here.

Thank you.

Louisa worked the black carpet like a pro. Miles was in awe of how each of her responses to the many questions about the event were expertly answered. She knew the photographers and journalists by name and managed to convey all the relevant information without sounding staged or rehearsed. *What were CASPO's future plans? What other events would be hosted? How was the money allocated? Who was benefitting from tonight's event? How did it feel being back in the UK? How did it feel to be taking over her mother's role?* The questions came at her in constant rapid fire and she answered everyone without breaking a sweat, reeling off facts, figures and future projections with charm and grace. Louisa introduced Miles to every journalist, even though they knew exactly who he was, mainly so he would know which publication he was talking to.

They were of course photographed together, but Miles noted that no one asked any inappropriate questions. When he'd done red carpets in the past, he'd always had some innuendo thrown at him about the women he was escorting. At this event there was none. Miles wondered whether the press had been warned not to, or maybe they just had respect for Louisa and her family, or perhaps they just weren't that interested in him. He wasn't the star of the show today, Lady Louisa Blackthorn was. Her absence from the UK and her return were obviously more interesting than anything he was connected to.

Miles let his gaze sweep over Louisa for a moment as she spoke to another journalist and she turned slightly, allowing her eyes to flit over to him. She gifted him with a small smile and continued. For a moment, Miles felt that maybe she'd forgotten the whole Lottie debacle.

They were then ushered into a small room where Melissa was waiting for them. She quickly poured and handed Louisa and Miles a glass of water from a side table, saying that they must be parched after all that talking, gushing at how well they'd done and how gorgeous they both looked. Louisa took a welcome sip and rolled her eyes at her ever enthusiastic and less than subtle friend.

"You looked good out there, like the perfect couple – even your outfits match," Melissa snorted, though her eyes sparkled with mischief as she said it. Miles tried to stifle his grin and failed, then took a gulp of his water. Melissa was right; his mouth had dried up.

"I'm not sure about that, I think I'm 15 years too old, I'm not a model, actress or singer, I'm not blonde or super-skinny and petite, and we all know that's more to Mr Keane's taste."

Miles choked on his water and Louisa turned to look at him, his eyes wide in surprise. "*Shit,* Louisa," he spluttered, caught off-guard by her flippant remark. Maybe he was wrong after all. It seemed that Louisa was still holding a grudge. Louisa picked up a napkin from the side table and handed it to him so he could dab his mouth. Melissa drew in her lips, trying hard not to laugh, enjoying watching the obvious sexual tension between her best friend and Miles.

"No point crying over spilt mineral water," Louisa said dryly and before Miles could say anything, the side door opened and in walked Hugh.

"My lady, all the guests are assembled in the lounge. Lady Blackthorn and Lady Celeste are about to go through."

"Thank you, Hugh." He gave a quick nod and exited the room.

"Right, I'd better go in. So, wait about a couple of minutes once I leave. Let Lady Alice and Celeste have their moment and then when you're ready, Mr Thomas will announce you." Melissa gave them both a big smile and then clenched her fist and shook it in front of her in a go-get-'em gesture, then left the room.

"Alone at last," Miles said dryly, then arched his brow at Louisa.

"Miles..." Louisa put her hand up in protest but from the devilish look in Miles's eye and the determined look on his face, she knew any resistance was futile. His smouldering eyes had darkened and the tension between them over the last few days was now at sizzling point.

"It's just you and me now." Miles had closed the distance between them, his eyes locked on hers. Louisa swallowed, totally mesmerized, and all thoughts of Lottie, distinguished guests and duty went flying out of the window.

"Only for a minute," she squeezed out and Miles's sculptured lips twitched.

"I'd better make it count, then."

Before Louisa could say a word, his lips crashed to hers. His hands flew up to frame her face, holding her steady but still mindful not to mess her up. Within a second Louisa gripped onto his lapels and pulled him as close as she could, allowing the tension to explode into this all-consuming kiss. There was no gentleness; this was a kiss born from frustration, anger and red-hot desire, and had there not been three hundred guests waiting for Lady Blackthorn in the lounge at Blacks Club, Miles would have knocked everything off the antique side table and taken her there and then, protocol be damned. They pulled away, gasping at the sound of a round of applause that had drifted in from the lounge, signalling the arrival of Lady Alice and Celeste.

Miles rested his forehead against Louisa's, his hands gentler on the side of her face now as they both allowed their breathing to calm. Miles slowly lifted his heavy lids and his gaze was met with Louisa's wide brown eyes staring back at him. "For the record and for future reference, you are exactly my taste: sweet and totally delicious," he said in a hoarse voice, then dropped a swift kiss on her swollen lips and stepped back.

Louisa's heart raced. This man was breaking her down with every candid word and every bold action and if she wasn't careful, he might just have the power to break her totally. She gave him a shy smile, registering her own words being thrown back at her, then handed him another napkin.

Miles furrowed his brow and she made a circling gesture in front of her mouth. Miles said a silent "Oh".

"Yes, dusky pink lipstick isn't your colour."

"Really?" He gave her a lopsided grin and she giggled. She turned to look in the mirror behind her and quickly touched up her makeup, catching Miles's admiring gaze in the reflection as he wiped his mouth. "You look absolutely stunning."

"Thank you." Her cheeks heated at his compliment.

"You and I need to have a serious talk, face to face, and with no one around."

Louisa gave him a nod and turned around to face him. He looked every part the superstar playboy in his bespoke tuxedo. "We do," she said with a sigh.

"Preferably naked." Miles deadpanned.

"Miles!" She choked out a laugh.

"Okay, I'll concede, semi-naked and we'll work it from there."

Louisa laughed again and shook her head, feeling like a huge weight had lifted from her. "Let's start with being alone first, shall we?" She let her fingers drift over his lapels and he caught her hand and kissed her palm.

"Good. Not right now though because I think our few minutes are up." He put out his arm. "Come on, my lady, your public awaits you."

"Such a gentleman," she said with a hint of sarcasm.

"I wasn't that much of a gentleman a couple minutes ago."

"I won't tell anyone if you don't."

Miles let out a husky laugh. "Come on. Game face on."

"Game face on."

Mr Thomas took his cue as the door opened and announced in a clear voice.

"May I present the Countess of Holmwood, Lady Blackthorn and Mr Miles Keane."

The room erupted into raucous applause and Miles flinched at the level of noise. Louisa tightened her grip on his arm and he was never more grateful that she was by his side. Louisa smiled at the guests, blindly walking through the mass of people glad she had Miles to lean on.

For the next 30 minutes, they moved around the room. Before introducing Miles to whomever they were about to speak to, Louisa whispered a quick rundown of who they were, so he wouldn't feel uncomfortable. Most of the guests she'd known for a very long time but for Miles, they were just faceless donators. Again he marvelled at how smoothly Louisa stroked each person's ego with her attention and still managed to slip in the importance of the work CASPO did. She balanced her well-versed sales pitch with compliments and genuine interest in each guest.

Lady Alice and Celeste were also working the room along with Margot, Melissa, Robert and the CASPO board members, ensuring all donators were spoken to and thanked. Miles scanned the grand room and noted that even though there were a fair number of guests over the age of 40, the majority of them were in their 20s, which he thought was strange, considering each ticket was £10,000, until Louisa began to introduce him to the various guests.

"Miles, may I introduce Lord and Lady Marlborough and their daughters, Phoebe, Milly and their son Edward." Hands were shaken and the women stared unashamedly at Miles.

"Miles, may I introduce The Earl of Wesson and Lady Broughton, it's lovely to see you. How are the Earl and Countess?" Louisa shook the hands of a tall young man and starstruck young woman.

"They're well, thank you. In Hong Kong at the mo though; that's why we're here, representing them with a table of our pals," the young man explained as his sister continued to stare at Miles.

"Miles, may I introduce you to Sir Henry Westmoreland and his wife Charlotte." The portly middle-aged man, who had the largest chain of frozen foods stores throughout the UK, introduced his two daughters and two sons plus their dates for the evening. Miles was faced with a set of blushing young women. He took the time to speak to each one and then was guided to the next guest. And so it went on, Lady this, Sir that, along with their heirs and heiresses to no doubt a billion-pound fortune, every name forgotten and every face morphed into another. Miles again was struck at how accomplished Louisa was at this role. By the time they'd reached the ballroom entrance, Miles had begun to understand why there were so many younger guests.

Mr Thomas announced that dinner would shortly be served and the guests made their way to their tables while Louisa and Miles hung back.

"Why do I get the distinct feeling that CASPO has subtly pimped me out again?" he whispered to Louisa, after he'd just been introduced and spoken to David Marks, owner of the famed shoe chain stores, and his two daughters.

"We're not being subtle, Miles. We filled this dinner within 24 hours of putting it up on our website. We had a waiting list of over two thousand people. As soon as it was announced you'd be here, every socialite, industry mogul's offspring and young aristocrat wanted a seat and thankfully, mummy and daddy paid."

"Wow."

"Indeed. We raised £3 million alone from the dinner and that's without the extra donations."

"Why the hell don't they just hand over the money anyway

and not go through all this?" Miles waved his hand towards the ballroom.

"Because how else can Sir Westmorland show off to David Marks that he bought a table too? Or that The Earl of Wesson paid for two tables to Lord Marlborough's one? It's all about show and sadly without that, the money won't come in."

"That's fucked up."

"Yep. Welcome to the world of the elite and aristocracy. It's basically what my father used to call 'a pissing contest'." Miles chuckled and Louisa grinned at him. "That's why Alistair stays away from these things. He hates the whole scene and can't stand to be diplomatic."

Miles let his gaze drift over the mass of guests who were making their way to their tables. "It's still a bit stuffy for all this lot though, isn't it?"

"Ordinarily yes, but this year we've mixed it up a bit, catered for the younger guests."

"You mean apart from pimping me out?" He arched his brow at her.

"Yes, is your ego hurt?"

"Terribly. I may cause a scene and have a tantrum if I don't have my quota of adoration and attention," he said in mock-horror and Louisa giggled. She loved the way he joked and didn't take himself seriously. It was a refreshing change from Gerard's more serious nature.

"When Melissa and I realised what was going on, we had to change our game plan."

"I don't understand."

"Well, we're happy that we filled the place, but we also wanted the new younger guests to have a good time. We want them to carry on coming and not only to this kind of event. So we had to swap our usual band for something a little more contemporary."

"So what's on the agenda?"

"Can you keep a secret?"

"Not as good as you, but yeah," he said with a cheeky smile, referring to their first date, and Louisa chuckled.

"TuKon is coming to play." Louisa tried not to sound too smug but she was excited that Konran was able to be there for her.

"What! But he's huge. How… he's on a world tour right now."

"Yeah I know, but he'll be arriving in about an hour. Alistair's flying him in from the airport."

"How the hell did you pull that off?" Miles asked, a little more in awe of the connections Louisa seemed to have. Louisa caught sight of Celeste walking towards them and smiled. She'd again behaved like a lady and spent the last 30 minutes accompanying her grandmother, making small talk to stuffy, middle-aged, rich donators and no doubt charming every one of them and their sons. Celeste was well practiced in the art of schmoozing. From a very early age, she'd attended functions and events with her parents, so tonight was all part and parcel of her life.

"It's a long story. I'll tell you about it sometime, but now let me introduce you to the first woman who ever stood you up."

"I believe I owe you an apology."

Miles turned around and was faced with a pretty blonde woman in a silver grey gown. Even without the introduction, Miles knew instantly who she was. Celeste's looks were a subtle combination of her mother and father. She had her mother's nose and mouth but her eyes and skin tone were definitely Gerard's. Her thick blonde hair, though, was inherited from her grandmother, Lady Alice. Celeste put out her hand for Miles to shake.

"No apology necessary. Your understudy did a fine job of entertaining me." He took her hand and she gave it a firm shake.

"Is that so?" Celeste arched her brow at him and darted her eyes towards her mother.

"Pleased to meet you, Lady Celeste."

"Likewise, Mr Keane. You're shorter than I remember you."

Miles chuckled at her forwardness and he remembered Louisa telling him that her daughter could hold her own in most situations. A few seconds in her company and he could see Louisa was completely right. She had a confidence beyond her years, but had a warmth about her that made her approachable, regardless of her title.

"That's probably because you're wearing heels and you're taller now," Louisa said with a roll of her eyes and wondered whether Miles had picked up on Celeste's comment about having already met him.

"Probably," Celeste said with a shrug.

Hugh slipped into through a side door, causing them to halt their conversation. "My lady, they're ready for you."

The dinner proceeded like most of these kinds of events, with exquisite food paired with fine wines, copious amounts of alcohol and a healthy dose of benign small talk. Louisa and Miles were seated at a table that Miles realised was more suited to him than any of the others. The eight guests comprised of the head of production at the Pinewood Group, the head of the National Theatre as well as two CEOs of the top film and TV production companies in the UK. It meant that Miles had a slight respite from the lustful looks from all the younger guests at the ball and was able to at least engage in a conversation. All the guests at their table showed a genuine interest in his future plans and he of course charmed them all with a few anecdotes from his past.

It had been a while since Louisa had last made a speech and she was surprised at how nervous she was. She was never gladder to have Miles at least take on the burden of entertaining their table. It wasn't long before Louisa was called up to the stage where her mother, Lady Alice, had made a short speech thanking everyone for attending and that she was pleased her daughter would be continuing the good work CASPO had done.

Louisa made her way to the stage to the sound of applause and took her place by the podium under the spotlight. She looked serenely over the guests as the applause died down and Miles couldn't help but admire her poise and beauty. As soon as the applause stopped, Louisa began.

"I have big shoes to fill – of course, I mean that figuratively." The guests laughed softly at her comment. "My parents began CASPO 30 years ago this September." Louisa paused as the guests applauded. "Over those years, the charity has helped hundreds of thousands of children and single-parent families, making a difference in their lives, not only for the short term but well into their future. A future that has meant they have safety and security rather than living in fear, that they have their own home rather than somewhere to live and that they have a successful career, rather than just a job." The guests murmured their approval. "These are privileges every one of us has in this room but for some though, it is an unattainable dream. My parents started CASPO so that those dreams could come true and it is an honour for me to be patron of such an admirable charity. Thank you all for your continuing and generous support. Without it, CASPO wouldn't be able to continue my parent's legacy. Tonight is not about my new position though, tonight is a celebration of the hard work and vision my parent's had and to the 30 years my mother has been the selfless patron."

Louisa turned to her mother as the whole room stood and applauded and for the first time, Lady Alice Blackthorn was rendered speechless. Louisa gave her mother a tight hug and Lady Alice tried to keep her emotions in check at the unexpected tribute. Once the applause died down, Louisa's attention was drawn to the window that overlooked the lawn where Alistair had just landed his helicopter. Konran and his three group members were heading towards the club in a golf cart.

"Now as a surprise, I'm proud to introduce our special guest for tonight. He's generously arranged to be here between his world tour dates." The guests strained in their seats to catch the first glimpse of who Louisa was referring to. Konran and his group jumped out of the cart and jogged in through the French windows to gasps and excited chatter. "It's my pleasure to welcome the number one, best-selling rap star artist of the year TuKon!"

As Konran ran up the few steps to the stage, the whole room erupted in applause and once again were on their feet. Konran lifted up his hands in greeting, then turned to shake Lady Alice's hand and kiss her cheek, saying a few words to her. He then stepped up to Louisa and engulfed her in a warm embrace, his large frame almost dwarfing her. "It's so good to see you, Lady B," he whispered in her ear.

"It's good to see you too. I'm so proud of you." Louisa stepped back and Konran caught her hand lifted up in the air and faced the guests, who applauded even louder. Louisa smiled widely, then walked backwards, clapping to let the superstar she'd seen grow up, from an awkward 14-year-old, have his moment.

Konran scanned the ballroom, taking in every face, searching for the one he'd yet to see, until he heard an unladylike whistle and laughed seeing his surrogate sister waving at him. He jumped down from the stage and jogged towards Celeste and lifted her up in a bear hug, to the delight of the guests. "Hey superstar."

"Hey, lady, I've missed you."

"I missed you more. Now shut up and go sing."

Konran laughed and kissed her cheek, then ran back up to the stage. "It's an honour to be here. Y'all having a good time?" The guests responded with a resounding cheer. "So, I'd like to introduce my good friends here: Margie, Ty and Roy, who I brought along especially to perform tonight. We're going to play some of our songs but just to ease you all in, we'll be playing something a little mellow to begin with." The audience chuckled at his comment as he took his place at the piano. He adjusted the microphone and gave a nod to his group, who'd positioned themselves on the tight stage, then began to play.

Miles stood clapping, flabbergasted at the moving scene that unfolded in front of him. *Lady Louisa Blackthorn had again surprised him – scratch that, she'd knocked him on his ass.* It was now obvious from what Miles had witnessed that Konran, aka TuKon, was someone very significant in Louisa's life, in all the Blackthorn's lives.

Louisa slipped into her seat next to Miles and he shook his head in wonder, then leaned to whisper, " Lady Blackthorn, you've managed to surprise me yet again."

Louisa shuddered at the feel of his warm breath against the shell of her ear and her eyes darted to their guests, whose attention was thankfully transfixed on the stage. Miles pulled back and she gave him that enigmatic smile he'd grown to love which only made him want to kiss her soundly. The fact he couldn't was driving him crazy; he wasn't used to all these restrictions. Miles was an in-the-moment kind of guy and holding back was both frustrating and a huge turn on. He was in awe of the stunning woman sitting next to him and every moment Miles spent in her company, his admiration for her grew.

Konran wasn't only a talented musician, he was a showman. He'd been classically trained, which was a little-known fact because of his meteoric rise to fame in the rap world, and for the next hour, he played a mashed-up medley of popular music through the ages, catering to his audience. He opened up with *Hound Dog,* pointing to Lady Alice, knowing that she'd been a huge fan of Elvis Presley. The guests lapped up his larger-than-life performance of *Why Do Fools Fall In Love, Respect* and *Mustang Sally*. Konran had them on their feet by the time he started playing the Beatles' *Twist And Shout* and when he sang out *We Are Family,* he ran down to Celeste and span her around and the whole room cheered at his total disregard for decorum. He had the crowd laughing as he sang the words to *Play That Funky Music,* making a mock shocked face as he sang "white boy". And then when he switched to *Isn't She Lovely,* he made a grand sweeping gesture with his arm in the direction of Louisa causing the guests to collectively say 'Ah'. His cleverly thought-out medley of songs had *Ladies Night,* to which the audience clapped.

He held up three fingers and called out. "Three Lady Bs are in the house!" Then smoothly swapped to *Once, Twice, Three Times A Lady,* and pointed to Lady Alice, Louisa and Celeste. Everyone laughed and cheered at his tongue-in-cheek homage to the three women.

Konran had the whole room dancing to *Get Up Off Of That Thing* and *I Wanna Dance With Somebody* and singing along with him and his band to *Don't Stop Believin'*. Louisa smiled widely when he played the Police's *Every Little Thing She Does Is Magic.* He gave her a wink and Miles laughed at the tribute to Louisa's favourite band. Konran then geared up his performance to include the few popular rap songs of *Gettin' Jiggy Wit It, Ice Ice Baby,* and *Thrift Shop,* before playing his own hits.

Louisa proudly watched Konran bow as he ended his energetic and captivating performance, her hands stinging from her vigorous clapping. He'd taken off his deep red jacket and was now just in a black T-shirt and his red suit trousers. Louisa noted his ever-present sneakers as he jogged down the steps to greet the various guests who were desperate for a photo and to meet him.

Once the guests realised Konran wasn't about to leave, they gave him some space and allowed him and his band to rest up before he did the rounds. Konran was ushered to Louisa's table, where space had been made for him and his band.

"You guys were amazing!" Louisa hugged him again, clearly overwhelmed. "Here, let me introduce you to Miles Keane."

Konran thrust out his hand and his eyes widened in awe. "Oh wow, I can't believe I'm in the same room with you. Pleased to meet you, my man," Konran gushed, shaking Miles's hand. "I grew up with your music. Celeste and I listened to it all the time. Respect, man."

Miles blinked at the heartfelt greeting, taken a back at Konran's genuine manner. "Really? The honour is mine. You guys killed it up there and from what I hear, you're killing it around the world." Miles shook hands with the rest of the band who seemed equally in awe of Miles.

"Yeah, it's all good, but we ain't quite reached your status." Konran's eyes darted to Louisa. "Sorry: *haven't*. Lady B here gets real cross when I get my grammar wrong."

Louisa chuckled and said, "You can take the boy outta the Bronx..." causing Konran to laugh, then he turned back to Miles.

"Man, you caused me such grief. I had to change the last part of my act and take out your songs when I knew you were gonna be here." Miles furrowed his brow at the comment. "Well, I couldn't play your songs with you in the audience, man, no way! But hey, it'd be a dream come true if we got to play together sometime." Konran saw Miles's face suddenly change and he quickly added, "Not now."

Miles let out a breath of relief and said, "I'd like that."

"Yeah? Wow, you hear that Lady B? Me and Miles Keane!"

"I heard," Louisa said, grinning at the excitement in his voice.

"I need to pinch myself," Konran said with a shake of his head as Celeste made it to their table. "There's my girl." Konran snaked his arm around her waist and pulled her close, then sat down on one of the chairs and placed her on his knee.

Celeste handed him a napkin. "You're sweaty."

"You're heavy," Konran teased.

"I'm not!"

"Okay, you're not." They both laughed and it became obvious to Miles that the two of them were close in a brother and sister way. "So, your best home boy here is gonna get to play with Miles Keane."

"Really?" Celeste looked expectantly over to Miles. From her expression, he could tell she thought Konran meant now.

"Not now, but we'll arrange it," Miles clarified and she made a silent "Oh".

"Cool!"

"Well, I'll let you two catch up. I think I need to go and do my duty." Louisa stood up from the table and Miles, along with all the men at the table, stood up.

"That goes for me too. You're staying a bit longer right?" he asked Konran.

"Yeah, we're crashing at Lady B's tonight."

Miles brow lifted in surprise. Somehow he couldn't quite put the Bronx rapper star and the quintessentially British countess in the same vicinity, let alone the same house. It seemed Miles still had a lot to learn about the intriguing Lady Louisa Blackthorn and he couldn't wait to see what other surprises she had in store for him.

21

GAME FACE ON

THE DISTINGUISHED AND PRIVILEGED guests were spoiled, having two superstars amidst them. Konran and Miles spent the next hour circulating and having their pictures taken. There were group photos and selfies galore, with the backdrop of the band playing a selection of well-known mellow music for the older guests to dance to.

Louisa moved around the room, taking time to speak to as many of the guests as she could, while Miles and Konran entertained the younger supporters. She spotted Alistair's friends' table and decided to take a bit of a respite from talking shop and relax a little with some familiar faces. They were always supportive of CASPO events, even if Alistair tended to avoid them. She wasn't very familiar with all the wives and girlfriends of Alistair's friends but knew enough about them to be able to ask about their families and partake in the usual small talk. They were all genuinely pleased to see her and Louisa wondered whether, now she was back for good, she should make more of an effort to get to know them better. After all, Melissa seemed to get on with all of them; it made sense that she should at least become more involved. Louisa noticed that Gordon wasn't at the table, yet she'd spotted his wife Emily at another earlier; one of which she'd still to go and greet. She was just about to ask about Gordon when she heard the distinct American drawl of Miles behind her.

"Lady Louisa, would you do me the honour?" Ten sets of eyes flitted between the handsome ambassador with the confident smile and the clearly bewildered Lady Blackthorn. She blinked at him, unsure of what he meant, until he put out his hand.

Shit, he was asking her to dance. Louisa looked back at the table and gave a tight smile as the guests stared back at her with amusement.

"If you'll excuse me," she said, then turned and placed her hand in his. Miles guided Louisa to the dance floor without saying a word, mindful that the whole room had suddenly focused on them. Miles slipped his arm around Louisa's waist, took her hand, then smoothly began to move around the floor to the sound of Sade's *This Is No Ordinary Love.*

"Do you ever get used to it?" Miles asked softly.

Louisa's eyes lifted to his and she tried hard to keep her expression as impassive as possible. The lighting had been dimmed but the guests would still be able to make out their expressions. "They're not looking at me, Miles," she said with a mild smile and he furrowed his brow. "They're looking at you."

"I think you'll find that they're looking at *us...* but I didn't mean that, I meant the lack of privacy."

"I've been around it my whole life, at differing degrees but all the same, it's been my life. You've had your share of invasion too."

"Yeah, but not once I was in my home. When you're outside, I suppose you're fair game but inside, that's a whole different level." Miles flexed his fingers against her back and Louisa's breath hitched but she tried her hardest to conceal the effect he was having on her.

"It bothers you?"

"Yeah." Miles gave her a crooked smile and squeezed her fingers a little.

"That's part of my life."

"I get that," he said with sigh. "Seeing as we're talking about lives, and I have your undivided attention: about Lottie..."

"Miles..." Louisa's eyes widened. He couldn't do this now, not while everyone was transfixed on them, watching every gesture and every move.

"We just happened to be at the same event," he carried on, ignoring her plea. "It was nothing more and the press... fuck, they just latched on to it, or Lottie's people exploited it. Either way, it was just a minute within a five-day event. Like you said, that's part of *my* life," he said with regret.

Louisa gazed into his pleading eyes and saw nothing but sincerity, and for a moment it was just the two of them. "Okay." She gave him a soft smile and he grinned widely, forgetting about his audience of hundreds. He quickly composed himself, then said, "I can't believe that I've finally got you in my arms and we've an audience, *again*."

"I can't believe you can dance so well," she countered with stifled grin.

"I was part of a band; dancing was part of our thing."

"Is that so? Amongst other things," she said dryly and Miles chuckled as he expertly moved her around the dance floor. They nodded to the other dancers, playing their role and tried hard not to let their eyes lock on each other's. But as the song progressed, they began to relax, swept away by the dulcet tones of the singer, their bodies almost touching now, betraying an intimacy that had yet to be fully realised.

"This is our third date," Miles said as the song drew to an end and he reluctantly released her.

"It is."

"Jesus, Louisa, you have no idea how much self-control I'm

battling with right now," he said through gritted teeth as he guided her back to their table.

"I think I can guess."

As was usual at these kinds of events, guards were slowly lowered as the alcohol consumption steadily rose. The guests became bolder and both Miles and Konran were accosted for more photos and to sign various objects, plus a few body parts. Konran gaped as one young woman asked Miles to sign her thigh. He carefully obliged, then once the woman was out of earshot, he said, "It takes some getting used to doesn't it?" Konran blew air up his face and shook his head in shock.

"I've been away for almost five years and I still can't believe people are interested in what I'm doing. It's like living in a constant goldfish bowl. But doing things like this, influencing people to do good, makes it worth it."

"Yeah. It's freaky though, right?"

"Yeah, totally." Miles chuckled just as he caught sight of Louisa smiling widely at someone hidden out of sight, obstructed by a wall. She disappeared behind it. He excused himself and crossed the floor in double quick time, anxious to see who had drawn her away.

Once he'd rounded the wall, Miles pushed open two heavy double doors that opened up into the hot kitchen. He came to an abrupt halt, seeing Louisa with Alistair. "Hello." Miles stepped up to them and extended his hand.

"Hello, nice to see you again. You caught me out skulking in the kitchen," Alistair said, shaking Miles's hand. His eyes darted to his sister's, then lit up with amusement. "Thought I'd discreetly pinch a bite to eat while I waited, but Louisa spotted me." Miles noted a half-eaten plate of food on the nearby stainless steel surface. The kitchen staff seemed unfazed to have three guests casually chatting while they cleaned down surfaces, but then again, the Blackthorns did own the club. "I hear it's been quite a success tonight."

"Well this is my first one, so I can't compare, but they all seem to be having a good time. Not your kind of thing?"

Alistair grinned and shook his head. It was obvious that Alistair wasn't about to make an appearance, dressed casually in a polo shirt and khaki shorts. "No, I'm not much of a diplomat, hence the skulking. I'm just waiting to take Mama back to Holmwood."

"She's going back in the helicopter?" Louisa asked in surprise.

"Yes she is. I told her it was a waste to fly back empty and use a car just for her to come back home. Appealed to her sensible side."

"Kind of like car-pooling, then, but with a helicopter?" Miles said with a smirk and Louisa stifled a grin at his reference to their earlier conversation.

Alistair's gaze shifted between his sister and Miles. He had a distinct feeling he was missing out on some private joke. "Yes, I suppose so," Alistair said with a chuckle. "Will you find out how long Mama wants to stay?"

"Sure, I'm surprised she's lasted this long." Louisa slipped out of the kitchen, leaving Miles and Alistair.

"I suppose I'd better go back in, it was nice to see you again."

"Likewise. You're coming to the activity weekend aren't you?"

"Yes. Margot sent me all the details this week. It looks like it's going to be quite an event."

"We're hoping so and now that Konran's going to come out too, it'll be extra special for the kids. Though they won't know, we're keeping it all hush hush. It's not a PR stunt like tonight. It's purely for the kids and their parents."

"More your kind of thing, I take it," Miles said wryly.

"Definitely." Alistair jerked his head towards the kitchen door. "That in there is more my mother's and Louisa's forte. Knowing me, I'll end up offending someone and putting my foot in it." He made a face, then added, "And I've only got one and it's a size 11, so…" he joked, and Miles chuckled at the blasé way he referred to his disability.

As their laughter died down their attention was drawn to raised voices just outside the kitchen door. Before either one of them could see who it was, the door of the kitchen swung open and a clearly shaken Louisa walked in with an animated Emily in tow.

"Don't tell me you didn't know." Emily sneered. "He's been in love with you since the day he clapped eyes on you."

"Gordon is a family friend, Emily. Any affection he has for me is purely as a friend," Louisa said calmly but whole demeanour was anything but.

"Tell her, Alistair. He knows." Emily pointed at a steely-faced Alistair and he stepped forward, taking Emily's arm in the hope of guiding her out of the kitchen and away from his sister. Emily shook him off and continued her slurred tirade. "He waited for you, waited to see if you and Gerard would last, what with all the rumours," she scoffed.

"Emily, shut up! You're drunk and embarrassing yourself." Alistair snapped back.

"Maybe I am, but it's still the truth. He realised you were never going to leave Gerard so he decided to marry the booby prize!" Emily said and flicked her hands down herself. Louisa blanched at Emily's acid tone and the revelations the bitter woman was spewing out. She was thankful that they were in the confines of the kitchen and only the few remaining staff and Miles could hear. Louisa stepped forward and tried to keep her voice as soothing as possible, not wanting to let the conversation escalated any further.

"Emily, you're just upset. I know you've been having problems but…"

"Our problem is *you*!" Emily jabbed her finger in Louisa's face and Louisa took a step back. Alistair grabbed her arm again and yanked her back with zero concern if he was hurting her, but his actions didn't stem the flow of her angry words. "You went and divorced, didn't you, after fucking 20 years! Who does that? The minute Gordon found out, it was like a switch." Emily snapped her fingers.

"Emily, shut the fuck up.," growled Alistair as he practically dragged her small frame towards the outside entrance.

"Fuck you, Alistair, you and your cosy clique of friends, all covering up his dirty secret." She struggled against him, refusing to be silenced.

"Emily, I'm sure you're mistaken..." Louisa pleaded.

"The only mistake I made was believing he was over you. You ruined my life, do you know that? I'm pregnant and he wants to divorce me... *for you*!"

"Jesus Christ, I don't care who you are but I think you've said more than enough..." Miles stepped in front of Louisa, effectively blocking her from Emily's sight.

"I haven't even started. You can't keep me quiet, *Lady* Blackthorn," she shouted as Alistair pulled her through the far fire exit.

Within a second, Hugh flung open the kitchen door and assessed the situation. His steely expression honed in on Louisa first, then Miles.

"Alistair's taken her out the back." Miles jerked his head towards the rear door.

Hugh gave a curt nod, then turned to Louisa. "My lady?"

"I'm fine, Hugh," she said still clearly shaken. After a second, he strode towards the door and left them alone.

"Are you okay?" Miles bobbed down to catch Louisa's gaze. She's closed hers eyes and covered her mouth, trying to compose herself. Miles scanned the kitchen, seeing the few remaining staff doing a stellar job of pretending they'd heard nothing, though he was sure they'd heard every word and been the ones to tip off Hugh. His instinct was to take her in his arms but with an audience of the kitchen staff, he hesitated, not knowing if he'd make the whole situation worse for Louisa. One look at Louisa's trembling hand made him throw caution to the wind. *Protocol be damned.* He enveloped her in his arms, pulling her close to his chest and she immediately sagged against him, stifling a sob.

"She cornered me as I came back towards the kitchen," Louisa sniffed. "I… I had no idea they were in so much trouble. And Gordon? I've known him my whole life… And she's pregnant. Oh God, this is just so awful."

"Hey, hey, this isn't your fault, Louisa. I'm sure they were having problems and she was just lashing out," Miles said, trying to placate her, but even he wasn't sure how much of what Emily had said was exaggeration or truth. After all, he'd seen Gordon's reaction with his own eyes. Louisa pulled back from him and took in a shaky breath and Miles handed her a napkin to dab her eyes. "Are you okay?"

She gave a nod, but Miles could see the lingering shadow of distress in her eyes. Her gaze flitted to the rear door and she blew out a breath. "We better go back in. They'll be wondering where we are."

Miles nodded, though the last thing he wanted was to go and socialise and he was more than sure Louisa left the same. He pressed a kiss to her forehead, then gazed down at her. "Okay?"

She gave him a weak smile and nodded. "Game face on."

Miles chuckled. "Yeah, game face on, baby."

They came back into the ballroom and were pleased to see that their brief absence hadn't been noticed. It probably had a lot to do with the fact that Konran and Celeste were tearing up the dance floor to the delight of the guests. The famed deejay they'd brought had started to spin the latest tunes and the ballroom at Blacks hadn't seen such revelry since the 80s. Most of the tables were empty of their occupants; either they had left or were enjoying the eclectic mix of current and classic hits on the dance floor.

Miles guided Louisa to their empty table and handed her a

glass of water, which she willingly took and sipped. He caught the attention of a waiter and asked for a couple of brandies, then ensured that Louisa sat down for a moment. From the corner of his eye, Miles caught sight of Hugh re-entering the ballroom and heading towards where they were sitting. There was nothing but concern in Hugh's expression and Miles gave him a reassuring nod, indicating Louisa was fine, before he'd reached the table.

"My lady, Mrs McKenzie has been put in one of our cars and is on her way home."

"Is she alright?"

Hugh paused before answering, his eyes darting to Miles. "She was a little agitated but the Earl managed to calm her down." Louisa pinched the bridge of her nose and closed her eyes. "My lady, she'd had a lot to drink. Our driver will ensure she gets home and the Earl has already called her husband."

"Thank you, Hugh."

"Our team will ensure that Mrs McKenzie will not be allowed back into Blacks or to your London residence or Holmwood, until further notice."

"Is that really necessary?" Louisa said, clearly uncomfortable with the extreme measures.

Hugh's eyes darted again to Miles before answering. "For the moment."

Louisa stood up and narrowed her eyes at him trying to grasp whatever it was his was hiding. "What is it you're not telling me, Hugh?"

"She made threats, madame."

"Threats?"

"Yes, my lady."

"Care to share?"

Hugh's eyes darted around the room and he shifted on his feet, not all together comfortable with disclosing the facts of Emily's rantings.

"Hugh?" Gone was the upset Louisa from the kitchen and in her place stood a confident Lady Blackthorn.

"She said she was going to ruin your life just as you had ruined hers," Hugh said quietly.

"I see. Thank you, Hugh. You do whatever you think is necessary."

Hugh gave her a curt nod, then turned and left them in contemplative silence.

Miles stood stunned at what had just been revealed and let his gaze drift over Louisa's pensive face. *What did that even mean?* "Louisa? Are you alright? What the fuc... what the hell just happened?"

"Apparently Emily McKenzie is going to ruin my life," she answered dryly and blew out a breath.

"Is she dangerous? How?" Miles asked, totally dismayed.

"I haven't the slightest idea," she said wearily. "You know what? I'm not going to worry about Emily and her drunken threats. Believe me, I've had to deal with far worse in my life." She gave a humourless laugh and gave a perplexed Miles a smile. "I've got a job to do." The waiter arrived with the two brandies Miles had ordered. Louisa took one of the heavy crystal glasses off the tray and Miles grabbed the other. Louisa clinked her glass against Miles's and said, "Here's mud in your eye." Miles chuckled and watched Louisa knock back half the glasses contents in one gulp as he took a sip. She placed the glass down, then jerked her head towards the dance floor. "Want to dance?"

"Sure," Miles said, totally in awe of how she was able to take things in her stride. "After you, my lady." He put out his arm for her to lead the way and then guided her to where Konran and Celeste were. The whole dance floor erupted into cheers as they stepped into the crowd, drawing the attention of all the guests.

At the far side of the ballroom, Lady Alice was sitting sipping her Champagne and taking in the whole scene as Margot chatted easily with the rest of their table. She discreetly nudged her dear friend and nodded to the dance floor. "Was that your doing?"

Margot squinted in the direction Lady Alice was looking at and smiled. "Not entirely; Melissa had a fair hand in it."

"Hmm."

"You don't approve?"

"I want my daughter to be happy. She hasn't been for over 15 years."

Lady Alice's gaze zeroed in on Louisa as she was whirled around the dance floor by Miles, to Celeste and Konran's whoops of encouragement. They were all dancing to *Girls Like You*. Konran and Miles mouthed the lyrics to Louisa and Celeste, pointing to them whenever Adam Levine sang "Girls like you", causing them to laugh as they danced alongside the other guests. Lady Alice hadn't seen her daughter laugh like that for a very long time.

"He seems to be doing a good job of it," Margot said with a smirk.

"You think he's up to the challenge?" Lady Alice's words were simple but implied so much more. The life of the aristocracy was complicated. Duty came first and Miles's life was so far removed from what Louisa was born into. There were so much to consider and Lady Alice wondered, as she watched Miles gaze adoringly at her daughter, whether he even understood what that life entailed.

"He's bulletproof, remember?" Margot chuckled.

Louisa watched as Miles shook the hand of another donator from across the ballroom. After the Emily episode and their unguarded dancing, Louisa and Miles parted company, working the room separately. Tonight was about raising money for CASPO and though Louisa enjoyed every second of the attention

Miles had bestowed on her, her duty came first and thankfully, Miles seemed to understand fully.

Miles had easily fallen into his role of ambassador. His relaxed and approachable manner made every guest he spoke to feel as though he'd become their personal friend. He joked freely and showed genuine interest in anything they had to say. He was sociable, charming and articulate, displaying a wider knowledge than the guests he spoke to expected. They soon began to realise that Miles wasn't just the pretty face of CASPO.

After a while, when half the guests had departed, Louisa headed back to bid the last of their table guests goodnight. Miles joined her and once they'd left, Louisa took a seat and ordered some coffee. It was only 10:30 but after the lead-up and preparation of the ball, Louisa was feeling tired. "How's it compared to the last balls?" Miles asked, sipping his coffee.

"Well I didn't come to many of them. It was hard to get away, with Celeste being at school. But from what Melissa tells me, this has been the best one yet. In terms of money collected and how everyone has enjoyed themselves. By this time, the party is usually over."

"Yeah? Well it looks like they'll be dancing for a while yet." Miles looked over to the dance floor, where Celeste, Konran and his band members were entertaining the guests. "Where are Melissa and Robert?"

"They left not long after Alistair took Mama home. I think she was exhausted. She really needs to slow down."

Miles nodded in agreement. "Good luck trying to convince her." Miles put down his cup and shifted closer to Louisa. "Philip from the production company said he'd heard about the TV series I've been approached to do. He wants to know if he can get involved."

"Really? Well that's good news."

"It's funny really. Each one of the guests at our table had a quiet word with me about my future plans. I've got meetings arranged, some of them next week. I thought tonight was about CASPO."

"It is about CASPO. But I suppose there are kick-backs." Miles's brows drew together. "Look the chances of you and those kinds of people being in the same room are quite slim. These are busy people, but in this relaxed environment, deals are often brokered, contacts made, without going through agents, managers and publicists. They saw you in a relaxed environment, liked what they saw and acted on it."

"I suppose so. I hardly think I'd move in their kind of circles."

"Maybe not now, but in the future. Tonight is sort of... well, think of it as the old-fashioned social media. A snapshot of yourself, looking your best, behaving well and accumulating more likes, just on a much smaller platform but with a few of the most powerful and influential people in the country." Miles chuckled at her crude analogy but he had to admit it had merit. These people wouldn't have even considered contacting him had he not been sitting at their table. As far as they were all concerned he was an ex-boy band member, and a recovering drug addict.

"You know I only care about how many likes I get from *one* influential person on this platform?"

"Is that so?"

"Uhuh" He pinned her with his gaze and she swallowed, caught off-guard by the sheer intensity. "I really want to kiss you right now but as usual, we have an audience," he growled.

"Well that wouldn't do, would it? We'd be viral in a heartbeat."

"I'm more *virile* in a heartbeat," he shot back and Louisa laughed softly.

"You're so bad."

"You have no idea." He arched his brow at her. "How long before we can blow this joint?"

"Another half an hour and then I need to get my daughter and guests back home," Louisa said with a sigh.

"Fuck," he muttered, knowing that they weren't going to have any time alone.

"Precisely."

Miles chuckled at her response, pleased she was just as disappointed as he was. He leaned closer and picked up her hand, encasing it in both of his. He slowly licked his sculptured lips and Louisa couldn't take her eyes off them. She wanted him to kiss her too but there were just too many people around, including her daughter. Her gaze lifted to his bright eyes, unsure of what he was doing but unable to put a stop to it.

"When and where, Louisa?" There was no subtlety in his meaning and Louisa's heart pounded against the blue silk of her gown.

"Tomorrow at yours?" she answered in a rush, before she could think it through. They'd danced around for what seemed like an eternity. The sexual tension between them escalated with every second they were in each other's company, and had Celeste and Konran not been here, Louisa would not have been going home alone tonight.

Miles unleashed that sexy smile that had women falling to his feet and nodded. He lifted Louisa's hand to his lips and kissed it, lingering for a few seconds before releasing it.

"Until tomorrow, my lady." His husky tantalising threat had every nerve of her body standing to attention.

22

MEETING

MILES COULDN'T BELIEVE HE was this nervous. This was the part he was good at. He'd slept with hundreds of women, for goodness sake; why was today making him so edgy? It probably had to do with the fact it was scheduled. This wasn't a spontaneous hook-up; like the ones he'd been used to in the past, the ones where they'd thrown themselves at him and he'd gladly obliged. This was an arranged, premeditated, organised… booty call? *Was it a booty call? Shit, he didn't even know.* The tables had certainly been turned. Usually it was him making the booty call, not the one on the receiving end. He'd always called the shots but today, this… whatever it was, wasn't anything like those experiences. This was, as Melissa had perceptively pointed out to him, unchartered territory. He hadn't really thought about it until that moment and he let out a humourless laugh. Miles paced around his lounge, checking over every detail. Louisa had been here before, of course, but then he didn't know who she was. *Were there rules about how you seduced a countess? Would he still need to seduce her or was it a done deal? Jesus, he was so out of his depth.* Miles shook his head.

It was just Louisa.

He had to get the notion out of his head that she was a countess. Miles stepped into his kitchen and opened the fridge looking for… he didn't even know what; inspiration or something to sooth his nervousness? He eyed the bottles of beer and thought about popping one open, but it was just after lunch and from the message Louisa had sent him, she was due any minute. The workout and swim had done nothing to calm his nerves. Even playing some music hadn't distracted him. Duke whimpered in his sleep, curled up in his basket, exhausted by the long walk in the local park, and Miles wished he could be so relaxed. Miles slammed the fridge shut. He couldn't smell of beer when she arrived.

He paced into the hallway and raced up the stairs, taking them two at a time, and stepped into his bedroom. His eyes scanned the bright tidy room. *It was too light.* It was a great room with a fabulous view of the park, decorated in soft hues of blue and cream but with the early afternoon sun shining through the windows, it wasn't exactly a romantic setting. He quickly drew the curtains and switched on the side lights, then dimmed them. *Much better,* he thought. He contemplated lighting a few candles, then changed his mind. It was 2:30 on a summer's day, for goodness sake; he didn't want it to look staged, though the drawn curtains were pretty much a giveaway to his intensions. Miles blew out a frustrated breath. *It was just Louisa,* he said to himself again, hoping if he said the words over and over, he wouldn't feel so daunted.

The doorbell rang and Duke immediately woke up and started to bark. She was here.

"You've got a meeting on Saturday afternoon?" Celeste narrowed her eyes at her mother as Louisa smoothed her hands down her trousers, peering back at her over the sitting room sofa.

"Yes. CASPO isn't a nine-to-five job, you know, Celeste,"

Louisa said, trying to avoid any eye contact. She hated lying to her daughter but she hadn't expected to be questioned on her plans for the day. She was already nervous and the way Celeste was looking at her, she felt as though her daughter knew what those plans really were.

"Hmm. And you're going to your meeting in that?" Celeste twirled her finger in the direction of her mother.

Louisa looked down herself. She'd put on a pair of slim black trousers, a cream sleeveless top and a pair of black stilettoes. *Smart casual, wasn't that what you wore on a date? Was this a date?* "Yes, why?"

"It's a bit casual for you, that's all."

Exactly, smart casual. That was the look she was going for! "Well it's a casual Saturday afternoon meeting," Louisa said tightly hoping Celeste would stop with the twenty questions.

"Hmm, who with?"

Fuck!

"Mr Keane. We need to go over some appearances and the activities weekend and… well, a few other things. He's a very busy man and this was the best time for him to… umm," she said in a rush.

"Hook up?"

What! Was it that obvious? She didn't mean... no, she was just using the term loosely. Louisa felt her face heat up. "Yes – I mean, have a meeting."

"Sure," Celeste said slowly, then rolled her eyes and added, "You can call him Miles, Mum. There's no one else here."

"Well, I'd better get off. You'll be okay here on your own? I can cancel if you'd like to do something." *Maybe this was really a bad idea after all.*

"I'm fine. Like you said, Miles is a busy man. I'll find something to do. How long will you be?"

Seriously? Jeez, this was awful. "I'm not sure."

"Well, I'll see you later then. Have a good meeting."

Louisa mumbled her thanks, feeling her cheeks redden even more, and stepped quickly towards the door, wanting to avoid anymore of her daughter's scrutiny. She felt as though there was a huge sign over her head saying "Off to have sex with Miles".

"Mum," Celeste called to her before she could escape.

What now? "Yes?"

"Your briefcase. Don't forget your briefcase." Celeste pointed to the antique chair where Louisa had left her case the day before.

"Oh yes, thanks." She quickly paced over to the chair, picked up her briefcase and scuttled out of the room.

Louisa stared out of the window as Hugh drove towards Miles's house. Maybe this wasn't such a good idea. She'd suggested today under emotional circumstances, in the heat of the moment, but now in the cold light of day, the idea of being alone with Miles had her stomach churning with nerves and her heart racing in anticipation. This was a man who'd slept with so many women, so many *young* women, what was she even thinking? Maybe he just wanted to bed an aristocrat, add that to his long list of conquests. Louisa sighed and looked down at her beautifully crafted briefcase and chuckled to herself. She wasn't even sure what she had in there. God only knew what Miles would think of her turning up with it.

She'd thought about cancelling throughout her morning but when Konran and his band left just after lunch, she bit the bullet and messaged Miles, telling him she'd be over in an hour. Maybe she wanted to add pop star to her list, she thought to herself; her shortlist of one person she'd ever slept with. Louisa blew air up her face and closed her eyes for a second. *What the hell was she doing? Was she really going to Miles Keane's house to finally sleep with him?* Because he'd made it perfectly clear that that was what he had on his mind. *What if she was...*

"Madame, we're here." Hugh's voice broke thought her erratic thoughts.

"Oh, sorry, I was miles away," Louisa muttered, then chuckled to herself at her use of words. Louisa looked up at the familiar black door that led into Miles's house and her stomach clenched tighter. *What if it was a total disaster? What if all the attraction and sexual tension between them fizzled out and was a huge disappointment?*

"Madame, is everything alright?"

"Yes, sorry Hugh. I'm not sure how long I'll be."

"That's fine. I have a 13-part series downloaded on my iPad. I'll be right here."

"Right." Louisa caught his questioning gaze in the rear view mirror and nodded. Hugh stepped out of the car and opened up her door. Louisa slipped out on to the pavement, made her way up the short path and up the four steps, took a deep breath and rang the bell.

"Hi," she said with a nervous smile.

Miles's gaze raked over her, taking in every detail of the beautiful woman standing on his doorstep. His lips curved into a wide smile. "Hi." His raspy voice gave the single word so much more meaning. He stepped back so Louisa could enter and she was immediately greeted by an excited Duke. As she bent down to greet the adorable puppy, Miles caught sight of Hugh standing by the car. Hugh gave him a nod; Miles reciprocated, then shut the door.

Louisa straightened, after giving Duke a good rub behind the ears, and stared at the heartrendingly gorgeous face of Miles.

"Alone at last." And before she could even reply, he grasped her face and branded his lips to hers. Louisa didn't register the thump of her briefcase falling from her hand as she let her arms cling on to him. He kissed her as though he'd thought he wasn't going to see her again, as though it had been days, rather than hours since they'd last been together. A low rumble in his chest made Louisa tremble. She'd never been kissed like this before and the sheer force had Louisa's head spinning and her pulse racing.

Miles reluctantly pulled away, his eyes still closed as though he was gathering himself. He hadn't meant to be so fierce, but the moment he'd set his eyes on her, protocol, patience and decorum had been blown out of the door as soon as it had been shut. He opened his eyes and gave a breathless Louisa a lazy smile. "As you can tell, I'm really pleased to see you." Louisa let out light laugh and he gave her a tender kiss on lips, then reluctantly let her go. "Come on through." He took her hand, then noticed the unceremoniously discarded briefcase and quirked his head.

"I told Celeste I was coming here for a meeting." Louisa scrunched up her nose in embarrassment at her lame excuse. Miles chuckled and went to pick it up. "Just leave it there, unless you want to discuss business," she said dryly.

"Nope, no business today." He gave her a wink and took her through to the kitchen with Duke following them, heading straight for his basket. "So, a drink? What would you like? Tea? Coffee?" He lifted her hand and kissed the back of it before releasing it.

"I think I need something stronger," she said slipping onto one of the bar stools and Miles turned, instantly catching her blow out a shaky breath.

"Louisa?"

Louisa lifted her gaze and he was up to her in second, cupping her cheek. "I…"

"Hey, we'll just have a drink, talk. Nothing has to happen if you don't want it to," he said softly. "Okay?"

"Okay" She gave him a nod.

"Good. Wine? I have Champagne if you prefer."

"That sounds wonderful." She gave him a shy smile and he

grinned back, glad she seemed to have relaxed. The last thing he wanted was to make her uneasy. He was just happy they were able to spend time together without someone looking at or over them.

"So Celeste's staying in London?" Miles opened up the fridge and pulled out a bottle of Veuve Clicquot Rose, then opened up a cupboard to retrieve two glasses.

"Yes, well until tomorrow, then she'll be back at Holmwood. She loves it there. She likes to help out Alistair."

Miles placed two elegant flutes on the breakfast bar and started to work on opening the Champagne. "My wine guy said this was 'enormously drinkable at any time of the day'." He put on a haughty English accent that made Louisa giggle. "Let's see if he's right, shall we?" He opened the bottle with a subdued pop. "And Konran left?" he asked pouring the subtle pink Champagne.

"Yes, he's in Frankfurt then Rome."

"Oh Rome is awesome. I played there on our last European tour. He's coming to the activities weekend?" Louisa gave a nod and accepted the flute. "That'll be a great surprise for the kids." Louisa agreed, then they clinked glasses and took a sip. Miles pulled out an oval platter with cut fruit, cheese and nuts from the fridge.

"Hungry?"

"Not really."

"You may change your mind. Grab the bottle and we can go into the lounge."

They moved to the sunny room and Louisa noted there were more pieces of furniture and soft furnishings. The room had already looked lovely but it had definitely taken on a more homely feel. There were silk cushions strategically placed on the large sofa and an enormous cream rug centred the room. The new side table had a modern lamp placed on it and there was a gilt mirror over the fireplace.

"You've bought more pieces."

"Yeah, it's getting there. I need some art for the walls, though," Miles said, placing the platter on the low coffee table.

"Any preference?" Louisa settled into the sofa and took a drink from her glass.

"Nothing too heavy. Maybe something that reminds me of home – the sea. I miss the sea. I haven't really thought about it." Miles lowered himself into the sofa and turned, resting his bent leg an inch way from her. His fingers caressed her leg. "I've never seen you in pants before."

"Oh, yes, well I was trying to be casual." She took another drink from her glass, draining it. Miles's eyes widened in surprise and took the glass from her hand placing it on the table. "God... can you tell I'm nervous? I've never done this before? Isn't that ridiculous?" She turned to him and made an exasperated face.

"What, date, you mean?" Miles reached over and took her hand and gently stroked over her knuckles.

"Date, spend time alone with a man who wasn't my family, sleep with anyone who wasn't my husband. Have secret meetings with pop stars," she said in a rush and Miles's mouth curved into a wide grin.

"That's quite a list."

"I'll say. Miles, I'm..." *scared, nervous, out of my depth, stupid to think this could even work...*

"Beautiful, you are beautiful, that's what you are," Miles interrupted as she struggled to find the words. Leaning over, he softly brushed back a stray lock of hair from her face. His eyes, transfixed on to hers, were so brilliantly blue that Louisa could easily have drowned in them. "Tell me about Konran." He stretched over and picked up the bottle of Champagne and poured some more into her glass, still keeping hold of her hand. "You told me last night you'd tell me about him."

Miles was determined to make her relax. When they'd spoken on the phone, she'd been candid and somewhat at ease. Here, in his home, alone, was a completely different scenario, especially now he knew who she was and there was the unsaid promise of more. He was trying to distract her so she'd forget whatever was making her so edgy. Miles had managed to keep his expression neutral when she'd revealed she'd only dated and slept with her husband. From the little he'd gleaned from their previous phone conversations, they'd never even dated as such.

"Well, he was at an after-school music program that one of the charities I supported had funded. He was this lanky pre-teen, with a smile too wide for his face, who was naturally musically talented. His father had been killed, shot actually, and he'd had to move into a smaller one-bedroomed apartment with his mother."

"And your charity rehoused them?" Miles picked up his glass and sipped it, keeping his eyes focused on Louisa. She went on to explain how originally that was what she'd wanted to do until she'd met Konran. He'd won her over with his remarkable talent and the songs he'd written, his way of coping with the tragic loss of his father. Louisa explained that she'd personally sponsored Konran and secured him a place in NYU, which meant he could fulfil his dream to study music.

Miles listened to Louisa talk about how Celeste had immediately struck up a conversation with Konran and spent most of their visit with him. Louisa's face lit up as she spoke about her daughter and over the next 30 minutes, Miles gradually saw Louisa begin to relax. He kept hold of her hand, only letting it go when he picked up the platter to offer her something to eat. He peppered their conversation with jokes and flirty comments as Louisa described the early years of Celeste and Konran's lives, hoping to coax away any of her unease.

"So he's family now. To be honest, he became family from very early on. He spent so much time with Celeste, even when he was at college. His mother was given a job in one of Gerard's companies, though now she doesn't need to work."

"That's so amazing. How come the press haven't latched on to any of this?" Konran, aka TuKon, was topping the rap charts globally and it was well documented that his father had been shot when he was young, yet there was nothing about the help Louisa had given.

"We kept it quiet. We didn't want Konran's success to be overshadowed by how he'd been helped. No one knew where the scholarship came from. It was put through the charity and though Gerard and I were linked to the charity, the association was never made."

"Well, you changed his life, Louisa. That's really something."

Louisa gave a small shrug. "He was talented and had such a positive attitude, even after the shitty card he'd been dealt. I think he would've made it eventually."

"Maybe. It's a hard business to be in but from the little I've seen, he seems to have his head screwed on right." Miles squeezed her hand. "Come on, let me show you what else I've done with the place." He bent down and prised off her shoes.

"What are you doing?"

"Making you more comfortable," he said as though it was obvious.

"Oh." Louisa watched as he pulled off her other shoe and set it neatly next to the other. She couldn't remember the last time she'd walked barefoot in someone's home. In fact she probably never had.

For a second, Miles focused on her bare feet, tipped with scarlet polish, then he stood up. "Even your feet are beautiful," he said almost to himself and Louisa blinked up at him blushing at his sweet comment. Miles reached down and took her hand. "Come, let me give you a proper tour this time."

They spent the next 15 minutes going around the bottom two floors of the house. Miles had bought more furniture for the music room, which admittedly made the room warmer. He showed her his wine cellar and pool, then took her to his cinema room.

"I put it in for Grace and Louis. They love to watch their films in here when they stay. And trash the place with popcorn!"

Louisa chuckled. It was obvious he adored his niece and nephew. "How often do they come down?"

"Twice a month, and I try to go up at least once. Duke loves it up there because they have a huge garden." They'd started to make their way up the stairs, back to the ground floor.

"It must be hard on them now you're not there."

"And on me." He huffed. "But it was Amanda who thought it would be better for me to move to London. Better for all of us: my career, the kids and for her. The kids are growing up and I'm sure Amanda wants to have her own life without me hanging around."

"Has she met someone?"

"No. Probably because I was always around." He laughed mildly. They'd reached the top of the stairs and were standing at the bottom of the next flight. "But I think it's more complicated than that. I hope she does, though. She deserves another shot at happiness."

Miles looked up the stairway, then stepped closer to Louisa. He lowered his head to hers and ever so softly kissed her. For the last hour and a half they'd talked and touched, he'd teased her and she'd tormented him and he'd lapped up every second. This slow and tantalising build up was so new to him. He'd never experienced it before. Every relationship he'd had in the past had been purely based on physical attraction, lust; he couldn't even class them as relationships, they were a long string of hook-ups. He'd never needed that kind of connection, he'd never been that interested in anyone, past getting them into his bed. But with Louisa, it was different. From the very first time he'd met her, he knew there was more to her than just her stunning good looks. She'd fascinated him right from the start, and the air of unattainability that oozed off her only made her more alluring and sexy as hell.

Over the last few weeks, he'd seen past that, and she'd slowly let down her guard. Her years of living in a world where privacy was everything and trust was paramount had made Miles's attempts to break through harder. But by some miracle she was here, in his home, alone and he didn't want to ruin this moment or have her running off to her forever-waiting Bentley.

Miles pulled away and cupped her face gently. "Want to see upstairs or shall we have some more Champagne?"

Louisa stared into those incomparable blue eyes and the doubts and fears that had been swimming around in her head vanished. From the very beginning she'd had the upper hand, and she'd called the shots – not because Miles was that kind of man; in fact, he was the opposite. Louisa knew he'd always been in control of any relationship he'd had. Louisa realised early on that Miles had allowed her be in control because he understood that what was developing between them was new to her. He'd made it obvious in his words and actions that he wanted more, much more, but he was letting her set the pace, and for an impulsive and impatient man, that was a lot to relinquish. His manner had been easy and he often used humour to diffuse awkward or difficult situations, which showed how perceptive he was. Miles observed everything, knowing what was expected of him in a given situation and where he could push. His well-documented rebellious side had been muted now but it often came out. His refusal to conform both amused and gained Louisa's respect, at the fact he didn't want to let that side of his personality go.

She should've instantly disliked him. He was the complete opposite to the men she'd been surrounded by. A different class and upbringing, and yet he made her feel more like herself than anyone had ever done. He made her feel a little reckless and carefree but most of all, he made her feel desirable again. This devastatingly handsome man wanted her, he wanted *just* Louisa, and she wanted nothing more than to be with him.

"More Champagne sounds good," she said softly and Miles

nodded but before he could release her, she added, “Maybe we could drink it upstairs though. You did promise me the full tour.”

He gave her that mega-watt smile that made his face crease up in the best possible way. “Whatever the lady wants.” He gave her a hard kiss, then paced to the lounge to collect the Champagne and flutes. He was back in a flash and motioned for her to go first. “One full tour coming up,” he said playfully and Louisa laughed as she took the first few steps, then turned to look at him over her shoulder.

“You do realise I don’t give a damn about a tour, right?”

“I didn’t tell you what kind of tour we were going on.”

“Oh, I see.”

“Yeah, you will.” He gave her a cheeky wink and ushered her up the stairs.

The few seconds it took them to get to Miles’s bedroom felt too long after the weeks of build-up. Miles placed the Champagne and glasses on the chest of drawers and took in the sight of Louisa standing close to his large bed. He couldn’t believe she was here. Her eyes scanned the stylish room, taking in every detail. He closed the distance between them in a few steps and cupped her face gently kissing away any lingering nervousness.

“No other woman has been in this room.”

His words wiped away the last seeds of unease Louisa had. She stepped away from his touch and lifted the hem of her top, pulling it over her head, and dropped it on the floor. Miles’s eyes were transfixed on the beautiful woman in front of him. His eyes widened at her sudden show of boldness. He couldn’t keep up. She’d surprised him again. One moment she was apprehensive and unsure, and then she switched to this confident and decisive woman. He was in awe of her, totally mesmerized. He kept hold of her gaze as she slowly began to shed her clothes, not wanting to break the intense connection.

Louisa unzipped her trousers and pushed them over her hips

until they slid voluntarily down her shapely legs, pooling at her feet. She'd worried and over thought every step of their relationship but once she'd stepped into his bedroom, she knew this was what she wanted. It was reckless and unprecedented, but she hoped he was worth the risk.

Miles's eyes lowered to slowly skim over her as she stood before him in her cream lace bra and panties. "You're breath-taking." He hastily pulled off his T-shirt, dishevelling his hair in the process, which somehow made him look even sexier. He quickly unfastened his jeans and shuffled out of them.

They collided like waves in a storm. His fingers spired into her hair, holding her to him as he attacked her mouth. She gripped his back, pulling him close, relishing the feel of his hot skin against hers. They fell on to the bed in a tangle of limbs without breaking contact. The soft silk duvet felt cool against Louisa's back as Miles held her body captive. His hand slid down her side and round to cup her behind, jerking her closer. Louisa gasped and let her hands slip under the waistband of his boxer shorts. She gave his behind a squeeze and Miles groaned.

"I need you naked," he said gruffly, urgently kissing down her neck. "I need to feel you, baby."

Louisa pushed down his boxers until they slid over the taut curve of his behind and then Miles yanked them off, leaving them to fall off the bed. Louisa moaned, feeling the weight of his hot erection against the silk of her panties and she struggled to pull them away. Miles reluctantly pulled his lips away from hers and grasped her hand, stilling her for a second. Her lids lifted and theirs eyes locked.

"Let me." Miles slowly lifted himself up so Louisa could take in the full force of naked Miles Keane. She swallowed as her eyes drifted over every sharp edge and every slab of muscle until she reached the sculptured troughs that ran under his hipbones. He was the poster boy for rebel *with* a cause. His dirty blond hair fell messily over his forehead and his eyes gleamed with a self-satisfied smirk. Miles hooked his fingers into the sides of her panties and pulled them down her legs, dropping them before slowly crawling up her. He lowered his face to the apex of her thighs and rubbed his nose against her, taking in her feminine scent. Louisa gasped and jerked upwards, but his hands held her still.

"You smell amazing." He planted soft sucking kisses across her pubic bone and down to the tender skin of her inner thigh. "Let's see if you taste as good as you smell."

"Oh God." Louisa squeezed her eyes shut and gripped on to the duvet as he got to work on the bundle of nerves that were vibrating against his ardent tongue. She felt herself losing the little control she had. If she'd believed for one moment she was the one calling the shots, seeing Miles between her thighs as he tortured her with bone-melting pleasure blew all those thoughts out of the water. She was at his mercy. He'd gifted her with setting the pace but once they smashed together, it was Miles who had taken the reins.

Her pent-up release blasted over her in an unexpected rush. Miles's groans vibrated against her flesh, prolonging the waves of pleasure. She let out a soundless cry as the last of her spasms rippled through her body. Before she'd even recovered, Miles was working his way up her body, kissing her sensitive skin until he reached her breasts. He pulled the straps away and reached around to unfasten the clasp. The lace undergarment was ripped away in a heartbeat and Miles's lips latched on to her hardened nipple, without a second for Louisa to catch her breath. Her hands found their way into his luxuriant hair, tugging it at the roots.

Miles was relentless in his possessive attack of all her senses, intent on drawing out as much pleasure as he could for her, without allowing her to think. He wanted her to feel desired in every way, to know that he understood what she needed and to accept that he was capable of giving it to her. Louisa writhed beneath him as he moved to the other breast and plumped it in his hand.

"Fuck, you're delicious." He pushed his steely erection against her thigh and kissed her hard. Their lips melded together and their tongues swept against each other in an erotic dance, a prelude to what was to come. Miles pulled away and grasped her face, looking into her stunned eyes. "I want you so badly, Louisa, but if you want to stop here, you need to tell me now."

Her chest heaved against his and her heart was pounding so hard it felt as though it would breakthrough her ribcage. "Don't stop," she said instantly, floored again by his concern.

Miles reached over to his bedside table and opened up the top drawer to retrieve a condom. His erection bobbed, brushing over Louisa's breasts. She bent down and kissed the tip.

"Fuck, Louisa." He jerked back. "I'm already struggling. Don't make this finish faster than I want." Louisa let out a giggle and he growled before ripping open the foil with his teeth and sheathing himself. "I'm going to take this slow baby," he said tenderly as he stroked back the hair from her face and positioned himself at her entrance. Miles lowered his lips to hers and kissed her, slowly pushing into her.

He had to will himself to take it slow, when every instinct in him wanted to thrust hard, claim her, make her his. Sweat beaded on Miles's brow, a sign that his control was costing him. Louisa groaned at the welcome invasion, which only made his restraint all the more difficult.

"Jesus, you're perfect," he said between kisses, withdrawing slowly before pushing back into her with a little more force.

The exquisite feeling of being stretched was incredible. Louisa felt her whole body blissfully vibrate as he kept up the unhurried rhythm that had her nerve endings spark with every thrust. Her hands roamed restlessly over his taut back, as his muscle rippled under his smooth skin. Louisa could feel his restraint in every movement. Every part of his body was solid with tension, begging for release, and she marvelled at his self-control. Hers had long gone the second they'd collided.

A slight shift in his position had Louisa splintering beneath him within a second. He didn't let up as she shuddered beneath him. Their sweat-slick bodies slipped effortless against each other, and Louisa struggled to catch a breath.

"Again, Louisa," he growled as he continued to plunge into her, his strokes becoming harder and faster.

"I can't, Miles, it's too much… I –"

Louisa exploded again before she could finish her protest and Miles's lips found hers. He kissed her thoroughly, letting out a tormented groan, finally allowing his release to crash over him. Their bodies finally fused together after the unstoppable collision course they'd been on from the very start. For Miles, it had never been the question of *if* they'd get together, but rather *when*. On that very first date, he knew no one would come even close to Louisa. She'd beguiled him from the get-go. Now, after only a few weeks, he knew Louisa was in a league of her own and he would move heaven and earth to feel worthy of her.

They held on to each other, not wanting to let go, break the spell or return to the world they'd closed themselves off from. Miles rested his damp forehead against hers and tried to level out his breathing, then let his eyes flutter open. He was met by her eyes lazily opening and she let out a soft sigh.

"Are you okay?" he asked hoarsely.

Louisa gave him a slight nod and let her lips curve into a coy smile. *Was she okay? She was more than okay. He'd blown her mind!*

Miles pulled back a little, trying to read her expression, and she smiled wider.

"I slept with a pop star," she said playfully and stifled her grin. Miles's mouth gaped open in surprise. "I'm so rock and roll. Does that make me a groupie now?"

Miles let out a laugh. Again she'd managed to shock him with her teasing and he revelled in every new facet of this priceless woman who was gracing his bed. "I feel so used." He feigned being hurt and she giggled, but he quickly silenced her with a fierce kiss. "I don't want you to leave," he said against her lips.

"I have to at some point."

Miles sighed. Of course she had to go but he wasn't ready for her to go yet. They had too much to catch up on and he had no idea when they'd be alone again. "How long?"

"I should call Celeste and see what's she's doing." Louisa shuffled under him and he reluctantly pulled out of her, losing the last of their connection.

"Where are you going?"

"To get my bag. My phone is in there." She stood up, stared at the open bedroom door and shook her head. This was the first time she'd ever had sex with the door wide open before. It was liberating.

Miles observed her as she looked for something to put on. "There's only you and me in the house, Louisa." She looked over her shoulder at him and he couldn't hide his amusement.

"Right. It's just… never mind." She looked back at the door and then quickly crossed the threshold, completely nude.

When she returned, she found Miles sitting up in bed, looking deliciously dishevelled. His hair, that was normally pushed back, had fallen over his forehead, making him look even more rebellious. He'd drawn back the duvet and sheets and had moved the Champagne and glasses to the bedside table.

"She went to Holmwood. She doesn't really have that many friends here. I think she'll be glad when her boyfriend comes out to stay."

"So you've nothing to rush back for?" he said with a wide smile.

Boy, that smile needed to come with a warning. Miles picked up her glass and motioned for her to come back to bed. "No, I suppose not." She slipped onto the cool sheets and took the glass of Champagne from his hand. She took a welcome drink from her glass, then placed it on the table next to her. "So, about that tour, then?" she said nonchalantly and Miles let out a laugh as he put his glass down. In a flash, he had her trapped beneath him and she let out a squeal. Miles let his face hover over hers, running his nose along hers and she stretched up to kiss him but he pulled back, teasing her.

"The only touring you'll be part of is me touring over this." He swept his hand down her body until he reached the top of her thighs and he cupped her. She gasped and he gave her a sexy smile that meant she was done for. "If my lady wants, that is."

"Yes she wants, she wants very much."

"Good."

"I'm not sure this is what Amanda had in mind when she told me to make up with you," Miles said dryly. He let his fingers drift rhythmically up and down her back.

"She told you to?" Louisa shifted, resting her chin on his chest so she could look at him.

"Yes, I spoke to her before the ball. Though I would've without her telling me to." He grinned at her and she rolled her eyes, then laid her cheek back on his chest.

"Good to know." Miles pulled her closer to his side, enjoying the intimacy of having her naked next to him. He knew it was getting late and she'd have to leave soon. The thought made his mood sink, but he wasn't about to ask how much longer they had. His mind drifted to Hugh and the ever-waiting Bentley and he was about to ask her if he was still there, when Louisa said, "You're very close with Amanda."

"Yeah." He gave a slight huff. "When... after the shooting... Well, everyone knows what happened. I don't think there was a media platform I wasn't plastered over. Kept them busy," he said with more than a hint of sarcasm. "I used whatever I could to block it out. Alcohol didn't do it for me, so, being who I was back then, I had whatever, whenever at my disposal. There wasn't anything I didn't try or anyone who wouldn't jump when I snapped my fingers. I sometimes wonder how I survived, all those risks I took." He rubbed his hand roughly over his face.

"I remember getting the call from Amanda's mother, telling me she'd gone into labour with Louis Junior. I was absolutely wasted, having partied all night. The call had kind of disturbed something, or rather someone I was doing."

Louisa turned to look at him again and he had the good grace to look embarrassed. She rested her chin on his chest and waited for him to continue.

"I'd promised Amanda I'd be there so, I got to the hospital, looking like shit. Somehow, I managed to sober up enough to be sort of supportive. It was a hard labour and after he was born, her parents and my parents left, so Amanda could rest. I passed out in her room, like the waste of space I was back then. The staff let me stay because Eric, my agent, made sure of it, seeing as there was a whole horde of paparazzi outside the hospital." He blew out a breath and let his eyes shift away from her gaze for a second, then shook his head. "The bastards never left her alone as it was, but I'd brought a whole new level of media frenzy, being there too. It must've got out that I was totally fucked when I'd arrived. I remember waking up and seeing Amanda in bed, holding Louis as she breast-fed him. She was crying and my heart literally ripped out of my chest."

He paused for a moment, needing a second to gather himself and Louisa shuffled up so she was level with him. It was obviously hard for him to talk about that time and she was about to tell him he didn't need to say any more, when he turned to look at her.

"All I wanted was another hit so I didn't need to witness her pain. Something that should've been so beautiful, joyful... was just so tragic. I made some excuse and left, managed to slip by the photographers around the back and went on another bender. I didn't see her or talk to her for three days. Such an asshole." He muttered the last sentence under his breath in disgust as he recounted his behaviour. "I got into a fight at a club because someone, rightly so, called me a loser. The press were all over it but thankfully, Eric came and took me away, took me back to his house and let me sleep it off.

"The next day I crawled my sorry ass out of his spare room and came down to face my parents, Josh and Mick from the band and Amanda. They'd set up an intervention.

"Fuck, I was appalled. I felt betrayed, when it was clearly me who had betrayed them all. I had to sit and listen to my parents say how losing one son was bad enough but they didn't want to lose another. Then it was Josh and Mick's turn to make me feel like utter crap and Eric too. Amanda sat quietly through the whole awful ordeal, tears constantly running down her face. I remember looking at her and seeing how pale and broken she was, and all I could think of was when would they all just fuck off so I could get my next fix to blot it all out." He swallowed hard, then rubbed his eyes with his thumb and forefinger. Louisa rubbed his chest gently, knowing this story was painful to relive.

"When Amanda's turn came around, I was almost relieved, because she'd always had my back. I thought, she'll go easy on me and then this whole shit-show would be over. She stood up and walked over to me. I was slumped in a chair at the time, and my head felt like it was splitting in two. Anyway she opened with, 'How are you feeling?' I said something on the lines of that I had a headache and felt like shit. She replied by saying, 'Good.' Which kind of shocked me but it was nothing to the berating I got from her. She wiped the fucking floor with me.

"Basically she said that she'd just had a baby, my nephew, and I had been wasted through his birth, after I'd promised I was going to be there for them. She told me if I wanted to kill myself, fine, but who the hell was going to tell Louis's children who their father was? Who was going to tell them about what he was like as a child, as a brother? Who was going to tell them stories of what he got up to when his parents weren't around? She told me I was the closest thing to a father Louis's children had right now and she'd never been so appalled. She was practically screaming at me and my parents tried to calm her down, but she didn't give a shit. She pulled out her phone and pushed it towards my face, showing me pictures of baby Louis and Grace, saying instead of her spending time with them, she was here trying to make me see what a fucking asshole I was. They needed her every minute right now, but she was here trying to help my sorry selfish ass out. She ended it by saying, 'Kill yourself if you want, right now I don't care. I wouldn't want you anywhere near my children and nor would Louis.'

"I checked into rehab the next hour, had a shit ton of therapy and came out after six months. I'd always been volatile before, quick-tempered, reacting before thinking. I vowed that would stop too. It's hard, really hard sometimes, and I battle with that, but Amanda saved my fucking life that day." Miles turned to look at Louisa and blew out a breath.

"I've only met her once but she seems like a very strong woman."

"You have no idea." He rolled his eyes and Louisa smiled.

"Is that why you came to the UK?"

Miles gave a nod. "She couldn't handle being in California anymore and I needed a change of scenery too, plus I couldn't be away from Louis and Grace. So we made the decision to come to here, away from everything."

Louisa rested her head on his shoulder, taking in this new information Miles had gifted her with. It was a miracle he'd survived the abuse and risks he'd put his body through. She remembered reading about various incidents at the time and there was always speculation that he was on a death wish. It was no wonder he was so close to Amanda; she really had saved his life. They stayed wrapped in each other's arms, Miles drawing lines up and down Louisa's back while she let her fingers trace over his chest in reflective silence. It had been an unexpected afternoon of normalcy, intimacy and revelations. It was something Louisa hadn't experienced in what seemed like an awfully long time, and it surprised her how much she'd missed just being.

"I don't want to ruin the mood, really I don't." Miles gave her tight squeeze and kissed the top of her head. "But is Hugh going to stay out there all the time?"

"As long as I'm here."

"Even if you stay the night?"

Louisa turned to look at him. "He stays with me wherever I am," she replied quietly, unsure of how to react to his words. *Stay the night?* She hadn't thought that far along. He clenched his jaw and she realised this was an issue for him. Her heart sank. This was her life, and though today she'd felt as close to being normal as possible, being who she was meant that the afternoon had been an exception rather than a rule.

"So he's just sitting there?" He furrowed his brow and Louisa nodded.

"He told me he has a 13-episode series downloaded."

Miles shuffled out of her arms and reached for his jeans and slipped them on, without his underwear. "He's been there five hours. He must be starving, or at least thirsty, and he probably wants a leak," he said as he put on his discarded T-shirt.

"What are you doing?"

"I may not like the fact you have a babysitter but I'm not comfortable having the poor guy suffering."

"Miles?"

"Give me a minute." Miles leaned down and gave her a swift kiss and then exited the room.

Louisa jumped out of the bed, paced to the door and strained to hear what Miles was doing. She heard the front door open so she rushed to the hallway and into the second bedroom that faced the road, then peered out of the window.

On the pavement, she could see Miles standing in his bare feet talking to Hugh. Miles motioned to the house and then after a bit of persuasion, Hugh locked up the car and followed Miles into the house. Duke was once again excited at a new visitor and Louisa could hear muffled conversation, in between excited barks, that faded as they moved further into the house. She stepped back from the window and looked down at herself, realising she was still naked, then quickly went back into Miles bedroom to dress.

She found Miles busily preparing a plate of sandwiches and an uncomfortable Hugh sitting on one of the barstools, drinking coffee. As soon as she entered the kitchen, Hugh stood up. "My lady…" Hugh's face tightened as he faced an ever-so-slightly dishevelled Louisa.

Before Hugh could explain, Miles interrupted. "I asked Hugh in. He refused at first but I told him he could at least come in for a bit, eat and drink something, seeing as… well, I wasn't sure how long you were going to stay." Miles twirled the chef's knife in her direction as he spoke. She arched her brow at him but he continued, unfazed, to prepare Hugh's snack.

"Madame, I realise this –"

"It's fine, Hugh. Sit down, please." Miles stifled a smirk but kept his eyes on the task in hand. "Shall I go and bring the platter? I'm a little hungry too." She tilted her head at Miles and his smile widened.

"Sure, thanks," he said, then he stopped what he was doing and watched her sashay into the lounge on bare feet. Miles chuckled, then turned his attention back to his guest, who had an amused expression on his rugged face.

"So, you served with Alistair?" Miles said, a little embarrassed he'd been caught out staring after her.

"Yes, Earl Blackthorn has employed many ex-service men."

"That's cool. I suppose it's because he served alongside you, he knows who he can trust."

"Yes. He's also a friend," Hugh said pointedly.

"Hmm... mustard?"

"Yes, thank you."

The click of Louisa's heels on the tiled floor drew Miles's attention to her coming back from the lounge, holding the platter. Miles gaze dropped to her shoes she'd put back on again.

"Going somewhere?"

"Eventually." She perched on a bar stool next to Hugh.

"Is that so?" Miles pushed the plate of sandwiches he'd prepared towards Hugh, who mumbled his thanks, feeling decidedly uncomfortable. "Hmm... I thought you didn't have any plans."

"I'm sure you have." Louisa plucked a grape and popped it into her mouth.

"Nope, nothing on my calendar for tonight." He tilted his head to the side and she saw the challenge in his eyes. "We've still got a lot to get through." Louisa's eyes darted to Hugh, who was doing an excellent job of ignoring their conversation, as he munched quickly through his sandwiches. "Our *meeting*. We're no way near finished," Miles explained with a cocky smirk.

"Are you sure we didn't finish off?" she said in that precise tone Miles loved so much.

"Quite sure. As soon as your man here is done, we need to get down to business." He punctuated his remark with an arch of his brow.

"I can take these to go.," Hugh said, scrambling off his stool suddenly.

They both spoke at the same time. "No, please finish," said Louisa.

"No, its fine," said Miles and Hugh darted his eyes between the two of them, before re-taking his seat. "A drink to go with the cheese?" Louisa gave Miles a nod and picked up a chunk of cheddar. "Wine?"

"Wine would be lovely," Louisa said graciously, then placed the cheese in her mouth and chewed.

"Whatever the lady wants."

23

ALONE AGAIN

"ALONE AGAIN." Miles's lips curved up into a cheeky smile. He'd just seen Hugh to the door and paced back into the kitchen. The early evening sun filtered in through the windows and caught the auburn flecks in Louisa's hair. She shook her head and got down from the stool.

"Well, that wasn't awkward at all."

"Maybe for Hugh." Miles stepped up to her and gave her a slow seductive kiss, pressing her against the counter. He pulled back and beamed at her. "He's seen us together in more awkward moments, and anyway, you should be used to him being around."

"Well I don't think for a minute he was fooled into thinking we were having *a meeting*."

"I wasn't trying to *fool* him. I was trying *spare* him more embarrassment. Maybe I should have just said I wasn't quite done fucking you yet." He arched his brow at her and Louisa's mouth gaped at his crude comment, but she had no doubt he wouldn't have thought twice about saying it, regardless of who was around. "What, does that go against protocol?" He couldn't hide his amusement at her reaction. Before Louisa could answer, he gave her a deep kiss that had her mind forgetting all about protocol. He hoisted her onto the kitchen counter and stepped between her open legs. "I really want you to stay." He reached down and prised off her shoes, letting them clatter to the floor.

"I can't."

"Why not?"

"I just can't."

He held her face between his palms and looked into her wide eyes. There were so many emotions flooding them that Miles had a hard time trying to figure out which one was her real reason she couldn't stay. "Because Hugh is waiting outside?" he asked and she twisted her mouth in response. "He can stay in the lounge. Or he can leave and we promise him that we won't leave the house. He can track you if he doesn't believe me." Louisa scrunched up her nose and allowed herself to feel a thrill at the lengths Miles would go to, just so she would stay. The truth was she wanted to, more than anything, more than the embarrassment of talking through logistics with Hugh, so it could happen. This whole scenario was so new to her. She'd never had to deal with clandestine trysts before, but seeing how important it was for Miles, she was willing to endure an uncomfortable conversation with her head of security. A conversation was just the tip of the iceberg though. There were other factors that were worrying Louisa.

"There are other ways around it."

"Like?" Miles said, narrowing his eyes and dropping his hands to rest on either side of her.

"Hugh can go bring in another one of his team to be here overnight, but outside. I can't expect him to work 24 hours."

"So why don't we do that?"

"Because," Louisa paused for a beat, "because that will mean more people know about us."

His brow furrowed, unsure of what she meant. "And you don't want that because… you don't want to be associated with me?" he said carefully.

"No, it's not that," she said emphatically.

"Then what is it?"

"The more people know, the more likely it'll get out. Celeste might find out before I tell her. And to be honest, what do I tell her? I'm not ready to put a label on whatever this is. I don't even know what this is, and there's CASPO and what affect us will have on that, plus so many other people and –"

Miles cupped her face in an attempt to calm the tirade of reasons, all of which were perfectly valid and thankfully nothing to do what he'd feared. "Okay, okay I get it. It's not as simple as making a snap decision."

"No it's not. Everything I do is planned," she said with a regretful sigh.

"Who do you plan it with... what I mean is, your schedule? Who do you go over it with?"

"Hugh. I trust him because Alistair trusts him. There are very few people I trust in this world, Miles." He gave a nod, remembering Melissa telling him the exact same thing.

"Right, so if Hugh can work around this, will you stay? Or is it that you don't want to?"

"I've never stayed over before."

"Ever?" He couldn't hide his astonishment.

Louisa shook her head and gave a half-shrug. "There are many things I haven't done that I find myself doing since I met you."

"Like?"

"Walking barefoot in someone else's home." She rubbed her bare feet against his legs and he grinned. "Walking around naked and... making love with the door open."

"Wow, that's, well that's a little sad, but I'm glad it's because of me you got to do those things." He placed a tender kiss on her lips and smoothed his hands around her hips. He rested his forehead against hers. "What else?"

"Secret rendezvous."

"Kissing in the rain," he countered with a smirk.

Louisa grinned back at him. "Yeah, kissing in the rain."

"Paying for a date?" Miles pulled back and chuckled. Louisa let out a soft laugh.

"Yes, that was definitely the first time I've ever done that."

"Yeah?"

"Yeah. Best £50,000 I've ever spent," she said, blinking up at him, and Miles's stomach clenched. His arms immediately banded around her as his lips melded with hers. He'd often thought about how they'd met, and the unusual circumstances of their very first date, and he'd always wondered if it had felt as significant to Louisa as it had to him. Hearing her candid statement put those doubts to rest.

"Oh God, Louisa, I really want you to stay. I don't know when I'm going to see you again. What do I need to do to make it happen?" he pleaded.

"You can't do anything. It's me who needs to." She urged him back so she could slip off the counter, then retrieved her phone from her bag and tapped the screen. "Hugh, can you come back into the house please? I need your help."

GERARD NURSED HIS DRINK, taking in the busy street below. New York really was the city that never slept, he thought to himself, but he had no desire to enjoy any of the huge charms his adopted hometown had to offer. He'd felt that way for over seven months. His stunning residence on one of the most prestigious addresses of the city felt empty but compared to the hollow feeling he had in his chest, it almost felt comforting. Since Louisa and Celeste had moved out, he'd consoled himself with the familiar surroundings of their home. It would always be *their* home because it had been Louisa's creation. Every furnishing, picture frame and colour swatch had been Louisa, and Gerard had no desire to change anything. There were 20 years of memories housed in these beautifully decorated walls: birthdays, Christmases and anniversaries, every one of them vivid in Gerard's mind and his only company over the last months.

The cognac did little to warm him and the recent phone call from Celeste had only highlighted what he'd lost. He'd masked his displeasure well, as his daughter recounted the events of the ball. Her candid comments and detailed description of the night had Gerard's interest piqued, when normally such an event would've been of little interest to him. He attended so many, they tended to merge into one, all of them unremarkable with the same guests, eating similar food, raising money for varying charities. Gerard hadn't taken much interest in CASPO. He'd donated generously but because it was a charity away from his home, he wasn't always informed with any of the latest developments. If there had been anything significant, Louisa always let him know. So when Celeste mentioned Miles Keane was their new ambassador, Gerard's interest shifted from indifference to surprised and then concerned.

The ex-pop star hadn't crossed his mind for a long time. He'd tolerated listening to his music for Celeste's sake, over the years she'd been a die-hard fan. Then, more recently, when Louisa had managed to arrange the charity date, he'd meant to look into him, purely for his daughter's safety. Apart from his infamous reputation, Miles Keane had behaved inappropriately towards Louisa all those years ago, when he'd arranged for the band to play Madison Square Gardens. His security had informed Gerard that very night and had they not been leaving for Europe, Gerard would have made things difficult for them. As it happened, Celeste didn't end up on the date and Gerard hadn't given Miles Keane a second thought – until now.

He'd originally worried about Celeste's exposure to the renowned playboy but having listened to his daughter recount the events of the evening, he'd decided to research into Miles's recent activities. The first thing Gerard noted was that Miles Keane had certainly cleaned up his act. There hadn't been any scandal related to him since his stint in rehab. There were articles on his move to England and a few pictures of him with his sister-in-law, until the announcement that he would be CASPO's ambassador.

Gerard scanned the photos of the garden party that were on the CASPO website and then searched for any more photos of the ball. A quick tap on a hashtag threw up a huge amount of uncensored photos, uploaded by the many socialites who had attended the ball. Gerard scanned the pictures feeling a twinge of resentfulness seeing Konran and Miles looking chummy, but that feeling paled when he fell on the handful of photos of Louisa and Miles together.

Gerard took in each photo of the handsome pop star and his stunning ex-wife, from their arrival, to the black carpet photo calls. He searched for the interviews and studied Miles's expressions and body language, trying to glean whatever he could from the few minutes of footage. Louisa was, of course professional and guarded with her movements and comments, well practiced in the art of public appearances and speaking. Miles, though, had yet to perfect his public social skills. There were gentle hand brushes against Louisa's back, he hung on her every word and gave her soft smiles that hinted at more than just a professional relationship. To the untrained eye, these small gestures would've gone undetected, but Gerard knew Louisa. If she hadn't welcomed the attention she would've stepped away and done the interviews separately. But what was more telling was in all their many telephone conversations over the last few months, she'd never once mentioned Miles Keane.

Gerard stepped away from the window of his office and quickly checked his engagements over the activities weekend Celeste had mentioned, in his calendar. He was of course fully booked with meetings and events, something he'd tried to ensure since Louisa had left. Any distraction was better than being alone again. He could reschedule; there was nothing that couldn't be postponed and with Konran also being there, it would be a perfect excuse for him to come out for a visit. Gerard knew Louisa would be suspicious but she wouldn't deny him time with his family. She'd never denied him that and he wasn't above using her good nature for his own means.

"HE'S A GOOD MAN. I can see why you trust him." Miles ambled barefoot across the bright kitchen after seeing Hugh to the door. He'd noticed that Louisa had already cleared up the few plates and cup from Hugh's breakfast. Her hair was pulled back into a ponytail and the few creases on yesterday's clothes were the only signs she'd stayed over. It was the only flaw in her usual impeccable appearance. "So we're alone again."

"Hmm, that's getting to become a habit," Louisa said with a smirk. She tried hard to focus on his face, but her eyes drifted over his tanned torso to where his lounge pants hung low.

"A good habit?" He quirked his eyebrow.

"Yeah. A good habit." Miles captured her lips in a slow sensual kiss. He was still couldn't believe she'd stayed the night. Hugh hadn't batted an eyelid when Louisa had explained her intention. Miles had insisted Hugh stay in the house, but only after Louisa had agreed did Hugh take up the offer. Otherwise he had been happy to stay in the car.

"So when am I seeing you again?"

"I think we have a meeting next week." Louisa let her hands roam over his shoulders.

"Somehow I think that meeting will be nothing like this *meeting* we've had," Miles said widening his eyes playfully. "Apart from recording and a few *actual* meetings next week, I'm free. So, Lady Blackthorn, it's up to you."

"Recording? Are you going back to your music?"

He gave a slight shake of his head. "It's the soundtrack for the watch company."

"They liked it then? Of course they liked it." She rolled her eyes at her ridiculous question. "That's brilliant news."

"Want to hear the final piece?"

"I'd love to," Louisa said sincerely and his eyes dropped to her feet.

"Take off your shoes," he demanded softly. After a beat she slipped them off, took his offered hand and headed barefoot for the music room.

When your whole life has been structured and under constant scrutiny, you become confined. There is no room for spontaneity, for freedom to do whatever, whenever in front of whoever. Everything is carefully co-ordinated and precise, and as Louisa watched Miles perform the moving piece of music, totally lost in that moment, she knew her life was at the farthest point in the spectrum to his.

He was an in-the-moment kind of guy. Whereas her fortune and title had restrictions, his wealth and fame had given him the opportunity to do and be whatever he wanted. He had choices that weren't weighed down with duty. Staying overnight could be an everyday occurrence for Miles, not a carefully co-ordinated plan, where safety was priority and anonymity was paramount. Everything he did was purely because he wanted to, not because it was expected. Louisa had forgotten which things she'd actually enjoyed doing, just because the mood or desire took her. She'd lost herself over the many years of being who her title expected her to be but the last few weeks with Miles had her thinking and yearning for more.

As Louisa watched Miles play his music, freely expressing himself, dressed only in a pair of pyjama bottoms, enjoying and living in that very moment, she both envied and craved his life. He was without a doubt a talented musician. The rich sound of the trumpet filled the room. Every square inch vibrated with the powerful notes of the beautifully melodic piece, but it was Miles himself who brought the music to life. He oozed magnetism. His music was almost a by-product of his hypnotic performance. Miles had always maintained that his brother had been the more talented of the two of them, which may have been true, but Miles had that something extra, something that couldn't be quantified. It wasn't just the music that filled the room, it was Miles. He dazzled, whether he was playing in a small 20-square-metre room or in the 20,000-capacity Madison Square Gardens.

Miles opened his eyes and gave her a reluctant smile as he lowered his priceless instrument.

"Incredible," she said, truly in awe of him. He gifted her with that radiant smile that beautifully creased his handsome face. "Do you think you'll ever perform again?" She wasn't the first person to ask him that billion-dollar question. Since the shooting, it was perhaps the most frequently asked question by anyone and, up until the night of the ball, it had been the farthest thing from his mind. Miles had not only avoided performing, he'd also avoided watching performances too. Seeing Konran play and elicit such a reaction from the guests had stirred up that part of him he'd locked away.

He gave a shrug and placed his treasured trumpet back in its box. "I honestly can't say. I…" he faltered trying to find the right words. "Performing has always been the part I enjoyed. Getting that instant feedback from the audience is so addictive. But after what happened, I don't know. There's just so much to deal with." He rested himself against the piano and crossed his arms before he continued. "The therapy helped with the fear, to an extent, but that's not the only reason. That day was a living nightmare. I live it every day. The thought of being up in front of thousands, I just don't think I could do it." He blew out a breath and looked down at his feet. Louisa nodded but stayed silent, giving him a moment, and just as she was about to give him some words of encouragement, he lifted his gaze and said, "It's the guilt I find hard to live with."

"Oh." Louisa furrowed her brow, unsure of what he meant. "So you feel what, guilty towards your fans?"

He shook his head. "I feel guilty for *surviving*. Louis had a family, a baby on the way, and he was the one who got killed. It should have been me." He put up his hand as Louisa was about to protest. "And before you say anything, I'm not being a martyr – believe me, I'm not that good a person. But the fact was he had so much more to lose and his family too. It's not fair he was taken."

"That's understandable. It was a horrific thing to go through. I know Alistair finds it hard. He lost friends in the war who had family, wives, and though it's not the same as what you went through, I see him struggle with that every day. He always says he got off lightly losing his leg."

Miles nodded and took in a deep breath as he ran his hand through his hair. "I often wonder if Amanda resents the fact I was the one that lived."

"I'm sure she doesn't," Louisa said immediately and Miles twisted his mouth, indicating he wasn't so sure. It suddenly became very clear to Louisa why he was so attached to his sister-in-law. It was guilt. It was his way of trying to make it up to her and the children for being the one who survived. Louisa remembered Miles saying it was Amanda who'd suggested he move to London. No doubt she'd realised he was battling with the guilt too and this was her way of trying to alleviate it. "I didn't know Louis but I can't imagine he'd ever want you to stop playing."

"Believe it to achieve it. God, that used to make me nuts. He'd say it all the time." Miles gave a humourless laugh.

"So believe it. You play so beautifully, it's a shame that your talent has been, for want of a better word… shelved," Louisa said softly, hoping she wasn't pushing him on an obviously touchy subject. "What about Grace and Louis Junior, have they heard you play?"

At the mention of his niece and nephew, Miles's pensive expression lifted. "Yeah, I taught Grace to play piano. She's good – scratch that, she's amazing – and Louis is starting to show an interest too."

Louisa gave him a bright smile of encouragement. "Well there you are, then. Do it for them, and do it for you too. Anyone watching you can see how important music is to you. It's part of you, Miles, a really important part of you. Don't quash it or lose it. Believe me, there's nothing worse than suppressing something you enjoy or are passionate about."

"I'm not sure I can be on stage without him next to me." His voice was hoarse with emotion and in that vulnerable moment, Louisa's heart broke for him. She rose from her seat immediately and stepped up to him, enveloping his hard strong body in her arms. He rested his chin on her head, relishing the closeness that had blossomed between them over the last 24 hours. Therapy had taught him to voice his feelings rather than bottling them up. It had taken him time and Amanda had often been his sounding board, but with Louisa, he found that it was easier to be more forthright.

"I'm so sorry for your loss, Miles. When you feel it's the right time to move on you will."

"Yeah. Today was good. You're the first person who isn't family who I've played in front of."

Louisa pulled back from his chest. "I am? Well it seems you and I are breaking through some personal barriers today. We've accumulated quite a list."

Miles blinked away his unshed tears and gave her a grin. "A never-have-I-ever list, in your case."

"Yes, and a get-back-on-the-horse list for you."

Miles let out a husky laugh at her quick comeback and kissed her soundly. "We're going to have to work on those lists."

"Well, I've never had sex on a piano before," Louisa said coyly, looking up at his surprised expression. "Want to help me cross that one of my list?"

In a flash he bent down, picked her up and seated her on top of the piano. "Whatever my lady wants."

24

WELCOME TO HOLMWOOD

AFTER LIVING IN CALIFORNIA for the majority of his adult life, Miles had been spoiled with good weather, blue skies and a sea view, but even he had to admit that England was glorious when the sun came out. It was just so green, every shade imaginable from moss green to bright emerald. It was as though the sun's rays brought the landscape to life, retouching its natural beauty.

The picturesque drive from London was about an hour to Holmwood House. Amanda and the children had come down to stay the night before and they'd all set off just after the morning traffic. Grace and Louis were just excited to be with their much loved uncle and Duke again, and the activities weekend was an added bonus.

Amanda eyed her brother-in-law as he tapped the steering wheel nervously. He was trying to act carefree, but Amanda knew this was a big deal for him. Over the last few weeks she'd seen a distinct change in Miles. He was embracing work again, taking meetings that a year ago he wouldn't have even entertained, let alone agree to. He'd been open to many proposals that had unexpectedly come his way, since being the ambassador for CASPO. And though Amanda was pleased she'd had a hand in his new role, she knew the reason he was finally embracing these new opportunities was because of a certain countess.

Miles and Louisa's relationship had its own challenges. Firstly there was the secrecy; only a handful of people knew that they were together. Louisa had yet to tell Lady Alice officially, but Amanda didn't doubt for a moment the shrewd woman hadn't figured it out. Louisa was worried the press would sensationalise their relationship, which would mean the spotlight would be taken away from the charity.

Secondly, because of the secrecy, they had to be over-vigilant, meaning they were limited to where they could be together. Miles had had extra cameras installed in his home, to appease Louisa's head of security, though she was rarely without her faithful bodyguard. Miles had joked to Amanda about there being three people in their relationship. He now took it in his stride and had formed an unsaid camaraderie with Hugh Thornton, but Amanda knew Miles would have much preferred not to be constantly under his watchful eye. Miles's home was the only place they could be together. He'd yet to visit Louisa's London residence, for fear of someone leaking it or spotting him there. His public profile had risen again after being off the radar for a few years. The various prestigious events he'd been part of had renewed the interest in his life and there was always constant speculation as to whom he was seeing.

Miles's recent collaboration on the six-part TV documentary had garnered interest from both the media and fans alike, which was another challenge Louisa and Miles's relationship had to face. He was photographed whenever he was out. If he walked Duke, someone would snap a shot of him. If he was entering CASPO offices, again it was documented. Shopping in the local supermarket took him twice as long because of the requests for celebrity selfies. He'd thought about employing a live-in housekeeper but he was already uncomfortable with Hugh's presence when Louisa came over, and he didn't want to add another person to their already crowded relationship. Plus Louisa was adamant that no one knew about them – not yet, anyway.

All these constraints were preying on Miles's mind. His rational side understood their unusual situation and he adjusted accordingly, but his emotional side was having a hard time catching up. Amanda was glad she was there for him to sound off to. He wasn't used to being restrained and for Miles to accept everything that was currently being thrown at him, it meant Louisa was someone he felt was worth the effort.

"Are you okay?"

"Hmm?"

"You seem a little uptight."

"I've never been in her… environment." Miles's eyes shifted for a second to Amanda and she gave him a reassuring smile.

"Well, you won't be alone."

"We're rarely alone," he said dryly.

"You know what I mean. We'll be there, and it's not formal either." Miles gave a sigh and kept his eyes glued to the road. "When Melissa invited us she said it was casual. No pomp and circumstance. Her words, so it's probably the best way for you to be there."

Miles nodded but stayed silent. His stomach was tightening with every mile he drove closer to Holmwood, his anxiety notching up so much that not even the chatter from his niece and nephew could distract him. Amanda was right, though, he was glad he wasn't facing this alone.

The last few weeks had been both wonderful and frustrating for Miles. Their secret rendezvouses at his home had been perfect. It was a novelty for both of them to just be alone in each other's company doing mundane, every day things. Preparing dinner together, talking over work projects and listening to music, just being them without the outside world or other people present. The constraints of their relationship meant they had no other focus but each other, which inevitably meant they'd built up a closeness that felt far too quick for such a new affair. The downside was that any time they spent together had to fit around their busy schedules, plus they couldn't be together outside of Miles's home.

This weekend was going to be a real test. They would have four days together but in the company of CASPO staff, Louisa's family and friends, and 32 children and their parents. When Miles had discussed the whole event with Louisa, she'd seemed less fazed about it. She'd been used to acting in front of an audience her whole life but Miles knew this would be a challenge for him. He also wanted to make a good impression on the people who were important to Louisa. It was a strange version of "meet the parents". Miles rarely cared what people thought of him but this weekend, he wanted to prove that he was worthy of Louisa. It was a getting-to-know visit, four days of being in her environment among her kind of people. He was lucky that the guests would take the full focus off them but nevertheless, it was still going to be a difficult.

Miles had researched Holmwood House when he'd first found out who Louisa was, but when his four-wheel drive Jaguar drove through the stoned gateway of the estate, nothing had prepared him for the magnificence of the house. Miles let out a low whistle as he drove slowly up the wide driveway, shaded by trees.

"I thought you'd googled it," Amanda said seeing his reaction.

"I did, but seeing it for real... she owns all of this. That seems so... weird." His eyes scanned the expanse of green that spread out like a thick rich carpet. In the far distance over the dips and rises he could see woodlands, which no doubt marked the end of the vast estate.

"Weird?" asked Amanda, turning to look at a clearly shocked Miles.

"Yeah. Having this passed down through generations. The

history of it all. It's daunting." Miles couldn't hide the apprehension in his voice. Holmwood was not only huge, it was grandiose, and though Miles knew the Blackthorns had a rich history, seeing their stately home in all its splendour brought it all to reality. Amanda patted his arm and turned to take in the beautiful landscaped gardens as they neared the grand house. The children were excited to be unbuckled out of their seats after their long journey. Duke jumped out onto the gravel pathway and ran around, stretching his legs to the joy of the house staff, who had come out to greet them. Miles popped open the boot of the car to retrieve their luggage, while Amanda introduced herself and children to the staff.

"Who's that?" Amanda asked shielding her eyes from the glare of the lake, where she'd spotted a man galloping along its shores towards them. Miles shut the car boot and looked to where Amanda was facing and saw the large frame of Alistair, dressed in what seemed to be his attire of choice, a white polo shirt, cargo shorts and walking boots.

"It looks like the Earl," Miles said, then he looked up at the house façade. "I'm not sure if this is where I should park up." He looked around for guidance, but no one seemed to be worried that he'd parked right outside the front steps.

The crunch of the gravel drew Miles's attention to Alistair's arrival. "Morning," he called to them and gave a salute, then shifted his attention to one of the staff, calling him by his name. "Park Mr Keane's car in the garage, would you please?" Miles handed over the keys and thanked the man, stepping back from the car and gathering up an excited Duke. "How was the drive up? Not too busy, I hope?" Alistair came to a halt by them and dismounted, before making his way around the impressive chestnut horse.

Miles caught the second Amanda saw his titanium blade but she covered up her surprise before Alistair noticed. He removed his hat, which was very similar to the kind Indiana Jones wore;

the battered leather was the exact same colour as his longer than usual hair. Considering Alistair had been a military man, Miles thought it was unusual that he preferred a trim beard rather than be clean-shaven, and his hair shaggy rather than a crew cut.

"It wasn't bad." Miles shook Alistair's hand and scanned the house behind him, hoping to see Louisa, but there was no one apart from the few staff. Grace and Louis were preoccupied with Duke as Miles greeted Alistair and introduced him to Amanda.

"Welcome to Holmwood," Alistair said as he shook Amanda's hand.

"Thank you. It's truly beautiful," she said genuinely and called over to her children who were immediately in awe of the horse.

"You ride like a cowboy!" Grace said and then her eyes dropped to Alistair's prosthetic leg.

"What happened to your leg?" asked Louis.

"Louis!" Amanda blushed at her son's outburst, but Alistair stepped forward and shook his head, indicating he wasn't offended.

"It's okay. I had an accident." He bent down so he was on the same level as Louis.

"On your horse?"

"No, I was in a war and there was an explosion."

"And it got blown off!" Louis said both in shock and awe.

Alistair let out a chuckle at his unfiltered reaction. "Yep. I lost my left leg, but I'm all *right* now," he said with a wink and Grace giggled, then slapped her hand over her mouth, worried that she shouldn't have laughed. "It's okay, you're supposed to laugh, it was one of my many bad leg jokes. There, you see? I just made another one. *Bad* leg joke… get it?" Alistair's eyes twinkled with mischief at the children who giggled freely, now they knew he wasn't offended. Alistair's eyes, then shifted to Amanda, who had just about recovered from her children's embarrassing behaviour. He gave her a wide smile and rose up from his crouching position. "Now I've got this titanium one." He knocked his knuckles against the metal.

"What's titanium?" asked Louis, looking up at Miles.

"It's a metal. You know, like iron or steel."

"Alistair's a war hero. He fought in a war," explained Amanda.

"You mean like Ironman and Superman?" Louis's eyes widened in awe as his head shot back to Alistair, who let out a laugh.

"They're *super*heroes," Grace said with a roll of her eyes.

"Umm." The five-year-old furrowed his small brow, then turned to his uncle. "Well, he has a metal leg, you said like iron and steel right?" Miles nodded and narrowed his eyes trying to work out where his nephew's train of thought was going. "Man of *Steel* and *Iron*man. See, he *is* a superhero!" he said as though it made perfect sense, causing everyone to laugh.

"Not quite," Alistair said with a shake of his head.

"But he's close. He also flies helicopters." Miles widened his eyes at his nephew who turned and looked at Alistair again.

"Wow! Can you take me up in one?"

"Louis!" Amanda chastised.

"If it's okay with your mum."

"Let's just see, shall we?" Amanda said softly and gave Alistair a thankful smile.

"I can take you all up if you like."

Grace beamed and nodded, then looked expectantly at her mother. "Well if they behave, that'd be very kind of you Mr..." She stuttered over what she should call him, forgetting his title and protocol, a little knocked off-kilter at how charming and approachable Alistair was.

"Alistair, just call me Alistair."

"Alistair," Amanda said with a shy smile.

"Shall we go inside?" Alistair asked one of the staff to take care of his horse and their luggage, then put out his hand, gesturing that they go into the house. "I think you talked me up, there," he muttered to Miles as they walked towards the steps.

"Not at all," Miles said sincerely. "What's that?" Miles spotted a number of large vans with the John Lewis logo emblazoned on their sides, parked up by a far section of the house.

"Makeover quarters. Well, it was the old dairy, but it's been converted into accommodation and is being used as makeover central," Alistair said with a smirk. "Louisa thought it'd be nice for the parents and the kids to get pampered. So we've set up a spa in the bathhouse over there." Alistair pointed to a grand building in the distance. "We have a team of stylists for anyone who wants help and then they can choose some clothes to take with them." Miles and Amanda looked at each other, a little in awe at what lengths the Blackthorns had gone to ensure the families were well looked after. "Don't ask me about any of it – as you can see, I live in work wear. I'm in charge of the outdoorsy stuff." Alistair chuckled. "But I think Louisa wanted the kids and parents to feel special for the big party on Saturday night."

"That's really something."

"Yeah, Louisa thinks of everything. There's so much going on, it's been a hell of a challenge. I feel like I'm back in the military."

Alistair made his way in through the grand entrance quickly followed by Grace, who had Duke on his leash now, and Louis.

"I'm so out of my depth here," Miles muttered to Amanda as he took in the huge hallway with sweeping staircases that curled upwards. There were antique statues and priceless art beautifully lit up with ornate period lighting. Miles felt as though he'd stepped back in time.

"Miles, she's just Louisa."

"But she owns this. She's a countess. I mean I knew that, but this shit just got real." He swallowed hard and tried not to look totally terrified.

"I know it's pretty grand, but most of this is for the visitors." Alistair waved his hand around vaguely, seeing the shock on

Miles's face. He gave them a minute to appreciate the room, knowing it was a lot to take in, fussing over Duke who was sniffing around, then continued. "So, once all the volunteers have arrived, we'll be having our first meeting at 11 in Louisa's private drawing room, then lunch. A grand tour of the estate follows that for you guys, and then tea. You know we British always stop for tea – that's one tradition we uphold religiously," Alistair said dryly, causing Miles to chuckle. Miles appreciated the Earl's easy and jovial manner. He was fast realising that Alistair was well versed in the art of putting people at ease. "We have coffee too, though," he added with a smirk.

"Good to know."

"Another debriefing, then the guests arrive and it's all hands on deck. There's an information pack in your rooms. Like I said, Louisa has everything covered." Alistair gestured for them to take the stairs and they all climbed up the wide, plush, blue-carpeted staircase.

Considering the size of the house and the period décor, Holmwood House didn't seem stuffy and somehow felt homely. Miles and Amanda took in the wide corridors that had various doors along them, all lit with warm lighting. Alistair pointed out certain features of the house, explaining some of its history and renovations that had been made over the years. It was clear that he loved his family home.

The main part of the house that they were now in was where Louisa stayed. The upstairs would normally have been closed off to the public but because it was the activities weekend, the whole house had been opened up.

"Let me show you to your rooms. We're all bunking in Louisa's suites. I've been evicted from my wing for all the guests and Mama's housing the volunteers in her wing – namely my friends and ex-colleagues." Alistair opened up one of the doors and revealed a grand room, complete with a king sized four-poster bed, small seating area and a second bedroom.

"This is your room. There are two beds in the second bedroom and the bathroom is through that door." Alistair pointed to a close door as he spoke to Amanda, who was openly gaping at the room. "Louisa thought this would be best suited to you, plus it has a fabulous view of the lake. Come and have a look."

"It's... wow. That bed is..." Amanda stepped up to the beautifully made bed. The room had been decorated in soft blues and gold, in keeping with the elegance of the house, but mixed in with antiques there were also modern accents.

"Yes, the frame is over 400 years old, but you'll be pleased to know that the mattress is new." Amanda let out a nervous laugh.

"I really should thank Louisa. Where is she?"

"She's just going over the final menus. She'll be along in a bit. I'm afraid I've been delegated as the welcoming committee."

"Well you're doing a great job so far. This room is stunning," Amanda said sincerely.

Alistair gave her a wide smile and joked. "Make sure you tell the boss – she's always having a go at me for being anti-social." He then reluctantly pulled his gaze away from Amanda and looked at an amused Miles. "Want to see your room? I'm afraid it's not as grand as this, but I have a feeling you'll like certain features in it," he said cryptically.

"Sure."

Miles left Amanda, the children and Duke in their room to settle in and followed Alistair further down the corridor, passing numerous doors until they reached his room. He opened the door to a comfortable more masculine room than the room Amanda had. It was subtly decorated in tones of rich browns and burgundy, which complimented the wooden panelling and again had spectacular views of the estate.

"So this is your room. It used to be where my great-great-grandmother used to stay before she married my great-great-grandfather. We've renovated all the house over the years, adding en suites and energy efficient heating and lighting, plus a few other extras."

"Thank you, it's a lovely room." Miles's eye caught sight of a stunning painting hanging up above the ornate fireplace and stepped towards it.

"Louisa had that put up for you." Miles span round to find an amused Alistair a few feet away from him. "It was hanging in the library but she asked the staff to hang it here. She thought it would make you feel more at home."

"It's stunning, so vivid." Miles turned back to look at the painting of a couple of sail boats on a deep blue sea, sailing near a white wooden white house. The painting was both calming and moving at the same time.

"Typical of the artist. He always captured the haunting drama and quiet tension in his best work."

"Who's the artist?" Miles asked, turning back to his host.

"Edward Hopper, an American." Alistair gave him a knowing smile. Miles stifled a grin, understanding why Louisa had put the painting in his room. Alistair thought it was because the artist was American but Miles knew it was because the painting was of the sea. She'd remembered that that was what he missed most from LA. Miles then stepped to the large window.

"The view is something else." Miles scanned the estate, noting various features he remembered seeing when he'd researched Louisa's family home. The lake spread out and at the far end was a pavilion nestled in a cluster of trees. Miles could see the bathhouse, which he remembered had a huge indoor swimming pool along with Jacuzzi, and to the left was another large period building with a glass roof which must have been the orangery. Miles still didn't know what that was, but it was grand all the same.

Miles was so engrossed with the view he didn't realise that Louisa had entered the room until Alistair spoke. "There you are.

Your special guests are settling into their rooms and I didn't botch it up," Alistair said with a smirk.

Miles turned away from the window and took in the stunning vision of Louisa. She was dressed casually in a pair of khaki silk trousers and soft cream top, but still had that undeniable air of elegance. She gave Miles a soft smile and stepped further into the room.

"Well let's hope you're on a roll, shall we?" Louisa said to her brother and he chuckled. "Hi, welcome to Holmwood."

"Thank you," Miles said and stepped closer, then stopped himself, remembering they had company.

"I think some of your gang have just arrived, but they know their way around."

Alistair gave a nod, taking the subtle hint that Louisa wanted to be alone with Miles. "Better go see they're not arguing over which room they're in. Mama will have them all cowering if they're too noisy." He gave Miles a curt nod and exited the room, closing the door behind him.

"Alone at last?" Miles said with a cheeky smile, then stepped up to her, kissing her thoroughly. They'd been apart for a few days and the late night phone calls were no substitute for the physical contact he'd been craving.

"Well, as alone as we can be," Louisa said with a huff and Miles squeezed her closer to his chest and rested his chin on the crown of her head.

"My room is lovely. Your house is incredible. I kinda thought I was the one who had to impress you. Alistair told me you put up that painting for me."

Louisa pulled back and looked into his handsome face. "Do you like it?"

"It's spectacular. I'm blown away. Everything is just so…"

"Too much?"

"It's a lot to take in." He gave a sigh and she watched as his eyes rested on the bed.

"Sorry about the sleeping arrangements. It's just Celeste will be here and…"

"Don't worry about it," he said dismissively. He knew they wouldn't be sharing a room. There would be too many people witnessing their every move. She squeezed his hand in silent gratitude of his understanding, then swallowed, worried how he would take the next piece of news.

"Gerard is coming on Saturday." Miles tensed at her words but before he could ask why, Louisa continued in a rush. "He wanted to help and see Celeste, and with Konran coming too, he thought it'd be the best opportunity."

"And he's staying here too?"

Louisa gave him a nod and he clenched his teeth. "My section is for family and VIP guests," she said apologetically.

Wonderful! It would be bad enough being around Louisa for four days and keeping their relationship in check, now he had her ex to contend with. Someone she'd loved and who was used to the kind of life Louisa was accustomed to. They had a history, a family and he was a total outsider. His stomach clenched at the thought. *How was he ever going to measure up?*

"Did Alistair show you all the features of this room?" Louisa tugged Miles's hand to the direction of the wall and he furrowed his brow. The last thing on his mind was the décor of his room. "Here, let me show you something." Miles watched as she pushed against a section of the panelling and the wood popped open to reveal a corridor behind it.

"Whoa, that's so cool. A secret passageway. Where does it lead to?" Miles stepped forward as Louisa opened up the door and switched on the light.

"Let me show you." She grasped his hand and led him through. It was a narrow corridor, just enough for one person to walk through, but the lighting was bright enough for Miles to see that it was fairly long with nothing on the walls. When they reached the far end, Louisa opened up the only door into what looked like a dressing room. Before Miles could ask where they were, Louisa tugged him through to a huge sumptuous bedroom, complete with four-poster bed.

"This is my suite," she said with a shy smile.

"This weekend just got a whole lot better," Miles said, grasping her by the waist and whirling her around, then kissing her hard. All thoughts of ex-husbands and constraints went flying out of his mind. He carried her over to the bed and roughly laid her on it, hovering over her. "Your ancestors knew what they were doing." He chuckled as he looked down at her, her dark hair fanning out on the ivory bedspread.

"It was made by my great-great-grandfather. Originally it was an escape route out of the house, but it passed by my soon-to-be great-great-grandmother's room. So he knocked through a door so he could be with her without being detected by anyone. It was then used in the world wars as an escape route when the house was used as a hospital for soldiers and high-ranking military."

"I feel like I'm in some fairy-tale novel… secret passages, clandestine meetings and furniture that is older than the country I was born in," he said with a shake of his head.

"I'm still just Louisa."

"I know, but the more I get to know about who you are, the harder it gets for me to get my head around it. It's a lot to take in." Louisa's face dropped and he brushed his knuckles over her flushed cheek. "But it's not *too* much. I just need to adjust a little – scratch that, a lot." He huffed, then dropped a quick kiss on her lips and pulled back. Louisa slipped her arms around his neck.

"Don't change for me. Don't ever change who you are," she said sincerely.

25

CHANGE OF PLANS

BY THE TIME MILES and Louisa entered her private drawing room, most of the volunteers and CASPO staff were already there. After greeting everyone, Louisa took her place at the front, with Alistair to her left. Miles took a seat next to Melissa, where the rest of the volunteers were scattered around the very large and grand room. There were over 20 volunteers with their own specific skills to help with the 32 children and 17 parents, plus the staff of Holmwood House. Louisa knew each and every one of them personally and spent the first 30 minutes introducing each one to the rest of the group, explaining their skills and duties for the weekend.

Miles watched her command everyone's attention, answering questions carefully and confirming her replies with various members of the team. She asked Alistair to outline certain facts and brought in Hugh to explain the extreme security measures Holmwood House employed. The whole weekend was well thought out, meticulously planned and carefully programmed, so that the guests would have a good time and feel special. Miles once again found himself in awe of Louisa.

The meeting was interrupted by the arrival of Lady Alice and

Celeste. Everyone immediately stood up, but Lady Alice ushered them to sit back down. The elegant lady perched herself on one of the antique sofas to the right of Louisa, and Celeste lowered herself next to her grandmother. Even in her worn jeans, plain white T-shirt and pink converse, Celeste looked like the perfect lady, mirroring her grandmother's posture. Miles gave the young lady Blackthorn a smile and she beamed back at him and for a split second, an image flashed through his memory, but it disappeared before he could grasp it. The sound of applause diverted his attention back to Louisa, who had now asked Lady Alice to say a few words.

Once Lady Alice finished her small welcome speech, they all filtered through to the dining room, where an informal buffet style lunch had been set up. It was the perfect opportunity for the volunteers to get to know one another in a casual setting and set the precedent for the rest of the weekend.

Amanda and her children were also brought to the dining room. Even though she wouldn't officially be one of the volunteers, she was included in all the functions. Miles took her around and introduced her to the few people he knew, including Celeste, who was happy to take over the introductions, leaving Miles the opportunity to mingle.

After a while, Miles helped Amanda sort out the children, then served himself lunch, hovering unsure where they should sit. He would have liked to sit with Louisa but he was mindful of drawing too much attention to himself. The decision was thankfully taken out of his hands when Alistair called him over to sit with him and Celeste, who had also insisted Amanda and the children join them.

The elegant dining room was buzzing with excitement and though it was an informal lunch, the crisp white linen, crystal glassware and delicate tableware added the ever-present sense of opulence. If this was informal, Miles couldn't imagine what formal dining at Holmwood was like.

Miles subtly kept his eye on Louisa. He noted she hadn't sat down to eat, preferring to speak to various staff and volunteers instead, moving around the room, still the consummate hostess. This was her role, the Countess of Holmwood, and even in this relatively informal setting she was on duty. The thought was both sobering and a little depressing. Miles couldn't imagine being constantly on his guard – and especially in his own home. Celeste and Alistair chatted easily, making Amanda feel welcome. It was obvious even she was a little in awe of her surroundings. Amanda gushed about her room and Celeste explained some history behind the beautiful suite, saying it was usually occupied by special guests of her mother's, which only made Amanda's eyes widen and blush.

"Which room are you in, Miles?" Celeste asked.

"I'm a few doors down from Amanda in your great-great-great-grandmother's old room, apparently."

Celeste shot a look at Alistair who stifled a smirk. "You mean granny's old room?"

"I've no idea?" Miles gave a shrug.

"My mother stayed in that particular room when she and my father were... courting."

"*Courting*?" Miles furrowed his brow.

"When they were dating, Miles," Amanda explained.

"Oh, okay."

Celeste's eyes widened in realisation, knowing the unique feature of that particular room, then she took a sip from her drink as she processed the surprising news.

"It's a lovely room," Miles said sincerely, unaware of Celeste's sudden unease, as his attention was drawn to the arrival of Gordon. He'd stepped into the room and immediately began scanning it, locking his sights on Louisa. Miles sensed the second Alistair saw Gordon and shot him a worried look. Alistair shook his head at Miles, indicating he shouldn't worry because Louisa was now only a few steps away from their table.

"Everything under control?" Alistair asked Louisa as he stood up.

"Yes, once lunch is done, we can take Miles and Amanda on the tour of the grounds."

Alistair nodded and was about to say something, when Gordon appeared at the table. He greeted everyone and Alistair introduced Amanda. Gordon politely shook her hand and acknowledged Miles but then turned his full attention to Louisa. "Louisa, could you spare me a moment?"

"Of course." She gave the table a tight smile, excused herself and made her way out of the dining room and into the drawing room. Miles looked to Alistair for guidance. He didn't want Louisa on her own with Gordon, not after what his wife had said.

"Louisa can handle him," Alistair said discreetly and Miles knew he was right, but it still made him uneasy.

Gordon shut the door behind him and took a deep breath.

"What can I help you with?"

"I came to apologise for Emily's behaviour," Gordon said as he stepped closer to Louisa. Louisa signalled to a chair for him to sit down and then she took the seat to his left.

"How is she?"

"She's staying with her parents at the moment." His light brown eyes fixed on Louisa's sympathetic expression and he knew this was the time he had to come clean. He'd waited long enough, missed opportunities and though he'd have preferred to declare his hand under better circumstances, he wasn't about to let this one go now. "About those things she said... I know that this is bad timing and all, but –"

Louisa cut him off before he carried on. "Gordon, please, before you say anything else, you need to know that I have only ever seen you as a friend – a dear friend, but a friend all the same."

"Louisa –"

"If you are under the impression there anything could be

more than that, I can assure there won't be. I'm sorry, but that's the truth. Had I known..." Louisa left the sentence hanging, seeing his devastated expression. She didn't want to hurt him but there was no point it giving him false hope, especially in the light of what had happened.

"I see."

"You have a baby on the way, Gordon." Louisa tried to sound comforting.

"Yes, but..."

Louisa leaned forward a little. "Gordon, if you're unhappy, get a divorce, work something out, have a new life. What you're doing isn't fair on her or you."

Gordon stood up and walked over to the large window. He couldn't bear her looking at him with pity. He wanted her to look at him and see a man she could have a future with. "How did you manage it?" he said after a moment.

"Manage what?" Louisa stood up and walked to where some papers had been left on her small antique bureau.

Gordon turned to look at the woman who had captivated his thoughts and heart for the last 30 years. "Being with Gerard for so long."

Louisa's gaze shot up to his and she answered. "I loved him."

"What changed?"

"I still love him.," she said clearly, not to hurt him, but because it was true. She loved Gerard and always would, but it wasn't the same as it had been right at the beginning.

"But you're not with him." Gordon narrowed his eyes at her and stepped closer. "What happened for you to finally decide to leave him? Was it true about –"

"My marriage and divorce are private, Gordon. We're talking about yours." She fussed over the papers and pressed the discreet button in her bureau, then turned back to face him. "Thank you for the apology, but you need to decide where your future is, but

I'm sorry it will never be with me." A knock at the door jolted Gordon. "Come in."

Hugh entered the room and fixed his attention firstly on Louisa, then Gordon.

"Now if you'll excuse me, I have a lot to organise." Louisa paced to the door where Hugh stood, and he stepped back for her to pass. Once out in the dining room, Louisa let out a breath and let her gaze search out Miles. He was already looking at her and he gave her a tentative smile, which she reciprocated. She needed some fresh air. It was time to show Miles Holmwood.

Miles was almost relieved to see Amanda was as awestruck as he was at the sheer expanse of the estate. Alistair had taken them around the perimeter in one of his Land Rovers and then worked their way back via the various features of the estate. Louisa explained some of the history and what the numerous buildings were originally used for and what they'd now been adapted to.

It was another world to Miles and though he was suitably impressed, he knew that this life Louisa had been born into was not only streets away from his, it was a whole other universe. It took them over an hour to skim around the estate. It would take more than the few days he had here for Miles to get at least a little bit acquainted with the grounds of Holmwood, but it was a start.

Once they returned to the house, Louisa and Alistair reluctantly excused themselves. They had a few last-minute meetings with their staff before their visitors arrived, leaving Amanda, Miles and the children an hour or so to leisurely take in the grounds before tea.

Teatime was another grand affair set up in the conservatory and spilling out on to the terrace that showcased the beautifully landscaped gardens. Lady Alice, Celeste and Margot played hosts, making everyone feel welcome. Miles reeled at the lengths the

Blackthorns had gone to and this was just for the staff and volunteers. His preconceived opinion of the aristocracy was changing with every moment he spent in the company of Louisa and her family.

Louis and Grace played with Duke on the lawn just off the adjoining terrace. The lively puppy was being spoiled with such a vast playground to run freely around. Lady Alice chuckled as she watched the children roll around with Duke. Her own dog, a King Charles Spaniel named Bella and Alistair's Golden Retriever Luna watched on as Celeste had now joined in the fun, throwing a ball for the puppy to chase.

"Your children are adorable," Lady Alice said from seat as she took in the scene.

"They're a handful," Amanda retorted and Miles rolled his eyes.

"Just the way children should be. Both of mine were always getting up to mischief on the grounds and Celeste carried on that particular family tradition."

Duke's attention was drawn to Alistair and Louisa, who had just returned and joined everyone out on the terrace. He sprinted towards Louisa and she dutifully bent down to give him a belly rub. Lady Alice smiled to herself and caught her daughter's eye.

"That puppy seems to be drawn to you." Lady Alice gave Louisa a knowing look, but she chose to ignore the underlying implication. Miles's eyes shot to Alistair, who smirked at him. Before Lady Alice could press further, Hugh arrived, informing Louisa she had a call.

Alistair picked up his teacup that Margot had poured for him and lifted it in a silent toast. "Saved by the bell," he muttered dryly to Louisa.

Louisa's relief was short lived, when she realised the phone call was from Gerard. He was due on Saturday and was staying for just one night, which was bad enough, but now it seemed he would be arriving on Friday with Konran and Nicholas, meaning he'd be there for two days. He had courteously rung to ensure that this wouldn't be a problem with Louisa or Lady Alice.

"Mother's fond of you."

"She tolerates me," Gerard replied. His relationship with the Blackthorns had always been amicable, mainly because Gerard behaved like the perfect son-in-law and father. He'd stood by the family in their time of need and took the reins when Louisa, Alistair and Lady Alice were unable to face the tragedy of the late Earl's death and Alistair's accident. But Gerard was under no illusion that Lady Alice was his biggest fan.

"You gave her her only grandchild, and to all intents and purposes, you made me happy. For that alone, she's grateful."

"Maybe she won't be that grateful now, *cherie.* We're divorced." His remark was met with silence. It was true; Louisa knew her mother was careful never to rock the boat in their seemingly calm marriage, even when she'd suspected it was turbulent. Lady Alice wasn't a fool, what she was though was a consummate diplomat. "Has she never asked you about why?"

"Oh, you know my mother. Discretion is her middle name. She'd never pry. I told her we grew apart and we were good friends, I spared her the details." It wasn't entirely the truth. Her mother had tried to find out and Louisa was sure she had her own suspicions but there was no need for Gerard to know.

"I suppose it's as close to the truth as you could get." Again his remark was met with silence because Louisa had no desire to rake over the breakdown of their marriage. He had had his chance to make amends and failed. She wasn't going to make him feel worse or better by commenting. If he wanted to be there this weekend, he was going to have to handle her mother and Alistair without any help from her. He was man enough for *that* challenge, at least.

"I'll be there tomorrow, then. I can't wait to see you and Celeste."

"I'll make sure everything's ready for you," Louisa said softly, unsure of why he was still being so persistent. Maybe it was his ego that had taken a hit.

"Cherie?"

"Yes."

"I've really missed you."

Louisa swallowed the instinctive reply of "Me too" and said, "Safe flight, Gerard," then ended the call. Twenty years of habits were hard to shake off and it seemed Gerard was determined to keep reminding her of them.

"Everything okay?"

Miles's raspy voice drew Louisa's attention to where he was leisurely leaning against the doorframe of the library. He'd asked Hugh where she was, hoping he'd have a few minutes alone with her, and heard the tail end of the phone call.

Louisa gave him a weary smile. This weekend was going to be a test in diplomacy as well as patience. She would be on display every minute, which would be pressure enough, but added to that, Gerard would be here, making things uncomfortable. On top of those stresses, she didn't want Miles to feel awkward or neglected. What she'd originally hoped would be a gentle introduction to her home life for Miles, and an informal setting for her family to meet him, was now turning into a precarious balancing act.

"Sure. That was Gerard." She stepped up to him as he walked towards her, seeing the slight stiffening of his relaxed stance. "He's decided to come tomorrow with Konran and Nicolas." She searched his brilliant blue eyes, trying to decipher what was going through his mind.

"Well, that'll mean there are more people to help out," he said with a wink and took hold of her elbow, gently pulling her towards him. She sagged in relief. Miles felt her whole body relax against his as he kissed the top of her head and gently wrapped his arms around her. He knew it was risky, but right now, her need for reassurance that he was fine was more important than being caught. He hated the idea she was stressing over Gerard coming and him being here. He hated that Gerard had put her in that position but most of all, he just hated Gerard. However, he was determined she would never know that.

"Don't sweat it, Louisa, I can handle Gerard."

"I know, it's just…"

"It just nothing. We're mature adults. I'll behave. Whatever he says or does, I'll be fine. It's 48 hours."

"Thanks. I'm not entirely sure what's behind this."

"I have a fair idea," Miles said dryly. "But whatever it is, I can handle it. I've handled worse. Remember, I'm bulletproof," he joked and Louisa chuckled.

A discreet cough had them jumping apart and for a split second, Miles's stomach clenched, thinking that their cover was blown, until he saw it was Hugh. Miles huffed to himself, thinking how things had changed. He was now relieved to see Hugh rather than irritated.

"Excuse me, my lady, but the first of the guests have arrived."

"Thank you, Hugh." He gave a curt nod and left.

Miles gave her a quick kiss on the lips, then added, "Game face on, baby."

Louisa knew what it was like to have attention. She avoided it as much as her status would allow, by keeping out of the limelight for a majority of her life. With her involvement in CASPO over the last few months, and her divorce, she was slowly becoming used to people's reaction to her. But nothing had prepared her for the attention Miles attracted and how it made her feel.

The total of 49 guests arrived in the early evening hours, 32 children aged between six and 17, five single fathers and 12 single mothers, all of whom were starstruck at meeting *the* Miles Keane. It said a lot for Keane Sense's popularity that the younger children were aware of who he was, seeing as they would've have been babies when their last number one single had been released.

The invited guests were introduced to Miles at the informal welcome dinner held in the library. The volunteers and staff waited for the guests to arrive after they'd been shown their rooms and settled in. The dinner was both a chance for the guests to meet everyone involved and to let them know about the various events the Blackthorns had arranged for their stay.

Louisa was adamant that the usual protocols were lifted, which meant their guests were free to chat with whomever they wanted. She was adhering to her mother's sound advice that a true lady or gentlemen always made someone feel comfortable, regardless of whom they were. This of course meant that their guests could freely approach Miles – well, flock to him would be a more accurate description. The children ran up to him, unguarded in their admiration, hugging him as though he was a long-lost friend. The mothers, on seeing him dressed in his light brown suit with dark blue shirt, straightened themselves out, gushed and flirted with him. The fathers eyed him up, a little in awe of his superstar looks and charm, shook his hand with respect for what he'd been through and what he was now doing. The whole spectacle was both amusing and an eye-opener. Louisa couldn't help but feel a little envious. She'd only been with Miles privately or at official functions, which were always controlled. Here he was free to be Miles the pop star, the charming and disarming celebrity surrounded by doting single swooning women. Louisa furrowed her brow. She hadn't really thought this part through at all. Would they be so swoony if they knew he was off the market? Their secrecy was always about how it affected her status, but as Louisa observed the mothers fawning over him, she wondered whether it was time to come out in the open.

Miles fell easily into his role of Miles Keane. He was used to his fame and how people reacted to him, comfortable with people approaching him and wanting to connect with him. It was something Louisa was still personally struggling with and she was in awe of how Miles slipped into it. His popularity meant his fans felt as though they knew him, which they did on the surface. A quick search on the Internet revealed everything about him, the good, the bad and the ugly. There were endless videos of interviews, shaky candid moments recorded on phones and uploaded, articles and editorials, all revealing something new about him in every possible situation. The majority of his adult life was under the spotlight and seeing how he comfortably handled all 49 guests, it became apparent that he was more than equipped to deal with this weekend.

"It's quite something, isn't it?" Louisa frowned as she turned to face an obviously amused Amanda. "He has them eating out of his hand. He's always been good at this. Louis and I used to just sit back and watch him when Keane Sense were at functions or in public."

"Oh, I see. Yes, he's got that…" Louisa twisted her mouth, unsure of the word.

"Magnetism."

"Yes, that's it. And he's so relaxed about it all."

"Hmm, not really. He just knows how to hide his anxiety, plus this situation is controlled. He's also doing it for a good cause too." Louisa nodded and turned to look back at Miles. He was crouching down and talking to a young boy who seemed to be shy.

"He also wants to make sure he measures up too."

Louisa's head shot back to Amanda. "Measures up?"

"Yeah, it's pretty daunting, being here for him. With all of this and… well, and you."

"I'm just Louisa."

"When you're alone, maybe; not over the next few days, though. Fame he can handle, celebrity he's gotten used to but this – this is a different league." Amanda waved her hand around and

Louisa sighed deeply. Amanda squeezed her arm in reassurance. "Just try and remember that. He won't say anything to you because he doesn't want to blow it. Under that light hearted, relaxed outside of his, he's still very vulnerable." Louisa nodded. She knew Amanda was right. This life was her normal and it was easy to forget that for an outsider it was anything but.

Dinner took over three hours. By the time the guests had met everyone and been given an informal introduction to what they'd be expecting over the next few days, it was late. The guests finally retired to Alistair's wing, leaving the volunteers to relax.

After the initial starstruck reaction the guests had to Miles, they had all mingled with the rest of the welcoming party. Alistair had received a sizeable amount of attention from the children and the parents, for differing reasons. His accident had been extensively documented when it had happened and he'd then become withdrawn from the public eye, so the parents wanted to meet the reluctant Earl and war hero. The children were just fascinated with his prosthetic leg, which Alistair took in his stride.

"He's found himself a fan there." Lady Alice gestured to Alistair, who was sitting with Louis on his lap, playing paper, scissors, rock. Lady Alice had asked the volunteers to come back to her wing for a nightcap after the guests had retired. She was sitting alongside Miles drinking her Armagnac, taking in the scene of the adorable five-year-old playing with her son. He'd hardly left his side all evening.

"Louis is convinced he's a superhero," Miles chuckled. "Which isn't too far from the truth. He's good with children. He has a lot of patience."

"Yes, Alistair's always been good with everyone, adults too," she smirked, "but especially with children, because of their honesty. It's refreshing. Celeste was instrumental to his healing, after the accident. She didn't hold back with him, not having a filter like we adults had. I think she still doesn't have one, to be honest." Miles let out a soft laugh. He couldn't argue with that statement. Of the little he'd seen of Celeste, she was quite the straight talker. "She made the loss of his leg a sort of game. Instead of ignoring it, she focused on it. We all cringed when she made some leg joke or robot joke, but it did break down the awkwardness."

"Yeah, I did notice that. Kids have a tendency to say it how it is."

"Out of the mouths of babes," Lady Alice said sagely as Celeste approached.

"Did Mum tell you Papa is coming tomorrow now instead?"

"Yes, she mentioned it," Lady Alice said, before taking the last sip of her drink.

"Alistair's picking him up with Konran and Nicolas. He said something about it making sense for Alistair to pick them all up at once. I'll have all my favourite men under one roof!" Celeste grinned and let her eyes flit over to Miles. "And when you think about it, it would be a waste to do two trips," she added as an after-thought.

"I didn't realise Gerard was so concerned about the environment," Lady Alice said dryly.

"Granny, his company pioneered the biodegradable disposable products." Celeste shook her head in exasperation, totally missing the sardonic undertone.

"Oh yes, so he did. Hmm, so that's the only reason he's coming earlier, so as not to increase his carbon footprint. How very commendable of him, I'm sure," Lady Alice answered with a healthy helping of sarcasm, but Celeste didn't seem to notice. Miles stifled a grin. He loved listening to Lady Alice and her witty comebacks. "Be a dear and get me a refill, I think your uncle's friends are hogging all the drink." Celeste rolled her eyes, then took her grandmother's glass and paced towards the drinks tray. "The fact Gerard flew over, alone on his private jet, seems to have escaped my grand-daughter completely," she muttered and

Miles chuckled, pleased she wasn't taken in by Gerard's obvious tactic.

"Maybe it's best not to point that out; she seems so happy."

"Yes, well at least someone is. I'm not sure how Louisa feels about having Gerard here so soon." Miles turned a little so he could look at the countess. Lady Alice gestured to Louisa, who was talking to one of Alistair's army buddies. She was laughing at something he said that was obviously at Alistair's expense because Alistair gave her a fake smile in retaliation. "She's been so much happier these last few weeks. It's like she's found a new lease of life and purpose."

Miles was caught between being pleased that Louisa's mother had noticed she'd changed for the better and concerned that she suspected it had something to do with him. So he decided to suggest it was because of her work. "She's very committed to CASPO."

"I think there's more to it than that," she answered with a slight lift of her brow.

Miles gave her a wide smile but chose not to comment. Lady Alice was no fool and he wasn't about to insult her intelligence by feigning ignorance.

Luckily, Lady Alice continued and Miles was sure the amount of alcohol she'd consumed over the evening had a lot to do with her candid remarks. "It takes a special kind of partner to accept her role. Louisa was stifled before. She was never keen on being in the limelight; that was definitely more Gerard's thing. He was always in the forefront." Lady Alice paused as Celeste handed her a freshly filled glass, and waited for her to pace over to where Alistair was now entertaining Grace and Amanda, as well as Louis. Their laughter every time Alistair lost was infectious.

Miles took a sip from his drink and pondered on why Lady Alice was revealing so much about her ex son-in-law. Louisa had not exactly been tight-lipped about Gerard, but they'd never really discussed him at any length either. She spoke about him in passing and in the context of being Celeste's father, never elaborating on their relationship. Miles hadn't really pushed to find out more, simply because he was in another country and the chances of being in the same company as Gerard were very slight... until this weekend. He knew Louisa was a private person and he'd wanted her to open up about her marriage when she was ready, but with Gerard's imminent arrival, Miles felt he needed as much ammunition as possible, so the odd snippets Lady Alice revealed were most welcome. "It was an adjustment when Louisa became the heir to Holmwood, suddenly she had to come out of the shadows, which was hard for her and Gerard. Being a countess has a great weight attached to it."

"Fame is overrated," Miles said quietly.

"You can say that because you've experienced both sides. In Louisa's case, though, it was more the life of privilege. She hasn't known anything different."

"Hmm, I suppose. I appreciate my fans; without them I wouldn't have what I have, but it comes at a price. One I feel is immeasurable. So I do understand Louisa's reluctance."

"The public are intrigued with title, history and the aristocracy. Granted, it was forced upon her, but she's always known what it encumbered. The cost for you and Amanda, though, was indeed immeasurable, and those adorable children. They're lucky to have you, Miles."

"I'm the lucky one," he answered softly.

"Yes, in more ways than one."

26

JUST MILES

STEAM FROM THE BATHROOM snaked around Miles's body as he stepped into the bedroom. A rich monogrammed towel hung over his hips while a second rested loosely over his shoulders. His thick damp hair was slicked back, and Louisa couldn't think of anything that looked more delicious. He stopped abruptly, seeing Louisa casually sitting on his bed, and beamed a mega-watt smile at her.

"Sorry about today," she said with a sigh.

"Why are you sorry?" He tilted his head and took in her anxious expression.

She shrugged. "Well I was busy, playing my role." She scrunched up her delicate nose and Miles instantly felt bad for her. Was this how she felt every time she had to be *the* Countess of Holmwood? Had Gerard made her feel guilty of her duties?

He took the few steps to reach her and crouched down on his haunches, taking her hands in his. "You're not *playing* your role, you *are* the countess. You're amazing." Her eyes widened at his comment and her plump lips curved into a shy smile. "I like seeing this side of you." Leaning forward, he kissed her softly. "You were born for this role," he said with the utmost sincerity.

Seeing her today, taking charge when needed, yet still keeping her sense of approachability to her staff, friends and the guests, Miles realised this was more than just a duty for Louisa. It was who she was and she was spectacular. Her eyes narrowed as she took in what he'd said. "You don't think so?" he asked, seeing doubt in her expression.

"It's just taken me a while to accept it that's all – the responsibility. I wasn't supposed to be the heir. I'm here by default."

"That might be how you got the role but you are not less capable because of it." He gave her hands a squeeze, then stood up. "Are you staying?"

"What do you think?" she said with a chuckle.

"Well, you might have snuck into my room, but you're wearing far too many clothes," he said with a cheeky wink, scanning over her body. That wink was going to be the death of her. That body was going to also send her to an early grave. He was just so ridiculously sexy.

"I didn't have time to shower yet," she said as he pulled her up with a tug of her hand.

"That's okay, I'm going to dirty you all up again anyway."

"Is that so?" She pulled on the towel from around his neck and let it fall to the ground.

"Yeah, is that a problem?"

"No complaints from me. Drop the other towel," she said as she smoothed her hand over his shoulders.

"Whatever my lady wants."

"IT'S BEEN QUITE AN eventful first day."

"Yes it has." Louisa propped her chin on Miles's chest and looked up at him. "I'm sorry about him coming." She didn't need to say *his* name; Miles knew she meant Gerard.

"Stop apologising for everything. He wants to see his family,"

Miles said as sincerely as possible, though he had his suspicions as to Gerard's real motive. "Does he know about us?"

"No one knows except Alistair and Melissa. I'm sorry."

"Again with the apologising," he playfully growled and gave her a squeeze. She was anxious enough he didn't need to add to it.

"I'll tell Celeste and Mama… and Gerard."

"You don't have to tell them for me, Louisa." He tenderly smoothed back her dishevelled hair from her forehead.

"I know, but to be honest, the secrecy is getting to me." She wasn't ready to admit that seeing him today being fawned over by the mothers had stirred up her own insecurities.

"Whenever you want you tell them is fine by me. I know we're together, I don't really care who else knows or doesn't – except for Hugh, because I'd hate to get shot!" Louisa giggled. He was doing that thing he did so well, making a difficult situation humorous, putting her at ease. "I'm not going to lie and say that I don't want everyone to know, but I get it's delicate."

"You're way too understanding." She huffed. Louisa knew she'd never be as accommodating as he was being.

"Not really. I'd love to be public. Be able to let my guard down around you when we're out. But I know that even if we were public, I'd still need to keep my distance. I'm sure it's not done for a countess to be publicly groped. At least I get you when you're off-duty, though." Louisa eyes dropped in regret. Miles shuffled to his side so that they were laid face to face. "And thank goodness your great-great-grandfather had the foresight to have secret passageways," he said with a bright smile and Louisa giggled, marvelling at how he was able to shake off her anxiety. He really did have a lot to put up with. She wondered how long he'd tolerate all these restrictions.

"I just want you to feel… I don't know, comfortable, at home here."

"Is that why you put that fabulously expensive painting in my room?" He gestured with his head to where the painting was hanging. "I googled it." Louisa's eyes widened and she cringed a little. "It's worth a cool 80 million."

"Well Papa paid less than that 30 years ago." Miles chuckled at her blasé comment. "I thought it would make you feel like you were at home."

"It's stunning. Thank you for doing that for me."

Louisa shrugged feeling a little embarrassed by her family's wealth. She then scrunched up her nose and said, "Gordon confessed to me."

"I realised. His timing sucks," Miles said with a roll of his eyes.

Louisa chuckled. "Yes. I've known him for 30 years and I didn't have a clue. I feel bad for him."

"Don't. He shouldn't have married Emily if he didn't love her and he should've made his move 20 years ago, like Gerard did. You snooze you lose."

"Snooze you lose?" she repeated with a chuckle.

"Yeah. He'd never have been good for you."

"No?"

"Uhuh. You need a go-getter, someone who'll fight for you, even if he fights dirty." He gave her a pointed look.

"Like Gerard?"

"Yeah." Miles had no doubt that Gerard was a dirty fighter but he was more than up for the challenge.

"Is that what you are, a go-getter?" she said teasingly.

"Well, you know I fight dirty" He nuzzled against her neck, causing her to squeal and wriggle, but his arms banded around her so she couldn't escape. He pulled back, allowing her to catch her breath and added, "And it depends whether I've got you or not."

"What do you think, have you got me?"

"I think I've got you for now." His arms tightened around her and Louisa focused on his glistening eyes.

"Just now?"

"I think that depends entirely on you, Louisa. Not sure I fit into all this quite as well as your ex and Gordon."

Louisa wriggled her arm free and placed her palm on his bristly cheek. "I don't want you to fit in. I want you to be just who you are, just Miles."

"Then that's what I'll be, just Miles."

"MUM?" Celeste opened the door to her mother's suite and peered in. The curtains hadn't been drawn yet, which was strange, seeing as it was 7:30 in the morning. She stepped further into the room and headed towards the bedroom, calling out again, but she was met with silence. *Had she already woken up and gone downstairs?* she thought, but then she remembered that all the curtains were still drawn.

Celeste crossed the threshold and took in the bed that looked as though it hadn't been slept in and the light was still on in the walk-in wardrobe. Tentatively, she stepped into the huge space that housed her mother's clothes and scanned it. Empty. Celeste's focus landed on the slightly open panel that led to the secret passageway and realisation dawned.

Her mother and Miles were sleeping together!

She blinked rapidly as she tried to process the information. She'd thought it was odd that her mother had put Miles in *that* particular room, but now it all made sense. God, she was so stupid! How had she not realised, and how long had *that* been going on? Her mind raced as it tried to calculate the timeline in her shocked brain. She knew they'd had the auction date on her birthday; that was almost two months ago. *Had it started then?* She'd been the one to suggest her mother went in her place.

Celeste slumped on the padded ottoman, trying to take it all in, then chuckled to herself. She'd set them up. They'd met because she didn't come back for the date. This was all because of her. *Way to go, Mum!*

27

THE MILES EFFECT

"WELL, I NEVER THOUGHT I'd see you doing the walk of shame."

Louisa's face dropped in horror, seeing Celeste sitting on her ottoman with her brow arched.

"Celeste, it's not..."

"Oh God, Mum, spare me the bull. I'm 19, not nine!" she said with a roll of her eyes

"I was going to tell you but to be honest, I didn't really know what there was to tell," Louisa said in a rush, horrified she'd been caught out by her daughter, no less. This was not how she wanted her daughter to find out. Apart from being extremely embarrassed, there was the major ten-year crush on Miles she'd had. Louisa's stomach plummeted. How did she ever think that this could ever work out?

"I see." Celeste furrowed her brow, unsure what her mother meant. Louisa stood awkwardly by the door, wondering how she could explain the situation, and worrying how Celeste was going to react.

Before she could say anything else, Celeste broke the silence.

"So, you and Miles, eh? I didn't see that one coming," she said, blowing out a breath.

Louisa closed the secret door and stepped up to where Celeste was, her stomach tightening at the thought of upsetting her daughter. "What are you doing here so early?"

"Excited about Nicolas coming today. I've really missed him."

Louisa nodded, then sat next to her. "So, about Miles. Like I said, I'm not exactly sure where it's going, or if it's going anywhere…"

"You really don't need to explain. I was only teasing you." Celeste grinned. "You have to admit it is a weird dynamic, *you* doing the walk of shame."

Louisa let out a sigh of relief and shook her head. She had to admit this wasn't something she'd ever expected. "Well technically, no one would have seen it."

"Yeah, sorry I screwed up your well-thought-out plans." She bumped her mother's shoulder. "Miles Keane and the Countess of Holmwood? That's a combination I never expected to see, seeing as you thought he was an arrogant arsehole."

"Well he's changed – or rather, he's mellowed."

"I can see."

Louisa scrunched her nose, still embarrassed that her daughter had caught her sneaking back from Miles's room. They'd always had a very open relationship and talked freely but nevertheless, this wasn't the kind of situation a mother wanted her daughter to see.

"So, *you're* sleeping with a pop star. How very rock and roll of you. And *I'm* dating a future investment banker and philanthropist. Somehow, I think that's a little bit ironic," Celeste said dryly.

"To be fair, Miles is also a philanthropist," Louisa deadpanned.

"Ah yes, that's what attracted you to him." Celeste let out a laugh and Louisa chuckled, pleased the awkwardness of the situation had evaporated. "You want my posters? I think I still have them somewhere in my closet."

"Very funny. Anyway, why would I need them when I have the real thing?"

"Mum, too much information!" Celeste gasped.

"Sorry. Seriously, though, this isn't weird for you?"

"Of course it's weird! But I'm okay with it. I'm kind of crazy about some other guy."

Louisa blew a breath up her face. "We're keeping it private. Alistair and Melissa know, and Amanda, but I haven't told Granny yet."

"You seriously think she hasn't worked it out yet? I can't believe I didn't." Celeste slapped her on her forehead.

"Well we are an unconventional match."

Celeste snorted. *Were they ever!* "But you like him, huh?"

"Yes, I like him, quite a bit actually. He's so different to me or anyone else I know."

"Well duh! He's at the other end of the spectrum to you and maybe that's why you like him… quite a bit."

"Maybe. Come on, I need to get ready. We've a full day ahead," Louisa said, standing up.

"It makes sense now."

"What does?"

"You've been so happy and relaxed. It's the Miles effect."

"The Miles effect?" Louisa liked the way that sounded. "So, you're okay with it?"

"Yeah, I'm okay with it." Celeste stood up and gave her mother a hug. She'd spent the last few years of her life in a lonely marriage. It was good to see her coming back to life again. Celeste pulled back and gave her mother a wide smile. "Quite a bit, eh?"

Louisa twisted her mouth and said, "Quite a lot, actually."

"Thought so."

IT WAS USUAL FOR smaller functions to be held in the library rather than the official dining room. The high, well-stocked bookshelves were an unusual backdrop and the lack of furniture meant that tables could easily be set up. But Louisa had decided that breakfast should be held in the conservatory as opposed to the library, which meant the guests could enjoy the open view of the grounds.

The guests would be given a grand tour of the grounds today before they split up to enjoy the various activities they'd signed up for. From horse riding, driving lessons, rock climbing and football to the gentler croquet, boules, billiards and enjoying of the pool. There was an activity to suit everyone's needs and capabilities. If any of the guests weren't interested in participating, there was also the media room.

Konran, Gerard and Nicolas were due to arrive in the afternoon. Miles was trying to be calm and unaffected but he would be lying if he said it wasn't eating him up that Louisa's ex could come and go as he pleased. Gerard was everything Miles wasn't: cultured, distinguished and accustomed to titles and all that they included. He'd stopped researching him, because reading about Louisa's past with him and his many business and philanthropic achievements only cemented his insecurities. Plus he had a daughter and close family ties with the Blackthorns. As if that wasn't enough to make Miles feel inadequate, by all accounts their divorce had been amicable. Louisa had never opened up about the reasons they'd split, other than to say they had grown apart but were still friends. He remembered one evening her candid remark about the aristocracy being well versed in being discreet and that she'd not wanted more children with Gerard. Those were the only hints that maybe all wasn't what it seemed. Regardless, Gerard was still welcome at Holmwood, the home of the Blackthorns, and no doubt was comfortable and familiar with its vast history, grandiosity and protocols. Miles was still trying to remember which fork to use for what course and still had no idea what an orangery was! The differences between him and Louisa's ex were excruciatingly pronounced: chalk and cheese, or night and day didn't even come close.

Miles stole a glance at Louisa from the football goal he was guarding, which was 50 metres away on the makeshift pitch. She laughed freely in delight as one of the children slowly began to trot around the pen. She looked carefree and totally at home, dressed in her cream jodhpurs, riding boots and black polo shirt, guiding the magnificent chestnut horse. Her hair was pulled into a ponytail, making her look ten years younger than she was. She was the most beautiful woman he'd ever seen and watching her unguarded and genuinely happy made Miles's heart expand to the point of bursting. He'd never felt like this before. He'd never revelled at the joy of another woman, and he wanted to witness it and do his utmost to ensure that happiness never faded.

Sensing Miles's eyes on her, Louisa turned towards him. Their eyes locked and she smiled widely at him, causing her nose to scrunch up in that adorable way and in that moment, it hit him like a football to his stomach: he was in love with her.

Louisa tilted her head in question, seeing his expression change as realisation hit him. He shook his head, clearing the glaringly obvious thought from his head and gave her a thumbs-up sign, indicating she was doing a great job teaching the nervous girl how to ride. She nodded back enthusiastically and mouthed "Everything okay?" He nodded and gave her a wink and he saw the relief flash across her stunning face. *Everything was perfect.*

MILES STOOD BY THE French windows of his room, holding his fine porcelain cup of coffee as he watched Alistair skilfully land the helicopter on the landing pad. He'd slipped upstairs to shower and change after a morning of football and then the afternoon playing cricket. A few of the guests had already come out onto the terrace to watch, unsure of who had arrived, while the Holmwood staff carried on setting up an informal bar-be-que for tonight's dinner. Miles smiled to himself as he watched Louis and Grace gape in awe. Louis was itching to go over and see the helicopter up close and he could see Amanda explaining that he couldn't just yet. He'd always marvelled at her parenting skills. How she'd managed all these years alone was something Miles admired in his beloved sister-in-law.

Before the blades had come to a complete halt, Miles saw Celeste running unceremoniously to the pad. A lanky young man with light brown hair stepped nervously out of the door and on seeing her, his face transformed into a huge smile. She hugged him tightly and gave him a quick kiss, disregarding etiquette and her audience of guests and staff. *This must be Nicolas,* thought Miles, taking comfort in the knowledge he wasn't the only American who felt awkward and out of his depth at Holmwood. Celeste's attention was then drawn to the next occupant who exited the helicopter. Miles took in a sharp breath as the tall dark distinguished figure of Gerard stepped confidently out onto the pad. Even in his casual dark slacks and polo shirt, he had an air of entitlement. His solemn expression scanned the grand building searching for someone, but before he could find them, Celeste caught his attention and his expression instantly changed upon seeing his daughter. They embraced tenderly and though Miles had only bad feelings towards the man he had yet to meet, there was no doubt about how deeply Gerard loved his daughter.

Once Gerard had greeted Celeste, he turned and, like a true gentleman, helped a young woman step down onto the ground, who was quickly followed by two more men, Konran's band members. All the guests had now all come out from the conservatory, where they'd been enjoying pre-dinner drinks, and were watching from the terrace, intrigued as to who else was going to emerge. As soon as Konran stepped out, there was a collected gasp from the older children and a sense of excitement rushed through the terrace. Celeste hugged and kissed her friend tightly, then he looked over to the terrace and gave a two-hand wave to the guests and smiled widely.

There was no holding them back. The children swarmed towards the megastar, closely followed by their parents, who were just as eager to meet their children's hero. Miles grinned from his distant position, revelling in their enthusiasm and Konran's ability to take his fame in his stride.

The only people left on the terrace were the staff and volunteers along with Lady Alice, Margot, Melissa and Louisa. Lady Alice and Margot took in the scene, clearly enjoying the excitement of the guests. Amanda had lost the battle of keeping Louis and Grace back, but contrary to the other guests, Louis and Grace had raced to greet Alistair, who had just shut down the helicopter. Miles watched on as Alistair lifted Louis into the helicopter and then helped up Grace and Amanda. Louis had been shadowing Alistair all morning. He'd taught him how to climb, as Amanda looked on nervously, even with all the harnesses, experts on hand and soft mats around him. Louis had been disappointed that he was unable to go with Alistair when it was time to go for the pick-up, but he'd promised Louis he could look around the cockpit when he returned. Alistair's superhero status was growing with every hour Louis spent with him, and though Miles felt that Louis was his, he was more than happy to see the attention Louis was giving the reluctant war hero.

Miles placed his cup down on a nearby table and was about to step out towards the door to go and join everyone, when he saw Gerard was now only a few metres from the terrace. He had made quick work of the remaining distance and jogged up the five steps to where Lady Alice, Margot, Melissa and Louisa were sitting. Gerard's face was transfixed on Louisa's but ever the gentleman, he firstly addressed and greeted his ex-mother-in-law, kissing her on both cheeks as she sat with a serene smile on her face. They spoke a few words, then Gerard greeted Margot and Melissa warmly. The greetings were genuine but it hadn't escaped Miles's attention that Lady Alice hadn't risen up from her seat to greet him; a subliminal message that there was a distance between them.

When Gerard turned, then stepped up to Louisa, Miles held his breath and waited to see Louisa's reaction. There was no doubt in Miles's mind that Gerard still loved Louisa. He'd flown over 10,000 miles to be here and was amongst her family, friends and staff. One look at the way his face transformed when he looked at her, and the possessive slip of his hand around her waist as he kissed her cheeks, sent a clear and powerful message: he was willing to do anything to get her back, even if he had to submit to her within her own environment. For a proud man this was a humble move, and Miles gave the arrogant French man kudos for his tactics. He'd picked the perfect situation to be on her turf. He had his daughter and Konran, who had split loyalties, and an audience of guests and volunteers to witness his good nature and support of his family. He looked like a hero, when all Miles could see was a cunning yet carefully disguised villain. He was here to fight dirty in a battle he didn't even know existed, well not *yet,* anyway. At least Miles had the element of surprise in his arsenal, plus he'd noted Louisa hadn't gone down to greet him like Celeste had done. She'd made him walk to her, made him seek her out. A subtle power play on her part, even if she did rise to greet him. Miles stepped back from the window. He'd had enough of being in the shadows. It was time to meet the infamous Mr Dupont. Game face on.

By the time Miles made it down to the terrace, Gerard had already been taken up to his room along with Konran, his band and Nicolas. He could sense the excitement of the guests at having the world famous TuKon in their midst. The informal dinner was a perfect setting for the guests and Konran to get acquainted. Before long, Miles was knee-deep in steaks, sausages and homemade burgers, helping out alongside the Blackthorn's chef and Alistair. Any children who wanted to help out were welcomed, to the delight of Louis and Grace, who immediately joined Miles and Alistair. The moment Konran stepped out on the terrace, everyone's attention was instantly diverted. It would take them a while to realise he wasn't going anywhere soon, but Konran took their incessant questions and requests for photos in his stride. He eventually made it over to where Miles was seasoning the steaks with the help of Grace.

"My man, good to see you again." Konran beamed at Miles as they shook hands and pulled each other into a man hug. "You ready to do this?" Over the last month they'd kept in touch, bouncing ideas off each other for their musical workshop, and had built up a friendship on mutual respect. They'd decided to compose a rap song with the children, backed with Miles's musical composition. They would all perform at the Saturday night karaoke party.

"Yeah, me and the top rapper, that's going to be something." Miles grinned at his new young friend.

Konran laughed freely at his comment and countered. "I'll say. Me and the superstar Miles Keane. I'm gonna be pinching myself."

"You going to help out with the grilling?"

"Grilling, now that's something I can do."

"Yeah, me too." Miles chuckled and handed Konran an apron and a bowl of sausages to put on skewers.

Celeste took photos of them cooking and they ended up roping Nicolas into the food prep too. The young man had begun to relax a little, now that there were plenty of people around him who were at least from the same side of the Atlantic as him. Miles felt for the guy, being thrown into such an event, surrounded by people he didn't know and thrust into a world that was so far from his suburban small life. Added to that, he was in the presence of a megastar and pop star, as well as aristocracy. If Miles thought he was overwhelmed, Nicolas was positively thunderstruck, though after a beer he had loosened up a bit.

Louisa hovered around the terrace, playing the perfect hostess, ensuring everyone was seen to with Celeste. The parents had become more at ease with each other and were beginning to let their guards down, socialising with Alistair's friends too. The children were either helping with the big cook out, on the boules or croquet green, or playing with Duke.

Miles was beginning to wonder whether Gerard was ever going to show up. He'd been ready to meet him head on, but he hadn't made an appearance since he'd arrived over an hour ago. Miles scanned the terrace again, just in case Gerard had come to join them when he spotted him walking back from the landscaped gardens with Lady Alice. Miles hadn't even realised she'd been missing. She seemed to be doing most of the talking, while Gerard kept a respectful distance and spoke whenever Lady Alice took a break. He couldn't work out if their conversation was casual or whether the tenacious Lady Alice was giving Gerard the third degree, but once they reached the steps leading up to the terrace, Gerard was again attentive and pulled out a chair for Lady Alice to sit next to Margot.

One of the staff immediately stepped through the various tables set up for al fresco dining and brought over her pre-dinner gin and tonic. Happy that the countess was comfortable, Gerard's attention was directed to Louisa. It didn't take him long to find her. She was overseeing the large buffet table that had been laden with salads and numerous side dishes to accompany the grilled meat and fish.

Miles tried not to make it obvious that he was keeping an eye on the couple and was grateful that there was enough activity around the large grills to distract him. He bent down and helped one of the children sprinkle some herbs on the chicken drumsticks, before passing the bowl to Konran to place on one of the grills.

"Miles." Louisa's voice beckoned and he turned around to see her standing a few feet away with Gerard at her side. His first thought was that they made a lovely couple, but he shook that thought from his mind and stepped towards them as he wiped his hands on a cloth he'd been given, ensuring his features gave nothing away. "I'd like to introduce you to Gerard. Gerard, this is Miles Keane, the ambassador of CASPO."

Gerard gave a curt nod and extended his hand to Miles. "Pleased to finally meet you, Mr Keane," he said as Miles clasped his hand and gave it a sharp shake. Miles was surprised to hear a slight accent in his voice.

"Likewise, Mr Dupont."

"Yes, our paths seemed to skim each other but never cross," Gerard said dryly and Miles narrowed his eyes, unsure of what he meant exactly, but he wasn't going to give him the satisfaction of knowing that.

"Well better late than never," he said lightly.

"Yes," Gerard answered with an insincere smile. "You look very comfortable there." He gestured to the grill.

"We Americans are all about outdoor cooking and keeping it casual," Miles drawled, purposely accentuating his accent, and his eyes shot to Louisa. He was sure she was thinking of the first time she'd been to his home. She blushed a little, confirming his thoughts. Gerard gave another slow nod. "And it's *just* Miles. Mr Keane sounds far too formal, don't you think, for this setting?"

"Of course. Please call me Gerard," he replied tightly.

The sound of laughter from the grills caught Miles's attention. "If you'll excuse me, duty calls. It was good to meet you, Gerard. No doubt our paths will be crossing over the next few days."

Gerard gave him a curt nod. "I look forward to it." He didn't even try to disguise the insincerity in his voice, but Miles smiled widely and went back to where Konran, Nicolas and Alistair were fooling around.

"He seems very comfortable here," Gerard said to Louisa.

"Oh that's just his way. It's his first time here at Holmwood but he's met everyone a few times."

"I see."

"He's certainly got the common touch."

Louisa caught his not-subtle dig at Miles's lack of lineage but refused to call him up on his snobbish comment, and replied politely, "Don't you mean friendly and approachable?"

"Of course."

"Yes, he's extremely friendly and has given so much support to CASPO. His influence has made an enormous difference to the charity." There was no way she'd allow Gerard to belittle Miles.

"Only the charity, *cherie*?" His brow rose in question as he watched Miles stride towards Lady Alice's table with a small plate of gourmet sausages. He caught him saying something about her needing to sample them and that Melissa probably was being driven mad with the smells. It was obvious his ex-mother-in-law and Melissa were part of Miles's fan club; he just wasn't sure how far that net spread.

Louisa chose to ignore his implication and excused herself, saying she needed to see to her guests, leaving him to watch over Miles, Konran, Nicolas and Alistair as they joked freely with each other. For the first time at Holmwood, Gerard felt like an outsider.

The longer summer nights meant that the guests were able to enjoy the casual outside dining and entertainment. The children and parents alike played boules and croquet along with Miles, Alistair, Konran and Nicolas. They were all still in awe that these megastars were in their presence, but as the evening wore on, everyone became more comfortable and less starstruck. Celeste was relieved to see Nicolas finally relax alongside her family and friends, though she didn't fail to notice that it was Miles who had made him feel more at home. It also didn't escape her attention that her father was monopolising her grandmother and trying his hardest to be around her mother. The tense set of Louisa's jaw spoke volumes and the furtive glances in Miles's direction confirmed that Louisa was feeling uncomfortable with Gerard's not-so-subtle attention.

Alistair announced that the next game of boules would be the last, seeing as they had a full day tomorrow and there was a collective moan from the children.

"Mum, fancy a last game? We can play doubles?" Celeste called over, hoping she could prise her mother away from Gerard. Louisa gave her a smile and nodded, then made her way down to where Alistair was setting up the game. Alistair teased her about her lack of skills as she lined herself up to throw her first ball. A small crowd had gathered around to see Lady Blackthorn play and when she bowled, everyone cheered as the ball stopped a couple of inches from the jack.

"Take that!" Louisa said with a smirk and Alistair laughed.

"It's early days, my lady." Then he turned to Nicolas, who was his partner. "Let's show them how it's done, shall we?"

The four of them played as the crowd around them grew. Miles had been asked to be umpire by Celeste because she said Alistair always bent the rules. The game continued with good-humoured teasing of each player who was taking their turn. Lady Alice made a point of keeping Gerard with her, asking him questions and relying on his impeccable manners not to leave her, even though it was obvious his attention kept drifting to the boules game.

The last ball was thrown by Nicolas and stopped close to the jack. Alistair insisted it was closer than their opposing team, even though it was hard to tell. Miles put up his hand to hush the crowd and players and took the special ruler to measure the distances handed to him by Konran. He chuckled at how competitive Alistair and Louisa were, as they did a good job of trash talking each other's playing skills.

"The results are in," Miles said with mock authority. "I am pleased to say that after careful measuring and conferring with Konran we are delighted that..." Konran did an air drum roll with sound effects and everyone laughed. "The winners are the Ladies of Holmwood."

Celeste squealed and jumped up, high-fiving her mother in a most unladylike fashion as the crowd cheered. Alistair let out a good-humoured grumble, then shook hands and hugged his niece and sister.

"You can't win every time, you know," Louisa said with a playful punch to his shoulder.

"Congratulations. I didn't realise how competitive you are." Miles shook Louisa's hand and she grinned.

"It's more a sibling thing. Alistair beats me at most things, but at boules we're pretty even." Louisa looked down at their joined hands and gave his a squeeze, which Miles reciprocated, then reluctantly let it go.

Everyone made their way back to the terrace and, after bidding each other goodnight, the guests went to their rooms.

Miles lifted a tired Louis and made his way into the house, with Amanda and Grace trailing behind him with Duke. The activities of the day had finally caught up on the children.

"He's adorable," Louisa said as she followed them in the house.

"Yes, especially when he's asleep," Amanda added with a chuckle. "I think he ran Alistair ragged today." Amanda's gaze flitted over to where Alistair was talking to the security guards.

"I wouldn't worry about that. He's big enough and ugly enough to handle it," Louisa said a little louder so Alistair could hear. He pulled a face at her and Amanda chuckled.

"*Cherie*, I'm sorry to interrupt, but I wondered if I could have a private word?" Gerard's deep authoritative voice travelled across the grand hallway. He was stood observing them from the top of the staircase. Miles stiffened at both the term of endearment and Gerard's audacity. He was obviously making a point of calling Louisa away from them, and Miles was thankful he was holding Louis and had Amanda by his side.

Louisa stopped in her tracks and gave Miles a worried look. "I'm sorry, I just need to –"

Miles cut her off before she could finish. She was being pulled in every direction, doing her duty, being Lady Blackthorn, a mother and a daughter; she didn't need to feel bad for him too. He never wanted her to have that look of worry or guilt on her face where he was concerned. "Don't worry. We've all had a packed day. I'll see you in the morning. You do what you need to do," he said softly. Louisa gave him a thankful smile, then bid everyone goodnight before she turned and walked up to where Gerard was patiently waiting.

28

THE PENNY DROPS

"GETTING YOURSELF A LITTLE snack there?"

"Fuck! You scared the shit out of me!" Celeste almost let go of the bowl of strawberries in shock. Miles had been carefully observing her for a few minutes, but she'd been so focused on her task, she hadn't noticed him sitting at the far table in the shadows.

Miles stifled his chuckle, amused at her outburst. "Not very ladylike."

Celeste rolled her eyes at him, then dropped her gaze over her scanty robe, checking she wasn't flashing him. "What are you doing here sitting in the dark?" she asked as she tightened her robe.

"I came down for a beer." Miles lifted up the bottle and she nodded. "Hugh told me where to get one. What's all that for? Looks like someone's having a midnight… party." Miles eyed the items she'd pulled out of the vast fridge: whipped cream, chocolate sauce, a bottle of Champagne and strawberries. He didn't need to guess what she had planned. Celeste's eyes widened and, if it wasn't so dark, Miles was sure her cheeks were reddening under his scrutiny.

"Erm... it's..."

"Don't sweat it; your secret's safe with me. At least someone's have a bit of fun tonight," he muttered and took a drink from his bottle.

Miles had helped Amanda settle the children, then had gone back to his room. He'd paced up and down for a bit and stared at the secret door, contemplating whether he should just go through to Louisa's private suite and brashly interrupt Gerard's little tête-à-tête, but that would only embarrass Louisa and put her in a difficult position. It would also make the rest of the weekend extremely awkward, and however much *he* could handle that, he couldn't do that to Louisa. He decided rather than brood in his room, he'd go in search of a beer, to take the edge off, plus it would mean he could legitimately pass by Louisa's door and hopefully hear what was being said.

On his way down, he'd seen the light under her doorframe and heard muffled voices, but he couldn't make out what they were saying. The sound of footsteps had him heading down the stairs, where he found Hugh coming up. It was thanks to Hugh that Miles knew where he could find himself a beer.

"Are you okay, Miles?" Celeste placed the items she'd taken from the fridge onto a tray as she spoke.

"Sure, couldn't be better." His reply tinged with sarcasm. Celeste furrowed her brow at his tone and stepped over to where he was sitting. He looked ticked off at something and Celeste knew in an instant that it was the appearance and behaviour of her father that had caused his bad mood.

"May I?" she said, indicating to the chair next him.

"It's your house, Celeste. I'm the guest, remember? Don't you need to be somewhere?" He jerked his head towards the laden tray.

"I can spare a couple of minutes. So, want to tell me why you're down here with a face like a slapped arse?"

Miles chuckled. "Man, I love your English turn of phrase." He used his foot to push the chair next to him away from the table as an invitation for her to sit down.

Celeste lowered herself into it and tilted her head at him. "Hmm… well, reading between the lines, I think my father turning up may have something to do with it." Miles's eyes darted to hers. She arched her brow at him and he shrugged, not ready to admit to anyone how out of sorts seeing Louisa with Gerard had made him. "They got divorced for a reason, Miles. If you're worried that he's here to get her back, don't be. He had his second chance; he won't get another. He's a good man, my dad. Just wasn't a brilliant husband." Miles nodded, still not comfortable voicing his opinion, but Celeste wasn't so easily deterred. "So, you and my mum, eh?"

"You don't pull any punches, do you?" he said, nearly choking on his drink.

"I am my mother's daughter." She smirked and rested her elbows on the table.

"Not your father's?"

"I have bits of him… my eyes, apparently, but I think I'm more Blackthorn than Dupont. So, my mum?"

"Not sure I'm comfortable talking about what's going on between your mom and me with you." He took another swig from his bottle and Celeste nodded.

"But you like her, don't you?"

"She's quite something."

"She's the best."

"I won't argue with that."

Celeste grinned at him, then pursed her lips and took a deep breath. "She's going to make it hard for you to get close to her. My mum's really good at keeping her distance, being in control. Don't let that put you off."

"You'd be okay with her seeing someone, then?"

"You mean you specifically or anyone?" she asked dryly, which caused Miles to let out a laugh before answering.

"Me."

"Yeah, I'd be cool with that. Not sure how my dad's going to react, though, but I think you could handle it."

Miles twisted his mouth at her frank comment. She really was her mother's daughter. "It doesn't bother you that they divorced?"

"Of course it *bothers* me, or rather bothered me, but I'll be doing my own thing soon enough and my mum needs to live her life. I think she sacrificed enough of herself." Miles gave her a nod, again not sure how much he should reveal to the tenacious Celeste. He fleetingly thought of her boyfriend and wondered if Nicolas was up to being in the future countess's shadow. "You realise you owe me?"

"Owe you?"

"Yeah, it was supposed to be me on that date."

"That's right, you stood me up."

"I was on the other side of the world. But yeah, I did. No offence, but I thought it was more important to see my philanthropic work through, rather than partake in small talk with a pop star," she said drolly and Miles let out a laugh.

"My ego should be wounded but believe it or not, it's not. You are definitely your mother's daughter, Lady Blackthorn."

Celeste gave him a huge smile and pushed herself up from her chair. "Thanks for the platinum disc, by the way, and don't worry, I won't sell it on eBay – just like I never sold the T-shirt you gave me," she said with a smirk.

Miles stood up. She may have been only 19 but she was the future Lady Blackthorn, even if she was dressed inappropriately in a red silky robe. "That's okay – I should thank *you*. If you hadn't stood me up, I'd never have met your mom."

"You'd already met her, Miles." Miles scowled at her, trying to work out what she meant and then it registered that she mentioned a T-shirt he'd given her. *What T-shirt?* "And anyway, I think you would have met her at some point without my help, because of CASPO."

"Wait a minute, what T-shirt? What do you mean?" Miles tried to bring into focus that niggling memory that kept fading. Something triggered in the deep recesses of his mind but it was always just out of reach.

"Wow, you really must've been wasted that night." Celeste shook her head and chuckled. "My mum and I came backstage to meet you on your last night at..."

"Madison Square Gardens. Fuck! Shit, I knew there was something about Louisa... and you. Yes, you were this sweet gracious girl. Fuck!" He slapped the heel of his hand against his forehead, as though he was trying to dislodge the memory.

"*Was?* I'd like to think I still am." Celeste joked and he laughed.

"Oh my god... I was..."

"An arse?"

Miles blanched at her comment and scrubbed his hand over his face. "Was I that bad?"

"Not really, not to me anyway. You tried really hard to act as though you weren't high as a kite, but looking back at that whole scene now, you were seriously off your face." She tried to stifle a grin. "I remember my mum talking to the security we had with us afterwards. She thought I hadn't heard but she was *so* pissed at you."

"Christ, I barely remember it. What did I do?"

"I think you flirted with her, like really obviously, and you were drunk and high too. I remember our head of security was livid that I'd been exposed to any of it. My mum asked him not to mention it to my dad though, because she knew he could make things really difficult for you."

"Fuck. No wonder she was so stand-offish on our first date. She never told me anything."

"Maybe she didn't want to embarrass you, bringing up the fact her ex-husband secured Madison Square Gardens for you or that your thank you was behaving badly."

Miles let what she said sink in. Gerard had secured their appearance? He needed to talk to Eric. "I think I need another beer."

"Well this was *fun,* but I need to be somewhere else."

"Good night, sweet Celeste."

"You remembered you called me that?" She beamed at him.

"Yeah, I do now. You really made an impression on me that night."

"Yeah, we Blackthorn women are hard to forget – well, as long as you're not wasted anyway." She let out a laugh as she picked up her tray. "Good night, Miles, and don't let my papa put you off. He had his second chance; don't blow yours."

Miles sat for a moment, mulling over what Celeste had revealed. He'd met Louisa before and he'd behaved appallingly, yet she'd seen past that. He thought back to that night, trying to clear the fog that alcohol and cocaine had misted over the memory. It had been a big deal for Keane Sense to play Madison Square Gardens on their first tour. He remembered how stoked they'd all been that Eric had managed to secure the last-minute venue that had sold out within hours of being announced. He also recalled Eric saying that they'd been lucky to get the venue and that favours had been pulled in. He'd been young and distracted at the time and didn't pay much attention, but now, looking back, that concert had been a huge coup. It catapulted Keane Sense's popularity and it was Gerard who had made it happen. His early comment about their paths skimming each other made sense now.

Miles pulled out his phone and scrolled to Eric's number. It was late here, but in New York, Eric would probably be still at his office.

"Miles, everything alright?" Miles could hear the apprehension in his agent's voice. He was probably trying to work out why he was calling him so late. He couldn't blame him; Miles had given more than his fair share of reasons to worry.

"Relax, everything's going fine."

"Good to hear. So, what's with the late-night call?"

"I met someone today that I think may have been the reason Keane Sense became so successful and so fast. Gerard Dupont – ring any bells?"

"I remember the name, though I never actually met him, I dealt with his people. He got your first night at Madison Square Gardens."

"Yeah well he's the Countess of Holmwood, Lady Blackthorn's ex-husband."

"Is he? Hang on, the patron of CASPO?"

"Yep, the very same."

"Well that… God, I knew his wife was some English aristocrat but I didn't put that together. It was over ten years ago, and to be honest, I had a lot more to worry about at the time. But now that you mention it, I remember the ridiculous amount of security they had. Didn't her brother die or something in the war?"

"He was badly injured but he's alive and kicking." Miles smirked to himself, thinking that Alistair would probably make a joke out of that comment. "Yeah, so Gerard is here at the activities weekend."

"Did he mention anything?"

"Not outright, but he hinted."

"I remember his staff were very difficult."

"I can believe it. He's not exactly a barrel of laughs either."

"Miles…"

"Don't worry. I won't say or do anything to rock the boat. Though I am kind of pissed it was him that helped us."

"That gig just got you guys there faster; you'd have got to where you ended up without his help, believe me."

"Thanks, Eric."

"Anytime."

Miles ended the call, after he promised Eric he'd meet up with him soon. He checked the time and frowned. It was late and he had a full day tomorrow. There was no point sitting here thinking about what Gerard had done in the past; it was done, over. Miles's concern should have been on what Mr Dupont was doing right now and what his plans were for the future.

The house was eerily quiet. Thankfully there were a few low lights on to guide him back to his room. Miles paused outside Louisa's heavy double door and strained to hear if there were any voices. He was met with silence. Maybe he should just use that secret passageway himself and check if Louisa was alright. Who was he kidding? He wanted to check and see that she was alone.

He paced quickly towards his door and opened it in a rush, his impulse to see Louisa clouding all his thoughts. A cluster of images flashed in his mind of Louisa with Gerard, but the second he entered his room, they disappeared. There, curled up in his bed, fast asleep, was Louisa. The hammering in his chest eased and in its place, warmth swelled. She'd come to him. Miles quickly undressed and slipped into the cool sheets. Louisa stirred, moving closer to him. He gently gathered her against his side and kissed the crown of her head. Celeste's words came to him. Gerard had had his second chance. Now it was his.

GERARD RUBBED HIS TIRED eyes, then looked out over the grounds of Holmwood. The morning dew glistered under the first sunrays. He'd hardly slept and after a couple of hours of tossing and turning, he'd decided to get up. He would have liked to blame the time change for his lack of sleep, but if he was being honest, it was last night's conversation with Louisa.

He wasn't used to losing. It happened very rarely, be it in business or life. If it ever did, it was because he had decided it, controlled the outcome. Even when Louisa had filed for divorce, he'd not made it hard for her, his sights set on reconciliation in the not-too-distant future. He believed in time she would miss him, and their privileged life in New York and once again return to him. His patience would, in the long run, pay off. He'd always been a strategist and it had served him very well. He didn't succumb to impulse, learning at an early age to rein it in and focus on the endgame. In this case, his endgame was Louisa. His arrival here was the first step to winning her back. Coming to Holmwood and being amongst her family and friends, supporting her work. He wanted her to see he was comfortable with her title and role. In their future, he saw them splitting their time between New York and Holmwood. It was a small price to pay if it meant they'd be together.

For the first time in his life, Gerard wasn't so sure if his carefully thought-out plans would work. Last night, he'd seen a different side to Louisa. Maybe it wasn't a different side, but rather a side she'd kept hidden. He'd tried to steer the conversation to some of her commitments in New York, using them as an excuse for her to spend more time in America. Before he could suggest how they could juggle her timetable, Louisa explained she'd already made the arrangements. There had been a time when Gerard would have been part of the planning process. No decision would have been made without his involvement. Louisa made it quite clear that she would decide how to address her commitments from now on, using the excuse that he was busy and wasn't privy to her schedule in the UK. Throughout their conversation, her manner was gentle yet professional, but more importantly, there was no room for any further discussion.

Rather than press her any further, Gerard commented on how well the weekend was going and then he reluctantly left, before she asked him to. There had been a distinct tip in the scales within their relationship. Maybe it was because she was on her home turf. Whatever the reason, it was obvious to Gerard that Louisa had found a new purpose and with that came a newfound confidence. She'd always been capable, and accomplished in so many ways. Everyone had seen it, her family and friends, as well as colleagues she'd worked alongside, but the difference now was that she knew it.

"GOOD MORNING."

Miles turned towards the familiar voice of Gerard, a little surprised to see that he was up so early, looking a little tired, but still impeccably dressed and groomed. "Morning."

"You're up early," the Frenchman said as he paced closer. His jaw twitched as his eyes darted to the slightly open door Miles had just stepped through. Miles quietly closed it and smirked to himself. He had no doubt that Gerard knew the specific feature his room had.

"I thought I'd get a run in before the madness starts. You? Are you jet-lagged?"

"Amongst other things."

"I find it's better powering through."

Gerard pursed his lips and nodded. The last thing he'd wanted to see this morning was Miles's pretty face, looking all fit and perky in his shorts and vest, when he was feeling anything but.

"Well, I'll see you later," Miles said, turning and jogging off down the corridor.

"Yes, you will," muttered Gerard, then let out a breath. He couldn't believe that the pop star he'd been worried about spending time with his daughter was in fact sleeping with his ex-wife. The ex-wife he'd flown 10,000 miles to get back. Gerard glanced back at the dark wooden door and gritted his teeth, then stormed towards the kitchen. He needed coffee – and lots of it.

Miles ran along the perimeter of the lake, taking in the impressive grounds of Holmwood. He usually ran listening to music, but today he had the beautiful landscape to take in. He still couldn't believe that all this land was Louisa's. The ground staff were already up, moving around in Land Rovers or golf buggies. Miles waved to them as he passed by them. What must it have been like growing up here? He'd had a good upbringing in a typical middle-class American family. He'd wanted for nothing, but what Louisa had been surrounded by was so far removed. He remembered Louis and he were the only kids at school who had had a cleaner that came in twice a week. He chuckled to himself as he jogged past the pavilion and down the other side of the lake. Louisa must have a staff of at least 25, if not more, and that wasn't including security and drivers. And there was also the London house – God only knew how many staff she had there. Miles scanned the grand house as he approached it. How could he ever get used to this: the size, the staff, the lack of privacy, the responsibility?

Miles slowed his pace to a gentler jog, reducing his heart rate as he approached the terrace. The lone figure of Gerard standing by the conservatory window caught his eye. It was too far away to see if he was looking at him, but Miles knew the Frenchman was keeping a close eye on him. Well he'd be doing the same. Like Celeste said, Gerard had had his chance and blown it. He wasn't going to do the same.

THE MORNING AT THE musical workshop flew by. It was refreshing and fun to work alongside Konran. Miles had only ever composed alone or with Louis and they'd had a unique dynamic. Louis had been the calm and Miles had provided the storm, a bond that only siblings could ever understand and accept. But Miles surprisingly found his role reversed with Konran. The young rapper was animated and charged, energy exuding from every pore, and Miles was soon chuckling to himself. If Louis could see him now, he'd get a real kick out of it. *Was this what it was like working with the Miles of ten years ago?* By the time lunch was ready, they'd mashed the rap lyrics with Miles's composed song. The children involved were bouncing with excitement as they entered the conservatory.

Alistair had thrown himself wholeheartedly into his role as mentor for some of the older children, teaching them to drive and completing assault courses he'd created with his army buddies. Some of the fathers had joined in too. Louisa also noted that her brother had carved out time to spend with Louis and Grace. She was surprised when she'd spotted him at the paddock, teaching them how to ride, as an anxious Amanda sat and watched on. The only other person he'd ever taught to ride was Celeste. Miles's niece and nephew were adorable, but Louisa had a distinct feeling that their mother had a lot to do with the added attention they were receiving.

Miles, Konran and his band sat together to eat, as the rest of the guests caught up with their children after the varying activities. There was an all-round sense of enthusiasm in the conservatory, and Louisa gave a relieved sigh that the first couple of days had gone so well. Parents were at ease and for the first time, enjoying being looked after while their children took part in unique experiences as well as learning new skills; all part and parcel of lifting their morale. She'd been so anxious about the weekend's success, she hadn't really had time to appreciate what an impact these few days were having on the guests. But one look around the sunny conservatory was enough to ease any doubts. The guests would not only leave with happy memories, they'd leave feeling worthy, stand a little taller and feel a little stronger – and that was something money couldn't buy.

"Ever think of performing again? I'd be happy to guest appear," Konran asked Miles as he pushed his plate away. They'd been joined by Melissa and Robert, who was shadowing his wife, worried that she was overdoing it at over seven months pregnant.

Miles chuckled. "I think it might be the other way round now, Konran. You're smashing it."

Konran gave an embarrassed shrug, a telling reaction of how humble he truly was. "So if I asked you to come and perform alongside me, you would?"

Miles rocked his head from side to side. The idea of performing was the furthest thing from his mind, but he didn't want to get into the whys while they were all in such a good mood. "I don't know. It's been a while."

"Sure, but I could ask you and one day you might want to, right?" Konran gave him a toothy hopeful smile.

"One day."

"If it was the right kind of gig, I mean?" Konran persisted.

"Maybe." Miles's eyes flitted to Melissa who was watching. She gave him a smirk, knowing that Konran's enthusiasm and tenacity was possibly pressing a still-too-raw nerve. Miles rolled his eyes and took a sip of his after-lunch coffee and wished it was something stronger.

Konran gave a nod, then picked up his water and gulped it down while he mulled over a thought. "Margi, when do we finish this leg of the tour?" Konran called down the table.

"Last weekend of August at Leedsfest, then Caribbean holiday, here we come!" The other band members whooped at her comment, but Konran twisted his mouth, then caught Alistair's eye further down the table.

"How quickly can you get a concert organised on the grounds here?"

"Erm… that depends. How quickly do you mean?" Alistair asked.

"First week in September."

"In ten weeks' time?" he said with a lift of his brow.

"Yep."

"Where are you going with this?"

Konran's eyes darted around the table. "I was thinking of a charity concert – us, maybe a few more bands and artists." His focus shifted to look at Miles. "All proceeds going to CASPO."

Alistair narrowed his eyes and leaned forward, seeing Melissa's sudden interest. "Well, I can set it up with help from Melissa; she has all the celeb contacts."

"This is just what CASPO needs." Melissa beamed.

"Calm down; you'll be either ready to pop by then or have a baby," Robert grumbled.

"I can still use a phone!" Melissa countered, causing Robert to let out a huff. He knew he was fighting a losing battle.

"I can ring round some of my friends."

"Friends?" Melissa asked Konran.

"Okay, bands – see who can spare the time."

"This is a fabulous idea. With Konran's input and Miles, we get all the demographics!" Melissa rubbed her hands together in glee, clearly excited at the prospect. Miles swallowed hard as the table discussion around him escalated. Konran and his band, Alistair and Melissa bounced ideas off each other while they culminated a plan, and Miles looked down at his empty coffee cup. He couldn't perform in front of thousands of people. He just couldn't do that – not yet, not without Louis. Suddenly, the walls of the conservatory felt as though they were closing in on him, and the sweat prickled at the back of his neck. Miles stood up abruptly, excusing himself, and headed out to the terrace. He needed fresh air.

Louisa searched the bright room but couldn't find Miles anywhere. She'd hardly seen him today. He'd left early in the morning for a run while she was sleeping, and then she'd left to get ready before he returned. They'd exchanged a few moments at breakfast and over the course of the morning, but they'd always had an audience. Louisa was hoping to see him over lunch, having spotted him with Konran earlier, but he seemed to have left the room, now that she was free. She walked towards the French doors that opened up on to the terrace and found him looking out over the grounds, deep in thought.

"There you are. I've been looking for you." Louisa's soft voice caused Miles to turn.

"I just needed some fresh air. A bit of quiet." He had to curb the urge to pull her towards him.

"Everything alright?" She searched his face and Miles instantly felt bad that she was worried about him. There were far more important things to concern herself with.

"Yeah, just... never mind." He brushed her concern off with a mild shake of his head.

Louisa gave a nod, but Miles could tell she wasn't convinced. "We've hardly spent any time together."

"That's not what this is about," Miles said, taking her hand in an attempt to reassure her.

"Oh."

"Shit, Louisa. Seriously this..." He stopped himself and dropped her hand as a few guests came out on to the terrace. They were just out of sight, but Miles didn't want to risk anyone seeing them. He gestured to an area further away and they stepped around the wall. "Look, honestly, this is nothing to do with you. It's also not the time to talk about it. I'm fine. Just some old demons, that's all." He cupped the side of her face, wanting her to understand this wasn't anything to do with her or the situation they were in.

"I promise you we'll get some time alone." Louisa leaned into his touch and sighed, slightly appeased.

"We could do with a vacation," he told her.

"That's sounds wonderful."

"Maybe I'd like to take you to *my* home, in Malibu," Miles said with an arch of his brow.

"You would?"

"It ain't as fancy as this but it's got the most fabulous view of the ocean," he drawled, and Louisa grinned. "And you know what the best part is?" He leaned in closer and rested his forehead on hers.

"What?"

"No one around to interrupt us."

"Sounds absolutely perfect." Louisa giggled and Miles gave her a soft kiss.

"Is that a yes, my lady?"

"It's a yes."

"Good." Miles pulled her towards his chest and held her for a moment. "Let's go show these kids a good time, shall we?"

"Thank you." She looked up into his eyes and he furrowed his brow.

"For what?"

"For just being... you."

Lady Alice looked down from her sitting room window and a smile curved over her lips. "Looks like Louisa has finally found her knight in shining armour after all."

Margot came and joined her at the window and peered down at the intimate scene. "So it seems. He's good for her."

"An unlikely couple, but you're right. She's been relaxed and happy these past few weeks." They watched as Miles moved Louisa to somewhere out of sight of the guests.

"An American with a dubious past?" Margot said dryly.

"Better than a Frenchman with a suspect past, present and no doubt future," Lady Alice huffed.

"I thought you liked Gerard."

"I do. I just don't like him for Louisa. He wasn't good for her. He had too much armour, too controlled and controlling, but she fell in love with him and you and I both know that you can't fight love."

Margot nodded sagely. "He's not going to like that."

"He won't have much choice," Lady Alice countered. "Gerard will have to bow out like the gentleman he is because the American isn't going to back down without a fight. He doesn't abide by the rules."

"No, he doesn't. And isn't that what makes him so attractive? The rebel in him? The devil-may-care attitude?"

"Yes, and his vulnerability. He's been broken and built himself back up again. He's a fighter. He'll fight for his lady, dirty if needs be. He won't be dissuaded, just like my James."

"Yes, James fought for you too." Margot patted her friend's arm, then looked down again as Miles pulled Louisa to his chest.

"Our Mr Keane here doesn't have any armour." Lady Alice gave Margot a knowing look. "He doesn't need it. Remember, he's bulletproof."

29

IT'S A RAP

"HOW LONG WERE YOU going to wait to tell me we'd met before?" Louisa's eyes widened as Miles caught her gaze in the mirror. He was glad that for once he'd caught her off-guard. "Celeste told me."

"Ah." Louisa dabbed her lipstick and turned around to face him. His tanned skin contrasted against his white shirt and light blue suit, ready for the evening party. He looked positively edible.

"Yes, ah. Jesus, I can't believe you never said anything." He narrowed his eyes at her and shook his head.

"Well, you didn't remember me… and I rather liked the fact you didn't have a clue who I was." She scrunched up her nose and gave an awkward one-shoulder shrug. "It was unusual. Everywhere I went, people knew me, or should I say knew who I was married to. And for all of my life here and in the US, my title or status preceded me, so when it was obvious you hadn't a clue who I was now or that back then, I wanted to just be me." Miles's face softened and he stepped up to her and dropped a chaste kiss to her lips. When they were alone, he kissed and touched her at every opportunity and Louisa eagerly reciprocated. She slipped her arms around his neck and he placed his hands on her waist, smoothing over the blue silk of her dress.

"I don't remember much of that night, after the performance that is, but I do recall you were sexy in an uptight kind of way and Celeste was sweet and ladylike. Eric bust a gut at my behaviour... rightly so, it seems. I was such an ass. And Gerard got us the gig there?" He pursed his lips, trying hard not to show how much that nugget of information bothered him.

"Celeste was going on about how she wanted to see you guys when you released your US tour dates. The Radio City Hall concert had sold out in seconds, at the beginning of your tour, and there was no way Gerard would have allowed her to go there anyway. He got his legal team to contact your people and secured Madison Square Gardens for your last added date."

"Wow." Miles knew Gerard was wealthy but he was a little stunned at what kind of connections he had.

"Yes. Gerard would and will do anything for Celeste. He may have his faults but he's a very good father."

"Yeah, I can see that. I'm surprised he allows Nicolas anywhere near her." He huffed.

Louisa tilted her head to the side and gave him that knowing smile. "Well, Gerard has done thorough checks on him, plus Celeste is no pushover. She makes up her own mind regardless of what her father thinks, or anyone for that matter."

"She's a tough cookie."

"She needs to be. She'll be the countess one day." Miles let out a soft laugh. Louisa was right about that. Just seeing Louisa in action over the weekend and the events they'd attended, tough was definitely a quality a countess needed. He still marvelled at Louisa's ability to be composed and unruffled. She had a reassuring presence for her staff at CASPO and at Holmwood House, even when she was under public scrutiny. She was new to her role, yet everyone gravitated to her for direction and he could see the same qualities in Celeste.

Louisa smoothed her fingers over the lapels of his jacket and tilted her head up to look at him. Even in her heels, he was still a few inches taller than her. "Want to tell me about this afternoon?"

Miles blew out a breath. He wasn't sure he wanted to get into his hang-ups just before they were due down for the evening party. "Is it anything to do with the concert Konran's been talking about?"

"You heard about that?"

"Melissa was practically bouncing about it. She cornered me this afternoon." Louisa rolled her eyes and Miles chuckled. He'd grown to love Melissa and her animated personality. He could just imagine her talking ten to the dozen and throwing facts and figures in Louisa's direction about what the potential could be.

"Look, when I took on this role as CASPO's ambassador, I didn't think it would… I didn't think it meant I'd have to perform." He stepped back and ran his fingers through his hair. "I mean appearing, doing press junkets, attending events… I can handle those." He started to pace around Louisa's dressing room, trying formulate his reasons. "But today, when Konran started on about the concert…"

"It's okay, you don't need to do it. You can be there just as the ambassador. We'd never pressure you to do that." Miles swallowed hard and nodded, grateful he didn't need to spell it out to her. "I'll talk to Konran."

"You don't need to make excuses for me, Louisa." He sighed. "I'll talk to him, explain. He's a good kid. It's coming from a good place. He wants to do as much as he can to help."

Louisa nodded, pleased Miles seemed to be pacified. "He's donating his earnings from any future songs to CASPO and the charity that helped him in the US."

"Wow, that's a huge donation."

"It is. He's going to help us help so many families." Louisa couldn't hide the pride in her voice.

"That's some 'paying it forward'."

"What you're doing, what you've done for CASPO… it's upped our profile. Melissa has shown you the figures. That's all you. And you being part of the concert will be more than enough." Miles gave her a small smile, though he still felt as if he was letting her down. "So, next week you start filming?" Louisa hoped talking about the six-part documentary Miles was presenting would change his thoughtful mood.

He immediately perked up. It was a project he was not only presenting, but also executive producing and Louisa knew he was excited about this new role. "I'm flying out at the end of next week. We've a few days of pre-production, then it's literally back-to-back filming."

"Sounds hectic but exciting."

"Hmm, you could come out and spend a few days with me. A vacation at Casa Keane."

"Won't you be busy?"

"We're scheduled to finish in ten days; you can come out after that. Plus, I think Melissa has already started the ball rolling for the concert, so she'll probably get me to schmooze some of my contacts." Miles ambled towards her with his eyes twinkling. "We can have a few days at my home…" He reached for her left hand and lifted it to his lips and kissed it, keeping his bright eyes on hers. "By the ocean…" he turned her hand over and kissed the inside of her wrist. "No interruptions. Just you and me… Walking around barefoot… And naked… All alone…" He punctuated his seductive words with soft, open-mouthed kisses up the length of her arm until he reached her exposed neck. "How does that sound?" he whispered against the shell of her ear, making goosebumps appear all over her body, in spite of the warmth of the room.

"That sounds perfect."

"WOW, THEY REALLY GO all out, don't they?"

"Yeah, looks like it." Miles smirked at Amanda. He was glad it wasn't only him who felt in awe of the grandeur. The Blackthorns had indeed gone all out, hosting the party in the formal ballroom of Holmwood House. The room looked fit for a royal visit. The chandeliers sparkled, the crystal glasses gleamed on brilliant white linen and the centrepieces were fragrant and elegant. Waiters walked around the reception area with silver trays of Champagne for the adults and fruity cocktails for the children. The volunteers and the Blackthorns mingled with the guests before they all sat down for dinner. They'd all been treated to special clothes for the party and each child had a small suitcase of clothes to take back home.

"It's like *Beauty and the Beast*," Grace gasped, taking in the room. "Where Belle dances with Beast."

"Yeah, it is." Miles chuckled. "Let's get settled at our table shall we?" He searched for their names on the seating plan and saw that Alistair and Louisa were both on their table. The remaining four seats were allocated to a single mother and her nine-year-old son and a single father with his seven-year-old daughter. Louisa had mixed the guests among the VIPs and volunteers. Miles noted that Gerard was sitting with Lady Alice and he wondered who had been responsible for the plan.

"Everything alright?" Melissa chirped behind him.

"Yes, of course. Where you in charge of the plan?"

"What do you think?" She gave him a cheeky smile and waddled over to where Robert was waiting impatiently for her.

"Hey there, champ." Alistair's voice dragged Miles and Amanda's attention away from the ballroom. He'd crouched down to greet Louis, who'd proceeded to fling himself at him. Alistair scooped him up and straightened, then beamed at Amanda and Miles. "Where are we sitting?" Miles eyes widened, seeing the Earl dressed for the first time in formal clothes. He'd donned a sharp, bespoke, dark blue suit, white shirt and silver tie.

"We're sitting on table three." Miles smirked, answering for an obviously surprised Amanda. "You scrub up well."

"Well, we can't let the side down. Plus Louisa would kill me if I turned up in shorts," he said rolling his eyes and as he took hold of Grace's hand. The antique gold signet ring on his right hand glinted as it caught the light from the large chandeliers.

"You look very –"

"Handsome." Grace interrupted her mother.

"Well in that case, it was worth the effort, if you think so." Alistair smiled softly at Grace and Amanda.

Miles stifled a grin, then cleared his throat. "Would you mind escorting them to the table? I just need to check on something."

"Of course, it'd be an honour." Alistair focused on a slightly bewildered Amanda. "I think it's this way." He indicated for her to step forward and to Miles's delight, he gently guided her to their table.

The ballroom soon filled up and after a quick welcome speech from Louisa, dinner was served. Louisa scanned the ballroom and felt a sense of pride at how well the weekend had gone. There was a distinct change in atmosphere from the very first evening the guests had arrived. The parents were now relaxed and letting themselves be spoiled. Their stress-free expressions and easy manner revelled in their children's joy of having experiences they'd never be able to provide. They were among people who were in similar circumstances, who could relate to their plight and even though the venue was grand, every member of the team and staff treated them as though they belonged there. The weekend was designed to give them all a treat, a break from the strains they encountered every day, but most of all, Louisa wanted them to leave happy and relaxed, with a bit more confidence.

As soon as dessert was served, Konran and his band played a few songs to warm them all up for the performance of their newly composed rap song. Louisa moved around the room, ensuring she spent time with everyone.

"You've done good." Louisa gave her mother a relieved smile. She hadn't been joking about filling big shoes in her speech all those weeks ago. Her parents had been a formidable team when they started the charity. It meant a lot to have her mother's approval.

"It was a team effort. Alistair has taken the brunt of it."

"Don't let him kid you; he's loved every second. Plus, I think there is a certain perk to working so closely with Miles Keane." Lady Alice indicated to where Alistair was deep in conversation with Amanda at their table. The rest of the guests had long abandoned the table for the dance floor, leaving them alone.

"I know; I didn't see that coming," Louisa whispered as they both observed them at the other end of the room.

"Well, I think it's early days but there certainly a real twinkle in his eye and he put on his big boy trousers. He must mean business," Lady Alice said with a chuckle, clearly thrilled her recluse son was finally coming out to play again.

"She's a lovely person, Mama," Louisa said sincerely.

"Yes, she is. So is her brother-in-law," Lady Alice said with a wry smile.

Louisa regarded her mother as she gave her a knowing smile. "He's very good for the charity."

Lady Alice patted the seat next to her and Louisa lowered herself into it, unsure of what her mother was going to say. "And for you... don't deny it." Lady Alice cut her off before she could even try and explain. "I'm not blind and neither is Gerard. He's going to find that a very bitter pill to swallow." Lady Alice nodded towards where Gerard was talking to Robert, yet his eyes kept darting to where Miles was laughing with Melissa. "He'll have to get over it. He had his chance, Louisa, and he misread and underestimated you. He has to live with his mistakes. You though, thankfully, do not." Lady Alice patted her leg.

"Thanks Mama."

"I didn't see *that* coming either, and one day, you'll tell me how it all happened."

"It was... kind of an accident."

"Hmm, a good accident though?" Louisa nodded. "Remind me to thank Melissa for her meddling."

A bubble of excitement spread over the ballroom as the children took their place by Konran and his band. Miles made his way to the piano and slipped into the seat, ready to play the refrain. Everyone took their seats and the staff of Holmwood adjusted the lighting to spotlight the performers.

"So, the guys here put together an awesome song for you to enjoy. Miles and I just guided them, the sentiment is all theirs, and I think I speak for all of us when I say we were blown away by their enthusiasm. It was a real joy. So... as they say... for one night only, here is their song, *Stand Tall*. Take it away, Miles!"

The applause echoed around the ballroom as the first child took the microphone from Konran and waited for Miles to start the intro. Miles nervously looked up from the keys and spotted Louisa standing to the side, directly in his line of vision. She gave him an encouraging smile and he took a deep breath and let his fingers move over the keys. Each of the children had a few lines, which they rapped in time to the mashed-up melody, sung by the band. They spoke of hopes and dreams, gratitude, love and new friends they'd made. Even with the few mistakes, their performance was met with a standing ovation and cheers. Konran and Miles high-fived them all and urged them to take a bow. It was a perfect finale to a memorable weekend.

"And now it's time to par-tay!" Konran announced. He turned to Miles and gave him a nod as he started to rap the intro to *Thrift Shop*. Miles picked up his trumpet and started to play the refrain, to everyone's delight. Celeste whooped as Konran started singing along, and the dance floor filled up.

Louisa stood in the shadows and watched Miles in his

element as he played the upbeat tune, while everyone around him stopped for a moment. He was mesmerising. His talent was astounding, his persona filling the huge room as he moved around the area, swapping from trumpet to piano with ease. Konran beamed his toothy smile at Miles and shook his head in disbelief. He was performing with one of his musical heroes. It might have been just for a few, but it felt as good as playing the huge stadiums on his world tour. The spotlight was directed on Miles but he didn't need it to shine. He dazzled. Miles wasn't just talented, he was gifted and Konran wanted more than anything for Miles to share his unique gift with the world again.

Miles caught Louisa's eye and she gave him a wide smile, and for a few seconds, it was just them in the room. Everything around them faded and Louisa had to catch her breath at the intense feeling that burst through her. This damaged man had put his fears to one side, just for tonight, for her cause, for the children it helped and to make the evening unforgettable. He was brave and he was fearless, and Louisa knew he was those things just for her.

The song came to an end and everyone in the room applauded wildly. "Mr Miles Keane is in the house, people!" Konran shouted and everyone cheered.

"Play something else!" called out Celeste.

"Play the Hawaii song!" shouted out Louis and Grace. Miles scrunched up his nose and cringed. "Pleeease!" they whined.

Konran looked over at his drummer, Ty, and quirked his eyebrow, a silent request asking if he knew how to play the intro. He gave a nod and turned to wait for Miles's instruction. Miles hesitated for a split second, until he refocused on Louisa. That was all the encouragement he needed. Konran counted them in, then Ty span his sticks dramatically and hit the drums, playing the iconic opening drum roll.

Louis and Grace squealed and started jumping about, dancing

animatedly, pretending to row a canoe as Miles belted out the tune on his trumpet. Amanda laughed loudly and joined them, along with the rest of the children, all inhibitions forgotten. Alistair, Celeste, Nicolas and practically everyone else soon followed. It was obvious that the particular song meant something to the Keane family. Lady Alice chuckled at the sight of the ballroom dance floor full of everyone, pretending to rapidly row in time to the music Miles played. Melissa laughed and was itching to join in but was pulled back by Robert, so she pretended to row in her seat. When the piece finished, everyone cheered and Louis and Grace ran to hug their uncle. Louisa stepped up to where they were, unable to hold back her emotions any longer, and gave Miles a swift hug and a peck on the cheek.

"That was incredible," she said in a rush.

"Thanks. It's one of their favourites." Miles blinked at her, his hand still resting on her waist. He gave it a squeeze, then released her, knowing that her show of affection was a huge step for her.

Konran clapped him on the back and pulled him into a man hug. "You just made my year, man." He pulled back and pretend rowed, then shook his head and chuckled. "That was surreal."

"Thanks," Miles muttered and carefully placed his trumpet in the box. "I think they want to hear some of your songs now, though. I'm getting too old for this." It was his discreet way of bowing out and letting Konran take centre stage.

At the back of the ballroom, Gerard sipped his drink, keeping his distance. His jaw ticked nervously as he watched on, noting every look, every touch and every move between Louisa and Miles. He'd seen that look in her eyes before; it was the way she used to look at him. He'd come here to win her back but it was obviously a lost cause. Gerard had to hand it to Miles, he'd come from nowhere and bowled her over. His easy manner and disarming charm had broken down Louisa's usual conservative nature and even he had to admit it looked good on her. She seemed to come alive when she was near him; he fanned her inner flame, drew it out and let it burn brightly. It was both wounding and astonishing to witness. If he were a better man, he would have bowed out like the gentleman everyone thought he was. Unfortunately, he wasn't.

MILES TOOK IN HER perfect profile as she slept soundly next to him. The subdued sunlight filtered through the slightly open curtains, casting a golden haze that kissed Louisa's delicate features. She looked angelic, nestled in the crisp, pure white linen of his bed. How could someone so restrained and ladylike be wild and passionate and downright dirty? Miles didn't care, as long as it was him who saw the other side of Lady Blackthorn.

They'd finally come to bed at 11, after all the guests had retired. Most of the children had fallen asleep earlier but a few of the older ones enjoyed listening to Konran and his band play some softer tunes, which allowed the adults to relax a little. With a little coaxing from Amanda and Celeste, Miles moved to the make shift stage and sat at the piano. There were no more than 30 people left in the ballroom – just a few parents, but mainly the friends of the Blackthorns. Amanda and Grace pulled their chairs a little closer along with Alistair, who was cradling a fast asleep Louis. Everyone followed suit, creating a more intimate atmosphere.

Miles gave Amanda a soft smile, then started to sing the classic Chet Baker song *I Fall in Love Too Easily*. His fingers moved over the keys as he soulfully sang, the bluesy after-hours-listening track. He switched to his trumpet, then effortlessly back to the piano with an ease that had always been his signature move, a move that had always wowed the crowds. His performance was hypnotically tender; every note had everyone under his spell. Miles had always been a showman, the spirited front man of Keane Sense who had their fans eating out of his hands, but when he performed like this, he was at his greatest.

Louisa stirred, feeling the weight of Miles's gaze.

"Morning," she croaked and his face lit up as she stretched. He dropped a gentle kiss on her lips. "What time is it?"

"Early. Too early. Go back to sleep."

"You're up."

"Yeah, I'm just deciding whether I should go for a run. Duke is going to need the bathroom. Though I have to say you gave me quite a workout last night."

"Well you shouldn't have been all sexy, singing and playing the piano."

Miles rolled over and pinned her down. "Is that so?"

"Oh, don't act all coy. You know what effect you have on women." Louisa playfully narrowed her eyes at him.

"I don't care about other women. I just care about what effect I have on you."

"Well, I think I showed you last night."

"In that case… *'I fall in love too easily. I fall in love too fast.'*" Miles sang softly, and Louisa drew in her lips and squirmed beneath him. Miles grinned at her. "Care to show me again this morning?"

"I thought you told me to go back to sleep."

"Change of plan, my lady. You can sleep after."

"After what?" she breathed.

"After this." Miles slowly sank into her and they both groaned.

"I hope Duke didn't destroy one of your priceless rugs."

"I'd be worth it," Louisa giggled while she watched Miles lace up his trainers. He leaned over and kissed her tenderly.

"Stay in bed until I can get back."

"Tempting as that is, I need to be up and ready. Duty calls," Louisa sighed.

"You're staying at mine tonight though, right?"

"That's the plan. Everyone is leaving after lunch, so we can head back to London."

"It'll be nice to have you all to myself."

"I thought you just did," she said with shy smile.

"Stop looking all sexy. I really need to go – or rather, Duke really needs to go." Miles growled into Louisa's neck as she squirmed. Then he shot up from the bed and patted his thigh. "Come on, boy." Duke bounded towards him as Miles paced over to the door and slipped on his leash before opening it. He took a last look at Louisa and gave her a cheeky wink. "Tonight can't come fast enough." Louisa giggled and he carefully closed the door behind him.

"Morning." Miles's huge grin faltered as he was greeted by Gerard walking down the corridor. He was like a bad penny turning up every morning in his face.

"Morning."

"You're a little later this morning," Gerard said through a strained smile.

"Yeah, we slept in."

"We?"

Miles smirked at his not-so-subtle question and after a beat, answered, "Duke and I."

"Ah yes, of course." Gerard's gaze darted to the closed door, then down to Duke. "Will you be joining us later on?" he asked curtly and Miles furrowed his brow, unsure of what the arrogant Frenchman meant. "Shooting. Clay pigeon with some of the fathers and the Earl's friends," Gerard added, seeing Miles's confused expression.

"Err, no. I'll pass. Shooting isn't really my thing." Miles narrowed his eyes at him, wondering if he was really that insensitive or he was being obtuse. The very idea of a gun or shooting made Miles want to throw up.

"Of course. Well, enjoy your run." Gerard gave a sharp nod and Miles stepped around him, gently guiding Duke.

"Thanks, enjoy your..." Miles waved his hand vaguely in the air and added, "Well, whatever." Then jogged down the stairs, glad to get away from him. At least he wouldn't be seeing Gerard anytime soon after today.

Gerard watched Miles run out on the grounds and towards the lake, then turned around and headed towards the door to Louisa's suite. He put his ear to the door but couldn't hear anything and he knew that by seven, Louisa was always up. It was almost eight and he hadn't seen her down in the main house, and the staff had said she hadn't come down yet. He knocked on the door and waited, but again, there was no sound. His eyes searched the corridor and landed on the door of Miles's room. The pop star's smug expression came into his mind, making his blood boil. Before he could talk himself out of it, Gerard pulled down on the handle and opened the door.

A quick sweep of the sitting area showed no signs of life. He stepped towards the bedroom, only to find the bed perfectly made up. A rustle from the dressing room caught his attention and he turned just as he spotted Louisa coming through the secret door panel.

She let out a soft squeal. "Jesus, Gerard, you gave me a fright." For a second, she forgot her dishevelled appearance, until she caught sight of Gerard meticulously taking in her knotted hair, red flush marks on her neck and yesterday's evening dress in her hands. She dropped her dress on a nearby chair and tightened Miles's robe she was wearing.

"What are you doing in here?" she asked, swallowing hard.

"I knocked and there was no answer. I was worried about you. You're usually up by now." He narrowed his eyes at her.

Louisa took a deep breath and straightened. "Well, as you can see, I'm perfectly fine. I slept in."

"You never sleep in."

"Well, I did today. I do a lot of things differently now," she said with an arch of her brow.

"Yes, I can see that." There was no mistaking his condescending tone. He gave a huff and shook his head.

"What's that supposed to mean?"

Gerard sucked on his top teeth and chose to ignore her question. "Unusually masculine robe." He reached over and fingered the dark blue lapel. The gesture was altogether too intimate and Louisa stepped back, turning her attention to the dress she'd previously discarded. "It looks big on you." There was no mistaking the hidden meaning to his observation. Gerard was very good at saying one thing and meaning something entirely different.

Rather than rise to the bait, Louisa followed his lead and ignored the implication. "Would you mind leaving? I'd like to get ready. I've a lot to organise and though it's nice of you to see that I'm alright, I do have things to do this morning, guests to see off – and I'm running late." She did her damnedest to sound casual as she busied herself finding a hanger for her dress. But even she could hear the tightness in her tone.

"Yes, you can't disappoint your *guests,* can you? Always the perfect hostess." Gerard said sharply. He was getting agitated at her being so dismissive. "Though I think some of them might be getting more attention than the rest," he goaded.

"I'll take that as a compliment. I think you know your way out." She nodded to the door.

"Always so ladylike, my *cherie.* He's a little young and reckless for you, no?" His accent thickened as he became more annoyed.

Louisa's gaze shot to his and he fixed her with his dark eyes, challenging her to deny it. "Aren't you a little old and prudent to judge?"

"I don't want you to be made a fool of," he bit out, stepping closer to her, a little taken back at her retort.

"Really?" She took a step back. "I was made a fool of for 15 years and it didn't bother you so much then."

"They meant nothing to me…" he all but growled.

"To you maybe, but to me they did," she snapped, then reined in her temper. "I'm not getting dragged into the same argument again, Gerard. It's in the past. Going over past mistakes won't solve anything. I'm moving on, as I'm sure you are too."

"And you think the playboy pop star is going to be faithful?" He flung his hand towards the secret door. "He has a wild and very public reputation. He has no idea how to fit into your life. What duty means. What discretion means. What that costs. He's from a different world that you don't belong in. And you were born into a life he can never comprehend," he gritted out, unable to hold back his frustration.

Part of what he said was true. Miles's reputation did still precede him. Louisa had almost gotten used to seeing "pop star playboy Miles Keane", whenever the media mentioned him. Almost. "It's none of your business, Gerard. What I do and whom I do it with doesn't concern you anymore," she answered quietly. She would've loved to put her ex-husband straight, telling him Miles was more than capable of stepping up, but the truth was Gerard had awakened the doubts she tried to push aside.

"I'm always concerned about you, *cherie*," he said sincerely. Louisa furrowed her brow. She knew Gerard cared for her, even after everything they'd been through. He'd always been reasonable, even when things between them were at their most strained. Gerard blew out a breath and reached for her hand. "Answer me this, though: if you were so sure of him, why are you sneaking around, keeping him a secret? I'll tell you why, because you're *not* sure of him. You know he could and can leave you at any time and a public break up is not something you want." Louisa swallowed hard and pulled her hand away at his harsh words. Every one of them was an unvoiced thought she'd had time and time again. "He's a playboy and you're nothing but a passing phase for him. He's never had a serious relationship other than with cocaine! I'm just looking out for you. I don't want you to get hurt. And just think about how bad it would look on CASPO, the Blackthorn name. You're playing a dangerous game – is the risk really worth it?"

Louisa dropped her gaze. She felt wretched that she couldn't defend herself or Miles because what Gerard had so brutally pointed out was true.

"I'm just worried for you, that's all." He bobbed down to catch her gaze. She blinked up at him, hoping he couldn't see how devastated she was.

"I need to get ready," she said sharply.

Not wanting to push her anymore. He could see that he'd planted the seed of doubt and if he knew Louisa at all, she would step back and put duty first – she always had and she always would; that was one thing Gerard was sure of.

"Of course." He stepped back and gave her a curt nod.

Louisa watched him leave, then slumped into the nearby chair. Gerard was right; if it ever got out about them, they'd be juicy gossip for every tabloid. If they split up, they'd be media fodder for years to come. Every time Miles did anything, her name would be linked to it. CASPO would be in the headlines for the wrong reasons. *What was she thinking?* Apart from all the public scrutiny, how would she ever cope with it all personally? Miles already meant too much to her, even with all the restrictions they had. She found herself thinking about him and missing him whenever they were apart. These past few days together were only going to make it harder when they went their separate ways next week.

Louisa stared down at the dark blue robe she'd borrowed and sighed. Last night and this morning had been wonderful, when they'd been alone, where no one knew about them. If their secret ever got out, they'd be forever under the spotlight. Miles had left his home and country to escape from that kind of intrusion and she'd avoided public life for so long. Maybe they were both just too naïve. This trip Miles was going on might be exactly what they needed – time apart. Time to reassess. Louisa shrugged out of the robe and with a heavy heart, stepped towards her bathroom.

30

ADIEU

THE MOMENT MILES STEPPED into his room, he realised Louisa had left. He spotted her shoes she'd left behind and he picked them up, smiling to himself. Louisa had walked back barefoot to her room but his missing robe meant she hadn't been naked. Well, she was certainly breaking a few of her rules, even in her own home.

It didn't take Miles long to shower and make it down to the conservatory for breakfast. It was the last few hours of the weekend, and though it was drawing to a close, the morning was still packed with activities. He was glad to see that Gerard wasn't around. No doubt he was showing off his ability to shoot innocent pieces of clay. He really was the epitome of an arrogant upper-class twit. He had no lineage or title, yet he behaved as though he did. He was in the company of the aristocracy and yet *he* acted entitled. Miles shook his head, ridding his thoughts of all things French, before spotting Amanda, Grace and Louis sitting with Alistair.

"Miles! Alistair is making soldiers," Louis said excitedly.

"Soldiers?"

"Toast strips to dip in the egg," Alistair explained, putting down his knife. "It's a British thing."

"Ah, I see. Very apt." Miles slipped into an empty seat. "What have you got planned this morning?"

"We're going in the helicopter!" Grace said excitedly.

"Yeah?"

"I'm dropping Konran and the guys to Heathrow. I said they could come along for the ride."

"Cool, how lucky are you?" Louis and Grace nodded excitedly at their uncle. "I thought we'd set off some time after three. The round trip will mean I'll be in London for six," Miles said to Amanda as he poured himself a coffee.

"Yeah sure, that'll be perfect," she replied.

"I could take them back if you like," Alistair offered casually. "Save you the round trip."

"Oh, I couldn't possibly ask you to do that," Amanda said in a rush.

Alistair tilted his head and gave her a smile. "You didn't. I offered. It's only 40 minutes from here. I'll be there and back in no time. It'll save Miles doing a three-hour drive."

"That's very kind of you, Alistair, but I don't want to put you out," she said politely, though it was obvious she more than happy at the offer.

"Not at all. It's settled. It'll be a nice drive and don't worry, we won't be going in one of the Land Rovers. It's about time I took out one of our other cars for a spin." Alistair chuckled.

Miles widened his eyes at a blushing Amanda as she thanked him, then she dropped her gaze to her plate. "Well, thank you," Miles said.

"You know, I hardly leave the grounds, so it'll be nice for me too," Alistair said softly, and Amanda looked up at him and nodded.

"Right, I better get some breakfast. Any recommendations?" Miles asked the children, diverting their attention to him,

"There's lots of things." Grace stood up from her seat and took Miles's offered hand.

"Want to show me? Maybe get some more toast to make more soldiers?" Miles stood up and gave a wink to Amanda. He had a distinct feeling that the earl and his sister-in-law wanted a little privacy.

"Okay!" Louis said and jumped up to help his uncle.

"Ooh, the croissants look good," Grace said. "There's chocolate ones too."

"Err, not for me, I don't think I can stomach anything French today," Miles said with more than a hint of sarcasm, which made Amanda and Alistair chuckle. "Those American pancakes look a lot more appetising, in my opinion," he continued, making Alistair let out a laugh.

Konran took his time talking to every child over breakfast, gifting them with signed merchandise from his tour and the latest tablet downloaded with all his music. Though the material items were received with enthusiasm, the greatest gift they'd received was his undivided attention. Everyone gathered on the terrace to wave off the rap star and his band as Alistair expertly flew the helicopter up and did a final sweep over the grounds, disappearing into the horizon.

The weather had reached an all-time high. With the sun shining down on the Holmwood grounds and bouncing off the still lake, it seemed a waste not to enjoy a swim and a makeshift game of water volley. Alistair's army colleagues organised the water games in his absence and everyone was happy to join in. Miles noted that Gerard had retreated to the house after Konran had left. The last thing he wanted was to play any form of sport or be in close quarters with the Frenchman, so Gerard's lack of presence pleased him until he realised that Louisa was also missing. He'd hardly seen her this morning. She'd fleetingly come into the conservatory at breakfast, then only reappeared to see off Konran. He knew she had a busy morning, ensuring all the guests had everything before they went back to their homes, but even at her busiest, she made time to say a quick hello or at least make eye contact. Miles tried to shake off the uneasy feeling that he'd missed something.

Grace and Louis were thrilled with their ride and Amanda seemed to be more comfortable around the Earl as every hour passed by. It was coming up to lunchtime, so Alistair began to take up small groups of the guests for their helicopter ride, circling the vast grounds of Holmwood. This was the guests' final treat before they had their lunch and headed back to their homes.

The last few hours seemed to fly by and were predominantly made up of packing and waving off the various helpers who had been part of the weekend. Miles kept himself busy with the children, along with Celeste, Alistair and Nicolas, while Louisa had informal chats with each parent. Before long, the guests were leaving Holmwood and the staff set to work on bringing the grand house back to its former glory.

Miles hugged his niece and nephew, then rubbed Duke's belly, before they climbed into the sleek Aston Martin that had been parked up ready for Alistair.

"Nice ride," Miles whistled out.

"Can't let the side down. No point in having a garage full of cars and never using them, right?"

"Well yeah." Miles shook Alistair's hand. "Thank you for taking them and for looking after the kids so well."

"It was my pleasure."

"So, we'll talk soon?"

"We've a lot of organising to do. A concert to get ready," Alistair said enthusiastically.

"Yes, we do," Miles laughed and shook his head. He'd really grown to like Alistair and his easy manner. Alistair got into the car, leaving Amanda to say her goodbyes to Lady Alice, Margot and Louisa.

Miles's heart sank as he watched Louisa disappear into the

house without so much as a backward glance, but he turned his full attention back to Amanda. "So, I'll see you when I get back from LA?"

"Uhuh. You're going to do a great job, Miles." Amanda gave him a reassuring smile. This six-part documentary was a huge step for him. Something he'd never done before, and his first time out in front of the public eye in over five years.

"Eh, we'll see." Miles tried to sound light hearted but she knew him too well – he was nervous.

"Give my love to Eric. It's been a while since I saw him."

"Well that might change. He said he had a few proposals for me."

"Yeah? Like what? You never said anything."

"That's because I've no idea. He said he'd tell me when I got there." Miles shrugged.

"Exciting stuff."

"Let's wait and see, shall we? Come on, your chariot awaits. Can't keep the earl waiting." Miles pulled her into a tight hug.

"You take care of yourself," she muttered as they pulled apart.

"You too." Miles's eyes darted to the waiting car. "He's a good man."

"Yes, he is." She smiled shyly, surprised it had taken him this long to bring it up, whatever *it* was. At the moment, it was two people getting to know one another, but there was definitely the promise of more.

"You let me know what happens, right?" She gave him a nod and tried hard to suppress her grin. "Go on. We'll speak soon." Miles opened the door for her and she settled into the luxurious leather seat. He stood back and waved them off, staying out on the gravel driveway until he couldn't see the car anymore. He jogged back into the house to pack up his things before he hunted down Louisa so he could find out what the hell was bothering her.

Gerard was the next to leave and Miles made a point of being at the front of the house when he was being seen off by Celeste, Nicolas and Louisa. He'd swanned around Holmwood as though it was his home for the last few days and pulled Louisa away privately on numerous occasions because he felt he still had the right to. There was no way Miles was going to allow Gerard to have another private moment, especially as there were no guests or staff around now.

Gerard's eyes hardened at the sight of Miles stepping through the front door and down the steps to where his car was waiting.

"I thought I'd missed you," Miles said in his cheery manner and held out his hand for Gerard. He took it and gave it a firm shake.

"No, I was just saying my last *adieu* to my family," he said curtly and Miles felt Louisa stiffen at his words but Miles didn't rise to the bait. He wasn't about to give the arrogant man the satisfaction in the last few minutes of the weekend. He was leaving and Miles would be here, with his ex-wife and his daughter. He was pretty sure that was more than enough punishment for Gerard to bear. Though Miles would have liked nothing more to punch that smug smile off his face.

"Well, have a safe trip."

Gerard gave a swift nod, then said, "Thank you for all your hard work."

Miles furrowed his brow at his comment. *Why on Earth did he think he think it was up to him to thank him?* "You don't need to thank me. I'm the ambassador for CASPO. It's a pleasure. I take my role very seriously."

"Yes, of course." Gerard then turned his attention to Nicolas and then Celeste, hugging her tightly. Miles stood back and turned his attention to a stoic Louisa, who was doing her best not to lock eyes with Miles. He sighed heavily. There was something wrong and Miles was more than a hundred percent sure that Gerard was the reason for her sudden change in mood.

Gerard stepped up to Louisa and pulled her into his embrace

and spoke softly to her before kissing her cheeks. She nodded and gave a stiff smile and pulled away. Reluctantly, Gerard let her go and slipped into the rear of the waiting car. The driver wasted no time in setting off down the sweeping driveway leaving Louisa, Miles, Nicolas and Celeste standing on the gravel. Celeste waved, then hooked her arm through Nicolas's and headed inside.

"Are you alright?" Miles asked Louisa as she turned to head back into the house.

"Yes, I'm fine. I just need to sort out…" she mumbled vaguely, then walked through the door, but Miles was hot on her heels.

"Louisa."

She walked briskly towards the staircase that led up to her suite. There were staff all around, busy putting the house in order ready for Monday morning. Miles held back from calling after her but he followed her, keeping a distance so as not to alert the staff, when all he wanted to do was sprint up the stairs two by two and yank her back. He was going to get to the bottom of this, one way or another. Something or someone had upset her and if it was him, he wanted to know what he'd done. If he'd learned anything about Louisa over the past few months, he knew this was how she dealt with things: she pulled away and avoided any confrontation. Well that wasn't going to happen, he wanted her to spell it out. If it was Gerard, then he wanted to know that too. This wasn't some trivial affair; he was in love with her and she couldn't just run off and hide behind her work or her duty when things got difficult.

Miles didn't bother to knock on her suite door. He flung it open, only to find Louisa standing by her desk with Hugh. "Hugh, would you mind giving us a moment?" Miles said sharply, his eyes fixed on Louisa.

Hugh waited for a beat and after not being told otherwise, he excused himself and exited the room.

"I told you I had something to sort out." Louisa crossed her arms. Her cool tone meant she was either annoyed or upset.

Miles strode to where she was standing. "What the hell, Louisa? Are you avoiding me?"

"I'm not avoiding you. I have things to…"

"Yeah, I heard you, *things to sort out.* Really? Because it feels like you are, or maybe you're playing me? Is this a game to you?"

"Me play you? Unbelievable." She huffed and stepped behind her desk.

"Well, yesterday you couldn't get enough of me. You were sweet, playful and downright dirty. But today, you can't even look at me." Miles rested his hands on the desk and leaned forward, his eyes laser focused on hers. "I feel as though I missed something. What did I miss, Louisa? What happened in the last 12 hours? Or maybe I should ask, who?"

"What? Nothing happened alright? I'm just… I'm…" her eyes widened in surprise at his implication.

"What? Tired of me? Had a better offer?" he said dryly.

"Ha, you're funny."

"I don't feel funny. I obviously did something to piss you off… Just tell me; I'm a big boy, I can take it, you know." He straightened up and arched his brow.

"You didn't do a thing, okay. This is all on me… so you don't need to worry."

"Seriously? It's me, not you? You're going to feed me that line?" Miles took in her stance, the way she swallowed, and when he searched her eyes for the answers, they glistened with unshed tears. She wasn't annoyed, she was upset, and his accusations were only making it worse. He let out a breath and ran his hand over his face. "Fuck, did I misread this so badly?"

"This?"

"Yes, this. You and me." He flicked his hand in the space between them. "Talk to me, God damn it. I deserve an explanation, Louisa." His voice softened and Louisa pulled her lips into her mouth and shook her head. He looked so lost. There was none of that swagger, no twinkle in his eye, no easy and relaxed manner, just a confused and, if she wasn't mistaken, hurt man. He'd done so much for her, been so much for her and this was how she repaid him. Again, he'd managed to call her up on her behaviour and he was right – he deserved so much more than an explanation.

"I'm afraid, okay? I'm petrified, in fact."

"Of me?" He couldn't disguise his shock.

"Of this."

"You mean what's happening between us?" Louisa gave him a nod and he smiled softly at her. "I won't hurt you..."

She cut him off. "You don't know that... not for sure."

"Okay, I'll rephrase it then. I promise to never willingly hurt you," Miles said sincerely as they stood staring at each other, with the large desk between them. Miles shook his head and stepped around the desk. He pulled her to his chest and felt her instantly soften against him. "Man, that ex of yours did a real number on you." He pressed a kiss on the crown of her head. "I'm scared, too. I don't want to fuck this up." They stood for a moment, holding each other, needing the connection but it still wasn't enough. Miles wanted to know what had spooked her – or rather, *who* had. "What did he say to you?"

Louisa pulled back and looked at him. "Miles... Oh God, I just don't know what to think about this, how it's going to end up."

"Louisa, baby, don't doubt us. Have I shown you that I'm not in this for the long haul?" He gently caressed her cheek with the back of his hand and she sighed. She searched his brilliant blue eyes and only saw his sincerity. It soothed her fractured soul. Miles didn't hide his feelings behind carefully chosen words; he'd always been candid, right from the start, even when it had been difficult.

"That lunch we had... the first time we met."

"Second," she corrected and he gave her a grin.

"Yes, sorry... though at the time, I was a stupid asshole, so it doesn't count." Louisa chuckled and the atmosphere in the room instantly changed. "You may have bought and paid for my time that day, but the second you walked through the doorway into the restaurant, I was totally sold. You were this gorgeous, sexy, confident woman and I realised that anyone before you had been just a silly girl and now, anyone after you would never match up. I was a jittering mess that day. And then you hit me with that line... What did you say?" Miles tilted his head to the side and narrowed his eyes at her. "Ah yes, how could I forget... 'I paid £50,000 for your undivided attention. I know everything about me; this date is all about you.'" Louisa let out a soft laugh as he relived that fateful day. "Fuck, I was a deer in the headlights. You oozed a steely confidence and I knew anyone who could make me feel so off-kilter had to be special."

"You held your own, if I remember."

"After a couple of stiff drinks, yeah. Then I saw that side of you. The passion you have for anything and anyone you feel strongly about, and I realised that I was wrong: you weren't special, you were exceptional." Louisa swallowed hard and her eyes filled with tears at his words. Miles kissed her lips softly. "Baby, I'm scared too. You know my track record."

"Everyone does." She blinked and a tear escaped. Miles chuckled and wiped it away with his thumb.

"Yeah... so if anyone should be scared, it's me. I won't recover from losing you. How would anyone ever match up to you?"

"Best £50,000 I ever spent," Louisa sniffed and Miles let out a husky laugh.

"You better believe." He clasped her face between his hands and kissed her hard. He pulled away and looked deep into her beautiful brown eyes and tilted his head to the side. "Tell me you love me."

"What?" Louisa stuttered.

"You heard me, Louisa. Tell me that you love me," he said

deliberately and Louisa's eyes widened. "Let me make this easier for you. I love you; I'm in love with you. Now tell me that you love me too…" He gave her his patented mega-watt no-holds-barred smile and she melted right there and had he not been holding her, she would've been reduced to a puddle on her priceless Persian rug.

"I love you," she whispered, because it was true, and his smile grew brighter than the sun.

"I know you do."

"How?"

"I recognise the signs… Now, let me show you how much I love you for a very long time." Before she could say anything else, he sealed the deal with his lips on hers. Whatever *things* Louisa had to sort out were instantly forgotten, along with any doubts she had too. He was here for her now, like he had always been. He was in it for the long haul and he loved her. That was all Louisa needed to know.

31

JUST US

MILES BREATHED IN THE late morning ocean air, filling his lungs with as much as he could. He loved England but he missed the ocean, the salty smell and the sound of the waves that sometimes crashed or sometimes lapped the shore. His home sat right on the famous Malibu beach. The coastline boasted ocean views for exclusive homes and was the most coveted address on the west coast. The inhabitants were the who's who of the rich and famous, Hollywood royalty and superstars living next to each other, which only meant their privacy was guaranteed. Miles had built his home early on in his career. It was situated on the Pacific Coast Highway and was one of the few homes that had distance between its neighbours. He'd originally bought the building that was situated on the road and converted it into a recording studio. The land behind the studio was also part of the plot, so Miles had built his home there. It meant that no one could see in from the road, seeing as the studio blocked the view, plus he hired out the studio whenever his band weren't using it.

He leaned on the railing of the upper deck that opened up from his bedroom and took in the uninterrupted views. There were a few joggers running along the shore, as well as dog walkers, and Miles immediately thought of Duke. He'd love it out here. He'd had to leave him with Amanda, to the delight of Grace and Louis, but next trip out, he'd definitely bring him.

Today was the first day since he'd arrived that he wasn't either filming or working. The past ten days had been gruelling, with back-to-back interviews and travelling. It was now up to the editing to polish up the six episodes they'd filmed. Miles knew he'd need to do voice-overs at a later date, but at least the lion's share of the work was done. He hadn't realised how draining the interviews would be. They worked to a script but on every occasion, the interview went off at a tangent. Most of the faded stars ended up revealing so much more of themselves, what had driven them to shoot to fame and what had made them crash and burn out. He remembered Louisa saying something about allowing people to talk about themselves was more revealing than asking direct questions, and he had to say this experience had definitely proved that. It was both moving and cathartic. It also opened up some of Miles's own demons and though he avoided focusing on his own past, it was obvious that he was more than sympathetic to their plight.

It had been a difficult ten days for him, both physically and mentally, but at the end of filming the last episode, Miles felt he'd achieved something he could be proud of. This was a completely different field in the world of entertainment for him and there were many others, more experienced, who could have done the interviews. Of course, he'd been asked because of his star status and his well-documented past, but once filming had started, the producers and director realised that Miles brought that something extra that an experienced interviewer couldn't. Empathy. Though he was a professional throughout, Miles brought a rawness to the interview, throwing out conventional polished performances, giving an almost fly-on-the-wall show. It had been a draining experience and he was both glad and relieved the worst of it was over.

Miles checked the time. It was nearing midday. In two hours, Louisa would be landing at LAX. They would have four days of uninterrupted time together and Miles couldn't think of anything else he'd rather be doing. They hadn't physically seen each other in almost three weeks. Though their video calls had been much needed, even for those few minutes every day, Miles craved the intimacy of just being around her. He was beginning to understand the true meaning of the saying "distance makes the heart grow fonder". Their relationship was testing it to the max. Two o'clock couldn't come fast enough.

"LADY BLACKTHORN, WE'LL BE landing in 30 minutes. Is there anything else I can get you?"

Louisa peered up from her laptop at the steward. He'd been attentive to their needs throughout the 11-hour flight. They'd been relatively lucky that the first-class section of their trans-Atlantic flight hadn't been full. Louisa had managed to sleep a little, in preparation for the long day ahead; when they arrived it would be early afternoon, but it would feel like the middle of the evening to her.

"I'm fine, thank you." Louisa replied and started to shut down the document she was reading in preparation for landing. Hugh and Pierce, one of Hugh's trusted security, were stretching their legs and talking at the far end of the cabin. Louisa hoped they'd also managed to rest on the plane because she wasn't entirely sure what was waiting for them in LA. They hadn't had much chance to discuss Hugh's role while she was taking a break with Miles. These few days were for the two of them, and she wasn't looking forward to having a constant presence. She'd decided to address it once she saw Miles's home. She wasn't a fool. If there was any threat to their privacy, she'd be the first to ask Hugh to step up security.

They were fast-tracked through passport control and whisked out to where a limo with blacked-out windows was waiting.

"This way, my lady." Hugh ushered her towards the car and the driver opened up the rear door for her to slip in. Pierce took care of the luggage and took the seat next to the driver, allowing Louisa and Hugh some privacy. Louisa scanned the interior of the luxurious car, a little disappointed not to see Miles there.

"Mr Keane wanted to be here but he knew it was a risk," Hugh said, seemingly reading her thoughts. He motioned to the photographers who were loitering just outside the entrance. "He didn't want any leaks, as you're adamant about not being public yet."

"Oh, I see. Of course." Louisa gave him a nod and looked out of the window as the car pulled away and into the heavy afternoon traffic.

"It's a 40-minute drive."

"I know, Miles told me," she said and then took a deep breath. "Hugh, these next few days will be a holiday and I appreciate that you have your job to do, but we will want some privacy."

"I am aware. Mr Keane and I have been liaising."

"Liaising?"

"Yes. Mr Keane has been very accommodating."

"What's that supposed to mean?"

"Let's say that we're on the same page with regard to your safety."

"Nothing is going to happen. We're going to be cocooned in his house," Louisa said with a sigh.

"I know. Mr Keane has given me and Pierce the top floor of the recording studio that looks over the street and the residence. So we're close enough, but not in the way. No one can get to the residence without going through the security gates."

"I see. I thought it was on the beach."

"The whole area is covered with cameras and sensors. He sent me the floor plans and the security measures and they are all satisfactory."

Louisa let out a breath. "Goodness me. All this fuss for four days in the sun."

"It's important to you, so it's important to him, my lady. He hasn't left anything to chance. If anyone asks, as far as anyone's concerned, you're here for the concert business."

"Oh, yes. That makes sense."

"He's got your back, my lady," Hugh said softly. He could see Louisa was a little uneasy.

"I know, thank you. You both have."

MILES"S LEG JUMPED IMPATIENTLY in anticipation as he sat on the terrace that spread out from the living room. The sun's rays bounced off the two pools the huge terrace boasted, and Miles was glad of the cover that shielded him. The LA summers could be quite brutal. He sipped his ice tea, wishing it was something stronger, but he didn't want to smell of alcohol when Louisa arrived. Miles stood up and paced back into the airy sitting room and over to the kitchen. He checked the food he'd prepared for the tenth time and then rearranged the glorious arrangement of flowers he'd placed in the wine bucket on the dining room table. He looked at his watch again. It was almost 3:30. She'd be here any minute. He scanned the area, making sure everything was how it should be, and then paced towards the stairs that led to the upper floor. Miles wasn't a patient man. If it were up to him, he'd have been at the airport waiting at the gate for her. But he knew that in Louisa's world, everything was controlled, programmed and meticulously orchestrated. He just hoped that they could become public soon. Experience had shown him that the longer you harboured a secret, the odds of it being exposed grew.

Miles stepped into his bedroom and went straight to the French windows. He opened them up so that the room filled with the ocean air; he straightened the new bedspread of his newly acquired bed, then gave himself a once-over in the mirror. The buzz of the intercom made his tense face split into a wide grin. She was here.

"IT'S JUST THAT BUILDING there." Hugh pointed out a rather plain-looking building with small blacked-out windows on the upper level. Louisa's brow creased. The driver pulled up to the huge solid gate and pressed the intercom.

"Hugh, when we get in there… can you give me a few minutes before you…"

"Yes, my lady. I can do that," Hugh said understanding exactly what she meant. Hugh dropped the partition. "Pierce, stay in the car until I tell you to get out. Lady Blackthorn would like a few minutes of privacy."

Pierce turned to Hugh and confirmed his request with a nod. The limo moved forward once the double gates opened and Louisa strained to see her first glimpse of Miles. He was standing barefoot just outside his doorway, dressed casually in blue shorts and a white polo T-shirt. The cover of the entrance way couldn't shade his megawatt smile.

The driver stopped, then got out of the car to open her door, but Louisa was already out and almost running the few steps to where Miles was. He laughed and rushed to meet her, protocol and decorum be damned. Miles grasped her in his arms and squeezed her tightly spinning her around, then kissed her thoroughly.

"Welcome to the Keane residence, baby. God, I missed you." He kissed her again because he just couldn't stop himself.

"Me too, too much. Let's not do that again. It's been three weeks!"

"I know. We need a two-week rule. I'd prefer a no-week rule, but that might be pushing my luck."

Louisa let out a giggle. A no week rule sounded exactly right to her.

"No Hugh to witness us kissing? I almost kind of miss him." Miles's eyes darted to the blacked-out rear windows of the limo. Louisa laughed at his playfulness, loving how he made light of everything.

"I asked him to give us a moment."

"Well, if we're left alone for any more time, he'll be staying in that limo until tomorrow." Miles lifted his brow suggestively. "Come on, let the poor guy out. Hey, Hugh." Miles waved in the direction of the car, indicating Hugh could come out now. The back door opened and Hugh stepped out into the afternoon sun, stifling a grin. Miles took Louisa by the hand and stepped towards him with his other hand outstretched. "Welcome to LA, Hugh."

"Thank you, sir. It's good to see you, Mr Keane. This is Pierce." Hugh introduced his second in command and then they collected their baggage from the car.

Miles showed Hugh and Pierce to their rooms above the studio. The top floor was a luxurious three-bedroom apartment. It was often used by artists who had booked out the studio, so it was as upscale as any five-star hotel. The street side of the apartment had small blacked-out windows, but the side that overlooked Miles's house and the ocean had large French doors leading onto a balcony.

The next half an hour was taken up with Hugh going through the house. He was familiar with it, seeing as Miles had forwarded the plans, but Hugh still wanted to check everything out for himself. Louisa sat patiently on one of the kitchen bar stools and waited until Hugh was satisfied.

"Well, everything is in order. I'll let you enjoy the rest of the day, my lady."

"Thank you, Hugh."

Miles walked Hugh out and bid him goodbye, then he shut the door and dead locked it. He quickly paced to where Louisa was now standing by the windows, taking in the magnificent view. She'd stayed downstairs while he'd shown Hugh around, not wanting to see the rest of his house with an audience.

"Alone at last." Miles took her hand and kissed each of her fingertips, giving her that sexy wink she loved so much. "Can I get you something to drink? Eat? Or maybe a tour?"

"Later."

"Later?" he said with a smirk and dropped down on his haunches. He tapped her foot and she lifted it, steadying herself by holding onto the window frame. Miles prised off her left court shoe, then removed the right one. He rose up slowly and cupped her face. "We won't be needing any shoes." Louisa smiled and leaned into his touch. "What do you want, Louisa?"

"Just you."

"You have me." He kissed her again, then took her hand and guided her towards the stairs.

"I could do with wearing less clothes and washing off the 11-hour flight."

"I'm on board with naked thing, but the wash can wait. Three weeks is long enough. I can't wait even three minutes." Miles swooped down and lifted her up bride-style, then jogged up the staircase. Louisa giggled into his neck, glad he was as anxious as she was to be together. He carefully set her down by the bed.

"The view is really something.," she said, staring out of the open windows. The light afternoon breeze had cooled the room enough, but it was still warm.

"Yes, it is. It's even better now that you're here." Miles reached behind to pull his T shirt off over his head, then dropped it. Louisa followed his lead and began to shed her slightly crumpled clothes, all thoughts of a shower vanishing at the sight of his tanned, toned torso. She stood still for a moment, just taking him in against the backdrop of the golden beach and the azure of the ocean. He looked perfect. He fit in so well here. This was Miles Keane, all-American California-boy pop star in his element, and he was just breathtaking.

Miles stepped up to her and cupped her face. "Are you okay?"

"Yes, it's just seeing you here. In your home. You're so relaxed and you look... well, you look like *the* Miles Keane."

"I'm just Miles, Louisa. And I'm relaxed because you're finally here. I wasn't joking about the two-week rule. This isn't happening again. I love you and we're together. *They* may not know out there, but we do. I can't be away from you so long ever again." He enveloped her in his arms and she relished the feeling of his warm body encasing her.

"It's been tough on me too, Miles, and as soon as the concert's done, we can stop with the secrecy."

Miles leaned back to look at her. "I don't care about the secrecy, Louisa. I just want us to be together. I can deal with being behind closed doors, but at least let us be behind the *same* closed door," he said with a smirk. Miles didn't want her to feel bad about keeping their relationship a secret. He knew it'd would be a media circus if and when it came out, so he was happy to be out of the gossip headlines too, but he needed to be with her more than a few days every month.

He reached out and pulled back the sheets of the huge bed, then shuffled out of his shorts. He'd conveniently forgotten to wear any underwear.

"I like this 'being naked'. Is it an LA thing?" Louisa said, stifling a grin as she removed her bra and panties.

"No, just a Miles thing. Now come here and let me show you how much I've missed you." Miles hooked his arm around her waist and dropped back onto the bed, so that she was sprawled over him. Louisa let out a little yelp in shock and Miles quickly flipped her over on to her back, trapping her beneath him. "Now I've got you exactly how I want you and where I want you, and there's no one here that can save you." He attacked her neck playfully, causing her to laugh as their limbs tangled together.

"Stop it! Stop it! That tickles." Louisa squirmed and Miles pulled back, grinning widely at her as she caught her breath.

"Man, you're really ticklish."

"I am, so stop it, you brute." She mock-pouted. "And anyway, you're wrong," she said quietly, and Miles furrowed his brow, unsure of what she meant. "You saved me."

Miles's face softened and he dropped a tender kiss on her lips. "No, you saved me more."

"WHATEVER HAPPENS, DON'T LET me fall asleep." Louisa yawned. "I need to power through the jet lag. Otherwise, I'll be sleeping away our time together."

"But you must be exhausted. You've been awake over 24 hours." Miles brushed back her hair from her forehead and her eyes closed lazily. She was flushed from their lovemaking and he'd never seen anything so beautiful.

"What time is it?" she mumbled. Miles reached over to where his phone was and checked.

"Five ten."

"Oh God," she groaned and forced her eyes open. She couldn't fall asleep. Her body clock would be totally out of sync with his. She pushed herself up from the bed and rested on her bent elbows and took in the glorious ocean view. "I had a nap on the plane but it doesn't seem to have made any difference." She looked over her shoulder at him still lying beside her, his hands behind his head unashamedly looking at her naked back. She narrowed her eyes at him and sat up. "So, it's your job to keep me awake and alert. Well at least until ten-ish, then let me flake out."

Miles sat up and trailed kisses over her shoulder. "Hmm, how will I keep you awake, I wonder?"

"We can't have sex the whole time because that'll tire me out." Louisa playfully patted his thigh and shuffled off the bed.

"Are you sure?" He pouted and she mock-glared at him and nodded. "You're no fun." Louisa chuckled, then yawned again.

"Come on get up. This room is too dreamy. If we stay here any longer, I'll collapse on the bed in a coma. How about a walk on the beach?"

"Okay, okay we can do that." Miles reluctantly swung his legs out of bed and stood up, stretching his arms upward. He'd have been quite happy to stay put until tomorrow morning. "And then something to eat. You must be hungry?" he suggested.

"Actually, food first, then the walk." Louisa bent down and picked up her discarded clothes, placing them on the chair. Miles followed her lead and collected his shorts and slipped them on.

"Come on then. Let's eat something."

"And a shower. I really need a shower." Louisa groaned as if the idea was just too much for her.

Miles chuckled and pulled her in his arms. She was so tired, she fell limply in his arms. He kissed the crown of her head. "Okay, shower first?"

Louisa nodded against his chest. "Yes, definitely." Then she stifled another yawn.

"Come on, let's get you in the shower." He patted her bottom and then took her hand, guiding her to his huge bathroom. Louisa eyed the sunken bath longingly as she traipsed behind him, but knew that would just make her even more sleepy. Miles stepped around the glass partition and turned on the overhead shower. Once he'd tested it was warm enough, he ushered Louisa under it and she moaned in appreciation.

"You stay under the spray and I'll get your suitcase, and then I'll come and scrub your back."

She leaned out of the spray so he could kiss her gently. "No sex, Miles, I'm dizzy from lack of sleep," she mumbled against his lips and he chuckled.

"Whatever you say, my lady. No sex, shower, food, then a walk, coming right up."

"Maybe an espresso? Do have some strong coffee?"

"Coffee is my speciality." He kissed her again and she closed her eyes and smiled sleepily as the water rained down on her. "No sleeping in the shower," he called out. "I'll be back before you know it."

"Okay."

Miles jogged down the stairs and set to work on making her a strong coffee. He quickly poured it into a cup, then went to haul her rather large suitcase upstairs. God only knew what she had in there that was so heavy. She was only here for four days.

"I'm back and I bring hot coffee to revive my lady!" Miles said as he entered to bathroom and he bowed dramatically, making Louisa giggle.

"My knight in shining armour." Louisa put out her arm and wiggled her fingers. "Gimme gimme." Miles handed it to her as she leaned away from the spray.

"Wow, that is strong," she said, taking a sip.

"Well, we've got to keep you awake for another four and a half hours." He slid off his shorts, stepped into the shower and banded her in his arms. Louisa took a few more swallows of the coffee and set it on the shelf, out of the stream of the water.

"Thank you. This shower is amazing." She turned in his arms and hooked her hands around his waist.

"Yeah, once you get in, it's hard to get out."

"Hmm, yes. I don't want to leave." Louisa kissed his neck, causing him to shiver.

"Louisa, if you carry on doing that, we won't be leaving here until I've fucked you against the tiles," he threatened mildly.

"Sounds good to me," she muttered kissing him across his chest.

"I thought you said no sex."

"Ignore me, I'm delirious, I don't know what I'm saying." Louisa stepped out of his arms and dropped to her knees. Before he could ask her what she was doing, Louisa took him in her hand and kissed the tip of his growing erection before sliding it through her lips.

"Jesus." He slapped his hand against the tiles to steady himself, then looked down at Louisa working her luscious lips over him. Just the sight of her, naked, wet and kneeling in front of him had his knees weakening and his toes curling against the shower floor. "Fuck." He threw his head back and looked up at the ceiling. He wasn't going to last five minutes if he carried on looking at her. The rumble of her moans from the back of the throat had him squeezing his eyes shut.

"Louisa, I don't want to blow in your mouth, baby," he said through gritted teeth, then took hold of her shoulders and pulled her up. His lips crashed against hers and she groaned, feeling his rock-hard erection press into her stomach. "Hold on to me." She put her arms around his neck and he hoisted her up and pressed her against the cool wall. Her legs automatically locked around his waist as he slid into her and they both moaned.

"Fuck, you feel so good." He slowly pulled out and then ground back into her.

"Harder," she gasped and he did as she asked, plunging in deeper, tightening his grip on her. Miles wasn't sure how long he'd be able to keep up the pace; she was driving him insane. How could such a proper and ladylike woman be so wild and uninhibited when they were together? It was the biggest turn-on ever, knowing she was only like this for him.

"Shit, you're going to make me come," he grunted, resting his forehead against hers.

"Don't stop, Miles," she panted and crushed her lips to his, falling apart against cold tile wall and Miles's heated body.

He fell over the edge just at the sound of her moans, tensing his whole body as the waves of his orgasm crashed over him. His eyes rose to meet hers and he let out a harsh breath. "You're going to kill me. If this is what you're like tired, heaven help me when you're rested." He gave her a hard kiss, then lowered her legs.

"I really like your shower."

Miles laughed loudly. "I hope you like the rest of my home just as much."

"This naked thing has its advantages."

"I know." He pulled her against him and kissed her thoroughly. He couldn't get enough of her. She was absolutely perfect. Every moment he spent with her was unexpected, exciting and just felt so right. He'd never felt like this before, never felt the desire to be with just one person because they filled you up in a way that you'd never experience before. With Louisa, he was filled to overflowing. This was what being in love was, what it felt like to be completely and unashamedly captivated by one person, and it scared the hell out of Miles. For the first time in his life, he wasn't in control.

"Come on, baby. Let me wash and feed you."

"I DIDN'T REALISE HOW hungry I was." Louisa sat back in her chair, replete after finishing off the last of her fillet steak.

"You've definitely perked up." Miles took a sip of the Lafite Louisa had brought, the mystery of the heavy suitcase now making sense. She'd brought four bottles with her, along with an Armagnac as a gift. Miles topped up her wine from the water jug

Louisa had decanted the celebrated wine into. “I need to buy a decanter if we’re going to be drinking this kind of wine here.”

“And a vase.” Louisa gestured to the flowers.

“Oh, I have vases. I was being nostalgic.”

She laughed softly at him and lifted her glass in a silent cheers. He’d practically recreated their first dinner at his home in London, even down to the menu. “I should check on Hugh, organise some dinner for them.”

“All taken care of. I’ve arranged with a local restaurant to have all their meals delivered. The place is stocked up with any drinks, snacks and food they might like too.”

“You’ve thought of everything.” She leaned over and gave him a kiss. He really had thought of everything to ensure their few days were special.

“Just want us to be left alone. Though I will need to speak with Eric at some point. He said he has a project he thinks would be good for me, but I told him I didn’t want to discuss anything until after I finished filming.”

“How do you feel, now it’s finished?” Louisa stood up and started to collect their plates and Miles picked up the salad bowl and serving dishes.

“You know, I had mixed feelings about that project. I was worried that it would feel staged, but filming in their own homes brought a raw substance to the interviews. It was more exposing and the conversations were… I don’t know, just…” Miles placed the dishes in the sink and turned to look at Louisa.

“More organic?” she offered, placing the plates on the work surface.

“Yeah. It was quite emotional, for everyone we interviewed and for me too. I keep thinking about Louis and his ‘Believe it to achieve it’ mantra. I really believed in this project.”

“It sounds like you did something very worthwhile.”

“I hope so.”

Louisa covered her mouth as she yawned, and Miles

chuckled. "Leave those. I'll sort them later. Let me show you around."

"I'd like that. Your home is really something."

Miles took her hand and led her out to the terrace. "Well, you've seen out here already but I wanted you to see it at sunset." The whole of the sky had a deep orange glow as the fiery sun began its slow decent into the sea. Miles wrapped his arms around her from behind and rested his chin on her shoulder.

"It's really beautiful."

"It is. I miss seeing this every night."

"You never wanted to come back here permanently?"

"I like my life in London. It's a different pace to here; it feels more real somehow. Do you understand what I mean?"

"I suppose. You get used to the different energy places have."

"Yeah. I didn't think I'd fit into the English way of life, but I'm happy there. I'm happier than I've been for a very long time." Miles squeezed her against him and kissed the side of her neck.

"Me too."

They watched the sun disappear over the horizon in a comfortable silence, just enjoying the sound of the waves and being with each other. It was a rare moment for them. Their relationship always felt like they had to pack as much as they could into the few hours they spent together. For the first time since they had started their affair, they had days of uninterrupted time to just be. Louisa let herself relax into his embrace, enjoying the kind of intimacy she'd longed for, and this unexpected man had gifted her with it. He was refreshingly candid. He didn't hide behind calculated grand gestures. He was honest and wore his feelings on his sleeve, for all to see, and that made him a rare breed of man.

Louisa's eyes grew heavy as the beach darkened by the second. The couple of glasses of wine and the warm air only made her even sleepier. She stifled another yawn and Miles chuckled.

"Come on baby, go to bed," he urged but she shook her head.

"No, no. Show me around. What time is it anyway?"

"Just gone eight."

"Two more hours and then I can zonk out. Come on, show me your home."

"You're a masochist. You're so tired, baby."

"That's because you keep showing me dreamy sunsets. You need to keep me alert, not be all swoony." She turned and mock-glared at him and he laughed.

"Swoony?"

"Yes. Your whole house is dreamy and swoony. I've never been so relaxed."

"So my house is to blame? And there was me thinking that it was the Lafite."

"Okay, and the Lafite. Don't let me drink any more." She pointed her finger at him and he pretended to bite it, causing her to giggle.

"Maybe if I throw you in the pool that would wake you up." He swooped down, threw her over his shoulder and stepped towards the pool.

She squealed and kicked her legs. "Don't you dare!"

Miles laughed loudly, then set her down. "Okay, no evening swim tonight, but tomorrow, we will be doing the naked swimming thing."

"Tomorrow." She sighed, then furrowed her brow. "Why do you have two pools?"

"One is shallow, for Grace and Louis. This one is deeper. And that there is a fire pit, though I didn't light it up tonight as it's too warm, but the kids make me, even in the summer. They love toasting stuff on it."

"You and Amanda lived here together?"

"We did, just before we came out to England. We all come out for holidays. Her home... well, she couldn't go back there. Not afterwards. It was too painful and she needed me around. So, I made this place child friendly and she sold their place." Miles took her hand and guided her into the living room. "She has her own side of the house. It's big enough not to be in each other's way, but we tend to hang out here and on the beach."

Miles wasn't kidding when he said it was large enough. From the outside, the house looked deceptively smaller, but it boasted five en suite bedrooms, a fully equipped gym and games room that doubled up as a cinema room. The house was decorated in light colours and the walls were adorned with a mixture of family photographs and artful images of musical instruments. There were also many pictures of him and Louis, Amanda and the children at varying times in their lives. Louisa wondered how he could be surrounded by them and not feel his tremendous sense of loss. Then again, from the few conversations they'd had about his brother, he always seemed to feel his absence.

There was an office just off the sitting room that housed the many awards he'd been given as well as a few of his instruments, all in glass cases. Her eyes drifted over the 11 Grammys that shone under the halogen lighting.

"Eleven. That's impressive." Louisa looked over her shoulder at him and he shrugged making light of his achievements.

"More than Bieber but not as many as Sting," he said with a smirk and Louisa giggled.

"No music room?" Louisa asked and Miles shook his head.

"I use the studio for playing – better acoustics." They stepped back into the airy sitting room and he guided her to the large couch. "And when I want to play just for me, I have the odd instrument here and the piano." He jerked his head to the dark grand piano that took up the far side of the room.

"Enough touring. Sit down, I have dessert." He gave her a sexy wink and she smiled sleepily up at him. "I found some delicious éclairs here too."

"I'd love some. You really thought of everything." She reached up and cupped his bristly jaw.

He leaned into her touch and kissed her palm. "I wanted your first time here to be special."

"It is because it's just us."

"You wait here. I'll get them."

"Thank you." Louisa slumped back into the soft couch and watched him amble over to the kitchen, then turned her attention back to the view. The subtly low lighting around the pools was easy on the eye, lighting up the terrace just enough. It really was a beautiful secluded setting, with the gentle crash of the ocean as background noise, which Louisa could still hear, even with the soft music Miles had put on.

Miles busied himself placing the various flavoured éclairs on a plate, then cutting them into four. He collected two plates and forks, adding them to the tray, as well as two crystal brandy glasses, ready for when they opened up the Armagnac.

"I'm not sure how good these are but they look and smell amaz –" He smiled to himself, seeing a fast asleep Louisa on the couch. Her dark hair fanned out over the cream cushion. He was glad she'd only put on a vest and panties to eat dinner. He'd have hated to wake her up to take off her clothes. Miles took the tray back to the kitchen, re-boxed the éclairs and stored them in the fridge, then turned off the lights and shut all the doors.

Miles picked up his phone and silenced it, then sprinted up the stairs to prepare the bedroom, shutting the glass doors, turning on the air conditioning and letting down the black-out shutters. The LA morning sun could wake the dead. By the time he came downstairs, Louisa had snuggled on to her side, deep in sleep. He carefully lifted her and walked towards the stairs. She'd lasted well, he thought to himself, it was almost nine.

Miles gently placed her in his bed and covered her, pressing a kiss to her forehead. Her eyes fluttered open and she gazed up at him. "Don't let me sleep," she mumbled.

"It's nine o'clock baby. You're exhausted."

She closed her eyes again and nodded, unable to keep them open. "Thank you for looking after me," she murmured drowsily.

"That's my job, baby. I'll always look after you."

LOUISA SLOWLY OPENED HER eyes and blinked, feeling slightly disorientated. It took her a minute to remember she was in Miles's bedroom. It was still so dark and she didn't have a clue what time it was. She reached out to the other side of the bed to find that it was empty. Louisa sat up and scanned the room. At the far end, she could see the door with light coming through at the bottom, indicating there was light outside, yet the room was almost pitch black. She reached over to her phone and checked the time. It was 8:15 in the morning. There were a few notifications which she ignored and a few messages from Celeste, Alistair and Melissa. She'd answer them later. She needed to wash the sleep from her face and go find Miles.

As soon as she opened the door to the en suite, the bright sunlight lit the room and it took Louisa a moment for her eyes to adjust. She quickly washed her face, brushed her teeth and tidied up her hair, then before she left the room, she straightened out the bed. Stepping out of the bedroom, she could hear singing that floated up the stairs. The closer Louisa got, the clearer the song became and she grinned to herself. From the top of the stairs, she could see Miles in his swimming trunks, chopping up fruit as he sang along to The Police.

He bobbed along in time with the music, singing to the lyrics, oblivious of his audience of one. Louisa lowered herself onto the step to watch, totally engrossed in her private performance of *the* Miles Keane singing *Everything Little Thing She Does Is Magic,* while he prepared breakfast. As the song came to the end, Miles caught sight of her sitting on the steps. His face transformed into a face-splitting smile.

"You're awake." He put down his knife and turned down the music as Louisa came down the stairs and he met her halfway.

"And what a way to wake up."

Miles gently clasped her face and kissed her. "You sleep okay?" he asked.

"Like the dead. I woke up and thought it was still night."

Miles chuckled. "Yeah, well I have black-out shutters because the sun blasts through in the summer. Come and sit; I've prepared breakfast." He guided her to where he'd set up the breakfast bar. "I made some fruit salad, there's yogurt, some granola. I can whip us up some eggs, bacon, whatever you want."

"Any tea?" she asked hopefully.

"Tea coming right up." He turned and opened up a cupboard and pulled out a box.

"I can make it."

"No, no you sit there. I'll just need to find the tea pot." He crouched down and opened up another cupboard and peered inside.

"You have a tea pot?"

"Amanda," he said as explanation.

"Oh yes. I'll have to thank her for training you."

"Yeah, you Brits take your tea very seriously," he said dryly.

"We do."

"Ah, here it is." He carefully pulled out a large white tea pot and placed it on the granite counter. "What do you want to do today?" he asked as he busied himself with the kettle.

"I'm not sure."

"Well we never had that walk on the beach."

"A walk sounds great."

"Then maybe be laze by the pool?" he suggested and she gave him a nod, thinking a lazy day sounded wonderful. "What do you want to eat?"

Louisa twisted her mouth as she looked at the fruit and granola, then scrunched her nose and said, "Éclairs."

Miles laughed. “Whatever my lady wants.”

“HOW’S LA?” Melissa asked.

“Hot, too hot.”

“And how’s my favourite CASPO ambassador?”

“Hot, too hot.”

Melissa snorted down the phone and Louisa giggled. “Ah, shush now. I’m already a mess of overactive hormones. What are you doing right now?”

“I’m lazing on a sun lounger after a walk along the beach. Miles is just cleaning up the bar-be-que, ready for us to cook on. He’s only in just his trunks.” Louisa peered over her sunglasses, letting her gaze linger on his sculptured back and tight behind.

“Oh my goodness, it sounds like a bad porno.”

Louisa sniggered at her friend’s comment. “Nothing bad about it.” Miles turned to see why she was laughing and she pointed to her phone and mouth that it was Melissa.

“Anyway, thought you should know and, sorry for the dampening of your good mood, but… Emily lost the baby.”

“Oh no. Poor Gordon.”

“Yes, he does rather blame himself, but it is what it is. Alistair and Robert are rallying around him. Emily is even more of a wreck. They think she’ll need psychiatric help. It seems she was on cocaine and other stuff. It is quite a mess.”

“Alistair never said anything.”

“Oh, you know how discreet he is.”

“Her poor parents must be besides themselves.”

“Quite. Anyway, just keeping you in the loop. I hope it’s not all fun in the sun; we need big names. Konran is steaming ahead and putting you guys to shame.” Miles had finished preparing the bar-be-que and joined Louisa. She shuffled over so he could sit on her bed. “He’s signed up some big names already, to be announced at the press conference at the end of next week," continued Melissa.

"Yes I saw, he sent me an email. Don't worry, I'll have news before we head back."

"You're heading back together?" Melissa asked.

"Yes, Miles needs to stop off in New York for the watch launch, which as luck would have it, coincides with my annual meeting and charity dinner, so..."

"A bit risky."

"Well we won't be at the same events."

"Still think you should just come clean."

Miles smiled, hearing Melissa's comment, and Louisa rolled her eyes. "Once the concert's done, that's the plan."

"Well, enjoy the next few weeks of secrecy because you know after that, all bets are off."

"Yeah, thanks for that," Louisa said dryly. She could always rely on Melissa to be blunt.

"Baby bump speculations, marriage speculations..."

Louisa's jaw dropped at Melissa's comment. "Okay, okay enough." She cut her off but Melissa continued.

"Baby's christening is going to be a circus!"

"Melissa!"

Miles chuckled, seeing Louisa's appalled expression, and grabbed the phone. "Melissa, are you trying to ruin our holiday?"

"Perish the thought. I'll leave you two lovebirds alone."

"Take it easy, Melissa." Miles handed back the phone to Louisa for her to say goodbye to her friend. Once she put her phone down, he leaned to kiss her.

"How hungry are you?"

"I'm not hungry for food," she said coyly.

"Hmm... Fancy a dip in the pool?" He smoothed his hand up her thigh and tugged at the string tie to her bikini bottoms. "We've got to do good on the naked swimming thing." He rubbed his nose along her collarbone and trailed open-mouth kisses up her neck.

"Well I do need to cool down."

The urgent buzz of the door had Miles pull back sharply. "Who the hell is that? No one knows I'm here."

Louisa shrugged. "Let's ignore it."

Miles leaned back down, but before he reached her lips, her phone started to ring. Miles cursed under his breath.

"Hugh, is everything alright?" Louisa asked him down the phone.

"Sorry to disturb you, madame, but there's someone at the gates. I called Mr Keane's phone but he didn't answer."

"I see. I'll pass him on." Louisa handed her phone to Miles.

"Hello, Hugh. Sorry, my phone was on silent after we talked this morning... Yes, no it's fine, I'll deal with it." Miles ended the call and blew out a breath.

"Who is it?"

"Eric. I'll get rid of him." Miles got up from the lounger and walked back into the house. Louisa swung her legs off her seat and followed him in.

"No, don't. He obviously thinks it's important to come unannounced."

Miles muttered something about him being a persistent pain in his ass as he picked up his phone and his face dropped. "Shit."

"What is it?"

"Four missed calls and a message from him. So much for just us," he said, clearly exasperated, putting his phone down a little harder than necessary.

"I better put some more appropriate clothes on." Louisa waved her hand down her body.

"And he ruined naked swimming!" Miles flung his hands out. "This better be good."

32

GATE CRASHERS

LOUISA HAD NEVER DRESSED so fast in her life. She was glad she'd packed at least a couple of sundresses, even though Miles had insisted they wouldn't be leaving his home. The few bits of clothing she had were what she needed for her official engagements in New York and certainly not appropriate for LA beach living. After quickly freshening up, she brushed and pulled her hair into a high ponytail, then checked her look in the mirror. She furrowed her brow at her fresh face, bare of makeup, then slipped on a pair of sandals. It would have to do. She was sure Eric Schultz couldn't care less what she looked like.

"I thought I told you I'd be in touch once filming finished," Miles said as soon as Eric stepped out of his car.

"Well hello to you too," he replied dryly.

"Sorry," Miles sighed and pulled his long-time agent and friend into a hug.

"Filming finished two days ago." Eric clapped him affectionately on his back, then entered the house. "Plus, I have to fly out to Berlin for two days tomorrow, so it was today or whenever you got back to England."

"You have heard of the phone."

"It only works if you answer it, smart ass." Eric rolled his eyes at him. "Anyway, these proposals warranted a face to face."

They both went straight to the kitchen. Miles opened the fridge while Eric made himself comfortable on one of the stools. He scanned the house, noting the fresh flowers and the towels on the sun loungers. The draining board also had two wine glasses and a tea pot on it.

"What can I get you?"

Eric's attention was pulled back to his host. "Ice tea, please." Miles nodded and pulled out a jug he'd freshly made earlier. The kitchen looked as though Miles was in the middle of preparing lunch. "Is Amanda here?"

"No, why?"

"The teapot."

"Oh, no – I have company."

"That explains you blanking me," Eric drawled.

"I'm just enjoying a bit of R n R," Miles said with smirk passing him his glass. Eric thanked him and they clinked glasses before he took a welcome drink.

"I spoke to Lionel. He said you did an excellent job. They were blown away."

"Yeah?" Miles tilted his head.

"Yeah. You weren't sure?"

"Well it's my first time being on the other side. You know, interviewing. It was weird."

"Weird in a good way, though."

"Yeah." Miles caught sight of Louisa coming down the stairs and his eyes lit up, seeing her glide down the stairs in her white halter-necked dress. "Here she is." He beamed and Eric swivelled in his chair to see who had made him look so happy. "Come here, baby, let me introduce you," Miles said stepping up to her.

Louisa walked up to a wide-eyed Eric who had slid off his stool and put out his hand.

"Eric this is Louisa. Louisa, meet Eric." Miles slipped his arm around her waist and gave her a squeeze.

"It's nice to see you again." Louisa smiled at Eric and shook his hand. He furrowed his brow for a second before realisation hit him.

"Err, it's nice to see you again, Lou… I mean Lady Blackthorn," he stammered, stunned that he was once again in the presence of the Countess of Holmwood and in Miles's Keane's kitchen.

"Please call me Louisa," she said with a soft smile.

Eric's eyes darted to Miles, then back to Louisa. A thousand questions swam around in his head but his good manners stopped him blurting them out.

"Louisa is here for a few days on holiday," explained Miles.

Eric gave a slow nod but kept his worries to himself. "That's nice," he said but his face had gone a shade of grey that matched the colour of his hair.

"We're together, Eric. It's been a few months now, so you can relax." Miles couldn't hide the amusement in his voice.

"Um, I see."

"Why don't you both go sit down in the lounge? It's maybe a little more comfortable. I'll just help myself to some ice tea," Louisa said trying to put a clearly shell-shocked Eric at ease. The poor man looked as though he was going to have a seizure.

"Sure. Come on, Eric, chill. You're raining on my parade," Miles said with a smirk, enjoying the fact he'd made his normally cool-headed agent so nervy.

Once Eric was seated, he glared at Miles. "What the fuck, Miles!" he hissed. "A heads up would've been nice. What the hell is going on?" He ran his fingers around the collar of his shirt and darted his eyes to the kitchen, making sure Louisa couldn't hear.

Miles chuckled. "It's all cool. We met in April at a lunch. It's a long story – I'll tell you it one day. Anyway, after I became ambassador for CASPO, things kind of developed."

"When you called me about her a couple of weeks ago, I thought it was strange, but this... I didn't expect this."

"Everything okay? Do you need some privacy to discuss business?"

Eric shot back in his seat and said, "Yes" at the same time as Miles answered "No".

Miles gave Eric an exasperated look. "Louisa knows everything, Eric, and I'd value her input." Miles patted the space next to him in invitation and Louisa settled into the spot.

"Of course. I didn't mean any offence; it's just usually we discuss work issues alone." Eric looked suitably embarrassed at his abrupt reaction.

"None taken," Louisa assured him and Miles clasped her hand and squeezed it, then gestured for Eric to continue.

"Okay, so I'll be honest. I've had a lot of enquiries about you starting recording again." Before Miles could protest, Eric put up his hand. "I'm not here to discuss those. Just letting you know that whenever or if ever that's in the cards, I got you covered." Miles pulled in his lips and nodded. "So, the first proposal is for a film."

Miles creased his brow. "What? I can't act in a film." He stared at his agent, waiting for him to say something, but he waited. Over the years, Eric had gotten to know Miles well. He needed time to digest and often to vent his thoughts before he was able to really evaluate proposals. Miles stood up abruptly. "You're kidding, right? I mean, music videos are one thing and the odd ad campaign... but a film?" He began to pace and Eric's eyes darted to Louisa, who gave him a sympathetic look. "And what kind of role would I even play? I'm not qualified for any of that!" He threw his hands up in the air. "I thought these were serious offers."

"They're very serious," Eric said calmly. "This film has been in the upping for over ten years but they haven't found the right person for the lead role, until now."

"And they want me?" Miles couldn't hide his astonishment. Eric gave him a nod. "What role is it? What kind of role could *I* possibly be right for?"

"The life story of Chet Baker."

Miles's face froze for a second. He stared at his agent, who gave him an encouraging smile. Eric knew how much Miles loved the trumpeter's music and style. He'd always idolised the musician's gift for soulful singing. While Miles Davis had always been his trumpet-playing hero, Baker's talent had mastered the art of combining those skills and made the trumpet look cool.

Eric reached for his phone and tapped the screen, before turning it in the direction of Miles. Miles's face dropped when he saw and heard his rendition of *I Fall in Love too Easy* he'd played at the activities weekend. "Who sent you that?"

"Amanda."

"What!"

"It was innocent. She sent it saying that she thought I'd get a kick out of seeing you perform again. That it took her back to the early days." Eric tapped the phone to stop the video and placed it on the coffee table. Miles slumped back into his seat and dragged his hand over his face. "But I'm glad she did, though."

"So, you showed that to... ?" Miles waved his hand vaguely at the phone.

Eric nodded. "I heard about the film a few years ago, but knew you were in no state to even think about it. When this came through, I sent it to one of the producers, saying I'd found their Chet Baker. He took one look at it and said now he understood why they'd never been able to cast it. They were waiting for you."

"Fuck. I can't act," Miles said wearily and leaned back into the couch and looked up at the ceiling. It was obvious that this was a dream role for him, something he could in reality accomplish, but his insecurities were holding him back.

"You can act just fine. A bit of coaching, you'll be as good as any seasoned actor." Eric tapped the table and Miles returned his pensive gaze back to him. "Plus, you know and love the music, and you can play the instruments. This role was meant for you, Miles."

"Jesus, Eric, this came out of left field. I mean it's a huge commitment too..."

"All projects are. Yes, normally a film like this would take a up to 12 weeks, but seeing as you don't need to rehearse and learn the music, or instruments, it'll be less."

"I live in England," Miles shot back as he rested his elbows on his knees.

Eric's eyes again darted to Louisa, who had kept quiet throughout their discussion. She gave him an encouraging smile and he leaned forward. "So? You'll be coached and rehearse out there, so as not to disrupt any commitments. Then, once you're ready, the filming will be done in two, maybe two and half months."

"Eric, I... I'm not sure." Miles let out a breath and dropped his gaze to the floor.

"Not sure you want to do it or not sure if you're able?" Miles's worried eyes shot back up to Eric's and he instantly knew the answer. "Miles, this isn't performing in front of people. It'll be in a studio with cameras. Very few people, 30 tops," he said softly.

"Miles?" Louisa rested her hand on his shoulder in support. He was in turmoil and all she wanted to do was hold him tightly and tell him she had his back, like he'd had hers. He turned to her and swallowed, holding her gaze, telling her so much with his eyes. *Thank you, I love you, I'm glad you're here.*

"Just give me a minute, will you?" Miles stood up suddenly and strode out on to the terrace.

Eric watched him leave and leaned back into the couch, wondering whether he'd pushed him too far. He'd seen a marked change in him over the last few months and he'd hoped that Miles had turned a corner. Eric might have been his agent, but he was his friend first and foremost, and he only ever wanted the best for him.

Before the shooting, Miles had been ambitious and cocky, thinking he could do whatever he wanted. He was always chasing the new project, the next album, the next tour. It had been Louis who'd had to ground him. Telling him to slow down and take a breath because they had all the time in the world in front of them and they needed to enjoy the moment. Well, Louis had been right on one of those points. Eric now realised that the recent change in Miles, and his willingness to start working again, probably had a lot to do with the woman sitting in front of him.

"It's a big step for him," Louisa said quietly, seeing Eric's pensive expression.

"I know. But…" He sighed and shook his head. "He's so goddamn gifted. So talented. Forget the success, the fame. When he performs, writes music, he's just so unbelievably good. They both were. The Miles I met was fearless – a pain in the ass, but totally fearless."

Louisa chuckled. "Yes, I think I remember that," she said dryly and he grinned back at her.

"Did he ever tell you how we met?"

"Yes, he told me the story."

"That night… well, the last thing I wanted to do was go to a student bar and listen to some mediocre musicians. If it wasn't for them being Richard's boys, I would have made some excuse and not bothered. But when they came on stage, I knew they had star quality." Eric gestured to his phone. "That video Amanda sent me is the first time I've heard him play since…"

"He feels guilty." Eric tilted his head at her, unsure of what Louisa meant. "For surviving."

"Christ." Eric closed his eyes in pain for his friend. When he opened them, they glistened with unshed tears as he searched the terrace for Miles. Louisa rose up from her seat and Eric stood too, remembering his manners. He was in the company of a countess after all.

"I'm just going to go to him," she said and headed through the doors to where Miles was staring at the ocean. "Hey."

Her voice pulled Miles out of his troubled thoughts. He took her in his arms and rested his chin on the top of her head. "I'm sorry."

"What are you sorry for?"

"This is supposed to be a fun few days and…"

"Shh… you've nothing to apologise for." She squeezed him, then decided to lighten his mood. "That look on Eric's face when he realised who I was." Louisa felt the rumble of his chortle. "You totally messed with him. Poor man, he went so pale. I thought you'd told him I was here."

Miles pulled back and Louisa was pleased to see the pensive expression had changed to that of mischievous amusement. "No, I didn't. It was fun though."

She shook her head at him, then pressed her palm to his cheek. "Talk to me, Miles." He sighed into her touch. She was the balm he needed. "Do you think the film is too much or are you just…"

"I'm scared," he said with an awkward one-shoulder shrug. "I know it's not a stage but it's still… I'm out there." She gave him a small nod to let him know she understood. She took both his hands in hers and gave them a squeeze. He let his gaze drift back to the ocean, unable to look at her concerned face. He didn't want to feel as if he was disappointing her.

"I can't tell you what to do, Miles, because this is something only you can work through. What I can tell, though, is that you have shown me how incredibly strong you are. How you put your fears to the side and made 32 children have an experience of a lifetime. You're so talented, so honest and generous." He swallowed hard at her heartfelt words and let himself look at her beautiful face. She gifted him with a warm smile. "This film offer is an opportunity for you to use your gifts in a different way. A new way. And if you think you can't do it right now, then see if they'll wait. They waited this long. But don't say no until you've thought about it long and hard. Take a meeting. See if you can work with them."

Miles pulled his lips into his mouth and nodded, then looked down at their joined hands and played with her fingers. "You know, I thought he was going to ask me to compose a film score or do some other ad campaign. A film wasn't even on the radar."

"I think things come to us when we're ready to receive them. Did you ever think you'd be an interviewer?" She pulled his hands to her lips and kissed them. His glorious blue eyes zeroed in on hers and he smirked. "Did you think you'd compose a rap song with TuKon?"

She was certainly right about that one. Never in a million years! he thought to himself. "I never thought I'd fall in love with a very proper and ladylike countess." He gave her a lopsided grin and she laughed softly.

"Exactly, and how scary is that?" Miles laughed and pulled her into his arms again. She'd taken a leaf out of Miles's book, diffusing any tension with humour. "Don't let fear stop you, Miles," she murmured against his bare chest. He bent down and kissed her tenderly, glad she was here to reassure him. "Come on, poor Eric is sat in there on his own."

Miles took her hand and lead her back into the sitting room. Eric's stood up as they came towards the couch. "I'll think about it."

Eric sighed in relief. "That's all I ask."

"Maybe I could take a meeting with the producers, director," Miles said carefully.

"I can arrange that."

"Do we know who the director is?"

"They mentioned James Mangold but it's not certain."

"Oh wow, he directed Joaquin Phoenix in *Walk the Line*, didn't he?" Eric gave him a nod. Miles sat back down and Louisa lowered herself next to him. "Any idea when they want to film?"

"That depends."

"Depends on what?"

"You." Eric took his seat opposite the couple and noticed Louisa was holding Miles hand. "They've stopped looking for someone to play the lead until you say no."

Miles stiffened at the comment, but before he could say anything, Louisa said, "Miles. Take the meeting. See how you feel after that, read the script. They have a script, right?" she asked Eric.

"I have it in my car."

"Even better. You can read that first, then decide whether you want a meeting."

"Okay. I'll read the script."

Eric beamed at Louisa, then immediately got up from his seat and practically jogged to the car.

"Well he seems happy," Miles said with more than a hint of sarcasm.

"We should ask him to stay for lunch."

"What! Why?"

"Because he cares for you. He came out to see you." Louisa glared at him, speaking to him as though he was a child.

"Yeah, I suppose you're right. He already gatecrashed our afternoon."

Eric strode back to where they both were sitting, holding a thick wad of paper. "You know your phone is ringing, right?" He gestured to Miles's phone that was flashing on the breakfast bar.

"Crap, I forgot to take it off silent." Miles marched up to where the phone was but it had already stopped. He picked it up and muttered a curse. He had four missed calls from his mother. *That couldn't be good,* he thought. He tapped his phone screen and mock-grimaced.

"Hi Mom, is everything alright? Sorry, my phone was on

silent." He blew out a relieved breath and Louisa and Eric chuckled. "Yeah, I've finished… Okay, I finished the day before yesterday. I just needed some time off to relax… it's been hectic." Miles rolled his eyes, then his expression blanched. "What now you mean? Eric is here." Miles listened to whatever his mother was saying and pinched the bridge of his nose. "Okay. Bye." He put his phone down but not before putting the ringer back on. "Looks like it's going to be five for that late lunch. Mom and Dad are on the way. They'll be here in an hour."

LOUISA HAD MET MANY different people throughout her life: film stars, pop stars, and dined alongside prime ministers and presidents. She'd had a privileged life, socialising with the elite, rubbing shoulders with international royalty, and had moved in the same circles as the royal family, but the idea of meeting Miles's parents was probably up there with one of the most daunting experiences she'd had.

Had she been in her own environment, things would have been different. Added to that, she'd had no time to prepare herself and she was pretty sure the Keanes had no idea she was here or what her relationship was with their son. Louisa was somewhat happier that Eric would also be here, so the burden didn't fall all on her shoulders.

Eric and Miles set to work on marinating the steaks and prawns, along with preparing a few salads and side dishes. It seemed that Eric was quite the chef and Louisa found herself laughing at the easy banter he had with Miles as she rustled up a salad dressing. It was obvious that the two men were close. Seeing as the cooking was under control, Louisa set the outside table and decanted the wine, hoping that if she kept busy, her nerves would subside. The sound of the ocean soothed her and she took a moment to take it in. It had to be difficult for Miles to leave this small slice of paradise he called home and come back to England, especially in the winter. The sound of the buzzer had Louisa's stomach clenching with nerves. *Game face on.*

"You're not too old for a telling off," teased Miles's mother as he let her hug him tightly. She was a tall slim woman with shoulder-length strawberry blond hair, elegant even in her tanned slacks and pastel green blouse. "You've been here for over two weeks and still haven't made time to come and see us."

"I was working, Mom."

"You had time for Eric, I see." She arched a brow at him, then greeted Eric with a kiss to his cheek.

"Eric gatecrashed," Miles muttered, then turned to the tall distinguished man, with a full head of blond greying hair. He was carrying a box but still managed to hug Miles with his free arm, his face crinkling up into a huge smile that looked way too familiar. "Hey, Dad."

"She's been insufferable." Miles's father rolled his eyes, then turned to greet his friend.

"Aw hush now, you were just as keen to see him as me," Miles's mother chided lightly. "We brought you all a pecan pie." Miles's father handed the box to Miles.

Louisa hung back, allowing the Keanes to have a moment with their son. It was amusing to watch their easy manner and light-hearted teasing.

"You made pie?" Miles said in disbelief, and Mr Keane chuckled at what must have been an inside joke, which earned him a playful slap to his arm.

"We *bought* pie." Mr Keane corrected and Miles mouthed "Ah". "So, what have you been doing with your..." Mr Keane stopped when he saw Louisa stepping closer to where they all were. "Oh, hello, I'm sorry, we didn't realise you had company."

Miles handed the pie to an amused Eric and held out his hand to Louisa, beckoning her to come closer. "Mom, Dad, I'd like to introduce you to Louisa, she's here for a few days holiday." Louisa smiled at them and took Miles's hand. "Louisa, these are my parents. Katherine and Richard."

"I'm very pleased to meet you, Mrs Keane," she reached out to shake her hand.

"Oh please call me Katy. You're British?"

"Yes, I am."

Louisa then turned to Mr Keane and shook his hand. He said, "Richard. We're very pleased to meet you, Louisa."

"Well this is a nice surprise," Katy said as they all walked into the lounge.

"I'm sorry we gatecrashed your holiday." Richard said sincerely, shooting Miles a look.

"Not at all. It's nice to finally meet you. Miles talks so much about you."

"He does, eh? Well forgive me, but he's told us nothing about you." Katy narrowed her eyes at her son.

"I have," Miles corrected his mother. "Louisa is the patron of CASPO that I'm the ambassador of." Both his parents looked puzzled as their eyes darted from Miles to Louisa.

"But she's a countess," his mother said slowly and Miles nodded, stifling a grin.

"So, you're the Countess of Holmwood," Richard asked, trying to keep the shock out of his voice. Eric chuckled behind them, glad it wasn't only him who had been awestruck.

"Oh, I'm… well." Katy put her hand over her mouth "And you two are… I mean. Oh my."

"I'm just Louisa," Louisa said softly and then glared at Miles, who was enjoying his parents squirm uncomfortably.

"A drink, anyone?" Eric chirped in from the kitchen.

"Yes!" his parents said in unison, making Miles chuckle.

"I'm sorry, it's just a bit of a surprise. A nice surprise," Katy said, trying to compose herself, shooting a sharp look at her son.

"If it's any consolation, I'm extremely nervous too." Louisa let out a soft laugh, feeling awful that Miles had made his parents feel awkward. "And I love pecan pie."

"Well, isn't that something," Katy sighed with relief.

"So that's how you two met each other – through the charity?" Richard asked Miles, trying to get his head around the fact his rebellious son was dating a British countess.

"Sort of. It's a long story."

"Well, we've all afternoon for you to tell us all about it."

THE AFTERNOON SEEMED TO fly by once everyone felt more comfortable. Miles recounted the story of how he and Louisa had met, with Louisa's occasional input. Eric even added to the story, describing the night at Madison Square Gardens. It was a lovely casual afternoon and Louisa got to see Miles surrounded by the people who loved and knew him the best. There was no talk of work. There seemed to be an unsaid rule that they avoided mentioning his performing or projects. Maybe it was because they knew Miles was still not ready, or maybe it was because they didn't want to pressure him. Whatever their reasons were, the Keanes didn't ask and took their son's lead as to which direction the conversation went. Miles filled them in on details of his role at CASPO and they spoke about Amanda and the children. They were due out for a visit, now that the school holidays had started. It was obvious that the Keanes adored Amanda and doted on their grandchildren.

It was early evening by the time Miles's parents left. Miles made them promise that they would come out to England before they started lecturing for the Autumn semester. They hugged Louisa tightly, saying they hoped to see her again soon. Louisa watched Miles walk them to their car and have a few private words with them before they waved them off.

Eric stepped into the entrance, where Miles and Louisa were

coming back in. “Time for me to go too.” He held out his hand for Louisa. “It was a real pleasure seeing you again.”

“For me too. You’re very welcome to come and visit Holmwood House.”

“Thank you, I may take you up on that.”

“Anytime,” Louisa said sincerely.

“I’ll see you out,” Miles said and followed him to his car. “You said there was more than one proposal.”

Eric nodded but didn’t elaborate. He wanted Miles to concentrate on one offer at a time. The second proposal was going to need a lot more convincing. “It can keep. Read the script, Miles.”

“Have you read it?”

“Yeah.”

“What do you think?”

“I wouldn’t have given it to you if I didn’t think it was good, but don’t let that persuade you – *you* have to like it.” Eric leaned in and hugged him tightly, then pulled away. “I know you have the concert to work on, but I’d like a meeting before that.”

“Okay, I’ll be in touch. Any idea when they want to film?”

“Ideally, filming could start at the beginning of next year, to be released the year after that.” Eric slipped into his car and looked up at Miles. “This role is perfect for you, Miles,” he said to him with an encouraging smile.

“Take it easy.” Miles shut the car door and waved him off.

“So much for just us,” Louisa noted.

Miles sauntered onto the terrace, where he found Louisa stretched out on one of the settees. He smiled, noticing she’d taken off her sandals, now that their company had left.

“It was certainly an eventful afternoon.” Miles chuckled and sat down next to her gathering her in his arms. “You were amazing. They think you’re wonderful.”

“Well, I’ve been brought up to be the perfect hostess.” Louisa answered in that proper way that Miles loved so much. “Though

I think my mother would have thrown a fit, seeing me dressed in a beach dress without a scrap of makeup on."

Miles laughed and kissed her temple, thinking Louisa was right on the money. "You look absolutely perfect to me, and right here, that's all that matters."

She turned her face up to look at him and smiled softly at him. It was him that was perfect. He looked so comfortable here, this was where he felt himself. "How do you feel about the film?"

"Honestly? The more I think about it, the more I'm interested."

"Hmm. Aren't you itching to read the script?"

His lips curled into a huge smile. "Absolutely."

Louisa laughed seeing his eyes twinkle with excitement. "Well what are you waiting for?" She sat up quickly, excited that he was seriously thinking about it.

"Naked swimming time," he growled and tackled her neck, making her squeal. "Then I'll read it."

33

WELCOME BACK

IT WAS SURPRISING HOW easy it was to forget what was just outside the security gates. Louisa and Miles had fallen into an effortless routine over the following few days of their holiday. They took pleasure in the mundane tasks, like preparing meals together, but at the same time, worked on reaching out to the many contacts Miles had in the music industry. Miles had read the script a number of times, discussing it at length with Louisa and even making notes. He'd even done some research, wanting to be as informed as possible for his scheduled meeting in New York with the producers. Once he'd expressed an interest, they'd wasted little time in arranging the earliest available slot while Miles was still stateside. That wasn't to say that their time together was all work – there was also an abundance of play too.

For Louisa, it was all so new. Lazing around in barely any clothes and being totally herself, never thinking of who was around or who might see. It was paradise. The longer she stayed there, the easier it became for her to get lost in Miles and everything that that included. For the first time, she felt free, even if it was in the confines of a half-an-acre beachfront property. Her only contact with the outside world was via email, the odd family phone call and the morning check-ins with Hugh. By the time their last day dawned, Louisa wondered whether she'd ever feel like this again.

"You okay, baby?" Miles caught Louisa wistfully looking out at the ocean from their bed.

"I'm going to miss this view." Miles kissed her temple and she sighed into him.

The four days they'd had together had been the best he could ever remember. It wasn't just the view he was going to miss. "We can come back whenever you want." Even as he said the words, he knew it wasn't going to be that easy. Their schedules and commitments over the next few months would mean they'd be lucky to spend an evening together once a week, and that would be after some serious juggling.

Miles reluctantly pulled himself away from her and sat up. "I need to get one last run in. I won't have that luxury in New York or the time. Plus, I need to fill my lungs with ocean air," he said with a twinkle in his eye.

"Are you excited about the meeting?"

"Yeah, I am. Thank you." He leaned down and kissed her tenderly. "I wouldn't have even looked at the script or agreed to a meeting without you."

"I'm excited for you too. Off you go." She patted his cheek as she smiled up at his handsome face. "I'll pack and we can make breakfast together when you get back."

"How very domesticated of us," he teased, giving her a wink as he rose up from the sex-mussed sheets.

"I know, right?" she giggled and watched his perfect naked form head to the bathroom.

By the time Miles returned, Louisa had packed her things, checked in with Hugh, cleared all her emails and spoken to Celeste, Alistair, Lady Alice and Melissa. The latter phone call taking a lot longer than normal. Louisa had found out that

Melissa's blood pressure was a little high and she'd been instructed to rest. She'd spent the best part of an hour reprimanding her dearest friend. giving her strict instructions to stay home in bed and to pass her workload to Margot until she was back in two days. Had Louisa not committed herself, she'd have been flying straight back to London that evening, instead of going to New York.

Louisa sighed as she looked at herself in the mirror. She was back in her "casual countess" uniform of fitted trousers and short-sleeved top. She'd styled her hair and applied minimal makeup, completing her flawless look. Her court shoes were set by the bed, ready for when they left for their flight. She'd decided she wasn't going to wear them until they left, clinging on to her last hours of freedom.

As she padded to the stairs, she could hear Miles's voice. He was talking to someone and Louisa wondered whether Hugh had come through to the house. She skipped down the stairs and came to an abrupt halt. There, casually sitting at the breakfast bar, drinking a glass of water and shirtless, was Sting.

Miles caught sight of her and blasted her with his all-American wide smile, momentarily eclipsing the megastar sitting comfortably on the bar stool. "Look who ran into – literally."

Sting looked up to where Louisa stood stunned, then immediately rose up from his seat and held out his hand. "Lady Blackthorn, it's a pleasure to meet you," he said in that familiar husky tilt of his.

Louisa managed to snap out of her daze and stepped towards the pop star to shake his hand. "I'm very pleased to meet you too, Mr Sumner," clicking herself into the well-practised role of the Countess of Holmwood. She suddenly became very aware of the cool granite under her bare feet.

"I was just explaining about the CASPO concert. I was running along the beach and there he was," Miles explained, holding out his hand in invitation for her to take – and she was never more grateful for something to hold onto.

"Oh, I see," she managed to squeeze out as she took her seat next to her pop idol, and he followed suit. *What were the odds?*

"I've heard a lot about your charity."

Louisa tried her hardest to keep her attention to his face but she was still reeling that her teenage crush was sitting at the breakfast bar, shirtless, discussing CASPO's concert as though this was an everyday occurrence. *Why did all the men in LA run shirtless?* she thought fleetingly. Miles did a brilliant job of explaining how the concert idea had come about and who TuKon and he had already managed to get commitments from. By the time Sting had left, he was also on board, and promised to ask some of his artist friends too.

Throughout the whole short visit, Louisa politely listened, occasionally commenting, giving an outward appearance of calm, but Miles knew she was awestruck. He did his best at keeping the light conversation flowing – something he was used to doing, but once the pop star bade them goodbye and jogged down the stairs back on to the beach, Louisa turned to an amused Miles.

"You know him?" She glared at him.

"He has a house about a mile up the beach." Miles jerked his chin in the direction Sting was running.

"All this time, when you've mentioned him, you didn't think to tell me?" she said incredulously.

"We're not best buddies. He uses the studio sometimes and I see him around."

"But you know Sting," she said with disbelief.

"You're not going to embarrass me are you? Going all fangirl on me?" Miles teased, pulling her into his arms.

"Oh, you're hilarious," she said, narrowing her eyes at him, and he laughed. "You bumped into him, just like that?" Her voice rose a little.

"This is Malibu. You can't not run into someone famous."

"You could've warned me."

"What, and miss that look on your face? It was priceless." Louisa made a frustrated noise and tried to struggle out of his hold, which only made Miles laugh. He tightened his arms and planted a hard kiss on her lips. "Worth it, though. He's going to be at the concert."

"I suppose so," she conceded, stifling a grin and pulling herself away from him.

"Suppose? Are you playing it cool, Lady Blackthorn? I just snagged your teenage crush for our concert," he said following her into the house.

"Who said it was just a *teenage* crush? He looks good for a man in his 60s," she said nonchalantly and Miles growled, running up behind her and swooping her in his arms, causing Louisa to squeal.

"Take that back," he said marching towards the pool as she squirmed.

"I take it back!" she laughed.

Miles stopped at the edge of the pool and took in her stunning, flushed face. "God, I'm going to miss this," he said earnestly, then kissed her deeply.

"Me too. Let's skip making breakfast."

"Breakfast is overrated." He grinned, then carried her back to bed.

MILES STARED OUT OF the 51st-floor windows that overlooked Central Park. The sun was still high enough to radiate its scorching heat – not that Miles could feel it. The presidential suite at the Four Seasons was set at a comfortable 20 degrees. There were no blue skies in New York in the summer; it was always tinged with the watery grey humidity that hung in the air. On a good day it was uncomfortable but on a bad day, like today, it was stifling. It had been 18 hours since he'd said goodbye to Louisa as she walked into the Mark Hotel last night, flanked by Hugh and Pierce, but it felt like days. He'd have to wait almost another 18 hours before they would be both boarding their plane back to London. The half a mile they were apart may as well have been 10,000. To be this close to each other but still apart seemed like the worst kind of torture.

As if that wasn't bad enough, Louisa would be in the company of her suave and sophisticated ex-husband for the majority of that time. The man was devious and Miles disliked everything about him. Gerard knew how to play his role, how to manipulate and use every weapon he had in his extensive arsenal, to chip away at Louisa's defences. On the outside, he was the perfect gentleman, but he couldn't be that perfect if Louisa had left him. Gerard used their 20 years of history and familiarity whenever he could, almost carrying on as though their separation was temporary. His appearance at Holmwood House was proof he still felt he was entitled to the perks he'd married into. He was either thick-skinned or just plain arrogant. Probably both. Miles couldn't wait to leave New York. He wanted to put the thousands of miles between Louisa and Gerard, to keep her close to him and as far as possible from the Frenchman's claws.

Miles checked the time, then held his phone to his ear and waited for his call to connect.

"Hey, baby."

Louisa smiled just from the sound of his voice. "Hey, are you ready to go to the launch?"

"Yeah, I'm hoping they've blasted the air-conditioning; today, it's brutal."

"Yes, New York is not the place to be in the height of summer."

"You okay? How was the meeting?" he asked tentatively. Louisa knew he wasn't asking about the content of the board meeting. This was Miles's tactful way of asking how Gerard had been. She didn't want to talk about her ex, especially not before Miles was due to be at his event.

"Oh, you know, just small talk with the board, a run through of revenue, expenditure, plans for the next year. But that's all boring. I'm dying for you to tell me about *your* meeting. How did it go?" She hoped that the producers were as excited as Miles was and they'd welcome any input he had. He'd dedicated time to the script and Louisa knew he wasn't about to step into a project without being part of the creative process.

"It went well, very well. Eric wasn't joking when he said they wanted me."

"I don't think Eric strikes me as a man who jokes about work."

"No, he isn't, and he was like a shark in the meeting."

"I can see that. He's good to have on your side. So, are you doing it?" she asked hopefully.

"Yeah, I'm doing it, subject to a few conditions." She could hear the smile in his voice.

"That so amazing. Congratulations. Conditions? What kind of conditions have they insisted on?"

"Not them, *me*." He chuckled.

"Oh, wow. It seems that Eric isn't the only shark."

"I learned from the best. I wanted certain things in my contract, aside from the creative input."

"Like what?"

"All rehearsals, coaching and prep will be done in England. I won't work more than 14 days straight, while we're filming on location. I wasn't kidding, Louisa, we will not be apart for that long again."

"Miles." Louisa couldn't believe he was willing to jeopardise a film role if he couldn't be with her.

"You're more important than any work I do. It was non-negotiable. They agreed to it all, even offered to foot the bill of a private jet to take me back and forth, which I said wasn't necessary. I can pay for my own flights." He huffed and Louisa chuckled.

"I love you, Miles."

"I know. I love you too and I know that it's harder for you to juggle your commitments. It's not a job for you – you have a duty and I understand that sometimes that will get in the way."

"Miles... I don't know what to say." She was in awe of how he was always willing to put her first. It was a new experience for her to have that level of understanding.

"I just want you to know that I'm in this for the long haul," he said sincerely.

"Me too. When we get back home, I'm going to make sure we have our time." It was a promise she was determined to keep.

"Just us."

"Just us."

"Now that sounds like a deal to me, my lady," he drawled.

"It does. Signed and sealed," Louisa countered.

"Good. Now tell me more about tonight's benefit."

"Urgh. It will be a boring dinner of benign conversations with donators who just want to say they've had dinner with a countess. I'll be in my room by 10:30," she said with a disdainful sigh.

Miles chuckled at her response. "How was Gerard today?" He tried to sound neutral but he knew Louisa was no fool. It was eating him up she was openly spending time with her ex and she knew it.

"Polite and a perfect gentleman," she said in a matter-of-fact tone, not wanting to waste their call on Gerard.

"So, you'll be going together?"

"He'll be picking me up in an hour." Louisa sighed after a beat, then added, "We're just car-pooling." She hoped it would lighten the mood and was pleased her comment had the desired effect. Miles chuckled at her reference to a conversation right from the beginning of their relationship.

"Is that so?"

"Yes. Don't worry about Gerard, Miles. There's nothing he can to do to me, to us."

"I don't trust him. Sorry, I shouldn't put you in a difficult position, but I need to be honest with you. He knows how to... get to you," he said evenly, worried that he might have overstepped the mark.

"He did, not any more. It's just a dinner. This one is the last event before the concert. Once that's over, we can become public and you can come with me to every boring, stuffy event and partake in small talk."

"You make it sound so appealing; how can I refuse," he said drolly.

The tinkle of her laughter made him grin. He was happy his candid remarks hadn't upset her. "Are you ready for the launch? Surrounded by rich, famous and fashionable people all looking gorgeous?"

"Yeah, I just need to stand around and look pretty."

"And you're so good at that!" she teased and his husky laugh made her stomach clench.

"You're funny for a countess."

"How many countesses do you know?" she chided.

"Three actually," he said with amusement. "But you're definitely my favourite."

"That's because I'm the funniest."

"Of course it is."

FOR THE LAST FOUR hours, Gerard had watched his ex-wife effortlessly charm every one of the many sponsors who had come over to speak to her. She'd been away from New York's society functions for seven months and she'd been missed. There was plenty of glamour in New York and an abundance of obscene wealth that functions such as these depended on. The New York glitterati knew how to razzle-dazzle, how to put on a show better than anything you'd pay to see on Broadway. The "old" money crawled out of their multi-million-dollar properties to pay back to the community, from money they'd probably never worked for. It made them feel worthy, it made them feel better about themselves and it made them above all, look good. These were the elite. But all the money and power they possessed, it paled into insignificance when they were in the company of a countess. There were pieces of furniture in Holmwood House that were older than the country they were born in. Louisa's lineage could be traced back to royalty. She possessed something the uber-rich could never have: class. To have a countess be patron of a charity gave it prestige. For the countess to be present at an event, the sponsors clambered to just be in her presence, as though her pedigree would rub off on them. She was a jewel in the crown and Gerard had underestimated her value both professionally and personally. She was undoubtedly priceless and he'd foolishly let this gem slip through his fingers.

He knew she'd spent four days with Miles. He didn't need to ask how it had gone; it was written all over her face in the tan she sported and the permanent wistful smile on her lips. Their talk at Holmwood had obviously done nothing to deter her and he was impressed with how they'd been able to keep their relationship under the radar. She'd been four days in LA and no one had noticed.

Louisa performed her role impeccably both at the board meeting that afternoon and at the dinner they attended. She knew how important it was for the sponsors to see her. It was all part of the marketing strategy. She thought back to her conversations with Miles about "pimping" him out and realised that she was in fact doing the same and she smiled to herself, thinking he'd get a real kick out of the idea.

"You look amused."

"Do I?" Louisa gave Gerard a puzzled look, then turned her attention back to the room, taking in the dance floor filled with couples that kept purposely dancing past them. She felt like she was part of a freak show. Louisa wasn't sure if they were just in awe of her being back or if they were trying to work out if she and Gerard were together again. On the first count, she didn't really care; she was used to that. On the second one, she thought it was fun to keep them guessing. Gerard had been attentive all evening, being by her side, shadowing her, which must have been a novelty for him and was probably the reason they were getting so many curious looks. No doubt they'd be the centre of all the gossip tomorrow. The New York society blabbermouths would have plenty to talk about at their brunches over the next few days, which was fine by Louisa – she wouldn't be here. "It looks like it's gone well."

"I didn't doubt that it would." Gerard nodded to some billionaire Louisa remembered he'd done business with as he danced with his over-made-up wife. "You were missed. Most of them didn't realise what your title actually meant until your new role at CASPO was announced." He couldn't disguise that it bothered him.

"I lived here for 20 years and no one was that interested in me," Louisa chuckled. She'd always known they'd overlooked her in favour of her debonair and wealthier-than-God husband. Once she'd stepped out of his shadow, though, they buzzed around her like hungry wasps. "Well, at least they dug into their deep pockets for the privilege." Gerard smiled at her dry comment, standing up as she rose from her seat. "If you'll excuse me." He gave her a nod and watched her glide towards the restrooms.

Louisa washed her hands, then opened up her clutch, pulling out her lipstick.

"Hello, Louisa."

Louisa looked up from her bag, hearing a familiar voice. "Oh

Tara, I didn't see you in there. How lovely to see you," Louisa said genuinely surprised to see her family friend. Tara was the oldest child of one of her late father's friends. Her brother Harry and her father had done business with Gerard over the years and Emily McKenzie was her younger sister. Their family had always supported their charity. Louisa gave her a kiss on the cheek. "Are you here with your parents?"

"No, I came with Harry, representing them." Tara gave her a tight smile and added, "They're with Emily."

Louisa grasped Tara's hand and gave it a squeeze. "It must be a very difficult time for all of you." Her concern was genuine and Tara gave her a small nod. "How is she doing?"

"She's getting the help she needs. This was her event. She used to love coming to this, with Gordon."

"I'm so sorry."

Tara gave a sad shrug. "She's always been a handful but I never realised how unhappy she was."

"Well, she's getting the help she needs."

"She is. Let's hope she sticks to it."

"I'm sure she will." Louisa gave her an encouraging smile.

"You know she blames you for everything."

"I didn't know about Gordon. I was over here for 20 years. I hardly saw any of the old crowd," Louisa said, hoping Tara believed her. After all, it was her sister who had lost a baby because she was so distraught after her husband asked for a divorce, and all because he was in love with her. She had every right to be upset.

Tara scanned Louisa's concerned face and gave a nod, satisfied that Louisa was in fact blameless, regardless of her sister's rantings. "I'm a little surprised to see you here."

Louisa knew she thought that since she'd divorced Gerard, she'd also removed herself of her involvement. "I'm on the board; I have duty and I'm happy to fulfil it." Louisa picked up her clutch and affectionately rubbed Tara's arm. "I better get back."

"Of course."

"It was lovely to see you, Tara. Give my best wishes to your parents, Harry and to Emily."

Louisa made her way back to her table in search of Gerard. It had been a long day and she was ready to go back to her hotel room. She had been sociable and talked to all the main sponsors, securing their hefty donations. She'd made her speech and had her picture taken numerous times with every socialite who wanted to show off that they knew the aristocracy. She'd gone over and above her duty and now she was done.

Gerard was talking to a couple but swiftly closed down the conversation when Louisa approached. After 20 years together, he knew that look on her face.

"Ready to go, *cherie*?"

"Yes, I asked Hugh to get the car." Gerard gave a nod, then turned to the couple and bid them goodnight. He guided her up the few stairs to the foyer in plain sight of the whole ballroom, and ushered her into the waiting limo.

"A nightcap, *cherie*?" he asked as they pulled away from the Plaza.

Louisa shook her head. "I'm tired and have a long flight in a few hours."

"You're leaving tomorrow?" Gerard asked, clearly surprised. He'd hoped she would be here for a few more days.

"Yes, I have commitments."

"I was hoping to see you." He tried not to sound annoyed.

"You did."

Her reply was curt and Gerard was caught off-guard. He shuffled closer. "*Cherie...*"

Before he could say anything else, Louisa dropped down the glass partition. "Any calls, Hugh?"

Hugh knew this was her code for asking after Miles. "Just one, my lady, 20 minutes ago." Louisa smiled to herself and Gerard instantly knew the call was from Miles.

"So, you're still seeing the American?"

Louisa's eyes shot to his and she answered. "Are you still seeing... well, whoever you're seeing at the moment?"

He sucked on his teeth and straightened. "Still seeing him in secret?" he said with more than a hint of mockery.

"It's not that hard to do Gerard, as you well know. You managed to keep all your liaisons secret and you were married," she countered; she wasn't in the mood for his criticisms. He'd lost that right a long time ago.

"They –"

She cut him off before he could use his well-versed excuse. "They meant nothing; I know you told me. But they meant something to me. I'm not rehashing this same argument," she said with a shake of her head. He wasn't going to get to her, not again, not ever.

"You think you can keep the American?" he challenged her, trying to tap into her insecurities.

She shifted around to face him and tilted her head to the side. "Maybe you should be asking whether the American can keep me."

"YOU'RE IN EVERY GOSSIP, magazine and newspaper site." Louisa pored over the pictures of Miles standing next to an array of models, TV stars and sports people. They'd boarded the first-class cabin and were settled in their private seats. She swiped through her iPad, reading every article, while Miles read through the script again. The event looked far more exciting than the dinner she'd attended – no stuffy businessmen and their wives in sight. Louisa watched the advert, which was now uploaded, and some video footage that had been put up on the various sites of the event. Miles look gorgeous in a sand-coloured linen suit and black shirt. The few days they'd spent at his beach house had brought out new natural highlights in his hair and made his blue eyes pop against his golden tan. Every pose was magazine worthy; he was a natural and the camera loved him.

"Stop looking at them all." Miles rolled his eyes.

"I wanted to see how it went."

"I told you. I just walked around and looked pretty. They played the advert, unveiled the range of watches, then I posed for pictures and made small talk. Eric did a great job of schmoozing, though."

"As he should," Louisa said wryly, putting her iPad down, and Miles chuckled.

"Exactly. They gave me one of each design for me to wear for the next six months. It's in the contract." He lifted up the sleeve of his shirt to reveal a sleek black and gold watch.

"Oooh, that's nice." Louisa took his arm and examined the designer timepiece.

"Yeah, it's pretty cool. There are another four designs." Louisa widened her eyes, clearly impressed. "I asked them if they'd be interested in sponsoring the concert."

"You did? And?"

"They said they'd let me know." He gave her a sexy wink and she grinned at him. Then, remembering where they were, they pulled back and checked the other passengers. Thankfully, no one could see them in the enclosed adjoining pods. "Once we do the press conference, they'll say yes. It'll be great international exposure."

"Eric really is rubbing off on you."

"I'd rather you were rubbing off on me," he said, raising his eyebrows lewdly at her, and she giggled. "I might insist on a private jet from now on, with a bedroom." He picked up her hand and gave it a kiss, keeping his eyes on her.

"Read your script, pretty boy," Louisa said with a grin and he blasted her with his smile.

"Yes, my lady."

"EVERYTHING ALRIGHT, HUGH?" Louisa took one look at his furrowed brow and knew something was wrong. They'd landed over 20 minutes ago but had yet to disembark. Pierce was standing by them as the few first-class passengers left the cabin.

Hugh leaned down to where Louisa and Miles were. "There's a number of reporters in the arrivals lounge. It seems word got out that Mr Keane is arriving back today."

Miles muttered a curse under his breath. "Probably from some journo at the launch."

"That's my guess." Hugh lifted his phone to his ear and listened to whoever was talking, then thanked them. He quickly gave some hushed instructions to Pierce, then turned back to Louisa and Miles. "I've organised for another car to take you, my lady." Louisa furrowed her brow. Their plan had been to leave in the same car. "The reporters have already spotted our car and are loitering by it. If you both get in it, they'll know you were on the same flight…" Hugh didn't need to explain further. The press would put two and two together and the proverbial cat would be out of the bag.

"Oh right, yes, of course."

"How many reporters are we talking?" asked Miles.

"My guess, around 20."

"Jesus." Miles scrubbed his hand over his face. What a nightmare. He'd been used to fan hysteria when he was at the height of his fame and then later, he was constantly hounded by the press. Since moving to England, he'd mainly been out of the limelight until he joined CASPO but even then, the press had been respectful. Now it seemed he was open for business again. He reached over and took hold of Louisa's hand and gave it a squeeze.

"Normally, Lady Blackthorn would disembark first. But I think it might be better if Mr Keane gets off beforehand." Miles furrowed his brow in confusion. "We need a diversion," Hugh explained.

"Oh, I'm the bait?"

Hugh gave him an apologetic look. "So we can make a quick escape, unseen."

"Oh no. He can't go out there alone," Louisa protested.

"I've three men from security out front for him, my lady, and Pierce will get him out of there." Hugh turned to Miles. "I need ten minutes to get Lady Blackthorn out and into the other car."

"Oh, good God." Louisa lifted herself out of her chair, appalled that Miles would have to face a gaggle of reporters.

"Hopefully we'll slip out unnoticed. As far as I'm aware, they don't know you're on the flight, my lady."

"Okay, ten minutes. I can distract the vultures for that," Miles said, getting up and slipping on his jacket.

"This is awful," Louisa said, looking at Miles.

He rounded the chairs and pulled her into his arms. "I'll do whatever it takes. I don't want you getting any exposure. Remember, I'm used to this shit." He kissed the top of her head, then bobbed down. "From now on, we need to work on keeping us as separate as possible." Louisa gave him a nod and sighed. "Okay, Pierce, let's do this."

Pierce and Hugh exchanged a few words, then Pierce lead Miles out of the cabin. Louisa waited impatiently while Hugh kept tabs on Miles's progress and with the security waiting outside. As soon as he was told that Miles had passed through passport control, he guided Louisa out of the plane. Most of the first-class passengers had moved through the baggage claim, so Hugh quickly collected Louisa's and his bags, placing them on the trolley. Louisa took the trolley from his hands – there was no way he could push it and shield her at the same time.

"Put your sunglasses on," he said softly and Louisa nodded, slipping them on. Hugh positioned himself at her side and spoke quietly into his sleeve as his eyes scanned the corridors leading to the arrivals lounge.

The loud sound of chatter caused Louisa to flinch and Hugh's eyes darted to the far end of the corridor.

"This way, my lady." He gently but firmly guided her through the automatic doors and they were faced with cameras flashing and questions being bombarded. At first, Louisa's step faltered, thinking their plan hadn't worked, but when she felt Hugh pushed her with more force, she realised the attention was directed at Miles. She kept her head down and scuttled towards the outer door.

"Mr Keane, are you recording again?"

"Miles, how was the watch launch?"

"Mr Keane, were you on holiday?"

"Miles, were you alone?"

"Miles, will you be presenting any more shows?"

The questions came as thick and fast as the flash bulbs exploding in Miles's face. He tried not to flinch and felt genuinely sorry for Pierce and the three other security who got the brunt of the attention. Miles pushed his trolley forward with a fixed smile on his face, not wanting anyone to realise how rattled he was. He could feel the sweat prickling at the back of his neck.

The rest of the people in the arrivals lounge had now joined the reporters and from 20, the crowd had grown to at least 50. Phones were being held up as his entrance to London Heathrow was recorded. In all the chaos, Miles managed to catch a glimpse of Hugh ushering Louisa towards the doors and he sighed to himself. *Nearly there.* Behind his sunglasses, he watched her approach the exit but then a single reporter, who'd obviously gotten wind of the story late, rushed in and came face to face with her. Hugh expertly blocked his view and manoeuvred the trolley out the door, but the reporter stopped for a moment and glanced back at them. It wouldn't take him much to work out who she was.

Before he could think his actions through, Miles stopped pushing his trolley and took off his sunglasses. "Good afternoon. This is quite a welcoming committee." He smiled widely at the stunned crowd and for a nanosecond, everyone ceased what they were saying or doing and focused on Miles Keane. The reporter at the door instantly forgot about the mystery woman and ran to where the 50-strong crowd were. The questions started again but with less urgency, now that Miles had stopped in front of them.

"How was LA?"

"How was the filming?"

"When is the series aired?"

Miles put up his hand in a silent request for some quiet. "LA was very hot and very productive." The crowd laughed as the clicking and the flashes kept going off. "I can't say more than that." There was a collective moan, but Miles continued. "But rest assured, the network will be putting out a statement very shortly." The chatter rose again and Miles put his sunglasses back on again. He checked the exit and saw Louisa's car had already left. "Now if you don't mind, I'd like to get home and rest after my long flight. Thank you all for your time."

He nodded to Pierce and the security cleared the way for him to push his trolley through.

"Did she get away okay?" he asked once they were in the car.

"Yes, sir."

He pulled out his phone and dialled her number. "Baby?"

"I'm so sorry you had to do that." He could tell she was shaken.

"Louisa, I told you I'll do whatever it takes to protect you."

"Still, it was awful."

"Part and parcel of my world. I've been through worse," he drawled, making light of what had been a stressful situation, for Louisa's benefit. He wiped the sweat from his hands on his trousers and pinched the bridge of his nose. In the past, he'd normally had the band with him, or Eric, and at least six security, but today he'd felt alone. His eyes caught sight of Pierce, who gave him a sympathetic look. Miles had never been more grateful of Hugh's overbearing security team.

"I'll come and see you tomorrow."

"Let's see what's waiting for me when I get home. I have a feeling there'll be some unwanted visitors outside my house," Miles said with a sigh.

"Hugh just told me there are."

"Awesome. What a welcome back."

34

SECRET RENDEZVOUS

MELISSA HUFFED AS SHE scrolled through various photos that had popped up on the many gossip sites. Miles Keane was front stage and centre again, landing in London with a bang. Melissa could only feel for him and her dear friend. She knew what this meant for them; no more clandestine dates at his home. He looked good, though, and he played the press perfectly. Melissa had grown very fond of the ex-pop star and in awe of how smoothly he handled obstacles. Thankfully, no one had picked up that Lady Blackthorn was also on the trans-Atlantic flight. She had to hand it to Hugh, he knew how to think on his feet. Melissa looked at the time and shifted a little to get comfortable. Three days of being cooped up in her house with her feet up was making her go stir crazy. To make it worse, Robert was hovering and if he didn't back off, she was going to throw her camomile tea at his head. There was so much to do and she was lying down under the strict instructions of her doctor. When the bell rang, she lifted herself up.

"Don't move, I'll get it," Robert called from the hallway and she huffed again. He seemed to always be around at the right time.

"Louisa, thank goodness you're back," Melissa said as her friend bent down to kiss her.

"How are you feeling?"

"I'm fine." Melissa waved her hand dismissively.

"She's not. Her blood pressure is still up," Robert chipped in and Melissa glared at him.

"That's because I'm worried about the office and who's dealing with it all!"

"Well I'm here now and that means I'll be dealing with it, so you can relax," Louisa said gently, giving Robert a sympathetic smile. He looked worried sick and her friend was only making things worse by being so bad tempered.

"You must be exhausted. You didn't need to come here straight away."

"Of course I did." Louisa darted her eyes to Robert. "Any chance of a cup of tea?"

"I'll get Gwen to organise it," he said taking his cue to leave.

"And get some cake. We can't have tea without cake," Melissa said, her tone decidedly warmer. Robert nodded and left the two of them to catch up.

"Miles made quite an entrance. I've been trolling the Internet. You'll be pleased to know there was nothing about you."

"Well that's a relief." Louisa settled back into the comfortable armchair next to the couch.

"So, tell me all about LA, and what's all this about Sting?!" Melissa couldn't contain her excitement. They'd both been huge fans through their teenage years and for a few moments, Louisa felt they'd been transported back to their time in Holmwood, listening to their CDs and dancing around her room.

Louisa gave Melissa a condensed version of her time in LA and brought her up to speed on the bands Miles had managed to secure for the concert. With the bands Konran had also managed to get signed up, they had a total of 15, which was more than enough to fill the seven hours.

Alistair was well on the way to organising the logistics of the concert. Holmwood House had hosted concerts in the past, so it wasn't uncharted territory, even if the timeline was a little tight.

"Here he is, the star of the show! And he brought cake." Melissa beamed and Louisa shifted round, only to be faced with the impossibly handsome Miles carrying a large box. Every time she saw him, it felt like sucker punch. His bright gaze made her heart pound and it took all her self-control not to get up and run to him. It had only been 12 hours since she'd seen him last but he had fast developed into a delicious habit she was addicted to. The thought of not spending time with him whenever she wanted depressed her. With the renewed media interest, their difficult situation was bordering on the impossible.

He lazily made his way to Melissa and kissed her cheek. "Éclairs, actually. How are you?" He couldn't disguise his concern.

"Oh, I'm fine," Melissa said lightly, which earned her another muttering of disapproval from Robert, who had followed Miles in.

Once Gwen, Melissa's housekeeper, had set down the tray of tea, Miles turned his attention to Louisa. He bent down and gave her an unhurried kiss. "Hey baby, how are you?"

"Better now."

He blasted her with his mega-watt smile. "Me too." Miles was glad they could be themselves around Melissa and Robert. Miles perched himself on the arm of her chair and took Louisa's hand, needing the contact. His home had felt so empty last night. He'd gotten used to having Louisa around and he even missed having the constant presence of Hugh. What made matters worse was he knew that things wouldn't be changing in the near future. They'd have to steal moments together and the thought of having even more restrictions made him feel wretched.

"How's it back at yours?" Louisa asked, while Robert busied himself pouring the tea.

"A nightmare. Though thankfully they didn't follow me. Hugh wants to assign me a team."

"I know, he told me."

"It's going to get worse when the show goes on air." He blew out a breath. The last thing he wanted was to go back to the life of being under a microscope, but at least he knew what to expect and at least Amanda and the children were far enough away.

"When's that?" Melissa asked, cutting through her éclair that Robert had handed her.

"Mid-September."

"It's all over the Internet." Melissa pursed her lips and sighed.

"Yeah, among other things," Miles said dryly. He'd tried not to look at the articles that described him as one-time bad-boy, drug addict pop star. He'd searched online to make sure Louisa hadn't been spotted and had inevitably seen articles on himself. Louisa gave his hand a squeeze and he lifted it to his lips.

"Okay, enough chit chat." Melissa put down her plate and rubbed her hands together, all business now. "The press conference. We're going to do it at the Four Seasons, seeing as it's not far from the offices. We've sent out a press release and it will be by invitation only."

"How does that work?" Miles asked.

"Various media networks, publications et cetera, ask to be present, and then we send them invitations. They've gone out and most have replied. There will be almost 50. It's going to be quite a circus," she said with an apologetic smile.

"Sounds delightful." Robert rolled his eyes and Miles chuckled. He'd grown to like Melissa's unassuming husband.

"There will be you two, obviously, plus Joel – he can handle the financial questions, and Darcy, who's in charge of the press office. Konran can't fly in for it but he will pre-record his statement and we will play it. Then we will allow a few questions. It should be over in 20 minutes. Then the real work starts.

Tickets will be available a month before the date on our official website only."

"How many?" Louisa asked.

"Alistair says 50,000."

Miles let out a low whistle. "Wow."

"Of course, the revenue of the tickets will be a huge amount, over five million. But it's more about the exposure and the potential of new sponsors that want to be part of the concert and then part of CASPO. I predict we'll double that."

"Anyone showed an interest so far?" Miles asked.

Melissa gave them a huge smile and reached for her laptop. "Not all of us have been sunning ourselves by the pool. Here, let me show you who's asked to sponsor."

For the next hour, Melissa, Miles and Louisa went through the various requests while Robert kept watchful eye on his animated wife.

"MY LADY." Louisa looked up from her computer and waved Hugh to come in.

"Come in. Sit down."

Hugh gave a curt nod and settled into the seat opposite her desk. "I just wanted to inform you that I've assigned Pierce to Mr Keane. There will also be another two members of our team as back up, Karl and Kurt."

"Oh right. Well, that makes sense. Miles seemed to like Pierce. How did he take it?"

"Mr Keane has been very understanding." He answered with wry smile.

"Well, I think his history has a lot to do with it."

"Maybe, but I think there's more to it than that." Hugh said with an arch of his brow. Louisa circled her hand in the air, indicating he should explain. "He knows this is important to you, madame."

Louisa pursed her lips and nodded. "It's going to get worse," she said with a sigh.

"I'm afraid it is." Hugh paused for a beat, then added, "You might need to take control of the situation."

"You mean become public?" Her trusted bodyguard gave her a sympathetic look, knowing this was something she was trying to put off. "Then it really will be a circus."

"Yes, but at least you'll be in that circus together and be the ringmaster. The concert is six weeks away." Louisa understood the hidden meaning in his statement. *Could they really do this for another six weeks?*

"It is a strain." Louisa slumped back in her chair. A strain was putting it lightly. She was used to it, but Miles might grow weary of it and he'd be right to.

"On both of you," Hugh said gently, confirming her fears. Her eyes shot up to his. Hugh had always been perceptive; it was part and parcel of his job. If he thought they should hurry along with becoming public, he had good reason and she'd be foolish not to listen.

"Okay, let's get this press conference out of the way at the end of the week. We can see when's the best time to come out, as it were. I think the network are releasing the dates for when the shows Miles is presenting are aired next week. So maybe after that?" She tilted her head at him and he gave her a nod.

"I think it's best."

MILES LOOKED AT THE feed from the security cameras. There were just two photographers out on the opposite side of the street. With any luck, they'd realise he wasn't going anywhere tonight and leave. The low rumble of Pierce's voice as he talked to one of the team Hugh had assigned to him caught his attention. He had three baby sitters. *Three.* He shook his head and pinched the bridge of his nose. Hugh was being overly cautious after the airport incident and Miles couldn't really blame him; it had rattled him too, but he'd learned how to cover it, years of experience. At the height of Keane Sense's fame, he'd had to deal with far worse. The band had had a team of ten security around them when they were out in public, to keep fans and reporters at bay, and they still seemed to get mauled. After the shooting, the fans had respected his privacy, but the reporters and paparazzi just became even more ruthless. His public meltdown only fuelled them, leading to his decision to leave the US and go practically into hiding. With any luck it would all blow over soon, like it did then, and he wouldn't feel as though he was a prisoner in his own home. Miles picked up his phone and dialled Amanda. He needed to see her and the children before they left for their holiday, and to pick up Duke. He'd missed them all, including Duke. The little guy was his sole company when he was at home.

Grace and Louis gave Miles a full rundown of Duke's antics over the three weeks he'd been away. Amanda managed to wrestle the phone from them and send them off so she could finally get to speak.

"They're so excited," Miles chuckled.

"Yeah, they missed you. This is the longest you've been away."

"I know, the downside of working again. Anyway, I thought I'd come up the day after tomorrow to see you guys and pick up Duke."

After a beat, Amanda answered. "I'm going to Holmwood the day after tomorrow."

"Oh. Care to elaborate?" Miles couldn't hide his amusement.

"Alistair invited us, seeing as we're leaving for LA," Amanda said carefully, and Miles realised from her tone she was nervous.

"I see."

"Maybe we could meet there," she suggested in a rush. Miles's instant thoughts went to a possible rendezvous with Louisa. It would be the perfect location, away from prying eyes. He just hoped Louisa could get away.

"Umm, sure, that could work. So, you've been in touch with Alistair, then?"

"Yes, just as friends," she added quickly.

"It's okay for you to find someone, Amanda."

"I know, it's just..."

"You feel guilty." He finished her sentence, knowing exactly how she felt. She'd been through so much, handled it all with dignity, supported him, his parents and brought up to perfect children. She had no reason to ever feel guilty. She was a hero in his eyes and he would be forever grateful for her being in his life at his worst and at his best. If anyone deserved a second chance at happiness, it was Amanda. Her selflessness knew no bounds and the thought of her feeling guilty for allowing herself to feel again broke Miles's heart. "Louis wouldn't want you to not go on with your life. You'll never forget him; he'll be part of all your lives, even Louis Junior's. We all love you, no matter what. You've *nothing* to feel guilty about."

"That goes for you too."

Miles smiled, even now she was thinking about him. "I'm working on it."

He heard her sniff and he squeezed his eyes shut, his heart breaking for her. Miles knew it was hard for her to admit she was taking a step forward, she didn't owe anyone an explanation, least of all him. He took a deep breath and did what he did best, diffuse the emotional air with a light hearted distraction. "Want to hear some exciting news?" he said playfully.

"Do I ever!"

"I got offered a film role."

"No way, that's amazing! What kind of film?"

Miles grinned to himself. She was excited, just like he knew she would be. "To play Chet Baker in his life story."

"Oh, Miles." He could hear the reverence in her voice, she knew what this meant to him.

"Yeah, I know, right? Totally your fault."

"Mine, how?"

Miles proceeded to tell her about how the film had been in the making for a while and Eric knew about it but the producers just couldn't cast the lead. "You sent that video to Eric and he showed it to the producers."

"Oh my god! But Chet Baker… I mean, you and Louis idolised him." He could visualise her animated face and feel how genuinely thrilled she was for him. It was infectious and for the first time since the film part had been offered, Miles realised just what a big deal this was for him.

"Yeah, I think they offered it to me because he was a drug addict, loser trumpet player… so I'm basically playing myself… no acting skills required," he said drolly.

"Miles, you're not any of those things, except for the trumpet player part anyway," she said with a chuckle but she knew there was some underlying insecurity in the way he joked. "Are you going to do it?"

"Yeah, I mean how could I not? It's Chet Baker and… well, if Louis was here, he'd kick my ass if I didn't."

Amanda laughed at his smart-aleck remark. "If Louis was here, he'd be playing him," she countered.

"No way! He'd never have acted in a film," he said in good humour.

"I know you're right. He left all that glam shit up to you. You're the pretty one and he was the brains." Amanda laughed and Miles joined her.

"Oooh, low blow!"

"Yeah it was, but seriously, Miles, that's amazing. You'll be great. Believe it to achieve it, Miles," she said with conviction.

"Yeah, that's what I keep saying to myself."

HOLMWOOD HOUSE ROSE UP on the horizon as Miles drove up the wide road lined with mature trees. It was his second visit to the house and he was caught off-guard at the sight of the extensive grounds filled with visitors, taking in the glorious surroundings of the grand stately home. It was the middle of summer and Holmwood House's busiest time. For some reason, Miles had forgotten that Holmwood was an attraction as well as Louisa's home, and he wondered whether it had been a good idea for them to meet here with so many people around. Louisa hadn't seemed concerned, or at least she hadn't voiced them when they'd made the arrangements. She'd only stipulated that he arrived early afternoon.

Pierce caught his worried expression in the wind mirror. "We'll be let in around the back, sir. There's a private entrance."

"Oh right, okay. I was wondering. It's pretty busy."

"Holmwood House is very popular. The earl has done a grand job of preserving his heritage and making it pay its way."

"I can see." Miles scanned the grounds, seeing various activities set up for the visitors. There was something for everyone, from boating on the lake to horse riding. There were games of croquet, giant chess, boules as well as a section for archery set up. Visitors sprawled on the vibrant green lawns on blankets, taking in the sun and enjoying their picnics. There were various refreshments stands and the old dairy had been converted into a café. It looked nothing like it had done when Miles was here last. It made him appreciate how much work had gone into transforming the grounds for the weekend.

A large solid double gate opened around the west wing of the house, letting Pierce drive through along with the second car with Karl and Kurt, the other two security men assigned to Miles.

They all headed to a highly polished black door where Pierce looked into an intercom. The door unlocked and they all filed into a small vestibule.

"If you go up those stairs, it will bring you up to Lady Alice's wing. At the top turn, left through the archway and you'll enter the top floor of the main house. Lady Blackthorn is in her suite. She's expecting you, sir."

"Oh right. You're not coming with me?" Miles asked.

"No sir, Hugh wants a debrief. You're both safe and private up there." Pierce shifted his eyes towards the staircase.

"And Alistair?"

"He's with Mrs Keane and the children. Once the house closes at 18:00 hours, you'll all meet for dinner." Pierce gave him a wide smile and a nod.

"Right. Well, see you later then," Miles said, a little bewildered but happy all the same. It would be good to be without a shadow for a while.

Miles reached the top of the staircase and took the left archway. Once he'd passed through, he recognised the wide passageway with various doors along it. Louisa's suite was in the centre. He stood outside the heavy wooden double doors and wondered whether he needed to knock. He chuckled to himself. They'd spent four days practically naked in LA; he was definitely beyond knocking on the door. He grasped the ornate handle and pushed open the door.

Louisa was sitting at her antique desk typing away on her computer. The moment the door opened her eyes shot up and locked onto his bright blues. He was breathtaking in his dark blue trousers and light blue shirt, and he'd rolled up the sleeves, showing off his tanned, toned forearms.

"I need a map," he said with a smirk, closing the door. He flicked the lock and gave her a sexy wink. Louisa was out of her chair and stepping towards him as he hastened their contact in two long strides, both of them eager to be in each other's arms. Miles grazed his knuckles across her cheek and then branded his lips to hers. He'd missed her but until that moment, he hadn't realised how much. Her presence brought something to him that he'd never had before, but now missed it when they were apart. It was a mixture of peace and fulfilment and at the same time, he had the compelling desire to protect and cherish her. A chaotic mix of emotions shot through him whenever he was with her or when she was in his thoughts, and every time they parted, it became so much harder.

"Sorry for all the cloak and dagger," Louisa sighed. "It's just –"

"I don't care. I get to be with you, alone." He wrapped his arms around her, holding her close, letting her scent and touch calm him. "How long do we have?"

"Until dinner at seven."

"Three hours should be long enough."

Louisa giggled, then toed off her shoes. "Let's not waste any more time, then." She looked up into his eyes and saw her desire reflected back at her.

"You won't get an argument from me." In one swift movement, Miles bent down and hoisted her over his shoulder. She let out a soft yelp and he marched straight to the bedroom.

"I could've walked," she said as her head swung over the top of his trousers, giving her an up close and personal view of his tight behind.

"Where's the fun in that?"

He let her down by the bed. Her hair all messed up, her dress a little askew and her face flushed from being upside down. She beamed up at him and his heart tightened. This was the Louisa he loved: sexy, playful and a little bit dishevelled because of him. He roughed up those smooth edges, smudged those fine lines that her impeccable breeding had given her. He was the only one who saw her like this and he loved her even more for allowing him to.

"Are you going to stand there and just look at me?" she said in that mock-clipped tone that never failed to turn him on.

"Just admiring the view," he drawled in his American accent and she instantly heated under the blaze of his molten gaze.

"Then I'd better give you some more to look at." Louisa gave him a gentle shove and he fell back onto her huge bed.

"You won't hear any complaints from me, my lady," he said, placing his hands behind his head as she started to unbutton the front of her casual shirt dress. Her confidence was totally captivating. Never had a woman who had been so gentle become so alluring. She was bold but not aggressive, soft but not a pushover and when they were together like this, just the two of them, she was everything he could ever want and so much more.

Louisa let her dress slide off her shoulders and drop to the floor. Miles instantly sat up and reached for her hips, drawing her to him. "God, you're so fucking beautiful." His voice hoarse with desire.

"Miles." His name a soft plea. The way he looked at her always floored her. Whether they were in a room full of people or alone, he looked at her as though she was the most precious thing in the world. He planted open-mouthed kisses across her stomach, leaving a trail of goose bumps in their wake. She took in a shuddery breath and speared her fingers into his thick hair. "I need you."

"I'm here, baby." Miles ran his fingers around the lace of her panties and swept them down her legs. In one fluid movement he lifted her, then placed her on the bed. He blanketed her body with his, taking her lips in a bone-melting kiss. He loved kissing her, the intimacy of it, the small delicate moans she let out and the way their lips moved so perfectly together in the most erotic of dances. Miles pulled away, leaving her breathless, like he always did.

"Let me taste you." He pinned her with his gaze as he slowly moved down her trembling body, ridding her of her bra as he went. She moaned as his lips explored every dip and every curve, until he reached the apex of her thighs.

Miles's eyes lazily closed at the first taste. She was like a rare delicacy, an elixir he was more than happy to get drunk on. "You're delicious," he murmured as his ardent mouth worked her over. She writhed beneath him but he gently steadied her, holding her hips until she cried out her climax.

"Jesus, Miles," she gasped. He kissed the inside of her thigh, then reluctantly pulled himself away so that her could rid himself of his shirt.

"I just can't get enough of you," he said, shuffling out of the rest of his clothes and shoes, leaving them in a heap on top of his shirt. He lowered himself over her, holding her captive with his body. "I love you," he said earnestly. "I hate being away from you. I want us to be like this every day."

Louisa stared into his stunning face, floored by his honestly, and felt herself fall even more in love with him. He was everything she shouldn't like in a man: cocky, a player, uncomfortably candid and a little bit unrefined. He was her little bit of rough and a match no one could ever have predicted, yet here they were, wrapped in each other's arms, totally and completely in love. He brought out her true self, the fun-loving, sexy self that had been hidden under layers of impeccable manners and cultivated restraint. With him she was free in every sense of the word, free to feel, do and be whoever she wanted to be. His love was the key that opened up her gilded cage and let her spread her trapped wings.

"I love you too, Miles, and I swear we will have this soon."

"Just us."

"Just us," she said emphatically.

He kissed her again, taking her breath away again, then with a deliberate thrust, Miles sank deep into her. He let out a tormented groan, feeling every part of her tighten around him like a vice.

"You're perfect baby, so fucking perfect." He pulled out, then slowly ground back into her, in a deliberate, unhurried rhythm that caused her to arch into him. Their pants and groans filled the stately bedroom as they edged closer to their release. Their bodies fused together as the light of the afternoon sun filtered across the bed, capturing the beads of sweat that had gathered on Miles's brow. They climaxed at the same time in a fiery burst, their lips locked together and their limbs intertwined.

"Wow," Miles croaked.

"That was..."

"Mind-blowing." He blew out a breath, then gave her that dazzling smile that lit up a whole room. She grinned back at him and pushed back the lock of hair that had fallen over his forehead.

"It was."

He closed his eyes and rested his forehead against hers, sighing as she played with his hair.

"I don't want to move."

"I don't want you to move."

She couldn't see his grin but she felt it. "Good, I'll just stay where I am then." He flexed his hips and she giggled.

The sound of people chattering and laughing drifted through the slightly open window, bringing them back to reality. Miles rolled onto his side, taking Louisa with him, still not wanting to break their connection. Miles's eyes drifted to the window. "I didn't realise how busy it would be."

"Yes, it's our peak time here," Louisa sighed.

"I was worried until Pierce told me there was a private entrance." He widened his eyes and mock-grimaced.

Louisa chuckled. "That's the only secluded entrance. Once you're up here, though, it's totally private."

"Your house is huge. I forget how big it is and that it's all yours. Your life is another world."

"Too much?" she asked softly.

"Yeah, but I'm getting used it. At least we have some times when it's just us." He playfully nuzzled her neck, causing her to squirm.

"I think I prefer being at your house," she said wistfully.

"Yeah?"

"Yeah, all that walking around practically naked. *I* could get used to that." Her eyes twinkled at him as her fingers gently drifted over the nape of his neck like a summer breeze. Miles captured her lips and kissed her deeply.

"God, I love you, Louisa."

"I love you too."

"SOMEHOW I THOUGHT YOU all got dressed up for dinner." Miles tucked in his fresh shirt, eyeing Louisa in the mirror.

"We do when we have official occasions but otherwise, we keep it simple. My father always liked to be informal. It's not like Downtown Abbey, you know." She arched her brow at him as she slicked on her lipstick.

"Eh, it kind of is, sometimes. All those rooms with fancy titles."

"Well our *casual* family dinner will be in Mama's wing. Drinks in her drawing room at seven."

Miles smirked and pointed at her. "See, right there: *drawing* room in your mother's *wing*."

"It's just another name for a living room and side of the house." Louisa chuckled, standing up from her seat. She was teasing him and he knew it.

"It's a lot different to the dinner we had with my parents," he huffed.

"Yes, at least my family know who you are, and you have Amanda on your side," Louisa said wryly.

"That's not what I meant and you know it." He shook his head, chuckling at her feigning to not understand what he meant. A casual dinner at Holmwood was streets away from a casual dinner in Malibu. "Though I'm pretty intrigued at the whole earl and my sister-in-law dynamic." He widened his eyes.

"Are you worried?"

"No, not at all. I really like your brother." His answer completely genuine and Louisa let out a breath in relief.

"Good, because this is the first woman he's ever shown any interest in since his accident."

"Really?"

"Uhuh."

"He's very… un-earl-like." Louisa furrowed her brow at his comment. Miles had seen photographs of Louisa's father in the press and around the house. He was always dressed smartly, with his hair cut short and clean shaven. "He was in the military, yet he has a beard and has long hair. I've only seen him in long trousers at the dinner over the activities weekend."

Louisa nodded. "He has a beard to cover up the burn scars on his face. His hair is long because it covers up a nasty scar above his left ear. As for the shorts…" Louisa gave an awkward shrug. "He'd rather people see his blade than try and speculate about it. Especially at the beginning. He found it hard to move around, so rather than let people think he was clumsy or useless, he had it on show."

"Oh right, I didn't know." Miles's admiration for the reluctant war hero hiked up even further.

"But other than that, he's very much like Papa." Louisa smoothed down her white silk dress and slipped on her nude heels. "He was devastated he couldn't have children. It took him a while to come to terms with it. Thankfully, he was close to Celeste."

"Is that why he's never been interested in dating?"

Louisa twisted her lips and nodded. "It's hard enough when you've got a title and you're somewhat well known. The women who were 'suitable' weren't interested once they knew. The ones that were not so suitable were interested only in his title and wealth. So, it was easier for him to become a recluse and throw all his energy into Holmwood."

"That's so sad."

"It is, because he's an amazing person. Mama was very worried about him. We all were. A few years ago, he… well, he was in a very bad place." Miles took hold of her hand, seeing the sorrowful look in her eyes. Reading between the lines, he instantly knew there was more to her statement but didn't push for an explanation. "You know we British don't do feelings. Stiff upper lip and all that, but he barely saw anyone, only when he had to work. I came out here with Celeste for the summer, which gave him a bit of a boost, but it was Robert and Melissa's struggle to get pregnant that helped him."

"Yeah?"

"Yes. It kind of put a perspective on everything for him. Robert was healthy and so was Melissa, but they still were finding it hard to have a baby. Robert and Melissa were quite matter-of-fact about it. Talking openly about their struggle, the IVF, possible adoption, surrogacy, all sorts really, and they always kept him in the loop. He's close to Robert. I think he realised that there were others with the same fate as him and yet they were trying to look at every possible scenario. It gave him hope too."

"So IVF worked for them?"

"No, not at all. They went through five rounds of it, at the best private clinic money could buy. Melissa gave up and said she needed a break from the constant pressure. They decided to have a year off from all things baby-related and then, by some miracle, she got pregnant."

"Wow. No wonder Robert never leaves her side."

"He was a little like that before, too. But yes, he's worse now." Louisa rolled her eyes and Miles said a silent "Ah".

"How did Alistair take it?"

"He was thrilled. He and I are going to be the godparents." Louisa gave Miles a quick kiss and gestured to the door. "Come on, they'll be wondering where we are."

"What about you?" Miles asked as they stepped towards the door.

"Me?"

"Want any more children?" He remembered a candid conversation they'd had where she'd confessed to not wanting any more children with Gerard. He still wasn't sure what that meant and at some point, he was going to have to bite the bullet and ask her about her relationship with the arrogant Frenchman. Now wasn't the time, but he was still intrigued as to whether the idea of more children was something she would consider.

Louisa stopped by the door. Her brow creased as she thought about his question. Six months ago, if she'd have been asked, she would have said no, without a doubt. Now, though, the possibility of having another child, in her present situation and frame of mind, felt more appealing. She turned to look at him and was surprised to see the worry etched across his handsome face. The answer to his question was important to him – the trouble was that she wasn't sure which answer he wanted to hear. They'd never really talked about a future because their relationship had always been in the dark. It made it easier not to focus on what might happen down the line, and to direct all their energy into trying to be together without being detected. Now, there was the possibility of them being public in the next few weeks, which meant the light would shine on them, and on questions they'd been avoiding. Maybe it was time for them to start opening up. Miles had always allowed her to take the reins and steer their relationship, careful not to push her too hard, but today, he'd made a tentative step over that imaginary line.

"If you'd have asked me six months ago, I would've said no." She gave him a gentle smile and watched his Adam's apple bob as he struggled with a swallow. "Now, though, I wouldn't rule out the possibility, age permitting," she said lightly, hoping her subtle joke about her age would ease the sudden tense atmosphere.

He gave her a small nod, trying hard not to show his emotions, but she saw the relief flash through his eyes and he gave her a huge smile. "You're not that old," he said jovially and she arched her brow at him.

"I'm four years older than you."

"Maybe, but I've lived a harder life, so physically, I'm older," he said with a cheeky smirk, reaching for the door handle.

Louisa let out a soft chuckle, then narrowed her eyes at him. "You never said if you wanted children."

He stared at her beautiful face, taking in every perfect feature, then bent down and gave her an unhurried kiss. He reluctantly pulled away and pinned her with his gaze. "If you'd have asked me six months ago, I would've said no, but I wouldn't rule out the possibility," he said with a smirk, widening of his eyes at her.

She laughed and shook her head, knowing that throwing her words back at her was his light-hearted way of saying they were on the same page.

35

REVEALED

FIFTY REPORTERS AND PHOTOGRAPHERS were what Miles had signed up for today. It might as well have been 500 or 5000, as far as he was concerned. He was putting himself up against a firing range both figuratively and, in his mind, physically. He had every faith in Hugh's security team – after all, it wasn't just him they were protecting. But the idea of sitting in front of an audience of unknowns was making his heart hammer against his ribcage. He couldn't seem to get his palms to stop sweating. As if that was enough, he wasn't sure if the line of questioning would turn personal. The press loved raking up his troubled past, shining a light on where he'd failed. There was also the possibility that they ask about the shooting. They'd have him exactly where they wanted him, a sitting duck. He'd been renownedly silent after Louis's death, refusing to talk to the press, hoping his lack of comment would make them back off. It hadn't – if anything, it had made it worse. He just hoped that the buzz over the concert would overshadow all his baggage this time. Melissa had assured him that the reporters had been warned that no questions about his past could be asked. The contract the publications had signed secured that. Their reward for their cooperation was coverage of the event. So technically, he was covered, but he still had that feeling of dread that had lodged itself in the pit of his stomach.

The deep rumble of Pierce's voice downstairs brought him out of his unsettling thoughts. Over the last few days, he'd struck up a form of friendship with his security detail. The three men assigned to him had been his constant company since leaving Holmwood. They accompanied him on his walks with Duke and to every meeting he had in the run-up to the press conference. They had even played cards with him on one night. Miles was thankful of their company. With Amanda and the children in LA, not being able to see Louisa and the constant presence of the paparazzi, he was feeling isolated.

Miles checked the time. He had ten minutes before they had to leave for the Four Seasons. He put on one of his designer watches, slipped on his dark blue linen sports jacket and picked up his phone and tapped it.

His call was answered on the second ring. "Hey," Amanda croaked.

"Did I wake you?"

"No, I was up, ready to see you do your thing on the live stream."

"It's an hour away," he drawled.

"Yeah well, my body clock is all over the place. Anyway, are you ready?"

"No, but I'm only admitting that to you." He blew out a breath.

"Miles, you're a pro. You've done hundreds of these things and this is so much more controlled. They're not going to ask questions about you; it'll be about the big names at the concert and CASPO."

"I feel better that Louisa is there and Joel from finance. Plus, they've put Margot's daughter Darcy in charge of the press office."

"Oh my, she's a chip off the old block. She'll take no shit, just like her mother." Amanda chuckled. She'd met Darcy a few times at the CASPO offices. She'd always been welcoming but, like her mother, she had a no-nonsense attitude.

"I know, right?"

"How's everything else?"

Miles knew Amanda was asking about Louisa. "Difficult. This 'having a relationship with an aristocrat' has some serious pitfalls."

"But some highs too, though, right? They make those lows worth it?"

"Yeah, well you should know," he answered wryly.

"I'm hardly in a relationship, Miles."

"Are you sure? Louisa mentioned that Alistair was thinking of taking a holiday, which coincidently falls at the same time as you being in LA." She could hear the amusement in his voice.

"I asked him to come out," she said softly.

"And he said yes?"

"He said yes."

"Awesome." Miles grinned widely because he was pleased at the news and because he knew Amanda would be blushing right now.

"It's still just as friends but… he's… I don't know."

"He's a really good man."

"He is."

"And he's got that British thing going on."

"British thing?"

"Yeah, kind of suave, kind of aloof, kind of outdoorsy, kind of funny. *And* he's a hero. Reluctant, maybe, but he really is."

Amanda laughed lightly at her tenacious brother-in-law's description. "That's *kind of* spot on."

"I know right, I'm so articulate," he joked.

"You're an idiot."

"I *kind of* am. Well I better get going. Wish me luck."

"You don't need luck, Miles, you're a natural."

LOUISA STEPPED INTO HER blue dress and struggled to zip up the back. She smoothed down the front of it and checked herself in the mirror. It was a chic dress that was both smart and edgy – just want she wanted to portray in front of the world press. This was a big moment for her, but more importantly, a huge step into the limelight for CASPO. Louisa sat down in front of her mirror, then picked up her phone, put it on speaker and called Melissa.

"Hey, how are you feeling?"

"Oh, I'm fine. Robert has me chained to the couch," Melissa muttered in frustration. Louisa could hear Robert's deep voice grumbling in the background, saying he'd gag her next and they both chuckled. "Oh shush, you oaf," she called to him, then turned her attention back to Louisa. "So are you ready?"

"Just putting my face on now."

"Excellent. How are you feeling?"

"Nervous."

"It's just like giving a speech. You've done that hundreds of times."

"Apart from the fact it's getting broadcast around the world," she said with a huff as she dabbed her face.

"Keep to the script. Remember stick to your topics of what the money will be used for. Defer all money questions to Joel – he's got all the facts and figures. Miles has the confirmed band list covered and the collaboration with Konran. It'll be short and concise. Darcy will be there to step in if any questions aren't covered by the three of you, or if they're not on point."

"Good, because you know this a big deal for Miles. I don't want him rattled." Louisa slicked on her mascara and scrutinized her face, looking for any smudges.

"I know. They've been warned: any questions about Miles's past are off limits. They don't want to miss out on coverage of the concert, plus we can sue the ass off them for breach of contract. Their publication will be closed down in seconds. He's covered."

Louisa smiled, hearing her dear friend turn into a hard-ass. Melissa was the sweetest person she knew but when it came to protecting her family, friends and work, she was a pitbull. "Good. They're getting over four weeks of news to fill their pages. They can at least respect the hand that's feeding them."

"Precisely."

Louisa and her family had never been fans of the press. She'd never needed them. Whereas some people had a love/hate relationship with the media, the Blackthorns had a hate/hate one. But for this concert to be a success, she knew they needed the coverage and that put her and her family in a vulnerable position.

"How's Celeste, enjoying Scotland?"

"Yes, I spoke to her this morning. Nicolas is getting the full tour of the British Isles while he's here. I told her to keep her head down because the press will dig about to see where she is. Though thinking about it, Scotland is probably the best place for her to be."

"Oh, to be young and carefree again," Melissa said in a theatrically wistful way, causing Louisa to giggle while she blotted her lipstick.

"Right, I'd better get going. Don't want to keep the vultures waiting." She stood up and gave herself a quick once over.

"That's the spirit! I'll be glued to the set while I'm shackled here. I wish I was there for you."

"Me too," Louisa said earnestly.

JOEL AND DARCY ENTERED the ballroom of the Four Seasons that had been sectioned into two parts for privacy. Joel headed to the small bar area, collected two glasses of water from the bartender and placed them on the table where Darcy had settled into a chair.

"I can't believe the press have been here for over three hours," he muttered, taking the seat next to Darcy. "We don't go on air until three," he said in frustration. Joel was part of the accounts company the Blackthorns employed. He headed up the office dedicated to CASPO. The only interaction he had with the CASPO office was with Margot and Darcy, via phone, and a weekly meeting with Louisa.

"We call it the Miles effect," Darcy said with an arched brow.

"We?"

"The staff at the CASPO office. Since he's become ambassador, it's been hell on wheels, but good for sponsors and donations."

"Yes, I've have seen the marked increase in funds."

Their attention was drawn to the door opening. The flustered general manager stepped into the room, followed by six of Hugh's security detail. They quickly greeted each other, then the security team began a sweep of the room they were in and the adjacent room, where the press conference was set up.

"Is everything alright?" the general manager asked as his eyes darted to the security men. Darcy almost felt sorry for him having to deal with Hugh's extreme demands, the pack of hungry press and camera-wielding photographers. As well as all that, his hotel was hosting a world press conference for a high-profile event headed by a member of the aristocracy. The pressure was showing in his tense jawline and worried eyes. She'd watched him over the last two hours oversee the set-up of the rooms, barking orders to his staff. *Just wait until the famous guest arrived*, she thought to herself.

"Just routine security," Darcy said lightly, hoping her tone would put the middle-aged man at ease.

"Right. We'll clear the reception area by 2:15, as per Mr Thornton's instructions," the general manager said tightly, darting his eyes to Joel, who was ignoring him and scanning through some notes, oblivious to his angst.

"Excellent. We need the press in the room before Lady Blackthorn and Mr Keane arrive."

"Of course. They arrive at 2:30 – is that still the case?"

"Yes, Lady Blackthorn is never late."

"Well, I'll leave you to, um, your preparations." He gave a curt nod and headed to the adjacent room.

Joel looked up from his file. "He seemed…"

"Stressed," finished Darcy. "Yep, that's the Miles effect *and* the Blackthorn name, mixed together. A sure recipe for a coronary." Darcy said sardonically and Joel rolled his eyes.

"IT'S THIS WAY, MY lady." Hugh guided Louisa through an empty reception area, with only the eyes of the two receptionists, the concierge and the general manager on her. She smiled her well-practiced public smile at them and stopped to speak briefly to the general manger. He basked in her attention before being shunned to the side by Hugh as he marched her and two of his team towards the ballroom.

Louisa entered the room and Miles instantly stood up from the table, eating up the floor space between them in a second. He'd been anxious to see her and didn't care who knew it. She looked stunning, dressed in her fitted blue dress and pewter-coloured heels; elegant as always with a hint of sexy. Her lush hair fell loosely but was perfectly styled.

"Hey," he said with a relieved smile, itching to kiss her but reluctantly holding back. Their two days apart had been difficult. He wished they were alone so he could hold her tightly, kiss her thoroughly and be damned with protocol. One look in Louisa's eyes, he knew she felt the same way.

"Hey, how are you?"

"Oh, you know." He widened his eyes and her public smile morphed into the genuine one Miles knew so well.

"Yes, I think I do," she said with a slight shake of her head. She took a deep breath, then gestured to where Darcy and Joel stood waiting. "Well let's go over everything again, shall we?"

"Sure." Miles turned and guided her to the table, where she quickly greeted Joel and kissed Darcy on the cheek, before sitting down in the chair Miles had pulled out for her.

Hugh cleared the room of all staff, giving the four of them some privacy, and took his post by the door leading to where the press conference was being held. Louisa read over her small speech again, making a few last-minute adjustments, and Miles rechecked his. Once they were both happy, Darcy went over the sequence and reassured them that should they be unable to answer the questions, she would intercept or they could refer to her.

"Remember, we are your back-ups. They're really here to see you two," Darcy said in her official tone that sounded so much like Margot. Miles had to remind himself that she was only 30 years old. He caught Louisa's eye and mouthed "pimping us out". She chuckled and Darcy's eyes shot up to them.

"Just a private joke," Louisa reassured Darcy.

"Oh, I see." Darcy looked back down at her file and continued. "We will be playing the pre-recorded message from Mr Kwon, and Mr Keane will say a few words about the artists. We added another one to the list. Dua Lipa confirmed late last night."

"That's great news," Louisa said, reaching for a glass of water and taking a sip.

"Right." Darcy caught Hugh's eye at the ballroom entrance and he nodded, indicating everyone was seated and ready. "I'll go out and give them the run down. Joel's going out there with me so once I'm done, he'll let Hugh know and I'll introduce you both. Lady Blackthorn first, then Mr Keane."

"Actually, we'll come out together," Louisa said in her official tone.

"Of course," Darcy said without a hint of surprise or hesitation. "See you in a moment and good luck."

Darcy picked up their speeches, tucked them under her arm, then followed Joel to the door. They heard a flurry of activity before Hugh closed the door again.

"Alone at last," Miles said taking her in his arms.

"Well… ish." Her eyes shifted to where Hugh was doing his best to look invisible, his six-foot four frame making it an impossible task.

"Eh, he doesn't count. He's seen me kiss you hundreds of times and hasn't drawn his gun on me yet."

Louisa giggled, glad they could have this private moment before they went out. She needed to see he was alright, that he didn't have any last-minute nerves. The change in their entrance was for him. Louisa didn't want him facing the cameras alone. "Well are you going to kiss me?" she said in that clipped tone he loved.

"I sure am, my lady," he drawled and pressed his lips to hers in the sweetest of kisses. The tender moment was cut short when they heard a discreet cough and instantly turned to Hugh.

"They're ready, my lady," he said with a stifled smile and Louisa straightened herself and looked into Miles's magnificent eyes.

"Game face on."

He gifted her with his sexy wink and mega-watt smile. "Game face on, baby."

LOUISA HAD OFTEN BEEN photographed at red carpet events she'd attended with Gerard. Always playing second to her powerful husband. When the Blackthorns had held gala dinners, she'd spoken to select reporters and made speeches, but nothing had prepared her for the fierce onslaught of cameras flashing as she stepped through the door. Miles was just a step behind her. He focused on the back of her head, ignoring the constant flashes and the rise of chatter. His footing faltered for a second, but when Louisa looked over her shoulder at him, he quickly fell in step with her. The short walk to their chairs felt endless. Joel and Darcy had both risen from their seats at each end of the podium, until Louisa lowered herself into the chair Miles had pulled out for her. He was pleased he had something to attend to before he faced the audience of the press. His eyes flitted over Louisa's tense shoulders and his stomach tightened, knowing she was as on edge as he was. He took a deep breath, unbuttoned his jacket and lifted his gaze to the sea of unfamiliar faces. The cameras flashed in rapid bursts like fireworks on the fourth of July and Miles met them head on, blasting them with his dazzling smile.

"Good afternoon everyone and welcome. How you all doing?" he drawled, playing up to his audience like a seasoned pro. He was met with a cheer and laughs, as well as a few good-humoured heckles, which he grinned at as he lowered himself into his seat.

Louisa shot him a thankful look, knowing he had put himself out there so that she had a minute to compose herself before she started her speech. "Good afternoon. It is my great pleasure to announce that on the second of September, this year, Holmwood House will be hosting a concert in aid of our charity CASPO." She paused as the reporters murmured in excitement. "All proceeds will go to help the many single parent families and children. I am pleased to say we have a 16-band line-up of world famous artists for this event." The reporters' murmurs grew louder, itching to ask their questions. "Fifty thousand tickets will go on sale for the concert and will be available as of next Monday, exclusively on our website."

Louisa took another pause before she continued. "We at CASPO are honoured that so many sponsors and artists are donating to our charity, in order to help those less fortunate. Our charity has always been generously supported throughout the years, helping thousands of families, and we are thankful for that. But this concert will give us the opportunity to help even more. Thank you." The reporters gave a round of applause and before they started their questions, Darcy reminded them that they'd have chance once all the speakers had finished.

Next up was Joel. For an accountant, he had a considerable amount of flair. Even though his address was mainly informative, giving the estimated revenue from tickets sales and sponsors, he peppered his speech with light-hearted comments, saying they were not above asking for more. He lifted up a few samples of the merchandise that would be on sale at the concert and on the website too, joking that he wouldn't be modelling them. Darcy once again interrupted any questions, directing the press to the website for a full press pack.

It was now Miles's turn to speak. He shuffled the papers in front of him, took a drink from his water and looked up into the lenses of the cameras. "I'd like to say that the idea for the concert was mine but it wasn't. All credit goes to TuKon, who I had the pleasure of meeting a few months ago." There was a collective gasp from the reporters. It was the first time Konran had been mentioned in association with CASPO – until now, he'd been a well-kept secret. "With his considerable contribution and determination to make this concert a success, I am beyond pleased to announce that he will be headlining the concert." The noise level rose considerably and Miles paused for them quieten down. "Along-side TuKon the following bands and artists will be playing: Lewis Capaldi, George Ezra, The Police, Dua Lipa, Pink, Ed Sheeran, Kendrick Lamar, French Montana, Maroon Five, Arctic Monkeys, Coldplay, Foo Fighters, Brian Adams, Alicia Keys and The Spin Doctors." There was a frenzy of chatter from the reporters but before anyone spoke out, Miles continued. "Now, as you might be aware, TuKon is on his world tour at the moment and sadly can't be here today but he sent us this video."

Darcy clicked on her remote control and the famous face of TuKon appeared on the screen behind them. He was sitting in what looked like a hotel room with his band members. He gave a toothy grin and started his speech. "You'll all know by now about the concert we will be holding at Holmwood House. I owe a lot to charities like CASPO. Without their help I wouldn't have had the opportunities I was lucky to have. We've an amazing line-up, which we're all so grateful for, and a truly beautiful venue, thanks to Lady Blackthorn and her family. See you all on the second of September, at Holmwood House. Stand up for CASPO's Stand Tall concert."

Once the video recording stopped, the reporters started to fire questions, but Darcy somehow managed to quieten them down, with a lift of her hand. "We will take questions now but one at a time, please." She pointed to a woman in the middle of the crowd.

"When did the idea come about?"

Miles took the question, explaining that he and TuKon had been at a private event and he'd asked Miles if he'd be interested in being part of it. The next question was directed at Louisa, asking her where the money would go.

"We're starting a few new projects to help single parent families, namely after-school activities. We are looking at setting up music workshops, therapy with music, dance and sports, as we've seen first-hand how beneficial these are. They are also close to both TuKon's and Miles Keane's hearts." Louisa turned briefly and smiled at Miles.

Joel then took the next question about ticket prices and how they would control mass buying. Joel explained that there would be a limit of four tickets per purchase and that the selling of tickets would be spread out over five days, which meant that they wouldn't sell out within minutes.

Darcy signalled to the next reporter to ask his question.

"Lady Blackthorn, how has it been working alongside Miles Keane as ambassador for CASPO?"

"Miles has brought an enormous amount of generosity to the organisation. When I say generosity, I'm talking about time, which is priceless for any charity. He has been extremely dedicated to our cause, which has meant that the children and families have seen an immediate effect from his involvement. All at CASPO are indebted to him and his selfless dedication." Louisa gave Miles a warm smile and he tried hard not to bask in her comments.

His attention was thankfully pulled back to his audience by the same reporter. "That's praise indeed for you, Miles," the reporter said wryly.

"Lady Blackthorn is as usual being too kind and generous with her praise. If it wasn't for Lady Blackthorn and her family, the charity wouldn't even exist. I'm happy to help in any small way I can, and always under her guidance."

"We have time for a couple more questions," Darcy said in her efficient manner and pointed to another reporter.

"How are you settling into life back in England after your 20-year stay in the US, Lady Blackthorn?"

"England has always been my home, so it wasn't hard. I look fondly on my time in the US – after all, my daughter was born there. I think I'm in a lucky position to regard both countries as home," Louisa answered without missing a beat. She was fully aware that her answer needed to be as diplomatic as possible. After all, it was going worldwide. Before Darcy could gesture to the next reporter, one of the reporters called out his question.

"Lady Blackthorn, do you still have fond memories of your time in the US, even though you left because of the alleged allegations of your husband's continuous infidelity?"

For a nanosecond, there was deathly silence, then a collective gasp. Louisa's face went from relaxed to stoic and Miles stiffened next to her.

Before Darcy could take control, the same reporter called out over the room's rising mutterings. "Is it true that Gerard Dupont, the billionaire, had a string of mistresses throughout your 20 years of marriage and that you endured it so that you could live in the lap of luxury in one of the most exclusive addresses in the world?" Every reporter was now shifting their attention between the brash reporter and the podium.

Darcy called out for him to stop. "Mr Stevens, please!" But he quickly fired out his next question as Hugh pushed through the crowd to where he was.

"Is it true that after your daughter left for her studies abroad, you were asked to leave your marital home and the only reason Mr Dupont allowed you to stay was for the sake of his daughter?" The reporter's voice was louder now, shouting over the chatter of the rest of the audience. Two of Hugh's team had managed to get hold of the reporter, effectively shutting him up, but the damage was done. He'd said his piece in front of a worldwide audience. Louisa's reaction had been recorded for all to see and even if the segment was cut out later, the damaging questions were out there for everyone to hear.

"Jesus Christ," Miles whispered, horrified that Louisa had been subjected to such an ordeal.

Miles reached out and took hold of Louisa's arm. For a second she seemed to be in a trance but then she stood up. Joel and Miles began to usher her off the podium, but she stayed rooted to her spot. Reporters were now talking loudly, caught between recording the reporter being manhandled and Louisa's reaction. Time seemed to stand still for her as she took in the cameras recording her and the flashes exploding in front of her. The volume of noise dropped a little, and Louisa's attention shifted to the man beside her, still holding onto her arm. Miles furrowed his brow at her, unsure of what she was thinking and then she stepped forward to where her microphone was.

"Mr Stevens." The whole room fell silent at her commanding tone. "I find the timing of these questions crass and classless, like the publication you represent. You are using an important and valuable press conference for your own personal platform to elevate the profile of yourself and the rag you work for, by sensationalizing my alleged private life. The work CASPO does is life changing – maybe you should be concentrating your efforts on shining the spotlight on the positive things our charity is achieving, rather than focusing on salacious gossip. I'm afraid we will have to cut this press conference short. Please direct any questions regarding our charity to the CASPO press office and we will endeavour to answer them as soon as possible. Good day to you all."

Before anyone could ask or say another word, Louisa walked off the podium and into the adjoining room with Miles and Joel following closely behind her.

The moment the door closed Louisa sagged against Miles.

"What the fuck just happened?" Miles said to no one in particular as he enveloped Louisa in his arms.

"Bastard," Joel muttered as he picked up a glass of water and handed it to Louisa. "Here, drink this." She took a quick sip and gave it back to him.

"Oh Miles, I'm so…"

"Shh baby, we got this, *I've* got this," Miles said, bobbing down so their eyes were on the same level. He held her face between his hands and dropped a kiss to her forehead, oblivious to whoever was there.

Darcy burst into the room with a face like thunder and clenched her jaw, seeing Louisa so upset.

"Lady Blackthorn, I'm so sorry. I have no idea how that happened. I'm so sorry…"

Louisa shook her head but said nothing, taking the glass again from Joel and sipping it.

It was the turn of the general manager to step into the room with Hugh behind him. "Lady Blackthorn, I don't know what to say…" he said in a rush.

"Leave her alone. Can't you see how shaken she is?" Miles bit out and turned his attention to Hugh, taking the glass she'd just drunk from and banging it on the table.

"The car's around the back with a pack of all the press too," he said to Miles.

"Fuck."

"Celeste… I need to talk to Celeste," Louisa said in a panic.

"In a moment, baby," Miles said in a soothing voice, his heart breaking at seeing her so shaken.

Pierce was the next to arrive, going straight to Hugh and giving him a rundown on where the offending reporter was. "It's pandemonium out there," he whispered.

"We need to get out of here *now*," Miles said through gritted teeth.

Hugh stepped up to where Louisa was being held by Miles and said calmly. "We need to get you out of here, my lady."

"Fuck, how the hell are we going to do this?" Miles asked Hugh. Hugh stared at him for a second, then gave him a nod. Miles narrowed his eyes and understood instantly what the head of security was thinking.

"Pierce, get Karl and Kurt. You're going out from the front. Bring the car around from the back." Pierce nodded and exited the room. Hugh then instructed another car to be on standby to drive to the back entrance.

"No, you can't they'll jump all over you!" Louisa cried, understanding that Miles was going to be a diversion for her again.

"Baby, I can handle it. I told you before: you come first. I'll always protect you."

The door opened and a stone-faced Pierce came in with Karl and Kurt.

"Karl, go out through reception and make sure every one of those fuckers sees you and hears you speak to the front staff. Tell them we're coming through and to clear the area. The limo should be around at the front. Go," barked Hugh.

"Can you get her out of here alone?" Miles asked Hugh and he nodded. "Okay, good."

Darcy and Joel quickly packed up their things and waited for Hugh's instructions. He spoke to the rest of his team via their radios, keeping them abreast of their decoy plans. Then as soon as Karl came back in, Hugh told them to leave via the front. The rest of his team would make sure they got out and into the first limo. Karl handed Louisa one of the hoodies Joel had shown the press, which was part of the merchandise display. She furrowed her brow in confusion but Miles instantly understood.

"Baby, put this on; put the hood up." Miles helped Louisa into it, then gave her a quick kiss. "Very sexy." Then he gave her a wink, hoping her face would lose that forlorn look. She gave him a reluctant smile to appease him but inside she was dying from shame. "I won't let them get to you, Louisa."

"They already did," her voice quivered and she swallowed back her tears. *How was she ever going to live this down?*

"Miles?" Hugh said in his hard tone that meant he was all business.

Miles pulled her close to him and murmured into her hair, "I love you, Louisa, I've got your back."

"I love you too. Be careful."

"Don't worry about me, I've handled worse. You forget, I'm bulletproof."

"Miles, you have to get going," Hugh said in a low voice.

Miles pulled away and bobbed down to look at her stunning face and dropped a sweet kiss on her lips. "Game face on, baby." She gave him a sad smile and he clenched his jaw. The last thing he wanted to do was leave her right now but he knew it was the only way. He gave Hugh a worried look but he reassured him with a nod. Miles turned to Pierce. "We ready to do this?"

"Yes, sir," he said with steely confidence.

"Let's do it, then." Pierce walked up to the door with Miles behind him flanked by Karl and Kurt, waited for a beat, then opened the door.

Louisa stood staring after them, knowing that they'd be swamped with reporters and probably a few more who had heard about the press conference, as soon as they went out on the pavement. Her perfect bubble had just been shattered.

"My lady?"

She closed her eyes, feeling wretched that she'd sent Miles out there to face the music, again.

"Louisa! We have to go now." Hugh said with urgency. If his plan was to work, they had to leave at the same time. He took her arm and she fell in step with her trusted bodyguard. Within a minute, they were running down some back stairs and exiting via a fire exit, where a modest car waited for them. Hugh opened the back door and guided a subdued Louisa into the back, then slipped in next to her.

"Head down, my lady, until we're in the clear," Hugh said gently, as the driver set off at a steady pace. The driver had no choice but to pass by the front of the hotel because of the one-way system. Louisa shuffled down and held her breath. She could hear loud undistinguished voices as they neared the entrance.

"Stay down, my lady."

"Is he okay?"

"Just getting into the limo now." Hugh said as they passed the chaotic scene.

Hugh felt the vibration of Louisa's phone in the inside of his jacket pocket and pulled it out. He turned the screen to face her. Louisa looked down at her phone and saw Gerard's number flash. She took it from Hugh and answered it.

"*Cherie,* I don't know how this happened. I swear I knew nothing about it. I was watching the press conference."

"Well someone knows something, Gerard," she said with a sob, unable to hold it back anymore. "I need to go. I need to speak to Celeste."

"I'm on my way to the airport. I'll be at Holmwood House in the morning."

"I'm not sure you coming is the best thing."

"I'm not letting you or Celeste have to deal with this alone. I don't care what they say about me, but you're never thinking about yourself. You've always protected me and Celeste; I won't sit by and have you and your reputation tainted, *cherie*."

"I think it's too late for that."

Miles let out a breath and shot a tense look at Pierce. "Please tell me she got away."

"Yes, sir, she's on her way to Holmwood."

"Thank fuck." He pulled out his phone and dialled her number as the limo driver drove through the busy streets, but was met with the engaged tone. "Damn it, she's on the phone." He immediately called Hugh. "Is she alright?" he asked without any pleasantries.

"Shaken, but fine. I'll ask her to call you once she's finished her calls."

"Thanks. And thank you for getting her away safely."

"I couldn't have done it without your help," Hugh said without hesitation.

Miles waited a second, taking in what he said before continuing. "Pierce says you're heading to Holmwood."

"Yes, no one can get to her there."

"Let's hope so."

Miles hung up, rested his head back and closed his eyes. He ran over the things the reporter had asked, wondering why he would have asked such questions. There was no way his publication would get away with it. Melissa had made them all sign a contract, stating that they couldn't ask personal questions. Miles opened his eyes and swallowed. The contract the press signed was to protect *him* from personal questions about *his* past, but it didn't mention Louisa. Surely the reporter knew it would mean career suicide, as well as being sued for slander, to even hint at any kind of false scandal. Unless the allegations were true. Unless his source was close to the family and knew the real story. Miles's thoughts instantly went to Gerard. Did he tip off the reporter? He needed to speak to Louisa. It was time to put all their cards on the table.

MILES PACED AROUND HIS lounge, anxiously waiting for Louisa to call. Pierce was keeping an eye out for any reporters but thankfully, they had left. They had a new victim to prey on now.

His phone rang in his hand and he answered it instantly. "Jesus, Miles what the hell!" said Amanda, clearly shaken.

"It's a mess. Louisa's on the way to Holmwood and I'm holed up here waiting for her to call."

"I know, I just got off the phone with Alistair. I've never heard him so angry."

"I know how he feels," Miles bit out.

"What he said, the reporter, is it true?"

"I've no idea. But if it is, only someone close to the Blackthorns would know."

"How are they going to handle it?"

"I don't know. Fuck, she was so shaken." Miles dragged his hand over his face in frustration.

"What she said, though… I can't believe she found the strength to answer him."

"Yeah, she amazes me every day."

"I'll call you later. Give her my love."

"I will, thanks." Miles ended the call and glared at it, willing it to call.

LOUISA CLOSED HER EYES and tried to level her breathing. She'd managed to get hold of Celeste, who was already on the way back from her trip. She'd watched the press conference and then immediately packed up and set off, knowing her mother needed her. Melissa had called her, practically thermo-nuclear. She'd already been in touch with the newspaper and called their lawyers for advice but Louisa told her to stop any action. The more they engaged, the more likely the story wouldn't go away. The knee-jerk reaction was to fight back. Louisa's retort at the press conference was exactly that but she knew that any reaction would be scrutinised and dissected by the public and the press. She should have kept quiet, stood up and walked away. That's what she'd always been told to do. Don't feed the fire.

In all the preparation for the press conference, she'd never once thought she'd be the one who would be exploited. Her focus had been Miles. Her thoughts shifted to the man she loved and her heart clenched. What must he think of her? From the look on his face, she knew he didn't believe the allegations. How would he feel, knowing she'd stayed in a sham of a marriage, for whatever the reason? He'd probably think she was weak and pathetic and he wouldn't be far wrong. Everything she'd worked hard for was falling apart. CASPO would most definitely be affected, the Blackthorn name would be in every paper and for the wrong reasons. Any respect she had in the public eye and in the work she did would be lost and she doubted Miles would see her in the same way again. She turned her phone in her hand, nervously knowing she had to call him, then looked out of the window at the familiar countryside roads that led to Holmwood.

Better to get it over with, she thought to herself, and tapped her phone."

"Baby, how are you?" She could hear the concern in his voice – or was it pity?

"I've been better."

Miles's heart broke hearing her so broken. She was always so strong and self-assured. "Look, I know it seems like the worse thing but it'll blow over. I'll come to Holmwood you can't face this…"

"No, Miles. I think it's best we have a break for a bit."

"What? No!"

"Miles, please. The press are going to be everywhere," she said wearily.

"Louisa, baby, I don't give a shit about the press." He'd handled so much worse than this, he'd shield her from anyone and everyone.

"I do, though. This is my family's name. I need to sort this out," she said with more force.

"How will you sort it out? By shutting me out? How will that help?"

"I need to lay low, be with my family. If we're seen together, it'll just make it worse."

"Louisa, I have been through this. I know it seems like the end of the world, but it isn't. They'll forget about it. Something else will capture their attention and you'll be old news," he said softly, hoping his reasoning would convince her, but he had a bad feeling that her worries would override any kind of rationale.

"It's not just me this affects. CASPO is going to lose money if all they focus on is my past marriage."

"It's just a blip, Louisa."

"It may be a blip to you but to me it's a huge bump!" Her voice cracked and she let out a sob.

"Christ, Louisa, please let me help you through this."

"I don't want your pity, Miles."

"It's not pity, it's empathy," he said emphatically.

"I just need to handle this alone."

"Louisa..." He spoke her name in a soft plea.

"I'm sorry. Please just let me do this. I'll call you."

"When?"

"I don't know. Bye, Miles."

Before Miles could answer, she ended the call and handed it to Hugh. Tears steadily rolled down her face and Hugh pulled out a handkerchief and passed it to her. The gesture only made Louisa feel even more vulnerable. She sobbed uncontrollably as the car drove closer to Holmwood House. Hugh slipped his arm over her shoulders, letting her rest her head on his shoulder, and he squeezed her. He felt as helpless as he was sure Miles felt, right now, but he was glad he was able to give her some comfort. Her phone vibrated in his hand and he showed the screen to Louisa. It was Miles.

"Don't answer it."

"My lady..."

"I can't talk anymore."

"Louisa..."

"I can't, Hugh. I feel so ashamed."

"You've nothing to feel ashamed about."

She huffed, then blew her nose. The phone stopped ringing and Hugh sighed. He liked Miles. He was good for Louisa and there was never any doubt about his feelings towards her. "He loves you," he said, hoping she'd change her mind.

"Well that might change when he realises most of what that reporter said was true," Louisa said with a shrug.

"I doubt it." Hugh's phone started to vibrate in his pocket and he struggled to get it out. "Is it him?" Hugh showed her the screen with Miles's name flashing on it. "Don't answer it."

Hugh nodded, then said, "I'll send him a message." Hugh quickly typed a message as they pulled up the driveway of

Holmwood House. He told Miles that she was upset but fine, and he would call him later.

"It must be bad if Mama's come out to greet me," Louisa sniffed, seeing her mother standing by the grand door. She wiped under her eyes and blew her nose again, and took a deep breath before the driver opened her door.

"FUCK!"

"What's wrong?" Pierce stepped into Miles's lounge after hearing him curse.

"She's shutting me out."

Pierce cringed and shook his head. In the few weeks he'd worked for Miles, they'd become more than just employer, employee.

"What the hell I'm going to do?" He ran his hands through his hair and stared out of the window.

"Don't let her."

Miles swung around to face Pierce.

"She's upset and probably feeling embarrassed. Don't let her pull away."

Miles nodded. He knew Pierce was right. This was her way. She hid from him every time things got hard or when she felt out of control. The Blackthorns always seemed to close ranks in a crisis. Well, she wasn't hiding from him ever again. He wasn't going to let her; he'd always fought for her, whatever the cost to him, and wasn't going to stop now. It was time for him to show Louisa what she was truly worth.

COMING SOON

Miles and Louisa's story continues in the second book of The Blackthorn Duet, ***Signed and Sealed.***

Please consider leaving a review.
It's the best way for readers like you help other readers discover new books!

NOTES FROM THE AUTHOR

One of the best things about writing novels is the interesting things you find out about while doing research. I came up with the subplot of Alistair being a war hero and losing his leg, who now threw himself into running his family's estate. I wanted him to find another purpose, so I decided he would fall in love with Amanda.

I like to visualise places and people when I write, so my next task was to find stately homes that would be suitable for Holmwood House. I came up with a few and took elements from each one but the main estate I used was Wrest Park. It's a gorgeous stately home with fabulous grounds. Reading up on it, I found out that it had been used as a military hospital in World War I and that a soldier, who had lost his leg, found love with a member of staff from the house. I was totally blown away at the uncanny coincidence.

PLAYLIST

Your Song – Elton John and Bernie Taupin
Singing in the Rain – Arthur Freed and Nacio Herb Brown
Hound Dog – Jerry Leiber and Mike Stoller
Why Do Fools Fall In Love – Frankie Lymon, Herman Santiago, Jimmy Merchant
Respect – Luther Ingram, Mack Rice
Mustang Sally – Mack Rice
Twist and Shout – Bert Berns, Phil Medley
We Are Family – Bernard Edwards, Nile Rodgers
Play That Funky Music – Rob Parissi
Isn't She Lovely – Stevie Wonder
Ladies Night – George M. Brown & Kool and the Gang
Three Times a Lady – Lionel Richie
Get Up Offa That Thing – Deanna Brown, Diedra Brown, Yamma Brown
I Wanna Dance with Somebody – George Merrill, Shannon Rubicam
Don't Stop Believin' – Steve Perry, Jonathan Cain, Neal Schon (Journey)
Every Little Thing She Does Is Magic – Sting

Gettin' Jiggy Wit It – Samuel Barnes, Bernard Edwards, Joe Robinson, Nile Rodgers, Will Smith
Ice Ice Baby – Vanilla Ice
Thrift Shop – Ben Haggerty, Ryan Lewis (Macklemore & Ryan Lewis)
This Is No Ordinary Love – Sade Adu, Stuart Matthewman
Girls Like You – Maroon Five
Hawaii Five-O Theme – Morton Stevens, Brian Tyler, Keith Power
I Fall in Love too Easily – Jule Styne, Sammy Cahn

ACKNOWLEDGMENTS

Bought and Paid For took far longer than I imagined and I'm sorry to all those readers who waited. To you guys: thank you for your patience. The idea for this book came to me about five years ago, all thanks to a lovely lady named Liz. We became friends because of a certain book, then bonded over writing, our love of Greece and lusting over various famous men. She was lucky enough to have a celebrity lunch she won on a charity auction, and though her experience was very enjoyable and entertaining, and the celebrity was respectful, I liked the idea of the date turning into something unexpectedly more. This is how Miles Keane and Lady Louisa Blackthorn's story was born.

A huge thank you to my mum, Helen. She's the first sounding board of all my books and without her encouragement and ass-kicking, I probably wouldn't finish them. To my dad, George, who always praises me no matter what.

My beta readers: Jaine who has shown me that miles don't matter, and Jackie, thank you for taking the time and effort to read my words so quickly, sending me your support – it means the world to me.

To Lucy, for your honesty and making me laugh. Sorry that

there's no instant gratification but glad you stuck it out until the end!

Emma, thank you for your randomness and endless encouragement, it has kept me going whenever I faltered.

To my crew: Mary for your overwhelming praise and faith in me, to Xenia who always knows exactly what to say to fire me up, and to Voula for our years of friendship and your relentless support, I am forever grateful for your love and endless encouragement – love you, girls.

This book wouldn't be here without the talented James Millington, Roi Ioakeimidou and Leanne Clugston, a huge shout-out to them for being so patient with me.

A special mention to my tech guys Savva, Harry and Christos, they saved me on far too many occasions – thanks again.

I am forever grateful for my husband Marios and sons George and Michael, who have put up with my mood swings and general craziness whenever I'm writing, but really, they should've got used to it by now!

Finally, I'd like to thank you, the readers. I love writing, putting my imaginary friends down on paper and watching them come alive. Without you, your constant support and feedback, I would just keep them in my head. I am forever grateful.

ABOUT THE AUTHOR

Anna-Maria Athanasiou is originally from Leeds in the UK but for the last 26 years she has lived in the heart of the Mediterranean on the island of Cyprus. Limassol is her adopted town, where she lives with her husband, two sons, Golden Retriever and eight cats. She had her debut novels, ***Waiting for Summer*** Book One and Two published in 2013 and 2014, having written the series in secret, never expecting to finish them or to be published.

Her dream was to have her own restaurant but seeing as it never came to be, Anna-Maria decided to create one within the pages of her next trilogy, ***La Casa d'Italia.***

Anna-Maria has been asked to guest write articles for The Glass House Girls, an online magazine for women, and contributed to a number of charity anthologies: *They Say I'm Doing Well, Break the Cycle, Poems to my Younger Self* and *Elements.*

Anna-Maria is a member of the Association of Authors and ***Bought and Paid For*** is the first book in the ***Blackthorn*** duet.

Loved *Bought and Paid For?*

Connect with Anna-Maria:

Facebook: www.facebook.com/annamariaathanasiouauthor

Twitter: @AMAthanasiou

Instagram: annamariaathansiou

OTHER BOOKS BY ANNA-MARIA ATHANASIOU

Waiting for Summer Book One

Waiting for Summer Book Two

La Casa d'Italia series

For Starters

Heavenly Fare

Just Desserts

COMING SOON...

Signed and Sealed

Printed in Great Britain
by Amazon

74759630R00338